# THE BAD PLACE

*Also by Dean R. Koontz*

MIDNIGHT

LIGHTNING

WATCHERS

STRANGERS

TWILIGHT EYES

DARKFALL

PHANTOMS

WHISPERS

THE MASK

THE VISION

THE FACE OF FEAR

NIGHT CHILLS

SHATTERED

# THE BAD PLACE

## DEAN R. KOONTZ

G. P. PUTNAM'S SONS
New York

G. P. Putnam's Sons
*Publishers Since 1838*
200 Madison Avenue
New York, NY 10016

Library of Congress Cataloging-in-Publication Data

Koontz, Dean R., date.
  The bad place / Dean R. Koontz.—1st American ed.
     p.  cm.
  ISBN 0-399-13498-0
  ISBN 0-399-13510-3 (Limited Edition)
  I. Title.
PS3561.O55B3     1990                    89-10861 CIP
813'.54—dc20

*Printed in the United States of America*
1  2  3  4  5  6  7  8  9  10

Teachers often affect our lives more than
they realize. From high school days to the
present, I have had teachers to whom I will
remain forever indebted, not merely because
of what they taught me, but because they
provided the invaluable examples of
dedication, kindness, and generosity of spirit
that have given me an unshakable faith in
the basic goodness of the human species.
This book is dedicated to:

David O'Brien
Thomas Doyle
Richard Forsythe
John Bodnar
Carl Campbell
Steve and Jean Hernishin

*Every eye sees its own special vision;*
*every ear hears a most different song.*
*In each man's troubled heart, an incision*
*would reveal a unique, shameful wrong.*

*Stranger fiends hide here in human guise*
*than reside in the valleys of Hell.*
*But goodness, kindness and love arise*
*in the heart of the poor beast, as well.*

—The Book of Counted Sorrows

# 1

THE NIGHT was becalmed and curiously silent, as if the alley were an abandoned and windless beach in the eye of a hurricane, between the tempest past and the tempest coming. A faint scent of smoke hung on the motionless air, although no smoke was visible.

Sprawled facedown on the cold pavement, Frank Pollard did not move when he regained consciousness; he waited in the hope that his confusion would dissipate. He blinked, trying to focus. Veils seemed to flutter within his eyes. He sucked deep breaths of the cool air, tasting the invisible smoke, grimacing at the acrid tang of it.

Shadows loomed like a convocation of robed figures, crowding around him. Gradually his vision cleared, but in the weak yellowish light that came from far behind him, little was revealed. A large trash dumpster, six or eight feet from him, was so dimly outlined that for a moment it seemed ineffably strange, as though it were an artifact of an alien civilization. Frank stared at it for a while before he realized what it was.

He did not know where he was or how he had gotten there. He could not have been unconscious longer than a few seconds, for his heart was pounding as if he had been running for his life only moments ago.

*Fireflies in a windstorm. . . .*

That phrase took flight through his mind, but he had no idea what it meant. When he tried to concentrate on it and make sense of it, a dull headache developed above his right eye.

*Fireflies in a windstorm. . . .*

He groaned softly.

Between him and the dumpster, a shadow among shadows moved, quick and sinuous. Small but radiant green eyes regarded him with icy interest.

Frightened, Frank pushed up onto his knees. A thin, involuntary cry issued from him, almost less like a human sound than like the muted wail of a reed instrument.

The green-eyed observer scampered away. A cat. Just an ordinary black cat.

Frank got to his feet, swayed dizzily, and nearly fell over an object that had been on the blacktop beside him. Gingerly he bent down and picked it up: a flight bag made of supple leather, packed full, surprisingly heavy. He supposed it was his. He could not remember. Carrying the bag, he tottered to the dumpster and leaned against its rusted flank.

Looking back, he saw that he was between rows of what seemed to be two-story stucco apartment buildings. All of the windows were black. On both sides, the tenants' cars were pulled nose-first into covered parking stalls. The queer yellow glow, sour and sulfurous, almost more like the product of a gas flame than the luminescence of an incandescent electric bulb, came from a streetlamp at the end of the block, too far away to reveal the details of the alleyway in which he stood.

As his rapid breathing slowed and as his heartbeat decelerated, he abruptly realized that he did not know who he was. He knew his name—Frank Pollard—but that was all. He did not know how old he was, what he did for a living, where he had come from, where he was going, or why. He was so startled by his predicament that for a moment his breath caught in his throat; then his heartbeat soared again, and he let his breath out in a rush.

*Fireflies in a windstorm. . . .*

What the hell did that mean?

The headache above his right eye corkscrewed across his forehead.

He looked frantically left and right, searching for an object or an aspect of the scene that he might recognize, anything, an anchor in a world that was suddenly too strange. When the night offered nothing to reassure him, he turned his quest inward, desperately seeking something familiar in himself, but his own memory was even darker than the passageway around him.

Gradually he became aware that the scent of smoke had faded, replaced by a vague but nauseating smell of rotting garbage in the dumpster. The stench of decomposition filled him with thoughts of death, which seemed to trigger a vague recollection that he was on the run from someone—or something—that wanted to kill him. When he tried to recall why he was fleeing, and from whom, he could not further illuminate that scrap of memory; in fact, it seemed more an awareness based on instinct than a genuine recollection.

A puff of wind swirled around him. Then calm returned, as if the dead night was trying to come back to life but had managed just one shuddering breath. A single piece of wadded paper, swept up by that insufflation, clicked along the pavement and scraped to a stop against his right shoe.

Then another puff.

The paper whirled away.

Again the night was dead calm.

Something was happening. Frank sensed that these short-lived whiffs of wind had some malevolent source, ominous meaning.

Irrationally, he was sure that he was about to be crushed by a great weight. He looked up into the clear sky, at the bleak and empty blackness of space and at the malignant brilliance of the distant stars. If something was descending toward him, Frank could not see it.

The night exhaled once more. Harder this time. Its breath was sharp and dank.

He was wearing running shoes, white athletic socks, jeans, and a long-sleeved blue-plaid shirt. He had no jacket, and he could have used one. The air was not frigid, just mildly bracing. But a coldness was in him, too, a gelid fear, and he shivered uncontrollably between the cool caress of the night air and that inner chill.

The gust of wind died.

Stillness reclaimed the night.

Convinced that he had to get out of there—and fast—he pushed away from the dumpster. He staggered along the alley, retreating from the end of the block where the streetlamp glowed, into darker realms, with no destination in mind, driven only by the sense that this place was dangerous and that safety, if indeed safety could be found, lay elsewhere.

The wind rose again, and with it, this time, came an eerie whistling, barely audible, like the distant music of a flute made of some strange bone.

Within a few steps, as Frank became surefooted and as his eyes adapted to the murky night, he arrived at a confluence of passageways. Wrought-iron gates in pale stucco arches lay to his left and right.

He tried the gate on the left. It was unlocked, secured only by a simple gravity latch. The hinges squeaked, eliciting a wince from Frank, who hoped the sound had not been heard by his pursuer.

By now, although no adversary was in sight, Frank had no doubt that he was the object of a chase. He knew it as surely as a hare knew when a fox was in the field.

The wind huffed again at his back, and the flutelike music, though barely audible and lacking a discernible melody, was haunting. It pierced him. It sharpened his fear.

Beyond the black iron gate, flanked by feathery ferns and bushes, a walkway led between a pair of two-story apartment buildings. Frank followed it into a rectangular courtyard somewhat revealed by low-wattage security lamps at each end. First-floor apartments opened onto a covered promenade; the doors of the second-floor units were under the tile roof of an iron-railed balcony. Lightless windows faced a swath of grass, beds of azaleas and succulents, and a few palms.

A frieze of spiky palm-frond shadows lay across one palely illuminated wall, as motionless as if they were carved on a stone entablature. Then the mysterious flute warbled softly again, the reborn wind huffed harder than before, and the shadows danced, danced. Frank's own distorted, dark reflection whirled briefly over the stucco, among the terpsichorean silhouettes, as he hurried across the courtyard. He found another walkway, another gate, and ultimately the street on which the apartment complex faced.

It was a side street without lampposts. There, the reign of the night was undisputed.

The blustery wind lasted longer than before, churned harder. When the gust ended abruptly, with an equally abrupt cessation of the unmelodic flute, the night seemed to have been left in a vacuum, as though the departing turbulence had taken with it every wisp of breathable air. Then Frank's ears popped as if from a sudden altitude change; as he rushed across the deserted street toward the cars parked along the far curb, air poured in around him again.

He tried four cars before finding one unlocked, a Ford. Slipping behind the wheel, he left the door open to provide some light.

He looked back the way he had come.

*12*

The apartment complex was dead-of-the-night still. Wrapped in darkness. An ordinary building yet inexplicably sinister.

No one was in sight.

Nevertheless, Frank knew someone was closing in on him.

He reached under the dashboard, pulled out a tangle of wires, and hastily jump-started the engine before realizing that such a larcenous skill suggested a life outside of the law. Yet he didn't feel like a thief. He had no sense of guilt and no antipathy for—or fear of—the police. In fact, at the moment, he would have welcomed a cop to help him deal with whoever or whatever was on his tail. He felt not like a criminal, but like a man who had been on the run for an exhaustingly long time, from an implacable and relentless enemy.

As he reached for the handle of the open door, a brief pulse of pale blue light washed over him, and the driver's-side windows of the Ford exploded. Tempered glass showered into the rear seat, gummy and minutely fragmented. Since the front door was not closed, that window didn't spray over him; instead, most of it fell out of the frame, onto the pavement.

Yanking the door shut, he glanced through the gap where the glass had been, toward the gloom-enfolded apartments, saw no one.

Frank threw the Ford in gear, popped the brake, and tramped hard on the accelerator. Swinging away from the curb, he clipped the rear bumper of the car parked in front of him. A brief peal of tortured metal rang sharply across the night.

But he was still under attack: A scintillant blue light, at most one second in duration, lit up the car; over its entire breadth the windshield crazed with thousands of jagged lines, though it had been struck by nothing he could see. Frank averted his face and squeezed his eyes shut just in time to avoid being blinded by flying fragments. For a moment he could not see where he was going, but he didn't let up on the accelerator, preferring the danger of collision to the greater risk of braking and giving his unseen enemy time to reach him. Glass rained over him, spattered across the top of his bent head; luckily, it was safety glass, and none of the fragments cut him.

He opened his eyes, squinting into the gale that rushed through the now empty windshield frame. He saw that he'd gone half a block and had reached the intersection. He whipped

*13*

the wheel to the right, tapping the brake pedal only lightly, and turned onto a more brightly lighted thoroughfare.

Like Saint Elmo's fire, sapphire-blue light glimmered on the chrome, and when the Ford was halfway around the corner, one of the rear tires blew. He had heard no gunfire. A fraction of a second later, the other rear tire blew.

The car rocked, slewed to the left, began to fishtail.

Frank fought the steering wheel.

Both front tires ruptured simultaneously.

The car rocked again, even as it glided sideways, and the sudden collapse of the front tires compensated for the leftward slide of the rear end, giving Frank a chance to grapple the spinning steering wheel into submission.

Again, he had heard no gunfire. He didn't know why all of this was happening—yet he did.

That was the truly frightening part: On some deep subconscious level he *did* know what was happening, what strange force was swiftly destroying the car around him, and he also knew that his chances of escaping were poor.

A flicker of twilight blue . . .

The rear window imploded. Gummy yet prickly wads of safety glass flew past him. Some smacked the back of his head, stuck in his hair.

Frank made the corner and kept going on four flats. The sound of flapping rubber, already shredded, and the grinding of metal wheel rims could be heard even above the roar of the wind that buffeted his face.

He glanced at the rearview mirror. The night was a great black ocean behind him, relieved only by widely spaced streetlamps that dwindled into the gloom like the lights of a double convoy of ships.

According to the speedometer, he was doing thirty miles an hour just after coming out of the turn. He tried to push it up to forty in spite of the ruined tires, but something clanged and clinked under the hood, rattled and whined, and the engine coughed, and he could not coax any more speed out of it.

When he was halfway to the next intersection, the headlights either burst or winked out. Frank couldn't tell which. Even though the streetlamps were widely spaced, he could see well enough to drive.

The engine coughed, then again, and the Ford began to lose

speed. He didn't brake for the stop sign at the next intersection. Instead he pumped the accelerator but to no avail.

Finally the steering failed too. The wheel spun uselessly in his sweaty hands.

Evidently the tires had been completely torn apart. The contact of the steel wheel rims with the pavement flung up gold and turquoise sparks.

*Fireflies in a windstorm. . . .*

He still didn't know what that meant.

Now moving about twenty miles an hour, the car headed straight toward the right-hand curb. Frank tramped the brakes, but they no longer functioned.

The car hit the curb, jumped it, grazed a lamppost with a sound of sheet metal kissing steel, and thudded against the bole of an immense date palm in front of a white bungalow. Lights came on in the house even as the final crash was echoing on the cool night air.

Frank threw the door open, grabbed the leather flight bag from the seat beside him, and got out, shedding fragments of gummy yet splintery safety glass.

Though only mildly cool, the air chilled his face because sweat trickled down from his forehead. He could taste salt when he licked his lips.

A man had opened the front door of the bungalow and stepped onto the porch. Lights flicked on at the house next door.

Frank looked back the way he had come. A thin cloud of luminous sapphire dust seemed to blow through the street. As if shattered by a tremendous surge of current, the bulbs in the streetlamps exploded along the two blocks behind him, and shards of glass, glinting like ice, rained on the blacktop. In the resultant gloom, he thought he saw a tall, shadowy figure, more than a block away, coming after him, but he could not be sure.

To Frank's left, the guy from the bungalow was hurrying down the walk toward the palm tree where the Ford had come to rest. He was talking, but Frank wasn't listening to him.

Clutching the leather satchel, Frank turned and ran. He was not sure what he was running from, or why he was so afraid, or where he might hope to find a haven, but he ran nonetheless because he knew that if he stood there only a few seconds longer, he would be killed.

# 2

THE WINDOWLESS rear compartment of the Dodge van was illuminated by tiny red, blue, green, white, and amber indicator bulbs on banks of electronic surveillance equipment but primarily by the soft green glow from the two computer screens, which made that claustrophobic space seem like a chamber in a deep-sea submersible.

Dressed in a pair of Rockport walking shoes, beige cords, and a maroon sweater, Robert Dakota sat on a swivel chair in front of the twin video display terminals. He tapped his feet against the floorboards, keeping time, and with his right hand he happily conducted an unseen orchestra.

Bobby was wearing a headset with stereo earphones and with a small microphone suspended an inch or so in front of his lips. At the moment he was listening to Benny Goodman's "One O'Clock Jump," the primo version of Count Basie's classic swing composition, six and a half minutes of heaven. As Jess Stacy took up another piano chorus and as Harry James launched into the brilliant trumpet stint that led to the most famous rideout in swing history, Bobby was deep into the music.

But he was also acutely aware of the activity on the display terminals. The one on the right was linked, via microwave, with the computer system at the Decodyne Corporation, in front of which his van was parked. It revealed what Tom Rasmussen was up to in those offices at 1:10 Thursday morning: no good.

One by one, Rasmussen was accessing and copying the files of the software-design team that had recently completed Decodyne's new and revolutionary word-processing program, "Whizard." The Whizard files carried well-constructed lockout instructions—electronic drawbridges, moats, and ramparts. Tom Rasmussen was an expert in computer security, however, and there was no fortress that he could not penetrate, given enough time. Indeed, if Whizard had not been developed on a secure in-house computer system with no links to the outside world, Rasmussen would have slipped into the files from beyond the walls of Decodyne, via a modem and telephone line.

Ironically, he had been working as the night security guard at Decodyne for five weeks, having been hired on the basis of elaborate—and nearly convincing—false papers. Tonight he had breached Whizard's final defenses. In a while he would walk out of Decodyne with a packet of floppy diskettes worth a fortune to the company's competitors.

"One O'Clock Jump" ended.

Into the microphone Bobby said, "Music stop."

That vocal command cued his computerized compact-disc system to switch off, opening the headset for communication with Julie, his wife and business partner.

"You there, babe?"

From her surveillance position in a car at the farthest end of the parking lot behind Decodyne, she had been listening to the same music through her own headset. She sighed. "Did Vernon Brown ever play better trombone than the night of the Carnegie concert?"

"What about Krupa on the drums?"

"Auditory ambrosia. And an aphrodisiac. The music makes me want to go to bed with you."

"Can't. Not sleepy. Besides, we're being private detectives, remember?"

"I like being lovers better."

"We don't earn our daily bread by making love."

"I'd pay you," she said.

"Yeah? How much?"

"Oh, in daily-bread terms . . . half a loaf."

"I'm worth a whole loaf."

Julie said, "Actually, you're worth a whole loaf, two croissants, and a bran muffin."

She had a pleasing, throaty, and altogether sexy voice that he loved to listen to, especially through headphones, when she sounded like an angel whispering in his ears. She would have been a marvelous big-band singer if she had been around in the 1930s and '40s—and if she had been able to carry a tune. She was a great swing dancer, but she couldn't croon worth a damn; when she was in the mood to sing along with old recordings by Margaret Whiting or the Andrews Sisters or Rosemary Clooney or Marion Hutton, Bobby had to leave the room out of respect for the music.

She said, "What's Rasmussen doing?"

Bobby checked the second video display, to his left, which

DEAN R. KOONTZ

was linked to Decodyne's interior security cameras. Rasmussen thought he had over-ridden the cameras and was unobserved; but they had been watching him for the last few weeks, night after night, and recording his every treachery on videotape.

"Old Tom's still in George Ackroyd's office, at the VDT there." Ackroyd was project director for Whizard. Bobby glanced at the other display, which duplicated what Rasmussen was seeing on Ackroyd's computer screen. "He just copied the last Whizard file onto diskette."

Rasmussen switched off the computer in Ackroyd's office.

Simultaneously the linked VDT in front of Bobby went blank.

Bobby said, "He's finished. He's got it all now."

Julie said, "The worm. He must be feeling smug."

Bobby turned to the display on his left, leaned forward, and watched the black-and-white image of Rasmussen at Ackroyd's terminal. "I think he's grinning."

"We'll wipe that grin off his face."

"Let's see what he does next. Want to make a bet? Will he stay in there, finish his shift, and waltz out in the morning—or leave right now?"

"Now," Julie said. "Or soon. He won't risk getting caught with the floppies. He'll leave while no one else is there."

"No bet. I think you're right."

The transmitted image on the monitor flickered, rolled, but Rasmussen did not get out of Ackroyd's chair. In fact he slumped back, as if exhausted. He yawned and rubbed his eyes with the heels of his hands.

"He seems to be resting, gathering his energy," Bobby said.

"Let's have another tune while we wait for him to move."

"Good idea." He gave the CD player the start-up cue—"Begin music"—and was rewarded with Glenn Miller's "In the Mood."

On the monitor, Tom Rasmussen rose from the chair in Ackroyd's dimly lighted office. He yawned again, stretched, and crossed the room to the big windows that looked down on Michaelson Drive, the street on which Bobby was parked.

If Bobby had slipped forward, out of the rear of the van and into the driver's compartment, he probably would have been able to see Rasmussen standing up there at the second-floor window, silhouetted by the glow of Ackroyd's desk lamp, staring out at the night. He stayed where he was, however, satisfied with the view on the screen.

Miller's band was playing the famous "In the Mood" riff, again and again, gradually fading away, almost disappearing entirely but . . . *now* blasting back at full power to repeat the entire cycle.

In Ackroyd's office, Rasmussen finally turned from the window and looked up at the security camera that was mounted on the wall near the ceiling. He seemed to be staring straight at Bobby, as if aware of being watched. He moved a few steps closer to the camera, smiling.

Bobby said, "Music stop," and the Miller band instantly fell silent. To Julie, he said, "Something strange here . . ."

"Trouble?"

Rasmussen stopped just under the security camera, still grinning up at it. From the pocket of his uniform shirt, he withdrew a folded sheet of typing paper, which he opened and held toward the lens. A message had been printed in bold black letters: GOODBYE, ASSHOLE.

"Trouble for sure," Bobby said.

"How bad?"

"I don't know."

An instant later he did know: Automatic weapons fire shattered the night—he could hear the clatter even with his earphones on—and armor-piercing slugs tore through the walls of the van.

Julie evidently picked up the gunfire through her headset. "Bobby, no!"

"Get the hell out of there, babe! Run!"

Even as he spoke, Bobby tore free of the headset and dived off his chair, lying as flat against the floorboards as he could.

# 3

FRANK POLLARD sprinted from street to street, from alley to alley, sometimes cutting across the lawns of the dark houses. In one backyard a large black dog with yellow eyes barked and snapped at him all the way to the board fence, briefly snaring one leg of his pants as he clambered over that barrier. His heart was pounding painfully, and his throat was hot and raw because he was sucking in great drafts of the cool, dry air through his open mouth. His legs ached. As if made of iron, the flight bag pulled on his right arm, and with each lunging step that he took, pain throbbed in his wrist and shoulder socket. But he did not pause and did not glance back, because he felt as if something monstrous was at his heels, a creature that never required rest and that would turn him to stone with its gaze if he dared set eyes upon it.

In time he crossed an avenue, devoid of traffic at that late hour, and hurried along the entrance walk to another apartment complex. He went through a gate into another courtyard, this one centered by an empty swimming pool with a cracked and canted apron.

The place was lightless, but Frank's vision had adapted to the night, and he could see well enough to avoid falling into the drained pool. He was searching for shelter. Perhaps there was a communal laundry room where he could force the lock and hide.

He had discovered something else about himself as he fled his unknown pursuer: He was thirty or forty pounds overweight and out of shape. He desperately needed to catch his breath—and think.

As he was hurrying past the doors of the ground-floor units, he realized that a couple of them were standing open, sagging on ruined hinges. Then he saw that cracks webbed some windows, holes pocked a few, and other panes were missing altogether. The grass was dead, too, as crisp as ancient paper, and the shrubbery was withered; a seared palm tree leaned at a precarious angle. The apartment complex was abandoned, awaiting a wrecking crew.

He came to a set of crumbling concrete stairs at the north end of the courtyard, glanced back. Whoever . . . whatever was following him was still not in sight. Gasping, he climbed to the second-floor balcony and moved from one apartment to another until he found a door ajar. It was warped; the hinges were stiff, but they worked without much noise. He slipped inside, pushing the door shut behind him.

The apartment was a well of shadows, oil-black and pooled deep. Faint ash-gray light outlined the windows but provided no illumination to the room.

He listened intently.

The silence and darkness were equal in depth.

Cautiously, Frank inched toward the nearest window, which faced the balcony and courtyard. Only a few shards of glass remained in the frame, but lots of fragments crunched and clinked under his feet. He trod carefully, both to avoid cutting a foot and to make as little noise as possible.

At the window he halted, listened again.

Stillness.

As if it was the gelid ectoplasm of a slothful ghost, a sluggish current of cold air slid inward across the few jagged points of the glass that had not already fallen from the frame.

Frank's breath steamed in front of his face, pale ribbons of vapor in the gloom.

The silence remained unbroken for ten seconds, twenty, thirty, a full minute.

Perhaps he had escaped.

He was just about to turn away from the window when he heard footsteps outside. At the far end of the courtyard. On the walkway that led in from the street. Hard-soled shoes rang against the concrete, and each footfall echoed hollowly off the stucco walls of the surrounding buildings.

Frank stood motionless and breathed through his mouth, as if the stalker could be counted on to have the hearing of a jungle cat.

When he entered the courtyard from the entrance walkway, the stranger halted. After a long pause he began to move again; though the overlapping echoes made sounds deceptive, he seemed to be heading slowly north along the apron of the pool, toward the same stairs by which Frank, himself, had climbed to the second floor of the apartment complex.

Each deliberate, metronomic footfall was like the heavy tick of a headsman's clock mounted on a guillotine railing, counting off the seconds until the appointed hour of the blade's descent.

# 4

As if alive, the Dodge van shrieked with every bullet that tore through its sheet-metal walls, and the wounds were inflicted not one at a time but by the score, with such relentless fury, the assault had to involve at least two machine guns. While Bobby Dakota lay flat on the floor, trying to catch God's attention with fervent heaven-directed prayers, fragments of metal rained down on him. One of the computer screens imploded, then the other terminal, too, and all the indicator lights went out, but the interior of the van was not entirely dark; showers of amber and green and crimson and silver sparks erupted from the damaged electronic units as one steel-jacketed round after another pierced equipment housings and shattered circuit boards. Glass fell on him, too, and splinters of plastic, bits of wood, scraps of paper; the air was filled with a virtual blizzard of debris. But the noise was the worst of it; in his mind he saw himself sealed inside a great iron drum, while half a dozen big bikers, stoned on PCP, pounded on the outside of his prison with tire irons, really huge bikers with massive muscles and thick necks and coarse peltlike beards and wildly colorful Death's-head tattoos on their arms—hell, tattoos on their *faces*—guys as big as Thor, the Viking god, but with blazing, psychotic eyes.

Bobby had a vivid imagination. He had always thought that was one of his best qualities, one of his strengths. But he could not simply imagine his way out of this mess.

With every passing second, as slugs continued to crash into the van, he grew more astonished that he had not been hit. He was pressed to the floor, as tight as a carpet, and he tried to imagine that his body was only a quarter of an inch thick, a target with an incredibly low profile, but he still expected to get his ass shot off.

He had not anticipated the need for a gun; it wasn't that kind of case. At least it hadn't *seemed* to be that kind of case. A .38 revolver was in the van glovebox, well beyond his reach, which did not cause him a lot of frustration, actually, because a single handgun against a pair of automatic weapons was not much use.

The gunfire stopped.

After that cacophony of destruction, the silence was so profound, Bobby felt as if he had gone deaf.

The air reeked of hot metal, overheated electronic components, scorched insulation—and gasoline. Evidently the van's tank had been punctured. The engine was still chugging, and a few sparks spat out of the shattered equipment surrounding Bobby, and his chances of escaping a flash fire were a whole lot worse than his chances of winning fifty million bucks in the state lottery.

He wanted to get the hell out of there, but if he burst out of the van, they might be waiting with machine guns to cut him down. On the other hand, if he continued to hug the floor in the darkness, counting on them to give him up for dead without checking on him, the Dodge might flare like a campfire primed with starter fluid, toasting him as crisp as a marshmallow.

He had no difficulty imagining himself stepping out of the van and being hit immediately by a score of bullets, jerking and twitching in a spasmodic death dance across the blacktop street, like a broken marionette jerked around on tangled strings. But he found it even easier to imagine his skin peeling off in the fire, flesh bubbling and smoking, hair *whooshing* up like a torch, eyes melting, teeth turning coal-black as flames seared his tongue and followed his breath down his throat to his lungs.

Sometimes a vivid imagination was definitely a curse.

Suddenly the gasoline fumes became so heavy that he had trouble drawing breath, so he started to get up.

Outside, a car horn began to blare. He heard a racing engine drawing rapidly nearer.

Someone shouted, and a machine gun opened fire again.

Bobby hit the floor, wondering what the hell was going on, but as the car with the blaring horn drew nearer, he realized what must be happening: Julie. Julie was happening. Sometimes she was like a natural force; she happened the way a storm happened, the way lightning happened, abruptly crackling down a dark sky. He had told her to get out of there, to save herself, but she had not listened to him; he wanted to kick her butt for being so bullheaded, but he loved her for it too.

# 5

SIDLING AWAY from the broken window, Frank tried to time his steps to those of the man in the courtyard below, with the hope that any noise he made, trodding on glass, would be covered by his unseen enemy's advance. He figured that he was in the living room of the apartment, that it was pretty much empty except for whatever detritus had been left behind by the last tenants or had blown through the missing windows, and indeed he made it across that chamber and into a hallway in relative silence, without colliding with anything.

He hurriedly felt his way along the hall, which was as black as a predator's lair. It smelled of mold and mildew and urine. He passed the entrance to a room, kept going, turned right through the next doorway, and shuffled to another broken window. This one had no splinters of glass left in the frame, and it did not face the courtyard but looked onto a lamplit and deserted street.

Something rustled behind him.

He turned, blinking blindly at the gloom, and almost cried out.

But the sound must have been made by a rat scurrying along the floor, close to the wall, across dry leaves or bits of paper. Just a rat.

Frank listened for footsteps, but if the stalker was still homing on him, the hollow heel clicks of his approach were completely muffled by the walls that now intervened.

He looked out the window again. The dead lawn lay below, as dry as sand and twice as brown, offering little cushion. He dropped the leather flight bag, which landed with a thud. Wincing at the prospect of the leap, he climbed onto the sill, crouching in the broken-out window, hands braced against the frame, where for a moment he hesitated.

A gust of wind ruffled his hair and coolly caressed his face. But it was a normal draft, nothing like the preternatural whiffs of wind that, earlier, had been accompanied by the unearthly and unmelodic music of a distant flute.

Suddenly, behind Frank, a blue flash pulsed out of the living room, down the hall, and through the doorway. The strange tide of light was trailed closely by an explosion and a concussion wave that shook the walls and seemed to churn the air into a more solid substance. The front door had been blasted to pieces; he heard chunks of it raining down on the floor of the apartment a couple of rooms away.

He jumped out of the window, landed on his feet. But his knees gave way, and he fell flat on the dead lawn.

At that same moment a large truck turned the corner. Its

cargo bed had slat sides and a wooden tailgate. The driver smoothly shifted gears and drove past the apartment house, apparently unaware of Frank.

He scrambled to his feet, plucked the satchel off the barren lawn, and ran into the street. Having just rounded the corner, the truck was not moving fast, and Frank managed to grab the tailgate and pull himself up, one-handed, until he was standing on the rear bumper.

As the truck accelerated, Frank looked back at the decaying apartment complex. No mysterious blue light glimmered at any of the windows; they were all as black and empty as the sockets of a skull.

The truck turned right at the next corner, moving away into the sleepy night.

Exhausted, Frank clung to the tailgate. He would have been able to hold on better if he had dropped the leather flight bag, but he held fast to it because he suspected that its contents might help him to learn who he was and from where he had come and from what he was running.

CUT AND RUN! Bobby actually thought she would cut and run when trouble struck—*"Get the hell out of there, babe! Run!"*—would cut and run just because he told her to, as if she was an obedient little wifey, not a full-fledged partner in the agency, not a damned good investigator in her own right, just a token backup who couldn't take the heat when the furnace kicked on. Well, to hell with that.

In her mind she could see his lovable face—merry blue eyes, pug nose, smattering of freckles, generous mouth—framed by thick honey-gold hair that was mussed (as was most often the case) like that of a small boy who had just gotten up from a nap. She wanted to bop his pug nose just hard enough to make his blue eyes water, so he'd have no doubt how the cut-and-run suggestion annoyed her.

She had been on surveillance behind Decodyne, at the far

end of the corporate parking lot, in the deep shadows under a massive Indian laurel. The moment Bobby signaled trouble, she started the Toyota's engine. By the time she heard gunfire over the earphones, she had shifted gears, popped the emergency brake, switched on the headlights, and jammed the accelerator toward the floor.

At first she kept the headset on, calling Bobby's name, trying to get an answer from him, hearing only the most godawful ruckus from his end. Then the set went dead; she couldn't hear anything at all, so she pulled it off and threw it into the backseat.

*Cut and run! Damn him!*

When she reached the end of the last row in the parking lot, she let up on the accelerator with her right foot, simultaneously tapping the brake pedal with her left foot, finessing the small car into a slide, which carried it onto the access road that led around the big building. She turned the steering wheel into the slide, then gave the heap some gas again even before the back end had stopped skidding and shuddering. The tires barked, and the engine shrieked, and with a rattle-squeak-twang of tortured metal, the car leaped forward.

They were shooting at Bobby, and Bobby probably wasn't even able to shoot back, because he was lax about carrying a gun on every job; he went armed only when it seemed that the current business was likely to involve violence. The Decodyne assignment had looked peaceable enough; sometimes industrial espionage could turn nasty, but the bad guy in this case was Tom Rasmussen, a computer nerd and a greedy son of a bitch, clever as a dog reading Shakespeare on a high wire, with a record of theft via computer but with no blood on his hands. He was the high-tech equivalent of a meek, embezzling bank clerk—or so he had seemed.

But Julie was armed on *every* job. Bobby was the optimist; she was the pessimist. Bobby expected people to act in their own best interests and be reasonable, but Julie half expected every apparently normal person to be, in secret, a crazed psychotic. A Smith & Wesson .357 Magnum was held by a clip to the back of the glovebox lid, and an Uzi—with two spare, thirty-round magazines—lay on the other front seat. From what she had heard on the earphones before they'd gone dead, she was going to need that Uzi.

The Toyota virtually *flew* past the side of Decodyne, and she wheeled hard left, onto Michaelson Drive, almost rising onto two wheels, almost losing control, but not quite. Ahead, Bobby's Dodge was parked at the curb in front of the building, and another van—a dark blue Ford—was stopped in the street, doors open wide.

Two men, who had evidently been in the Ford, were standing four or five yards from the Dodge, chopping the hell out of it with automatic weapons, blasting away with such ferocity that they seemed not to be after the man inside but to have some bizarre personal grudge against the Dodge itself. They stopped firing, turned toward her as she came out of the driveway onto Michaelson, and hurriedly jammed fresh magazines into their weapons.

Ideally, she would close the hundred-yard gap between herself and the men, pull the Toyota sideways in the street, slip out, and use the car as cover to blow out the tires on their Ford and pin them down until police arrived. But she didn't have time for all of that. They were already raising the muzzles of their weapons.

She was unnerved at how lonely the night streets looked at this hour in the heart of metropolitan Orange County, barren of traffic, washed by the urine-yellow light of the sodium-vapor streetlamps. They were in an area of banks and office buildings, no residences, no restaurants or bars within a couple of blocks. It might as well have been a city on the moon, or a vision of the world after it had been swept by an Apocalyptic disease that had left only a handful of survivors.

She didn't have time to handle the two gunmen by the book, and she could not count on help from any quarter, so she would have to do what they least expected: play kamikaze, use her *car* as a weapon.

The instant she had the Toyota fully under control, she pressed the accelerator tight to the floorboards and rocketed straight at the two bastards. They opened fire, but she was already slipping down in the seat and leaning sideways a little, trying to keep her head below the dashboard and still hold the wheel relatively steady. Bullets snapped and whined off the car. The windshield burst. A second later Julie hit one of the gunmen so hard that the impact snapped her head forward, against the wheel, cutting her forehead, snapping her teeth together forcefully enough to make her jaw ache; even as pain needled through her face, she heard the body bounce off the front bumper and slam onto the hood.

With blood trickling down her forehead and dripping from her right eyebrow, Julie jabbed at the brakes and sat up at the same time. She was confronted by a man's wide-eyed corpse jammed in the frame of the empty windshield. His face was in front of the steering wheel—teeth chipped, lips torn, chin slashed, cheek battered, left eye missing—and one of his broken legs was inside the car, hooked down over the dashboard.

Julie found the brake pedal and pumped it. With the sudden drop in speed, the dead man was dislodged. His limp body rolled across the hood, and when the car slid to a shaky halt, he vanished over the front end.

Heart racing, blinking to keep the stinging blood from blurring the vision in her right eye, Julie snatched the Uzi from the seat beside her, shoved open the door, and rolled out, moving fast and staying low.

The other gunman was already in the blue Ford van. He gave it gas before remembering to shift out of park, so the tires screamed and smoked.

Julie squeezed off two short bursts from the Uzi, blowing out both tires on her side of the van.

But the gunman didn't stop. He shifted gears at last and tried to drive past her on two ruined tires.

The guy might have killed Bobby; now he was getting away. He would probably never be found if Julie didn't stop him. Reluctantly she swung the Uzi higher and emptied the magazine into the side window of the van. The Ford accelerated, then suddenly slowed and swung to the right, at steadily diminishing speed, in a long arc that carried it to the far curb, where it came to a halt with a jolt.

No one got out.

Keeping an eye on the Ford, Julie leaned into her car, plucked a spare magazine from the seat, and reloaded the Uzi. She approached the idling van cautiously and pulled open the door, but caution was not required because the man behind the wheel was dead. Feeling a little sick, she reached in and switched off the engine.

Briefly, as she turned from the Ford and hurried toward the bullet-riddled Dodge, the only sounds she could hear were the soughing of a faint breeze in the lush corporate landscaping that flanked the street, punctuated by the gentle hiss and rattle of palm fronds. Then she also heard the idling engine of the Dodge, simultaneously smelled gasoline, and shouted, "Bobby!"

Before she reached the white van, the back doors creaked open, and Bobby came out, shedding twists of metal, chunks of plastic, bits of glass, wood chips, and scraps of paper. He was gasping, no doubt because the gasoline fumes had driven most of the breathable air out of the Dodge's rear quarters.

Sirens rose in the distance.

Together they quickly walked away from the van. They had gone only a few steps when orange light flared and flames rose in a *woooosh* from the gasoline pooled on the pavement, enveloping the vehicle in bright shrouds. They hurried beyond the corona of intense heat that surrounded the Dodge and stood for a moment, blinking at the wreckage, then at each other.

The sirens were drawing nearer.

He said, "You're bleeding."

"Just skinned my forehead a little."

"You sure?"

"It's nothing. What about you?"

He sucked in a deep breath. "I'm okay."

"Really?"

"Yeah."

"You weren't hit?"

"Unmarked. It's a miracle."

"Bobby?"

"What?"

"I couldn't handle it if you'd turned up dead in there."

"I'm not dead. I'm fine."

"Thank God," she said.

Then she kicked his right shin.

"Ow! What the hell?"

She kicked his left shin.

"Julie, dammit!"

"Don't you ever tell me to cut and run."

"What?"

"I'm a full half of this partnership in *every* way."

"But—"

"I'm as smart as you, as fast as you—"

He glanced at the dead man on the street, the other one in the Ford van, half visible through the open door, and he said, "That's for sure, babe."

"—as tough as you—"

29

"I know, I know. Don't kick me again."

She said, "What about Rasmussen?"

Bobby looked up at the Decodyne building. "You think he's still in there?"

"The only exits from the parking lot are onto Michaelson, and he hasn't come out this way, so unless he fled on foot, he's in there, all right. We've got to nail him before he slides out of the trap with those diskettes."

"Nothing worthwhile on the diskettes anyway," Bobby said.

Decodyne had been on to Rasmussen from the time he applied for the job, because Dakota & Dakota Investigations—which was contracted to handle the company's security checks—had penetrated the hacker's highly sophisticated false ID. Decodyne's management wanted to play along with Rasmussen long enough to discover to whom he would pass the Whizard files when he got them; they intended to prosecute the money man who had hired Rasmussen, for no doubt the hacker's employer was one of Decodyne's primary competitors. They had allowed Tom Rasmussen to think he had compromised the security cameras, when in fact he had been under constant observation. They also had allowed him to break down the file codes and access the information he wanted, but unknown to him they had inserted secret instructions in the files, which insured that any diskettes he acquired would be full of trash data of no use to anyone.

Flames roared and crackled, consuming the van. Julie watched chimeras of reflected flames slither and caper up the glass walls and across the blank, black windows of Decodyne, as if they were striving to reach the roof and coalesce there in the form of gargoyles.

Raising her voice slightly to compete with the fire and with the shriek of approaching sirens, she said, "Well, we thought he believed he'd circumvented the videotape records of the security cameras, but apparently he knew we were on to him."

"Sure did."

"So he also might've been smart enough to search for an anticopying directive in the files—and find a way around it."

Bobby frowned. "You're right."

"So he's probably got Whizard, unscrambled, on those diskettes."

"Damn, I don't want to go in there. I've been shot at enough tonight."

*30*

A police cruiser turned the corner two blocks away and sped toward them, siren screaming, emergency lights casting off alternating waves of blue and red light.

"Here come the professionals," Julie said. "Why don't we let them take over now?"

"We were hired to do the job. We have an obligation. PI honor is a sacred thing, you know. What would Sam Spade think of us?"

She said, "Sam Spade can go spit up a rope."

"What would Philip Marlowe think?"

"Philip Marlowe can go spit up a rope."

"What will our client think?"

"Our *client* can go spit up a rope."

"Dear, 'spit' isn't the popular expression."

"I know, but I'm a lady."

"You certainly are."

As the black-and-white braked in front of them, another police car turned the corner behind it, siren wailing, and a third entered Michaelson Drive from the other direction.

Julie put her Uzi on the pavement and raised her hands to avoid unfortunate misunderstandings. "I'm *really* glad you're alive, Bobby."

"You going to kick me again?"

"Not for a while."

# 7

FRANK POLLARD hung on to the tailgate and rode the truck nine or ten blocks, without drawing the attention of the driver. Along the way he saw a sign welcoming him to the city of Anaheim, so he figured he was in southern California, although he still didn't know if this was where he lived or whether he was from out of town. Judging by the chill in the air, it was winter—not truly cold but as frigid as it got in these climes. He was unnerved to realize that he did not know the date or even the month. Shivering, he dropped off the truck when it slowed and turned onto a serviceway that led through a warehouse district. Huge, corrugated-metal buildings—some newly painted and some streaked with rust, some dimly lit by security lamps and some not—loomed against the star-spattered sky.

Carrying the flight bag, he walked away from the warehouses. The streets in that area were lined with shabby bungalows. The shrubs and trees were overgrown in many places: untrimmed palms with full skirts of dead fronds; bushy hibiscuses with half-closed pale blooms glimmering softly in the gloom; jade hedges and plum-thorn hedges so old they were more woody than leafy; bougainvillea draped over roofs and fences, bristling with thousands of untamed, questing trailers. His soft-soled shoes made no sound on the sidewalk, and his shadow alternately stretched ahead of him and then behind, as he approached and then passed one lamppost after another.

Cars, mostly older models, some rusted and battered, were parked at curbs and in driveways; keys might have dangled from the ignitions of some of them, and he could have jump-started any he chose. However, he noted that the cinderblock walls between the properties—as well as the walls of a decrepit and abandoned house—shimmered with the spray-painted, ghostly, semi-phosphorescent graffiti of Latino gangs, and he didn't want to tinker with a set of wheels that might belong to one of their members. Those guys didn't bother rushing to a phone to call the police if they caught you trying to steal one of their cars; they just blew your head off or put a knife in your neck. Frank had enough trouble already, even with his head intact and his throat unpunctured, so he kept walking.

Twelve blocks later, in a neighborhood of well-kept houses and better cars, he began searching for a set of wheels that would be easy to boost. The tenth vehicle he tried was a one-year-old green Chevy, parked near a streetlamp, the doors un-locked, the keys tucked under the driver's seat.

Intent on putting a lot of distance between himself and the deserted apartment complex where he had last encountered his unknown pursuer, Frank switched on the Chevy's heater, drove from Anaheim to Santa Ana, then south on Bristol Avenue to-ward Costa Mesa, surprised by his familiarity with the streets. He seemed to know the area well. He recognized buildings, shopping centers, parks, and neighborhoods past which he drove, though the sight of them did nothing to rekindle his burnt-out memory. He still could not recall who he was, where he lived, what he did for a living, what he was running from, or how he had come to wake up in an alleyway in the middle of the night.

Even at that dead hour—the car clock indicated it was 2:48—he figured his chances of encountering a traffic cop were greater on a freeway, so he stayed on the surface streets through Costa Mesa and the eastern and southern fringes of Newport Beach. At Corona Del Mar he picked up the Pacific Coast Highway and followed it all the way to Laguna Beach, encountering a thin fog that gradually thickened as he progressed southward.

Laguna, a picturesque resort town and artists' colony, shelved down a series of steep hillsides and canyon walls to the sea, most of it cloaked now in the thick fog. Only an occasional car passed him, and the mist rolling in from the Pacific became sufficiently dense to force him to reduce his speed to fifteen miles an hour.

Yawning and gritty-eyed, he turned onto a side street east of the highway and parked at the curb in front of a dark, two-story, gabled, Cape Cod house that looked out of place on these Western slopes. He wanted to get a motel room, but before he tried to check in somewhere, he needed to know if he had any money or credit cards. For the first time all night, he had a chance to look for ID, as well. He searched the pockets of his jeans, but to no avail.

He switched on the overhead light, pulled the leather flight bag onto his lap and opened it. The satchel was filled with tightly banded stacks of twenty- and hundred-dollar bills.

# 8

THE THIN SOUP of gray mist was gradually stirring itself into a thicker stew. A couple of miles closer to the ocean, the night probably was clotted with fog so dense that it would almost have lumps.

Coatless, protected from the night only by a sweater, but warmed by the fact that he had narrowly avoided almost certain death, Bobby leaned against one of the patrol cars in front of Decodyne and watched Julie as she paced back and forth with her hands in the pockets of her brown leather jacket. He never got tired of looking at her. They had been married seven years, and during that time they had lived and worked and played together virtually twenty-four hours a day, seven days a week. Bobby had never been the kind who liked to hang out with a bunch of guys at a bar or ball game—partly because it was difficult to find other guys in their middle thirties who were interested in the things that he cared about: big-band music, the arts and pop culture of the '30s and '40s, and classic Disney comic books. Julie wasn't a lunch-with-the-girls type, either, because not many thirty-year-old women were into the big-band era, Warner Brothers cartoons, martial arts, or advanced weapons training. In spite of spending so much time together, they remained fresh to each other, and she was still the most interesting and appealing woman he had ever known.

"What's taking them so long?" she asked, glancing up at the now-lighted windows of Decodyne, bright but fuzzy rectangles in the mist.

"Be patient with them, dear," Bobby said. "They don't have the dynamism of Dakota and Dakota. They're just a humble SWAT team."

Michaelson Drive was blocked off. Eight police vehicles—cars and vans—were scattered along the street. The chilly night crackled with the static and metallic voices sputtering out of police-band radios. An officer was behind the wheel of one of the cars, and other uniformed men were positioned at both ends of the block, and two more were visible at the front doors of Decodyne; the rest were inside, looking for Rasmussen. Meanwhile, men from the police lab and coroner's office were photographing, measuring, and removing the bodies of the two gunmen.

"What if he gets away with the diskettes?" Julie asked.

"He won't."

She nodded. "Sure, I know what you're thinking—Whizard was developed on a closed-system computer with no links beyond Decodyne. But there's another system in the company, with modems and everything, isn't there? What if he takes the diskettes to one of *those* terminals and sends them out by phone?"

"Can't. The second system, the outlinked system, is totally different from the one on which Whizard was developed. Incompatible."

"Rasmussen is clever."

"There's also a night lockout that keeps the outlinked system shut down."

"Rasmussen is clever," she repeated.

She continued to pace in front of him.

The skinned spot on her forehead, where she had met the steering wheel when she'd jammed on the brakes, was no longer bleeding, though it looked raw and wet. She had wiped her face with tissues, but smears of dried blood, which looked almost like bruises, had remained under her right eye and along her jawline. Each time Bobby focused on those stains or on the shallow wound, a pang of anxiety quivered through him at the realization of what might have happened to her, to both of them.

Not surprisingly, her injury and the blood on her face only accentuated her beauty, making her appear more fragile and therefore more precious. Julie *was* beautiful, although Bobby realized that she appeared more so to his eyes than to others, which was all right because, after all, his eyes were the only ones through which he could look at her. Though it was kinking up a bit now in the moist night air, her chestnut-brown hair was usually thick and lustrous. She had wide-set eyes as dark as semi-sweet chocolate, skin as smooth and naturally tan as toffee ice cream, and a generous mouth that always tasted sweet to him. Whenever he watched her without her being fully aware of the intensity of his attention, or when he was apart from her and tried to conjure an image of her in his mind, he always thought of her in terms of food: chestnuts, chocolate, toffee, cream, sugar, butter. He found this amusing, but he also understood the profundity of his choice of similes: She reminded him of food because she, *more* than food, sustained him.

Activity at the entrance to Decodyne, about sixty feet away, at the end of a palm-flanked walkway, drew Julie's attention and then Bobby's. Someone from the SWAT team had come to the doors to report to the guards stationed there. A moment later one of the officers motioned for Julie and Bobby to come forward.

When they joined him, he said, "They found this Rasmussen. You want to see him, make sure he has the right diskettes?"

"Yeah," Bobby said.

"Definitely," Julie said, and her throaty voice didn't sound at all sexy now, just tough.

# 9

KEEPING A LOOKOUT for any Laguna Beach police who might be running graveyard-shift patrols, Frank Pollard removed the bundles of cash from the flight bag and piled them on the car seat beside him. He counted fifteen packets of twenty-dollar bills and eleven bundles of hundreds. He judged the thickness of each wad to be approximately one hundred bills, and when he did the mathematics in his head he came up with $140,000. He had no idea where the money had come from or whether it belonged to him.

The first of two small, zippered side compartments in the bag yielded another surprise—a wallet that contained no cash and no credit cards but two important pieces of identification: a Social Security card and a California driver's license. With the wallet was a United States passport. The photographs on the passport and license were of the same man: thirtyish, brown hair, a round face, prominent ears, brown eyes, an easy smile, and dimples. Realizing he had also forgotten what he looked like, he tilted the rearview mirror and was able to see enough of his face to match it with the one on the ID. The problem was . . . the license and passport bore the name James Roman, not Frank Pollard.

He unzipped the second of the two smaller compartments, and found another Social Security card, passport, and California driver's license. These were all in the name of George Farris, but the photos were of Frank.

James Roman meant nothing to him.

George Farris was also meaningless.

And Frank Pollard, whom he believed himself to be, was only a cipher, a man without any past that he could recall.

"What the hell am I tangled up in?" he said aloud. He needed to hear his own voice to convince himself that he was, in fact, not just a ghost reluctant to leave this world for the one to which death had entitled him.

As the fog closed around his parked car, blotting out most of the night beyond, a terrible loneliness overcame him. He could think of no one to whom he could turn, nowhere to which he could retreat and be assured of safety. A man without a past was also a man without a future.

# 10

WHEN BOBBY and Julie stepped out of the elevator onto the third floor, in the company of a police officer named McGrath, Julie saw Tom Rasmussen sitting on the polished gray vinyl tiles, his back against the wall of the corridor, his hands cuffed in front of him and linked by a length of chain to shackles that bound his ankles together. He was pouting. He had tried to steal software worth tens of millions of dollars, if not hundreds of millions, and from the window of Ackroyd's office he had cold-bloodedly given the signal to have Bobby killed, yet here he was pouting like a child because he had been caught. His weasel face was puckered, and his lower lip was thrust out, and his yellow-brown eyes looked watery, as though he might break into tears if anyone dared to say a cross word. The mere sight of him infuriated Julie. She wanted to kick his teeth down his throat, all the way into his stomach, so he could re-chew whatever he had last eaten.

The cops had found him in a supply closet, behind boxes that he had rearranged to make a pitifully obvious hiding place. Evidently, standing at Ackroyd's window to watch the fireworks, he had been surprised when Julie had appeared in the Toyota. She had driven the Toyota into the Decodyne parking lot early in the day and had stayed far back from the building, in the shadows beneath the boughs of the laurel, where no one had spotted her. Instead of fleeing the moment he saw the first gunman run down, Rasmussen had hesitated, no doubt wondering who *else* was out there. Then he heard the sirens, and his only option was to hide out in the hope they would only search the building casually and conclude that he had escaped. With a computer, he was a genius, but when it came to making cool decisions under fire, Rasmussen was not half as bright as he thought he was.

Two heavily armed cops were watching over him. But because he was huddled and shivering and on the verge of tears, they were a bit ludicrous in their bulletproof vests, cradling automatic weapons, squinting in the fluorescent glare, and looking grim.

Julie knew one of the officers, Sampson Garfeuss, from her own days with the sheriff's department, where Sampson also served before joining the City of Irvine force. Either his parents had been prescient or he had striven mightily to live up to his name, for he was both tall and broad and rocklike. He held a lidless box that contained four small floppy diskettes. He showed it to Julie and said, "Is this what he was after?"

"Could be," she said, accepting the box.

Taking the diskettes from her, Bobby said, "I'll have to go down one floor to Ackroyd's office, switch on the computer, pop these in, and see what's on them."

"Go ahead," Sampson said.

"You'll have to accompany me," Bobby said to McGrath, the officer who had brought them up on the elevator. "Keep a watch on me, make sure I don't tamper with these things." He indicated Tom Rasmussen. "We don't want this piece of slime claiming they were blank disks, saying I framed him by copying the real stuff onto them myself."

As Bobby and McGrath went into one of the elevators and descended to the second floor, Julie hunkered down in front of Rasmussen. "You know who I am?"

Rasmussen looked at her but said nothing.

"I'm Bobby Dakota's wife. Bobby was in that van your goons shot up. It was my Bobby you tried to kill."

He looked away from her, at his cuffed wrists.

She said, "Know what I'd like to do to you?" She held one of her hands down in front of his face, and wiggled her manicured nails. "For starters, I'd like to grab you by the throat, hold your head against the wall, and ram two of these nice, sharp fingernails straight through your eyes, all the way in, deep, real deep in your fevered little brain, and twist them around, see if maybe I can unscramble whatever's messed up in there."

"Jesus, lady," Sampson's partner said. His name was Burdock. Beside anyone but Sampson, he would have been a big man.

38

"Well," she said, "he's too screwed up to get any help from a prison psychiatrist."

Sampson said, "Don't do anything foolish, Julie."

Rasmussen glanced at her, meeting her eyes for only a second, but that was long enough for him to understand the depth of her anger and to be frightened by it. A flush of childish embarrassment and temper had accompanied his pout, but now his face went pale. To Sampson, in a voice that was too shrill and quaverous to be as tough as he intended, Rasmussen said, "Keep this crazy bitch away from me."

"She's not actually crazy," Sampson said. "Not clinically speaking, at least. Pretty hard to have anyone declared crazy these days, I'm afraid. Lots of concern about their civil rights, you know. No, I wouldn't say she's crazy."

Without looking away from Rasmussen, Julie said, "Thank you so much, Sam."

"You'll notice I didn't say anything about the other half of his accusation," Sampson said good-naturedly.

"Yeah, I got your point."

While she talked to Sampson, she kept her attention on Rasmussen.

Everyone harbored a special fear, a private boogeyman built to his own specifications and crouched in a dark corner of his mind, and Julie knew what Tom Rasmussen feared more than anything in the world. Not heights. Not confining spaces. Not crowds, cats, flying, insects, dogs, or darkness. Dakota & Dakota had developed a thick file on him in recent weeks, and had turned up the fact that he suffered from a phobia of blindness. In prison, every month with the regularity of a true obsessive, he had demanded an eye exam, claiming his vision was deteriorating, and he'd petitioned to be tested periodically for syphilis, diabetes, and other diseases that, untreated, could result in blindness. When not in prison—and he had been there twice—he had a standing, monthly appointment with an ophthalmologist in Costa Mesa.

Still squatting in front of Rasmussen, Julie took hold of his chin. He flinched. She twisted his head toward her. She thrust two fingers of her other hand at him, raked them down his cheek, making red welts on his wan skin, but not hard enough to draw blood.

He squealed and tried to strike her with his cuffed hands, but he was inhibited by both his fear and the chain that tethered his wrists to his ankles. "What the hell you think you're doing?"

She spread the same two fingers with which she'd scratched him, and now she poked them at him, stopping just two inches short of his eyes. He winced, made a mewling sound, and tried to pull loose of her, but she held him fast by the chin, forcing a confrontation.

"Me and Bobby have been together eight years, married more than seven, and they've been the best years of my life, but you come along and think you can just squash him the way you'd squash a bug."

She slowly brought her fingertips closer to his eyes. An inch and a half. One inch.

Rasmussen tried to pull back. His head was against the wall. He had nowhere to go.

The sharp tips of her manicured fingernails were less than half an inch from his eyes.

"This is police brutality," Rasmussen said.

"I'm not a cop," Julie said.

"*They* are," he said, rolling his eyes at Sampson and Burdock. "Better get this bitch away from me, I'll sue your asses off."

With her fingernails she flicked his eyelashes.

His attention snapped back to her. He was breathing fast, and suddenly he was sweating too.

She flicked his lashes again, and smiled.

The dark pupils in his yellow-brown eyes were open wide.

"You bastards better hear me, I swear, I'll sue, they'll kick you off the force—"

She flicked his lashes again.

He closed his eyes tight. "—they'll take away your god-damned uniforms and badges, they'll throw *you* in prison, and you know what happens to ex-cops in prison, they get the shit kicked out of them, broken, killed, *raped!*" His voice spiraled up, cracked on the last word, like the voice of an adolescent boy.

Glancing at Sampson to be sure she had his tacit if not active approval to carry this just a little further, glancing also at Burdock and seeing that he was not as placid as Sampson but would probably stay out of it for a while yet, Julie pressed her fingernails against Rasmussen's eyelids.

He attempted to squeeze his eyes even more tightly shut.

She pressed harder. "You tried to take Bobby away from me, so I'll take your eyes away from you."

"You're *nuts!*"

She pressed still harder.

"Make her stop," Rasmussen demanded of the two cops.

"If you didn't want me to have my Bobby to look at, why should I let you look at anything ever again?"

"What do you want?" Perspiration poured down Rasmussen's face; he looked like a candle in a bonfire, melting fast.

"Who gave you permission to kill Bobby?"

"Permission? What do you mean? Nobody. I don't need—"

"You wouldn't have tried to touch him if your employer hadn't told you to do it."

"I knew he was on to me," Rasmussen said frantically, and because she had not let up the pressure with her nails, thin tears flowed from under his eyelids. "I knew he was out there, tumbled to him five or six days ago, even though he used different vans, trucks, even that orange van with the county seal on it. So I had to do something, didn't I? I couldn't walk away from the job, too much money at stake. I couldn't just let him nail me when I finally got Whizard, so I had to do something. Listen, Jesus, it was as simple as that."

"You're just a computer freak, a hired hacker—morally bent, sleazy, but you're no tough guy. You're soft, squishy-soft. You wouldn't plan a hit on your own. Your boss told you to do it."

"I don't have a boss. I'm freelance."

"Somebody still pays you."

She risked more pressure, not with the points of her nails but with the flat surfaces, although Rasmussen was so swept away by a rapture of fear that he might still imagine he could feel those filed edges gradually carving through the delicate shields of his eyelids. He must be seeing interior starfields now, bursts and whorls of color, and maybe he was feeling some pain. He was shaking; his shackles clinked and rattled. More tears squeezed from beneath his lids.

"Delafield." The word erupted from him, as if he had been trying simultaneously to hold it back and to expel it with all his might. "Kevin Delafield."

"Who's he?" Julie asked, still holding Rasmussen's chin with one hand, her fingernails against his eyes, unrelenting.

"Microcrest Corporation."

"That's who hired you for this?"

He was rigid, afraid to move a fraction of an inch, convinced that the slightest shift in his position would force her fingernails into his eyes. "Yeah. Delafield. A nutcase. A renegade. They don't understand about him at Microcrest. They just know he gets results for them. When this hits the fan they'll be surprised by it, blown away. So let go of me. What more do you want?"

She let go of him.

Immediately he opened his eyes, blinked, testing his vision, then broke down and sobbed with relief.

As Julie stood, the nearby elevator doors opened, and Bobby returned with the officer who had accompanied him downstairs to Ackroyd's office. Bobby looked at Rasmussen, cocked his head at Julie, clucked his tongue, and said, "You've been naughty, haven't you, dear? Can't I take you anywhere?"

"I just had a conversation with Mr. Rasmussen. That's all."

"He seems to have found it stimulating," Bobby said.

Rasmussen sat slumped forward with his hands over his eyes, weeping uncontrollably.

"We disagreed about something," Julie said.

"Movies, books?"

"Music."

"Ah."

Sampson Garfeuss said softly, "You're a wild woman, Julie."

"He tried to have Bobby killed," was all she said.

Sampson nodded. "I'm not saying I don't admire wildness sometimes . . . a little. But you sure as hell owe me one."

"I do," she agreed.

"You owe me more than one," Burdock said. "This guy's going to file a complaint. You can bet your ass on it."

"Complaint about what?" Julie asked. "He's not even marked."

Already the faint welts on Rasmussen's cheek were fading. Sweat, tears, and a case of the shakes were the only evidence of his ordeal.

"Listen," Julie told Burdock, "he cracked because I just happened to know exactly the right weak point where I could give him a little tap, like cutting a diamond. It worked because scum like him thinks everyone else is scum, too, thinks *we're* capable of doing what he'd do in the same situation. I'd never put out his eyes, but he might've put mine out if our roles were reversed, so he thought for sure I'd do him like he would've done me. All I did was use his own screwed-up attitudes against him. Psychology. Nobody can file a complaint about the application of a little psychology." She turned to Bobby and said, "What was on those diskettes?"

"Whizard. Not trash data. The whole thing. These have to be the files he duplicated. He only made one set while I was watching, and after the shooting started he didn't have time to make backup copies."

The elevator bell rang, and their floor number lit on the board. When the doors opened, a plainclothes detective they knew, Gil Dainer, stepped into the hallway.

Julie took the package of diskettes from Bobby, handed them to Dainer.

She said, "This is evidence. The whole case might rest on it. You think you can keep track of it?"

Dainer grinned. "Gosh, ma'am, I'll try."

# 11

FRANK POLLARD—alias James Roman, alias George Farris—looked in the trunk of the stolen Chevy and found a small bundle of tools wrapped in a felt pouch and tucked in the wheel well. He used a screwdriver to take the plates off the car.

Half an hour later, after cruising some of the higher and even more quiet neighborhoods in fogbound Laguna, he parked on a dark side street and exchanged the Chevy's plates for those on an Oldsmobile. With luck, the owner of the Olds would not notice the new plates for a couple of days, maybe even a week or longer; until he reported the switch, the Chevy would not match anything on a police hot sheet and would, therefore, be relatively safe to drive. In any case, Frank intended to get rid of the car by tomorrow night and either boost a new one or use some of the cash in the flight bag to buy legal wheels.

Though he was exhausted, he didn't think it wise to check into a motel. Four-thirty in the morning was a damned odd hour for anyone to be wanting a room. Furthermore, he was unshaven, and his thick hair was matted and oily, and both his jeans and checkered blue flannel shirt were dirty and rumpled from his recent adventures. The last thing he wanted to do was call attention to himself, so he decided to catch a few hours of sleep in the car.

He drove farther south, into Laguna Niguel, where he parked on a quiet residential street, under the immense boughs of a date palm. He stretched out on the backseat, as comfortably as possible without benefit of sufficient legroom or pillows, and closed his eyes.

For the moment he was not afraid of his unknown pursuer, because he felt that the man was no longer nearby. Temporarily, at least, he had given his enemy the shake, and had no need to lie awake in fear of a hostile face suddenly appearing at the window. He was also able to put out of his mind all questions about his identity and the money in the flight bag; he was so tired—and his thought processes were so fuzzy—that any attempt to puzzle out solutions to those mysteries would be fruitless.

He was kept awake, however, by the memory of how *strange* the events in Anaheim had been, a few hours ago. The foreboding gusts of wind. The eerie flutelike music. Imploding windows, exploding tires, failed brakes, failed steering . . .

Who had come into that apartment behind the blue light? Was "who" the right word . . . or would it be more accurate to ask *what* had been searching for him?

During his urgent flight from Anaheim to Laguna, he'd not had the leisure to reflect upon those bizarre incidents, but now he could not turn his mind from them. He sensed that he had survived an encounter with something unnatural. Worse, he sensed that he knew what it was—and that his amnesia was self-induced by a deep desire to forget.

After a while, even the memory of those preternatural events wasn't enough to keep him awake. The last thing that crossed his waking mind, as he slipped off on a tide of sleep, was that four-word phrase that had come to him when he had first awakened in the deserted alleyway: *Fireflies in a windstorm. . . .*

# 12

BY THE TIME they had cooperated with the police at the scene, made arrangements for their disabled vehicles, and talked with the three corporate officers who showed up at Decodyne, Bobby and Julie did not get home until shortly before dawn. They were dropped at their door by a police cruiser, and Bobby was glad to see the place.

They lived on the east side of Orange, in a three-bedroom, sort-of-ersatz-Spanish tract house, which they had bought new two years ago, largely for its investment potential. Even at night the relative youth of the neighborhood was apparent in the landscaping: None of the shrubbery had reached full size; the trees were still too immature to loom higher than the rain gutters on the houses.

Bobby unlocked the door. Julie went in, and he followed. The sound of their footsteps on the parquet floor of the foyer, echoing hollowly off the bare walls of the adjacent and utterly empty living room, was proof that they were not committed to the house for the long term. To save money toward the fulfillment of The Dream, they had left the living room, dining room, and two bedrooms unfurnished. They installed cheap carpet and cheaper draperies. Not a penny had been spent on other improvements. This was merely a way station en route to The Dream, so they saw no point in lavishing funds on the decor.

The Dream. That was how they thought of it—with a capital *t* and a capital *d*. They kept their expenses as low as possible, in order to fund The Dream. They didn't spend much on clothes or vacations, and they didn't buy fancy cars. With hard work and iron determination, they were building Dakota & Dakota Investigations into a major firm that could be sold for a large capital gain, so they plowed a lot of earnings back into the business to make it grow. For The Dream.

At the back of the house, the kitchen and family room—and the small breakfast area that separated them—were furnished.

This—and the master bedroom upstairs—was where they lived when at home.

The kitchen had a Spanish-tile floor, beige counters, and dark oak cabinets. No money had been spent on decorative accessories, but the room had a cozy feeling because some necessities of a functioning kitchen were on display: a net bag filled with half a dozen onions, copper pots dangling from a ceiling rack, cooking utensils, bottles of spices. Three green tomatoes were ripening on the windowsill.

Julie leaned against the counter, as if she could not stand another moment without support, and Bobby said, "You want a drink?"

"Booze at dawn?"

"I was thinking more of milk or juice."

"No, thanks."

"Hungry?"

She shook her head. "I just want to fall into bed. I'm beat."

He took her in his arms, held her close, cheek to cheek, with his face buried in her hair. Her arms tightened around him.

They stood that way for a while, saying nothing, letting the residual fear evaporate in the gentle heat they generated between them. Fear and love were indivisible. If you allowed yourself to care, to love, you made yourself vulnerable, and vulnerability led to fear. He found meaning in life through his relationship with her, and if she died, meaning and purpose would die too.

With Julie still in his arms, Bobby leaned back and studied her face. The smudges of dried blood had been wiped away. The skinned spot on her forehead was beginning to scab over with a thin yellow membrane. However, the imprint of their recent ordeal consisted of more than the abrasion on her forehead. With her tan complexion, she could never be said to look pale, even in moments of the most profound anxiety; a detectable grayness seeped into her face, however, at times like this, and at the moment her cinnamon-and-cream skin was underlaid with a shade of gray that made him think of headstone marble.

"It's over," he assured her, "and we're okay."

"It's not over in my dreams. Won't be for weeks."

"A thing like tonight adds to the legend of Dakota and Dakota."

"I don't want to be a legend. Legends are all dead."

"We'll be *living* legends, and that'll bring in business. The

46

more business we build, the sooner we can sell out, grab The Dream." He kissed her gently on each corner of her mouth. "I have to call in, leave a long message on the agency machine, so Clint will know how to handle everything when he goes to work."

"Yeah. I don't want the phone to start ringing only a couple of hours after I hit the sheets."

He kissed her again and went to the wall phone beside the refrigerator. As he was dialing the office number, he heard Julie walk to the bathroom off the short hall that connected the kitchen to the laundryroom. She closed the bathroom door just as the answering machine picked up: *"Thank you for calling Dakota and Dakota. No one—"*

Clint Karaghiosis—whose Greek-American family had been fans of Clint Eastwood from the earliest days of his first television show, "Rawhide"—was Bobby and Julie's right-hand man at the office. He could be trusted to handle any problem. Bobby left a long message for him, summarizing the events at Decodyne and noting specific tasks that had to be done to wrap up the case.

When he hung up, he stepped down into the adjoining family room, switched on the CD player, and put on a Benny Goodman disc. The first notes of "King Porter Stomp" brought the dead room to life.

In the kitchen again, he got a quart can of eggnog from the refrigerator. They had bought it two weeks ago for their quiet, at-home, New Year's Eve celebration, but had not opened it, after all, on the holiday. He opened it now and half-filled two waterglasses.

From the bathroom he heard Julie make a tortured sound; she was finally throwing up. It was mostly just dry heaves because they had not eaten in eight or ten hours, but the spasms sounded violent. Throughout the night, Bobby had expected her to succumb to nausea, and he was surprised that she had retained control of herself this long.

He retrieved a bottle of white rum from the bar cabinet in the family room and spiked each serving of eggnog with a double shot. He was gently stirring the drinks with a spoon to blend in the rum, when Julie returned, looking even grayer than before.

When she saw what he was doing, she said, "I don't need that."

"I know what you need. I'm psychic. I knew you'd toss your

cookies after what happened tonight. Now I know you need
*this.*" He stepped to the sink and rinsed off the spoon.

"No, Bobby, really, I can't drink that." The Goodman music
didn't seem to be energizing her.

"It'll settle your stomach. And if you don't drink it, you're not
going to sleep." Taking her by the arm, crossing the breakfast
area, and stepping down into the family room, he said, "You'll
lie awake worrying about me, about Thomas"—Thomas was her
brother—"about the world and everyone in it."

They sat on the sofa, and he did not turn on any lamps. The
only light was what reached them from the kitchen.

She drew her legs under her and turned slightly to face him.
Her eyes shone with a soft, reflected light. She sipped the eggnog.

The room was now filled with the strains of "One Sweet
Letter From You," one of Goodman's most beautiful thematic
statements, with a vocal by Louise Tobin.

They sat and listened for a while.

Then Julie said, "I'm tough, Bobby, I really am."

"I know you are."

"I don't want you thinking I'm lame."

"Never."

"It wasn't the shooting that made me sick, or using the Toyota
to run that guy down, or even the thought of almost losing
you—"

"I know. It was what you had to do to Rasmussen."

"He's a slimy little weasel-faced bastard, but even he doesn't
deserve to be broken like that. What I did to him stank."

"It was the only way to crack the case, because it wasn't near
cracked till we'd found out who hired him."

She drank more eggnog. She frowned down at the milky
contents of her glass, as if the answer to some mystery could be
found there.

Following Tobin's vocal, Ziggy Elman came in with a lusty
trumpet solo, followed by Goodman's clarinet. The sweet
sounds made that boxy, tract-house room seem like the most
romantic place in the world.

"What I did . . . I did for The Dream. Giving Decodyne
Rasmussen's employer will please them. But breaking him was
somehow . . . worse than wasting a man in a fair gunfight."

Bobby put one hand on her knee. It was a nice knee. After all these years, he was still sometimes surprised by her slenderness and the delicacy of her bone structure, for he always thought of her as being strong for her size, solid, indomitable. "If you hadn't put Rasmussen in that vise and squeezed him, I would've done it."

"No, you wouldn't have. You're scrappy, Bobby, and you're smart and you're tough, but there're certain things you can never do. This was one of them. Don't jive me just to make me feel good."

"You're right," he said. "I couldn't have done it. But I'm glad you did. Decodyne's *very* big time, and this could've set us back years if we'd flubbed it."

"Is there anything we won't do for The Dream?"

Bobby said, "Sure. We wouldn't torture small children with red-hot knives, and we wouldn't shove innocent old ladies down long flights of stairs, and we wouldn't club a basketful of new-born puppies to death with an iron bar—at least not without good reason."

Her laughter lacked a full measure of humor.

"Listen," he said, "you're a good person. You've got a good heart, and nothing you did to Rasmussen blackens it at all."

"I hope you're right. It's a hard world sometimes."

"Another drink will soften it a little."

"You know the calories in these? I'll be fat as a hippo."

"Hippos are cute," he said, taking her glass and heading back toward the kitchen to pour another drink. "I love hippos."

"You won't want to *make* love to one."

"Sure. More to hold, more to love."

"You'll be crushed."

"Well, of course, I'll always insist on taking the top."

# 13

CANDY WAS going to kill. He stood in the dark living room of a stranger's house, shaking with need. Blood. He needed blood.

Candy was going to kill, and there was nothing he could do

to stop himself. Not even thinking of his mother could shame him into controlling his hunger.

His given name was James, but his mother—an unselfish soul, exceedingly kind, brimming with love, a saint—always said he was her little candy boy. Never James. Never Jim or Jimmy. She'd said he was sweeter than anything on earth, and "little candy boy" eventually had become "candy boy," and by the time he was six the sobriquet had been shortened and capitalized, and he had become Candy for good. Now, at twenty-nine, that was the only name to which he would answer.

Many people thought murder was a sin. He knew otherwise. Some were born with a taste for blood. God had made them what they were and expected them to kill chosen victims. It was all part of His mysterious plan.

The only sin was to kill when God and your mother did not approve of the victim, which was exactly what he was about to do. He was ashamed. But he was also in need.

He listened to the house. Silence.

Like unearthly and dusky beasts, the shadowy forms of the living-room furniture huddled around him.

Breathing hard, trembling, Candy moved into the dining room, kitchen, family room, then slowly along the hallway that led to the front of the house. He made no sound that would have alerted anyone asleep upstairs. He seemed to glide rather than walk, as if he were a specter instead of a real man.

He paused at the foot of the stairs and made one last feeble attempt to overcome his murderous compulsion. Failing, he shuddered and let out his pent-up breath. He began to climb toward the second floor, where the family was probably sleeping.

His mother would understand and forgive him.

She had taught him that killing was good and moral—but only when necessary, only when it benefited the family. She had been terribly angry with him on those occasions when he had killed out of sheer compulsion, with no good reason. She'd had no need to punish him physically for his errant ways, because her displeasure gave him more agony than any punishment she could have devised. For days at a time she refused to speak to him, and that silent treatment caused his chest to swell with pain, so it seemed as if his heart would spasm and cease to beat. She looked straight through him, too, as if he no longer existed. When the other children spoke of him, she said, "Oh, you mean your late brother, Candy, your poor dead brother. Well, remember him if you want, but only among yourselves, not to me, never to me, because I don't want to remember him, not that bad seed. He was no good, that one, no good at all, wouldn't listen to his mother, not him, always thought he knew better. Just the sound of his name makes me sick, *revolts* me, so don't mention him in my hearing." Each time that Candy had been temporarily banished to the land of the dead for having misbehaved, no place was set for him at the table, and he had to stand in a corner, watching the others eat, as if he was a visiting spirit. She would not favor him with either a frown or a smile, and she would not stroke his hair or touch his face with her warm soft hands, and she would not let him cuddle against her or put his weary head upon her breast, and at night he had to find his way into a troubled sleep without being guided there by either her bedtime stories or sweet lullabies. In that total banishment he learned more of Hell than he ever hoped to know.

But she would understand why Candy could not control himself tonight, and she'd forgive him. Sooner or later she always forgave him because her love for him was like the love of God for all His children: perfect, rich with forbearance and mercy. When she deemed that Candy had suffered enough, she always had looked *at* him again, smiled for him, opened her arms wide. In her new acceptance of him, he had experienced as much of Heaven as he needed to know.

She was in Heaven now, herself. Seven long years! God, how he missed her. But she was watching him even now. She would know he had lost control tonight, and she would be disappointed in him.

He climbed the stairs, rushing up two risers at a time, staying close to the wall, where the steps were less likely to squeak. He was a big man but graceful and light on his feet, and if some of the stair treads were loose or tired with age, they did not creak under him.

In the upstairs hall he paused, listening. Nothing.

A dim night-light was part of the overhead smoke alarm. The glow was just bright enough for Candy to see two doors on the right of the hall, two on the left, and one at the far end.

He crept to the first door on the right, eased it open, and slipped into the room beyond. He closed the door again and stood with his back to it.

Although his need was great, he forced himself to wait for his eyes to adjust to the gloom. Ashen light, from a streetlamp at least half a block away, glimmered faintly at the two windows. He noticed the mirror, first, a frosty rectangle in which the meager radiance was murkily reflected; then he began to make out the shape of the dresser beneath it. A moment later he was also able to see the bed and, dimly, the huddled form of someone lying under a light-colored blanket that was vaguely phosphorescent.

Candy stepped cautiously to the bed, took hold of the blanket and sheets and hesitated, listening to the soft rhythmic breathing of the sleeper. He detected a trace of perfume mingled with a pleasant scent of warm skin and recently shampooed hair. A girl. He could always tell girl-smell from boy-smell. He also sensed that this one was young, perhaps a teenager. If his need had not been so intense, he would have hesitated much longer than he did, for the moments preceding a kill were exciting, almost better than the act itself.

With a dramatic flick of his arm, as if he were a magician throwing back the cloth that had covered an empty cage to reveal a captive dove of sorcerous origins, he uncovered the sleeper. He fell upon her, crushing her into the mattress with his body.

She woke instantly and tried to scream, even though he had surely knocked the wind out of her. Fortunately, he had unusually large and powerful hands, and he had found her face even as she began to raise her voice, so he was able to thrust his palm under her chin and hook his fingers in her cheeks and clamp her mouth shut.

"Be quiet, or I'll kill you," he whispered, his lips brushing against her delicate ear.

Making a muffled, panicky sound, she squirmed under him, though to no avail. Judging by the feel of her, she was a girl, not a woman, perhaps no younger than twelve, certainly no older than fifteen. She was no match for him.

"I don't want to hurt you. I just *want* you, and when I'm done with you, I'll leave."

That was a lie, for he had no desire to rape her. Sex was of no interest to him. Indeed, sex disgusted him; involving unmentionable fluids, depending upon the shameless use of the same organs associated with urination, sex was an unspeakably repulsive act. Other people's fascination with it only proved to Candy that men and women were members of a fallen species and that the world was a cesspool of sin and madness.

Either because she believed his pledge not to kill her or because she was now half-paralyzed with fear, she stopped resisting. Maybe she just needed all of her energy to breathe. Candy's full weight—two hundred and twenty pounds—was pressing on her chest, restricting her lungs. Against his hand, with which he clamped her mouth shut, he could feel her cool inhalations as her nostrils flared, followed by short, hot exhalations.

His vision had continued to adapt to the poor light. Although he still could not make out the details of her face, he could see her eyes shining darkly in the gloom, glistening with terror. He could also see that she was a blonde; her pale hair caught even the dull gray glow from the windows and shone with burnished-silver highlights.

With his free hand, he gently pushed her hair back from the right side of her neck. He shifted his position slightly, moving down on her in order to bring his lips to her throat. He kissed the tender flesh, felt the strong throb of her pulse against his lips, then bit deep and found the blood.

She bucked and thrashed beneath him, but he held her down and held her fast, and she could not dislodge his greedy mouth from the wound he had made. He swallowed rapidly but could not consume the thick, sweet fluid as fast as it was offered. Soon, however, the flow diminished. The girl's convulsions became less violent, as well, then faded altogether, until she was as still beneath him as if she had been nothing more than a tangled mound of bedclothes.

He rose from her and switched on the bedside lamp just long enough to see her face. He always wanted to see their faces, after their sacrifices if not before. He also liked to look into their eyes, which seemed not sightless but gifted with a vision of the far place to which their souls had gone. He did not entirely understand his curiosity. After all, when he ate a steak, he did not wonder what the cow had looked like. This girl—and each of the others on whom he'd fed—should have been nothing more than one of the cattle to him. Once, in a dream, when he had finished drinking from a ravaged throat, his victim, although dead, had spoken to him, asking him why he wanted to look upon her in death. When he had said that he didn't know the answer to her question, she had suggested that perhaps, on those occasions when he had killed in the dark, he later needed to see his victims' faces because, in some unlit corner of his heart, he half expected to find his own face looking up at him, ice-white and dead-eyed. "Deep down," the dream-victim had said, "you know that you're already dead yourself, burnt out inside. You realize that you have far more in common with your victims after you've killed them than before." Those words, though spoken only in a dream, and though amounting to the purest nonsense, had nevertheless brought him awake with a sharp cry. He was alive, not dead, powerful and vital, a man with appetites as strong as they were unusual. The dream-victim's words stayed with him over the years, and when they echoed through his memory at times like this, they made him anxious. Now, as always, he refused to dwell on them. He turned his attention, instead, to the girl on the bed.

She appeared to be about fourteen, quite pretty. Captivated by her flawless complexion, he wondered if her skin would feel as perfect as it looked, as smooth as porcelain, if he dared to stroke it with his fingertips. Her lips were slightly parted, as if they had been gently prised open by her spirit as it departed her. Her wonderfully blue, clear eyes seemed enormous, too big for her face—and as wide as a winter sky.

He would have liked to gaze upon her for hours.

Letting a sigh of regret escape him, he switched off the lamp.

He stood for a while in the darkness, enveloped by the pungent aroma of blood.

When his eyes had readjusted to the gloom, he returned to the hall, not bothering to close the girl's door behind him. He entered the room across from hers and found it untenanted.

But in the room next to that one, Candy smelled a trace of stale sweat, and heard snoring. This one was a boy, seventeen or eighteen, not a big kid but not small either, and he put up more of a struggle than his sister. However, he was sleeping on his stomach, and when Candy threw back the covers and fell upon him, the boy's face was jammed hard into the pillow and mattress, smothering him and making it difficult for him to shout a warning. The fight was violent but brief. The boy passed out from lack of oxygen, and Candy flopped him over. When he went for the exposed throat, Candy let out a low and eager cry that was louder than any sound the boy had made.

Later, when he opened the door to the fourth bedroom, the

first pewter light of dawn had pierced the windows. Shadows still huddled in the corners, but the deeper darkness had been chased off. The early light was too thin to elicit color from objects, and everything in the room seemed to be one shade of gray or another.

An attractive blonde in her late thirties was asleep on one side of a king-size bed. The sheets and blanket on the other half of the bed were hardly disturbed, so he figured the woman's husband had either moved out or was away on business. He noted a half-full glass of water and a plastic bottle of prescription drugs on the nightstand. He picked up the pharmacy bottle and saw that it was two-thirds full of small pills: a sedative, according to the label. From the label, he also learned her name: Roseanne Lofton.

Candy stood for a while, staring down at her face, and an old longing for maternal solace stirred in him. Need continued to drive him, but he did not want to take her violently, did not want to rip her open and drain her in a few minutes. He wanted this one to last.

He had the urge to suckle on this woman as he had suckled on his mother's blood when she would permit him that grace. Occasionally, when he was in her favor, his mother would make a shallow cut in the palm of her hand or puncture one of her fingers, then allow him to curl up against her and be nursed on her blood for an hour or longer. During that time a great peace stole over him, a bliss so profound that the world and all its pain ceased to be real to him, because his mother's blood was like no other, untainted, pure as the tears of a saint. Through such small wounds, of course, he was able to drink no more than an ounce or two of her, but that meager dribble was more precious and more nourishing to him than the gallons he might have drained from a score of other people. The woman before him would not have such ambrosia within her veins, but if he closed his eyes while he suckled on her, and if he let his mind reel backward to memories of the days before his mother's death, he might recapture at least some of the exquisite serenity he had known then . . . and experience a faint echo of that old thrill.

At last, without casting the covers aside, Candy gently lowered himself to the bed and stretched out beside the woman, watching as her heavy-lidded eyes fluttered and then opened. She blinked at him as he cuddled next to her, and for a moment she seemed to think that she was still dreaming, for no expression tightened the muscles of her slack face.

"All I want is your blood," he said softly.

Abruptly she cast off the lingering effects of the sedative, and her eyes filled with alarm.

Before she could spoil the beauty of the moment by screaming or resisting, thereby shattering the illusion that she was his mother and was giving voluntarily of herself, he struck the side of her neck with his heavy fist. Then he struck her again. Then he hammered the side of her face twice. She slumped unconscious against the pillow.

He squirmed under the covers to be close against her, withdrew her hand, and nipped her palm with his teeth. He put his head on the pillow, lying face to face with her, holding her hand between them, drinking the slow trickle from her palm. He closed his eyes after a while and tried to imagine that she was his mother, and eventually a gratifying peace stole over him. However, though he was happier at that moment than he had been in a long time, it was not a deep happiness, merely a veneer of joy that brightened the surface of his heart but left the inner chambers dark and cold.

# 14

AFTER ONLY a few hours of sleep, Frank Pollard woke in the backseat of the stolen Chevy. The morning sun, streaming through the windows, was bright enough to make him wince.

He was stiff, achy, and unrested. His throat was dry, and his eyes burned as if he had not slept for days.

Groaning, Frank swung his legs off the seat, sat up, and cleared his throat. He realized that both of his hands were numb; they felt cold and dead, and he saw that he had curled them into fists. He had evidently been sleeping that way for some time, because at first he could not unclench. With considerable effort, he opened his right fist—and a handful of something black and grainy poured through his tingling fingers.

He stared, perplexed, at the fine grains that had spilled down the leg of his jeans and onto his right shoe. He raised his hand to take a closer look at the residue that had stuck to his palm. It looked and smelled like sand.

*Black* sand? Where had he gotten it?

When he opened his left hand, more sand spilled out.

Confused, he looked through the car windows at the residential neighborhood around him. He saw green lawns, dark topsoil showing through where the grass was sparse, mulch-filled planting beds, redwood chips mounded around some shrubs, but nothing like what he had held in his tightly clenched fists.

He was in Laguna Niguel, so the Pacific Ocean was nearby, rimmed by broad beaches. But those beaches were white, not black.

As full circulation returned to his cramped fingers, he leaned back in the seat, raised his hands in front of his face, and stared at the black grains that speckled his sweat-damp skin. Sand, even black sand, was a humble and innocent substance, but the residue on his hands troubled him as deeply as if it had been fresh blood.

"Who the hell am I, what's happening to me?" he wondered aloud.

He knew that he needed help. But he didn't know to whom he could turn.

# 15

Bobby was awakened by a Santa Ana wind soughing in the trees outside. It whistled under the eaves, and forced a chorus of ticks and creaks from the cedar-shingle roof and the attic rafters.

He blinked sleep-matted eyes and squinted at the numbers on the bedroom ceiling: 12:07. Because they sometimes worked odd hours and slept during the day, they had installed exterior Rolladen security shutters, leaving the room coal-mine dark except for the projection clock's pale green numerals, which floated on the ceiling like some portentous spirit message from Beyond.

Because he had gone to bed near dawn, and instantly to sleep, he knew the numbers on the ceiling meant that it was shortly past noon, not midnight. He had slept perhaps six hours. He lay unmoving for a moment, wondering if Julie was awake.

She said, "I am."

"You're spooky," he said. "You knew what I was thinking."

"That's not spooky," she said. "That's married."

He reached for her, and she came into his arms.

For a while they just held each other, satisfied to be close. But by mutual and unspoken desire, they began to make love.

The projection clock's glowing green numerals were too pale to relieve the absolute darkness, so Bobby could see nothing of Julie as they clung together. However, he "saw" her through his hands. As he reveled in the smoothness and warmth of her skin, the elegant curves of her breasts, the discovery of angularity precisely where angularity was desirable, the tautness of muscle, and the fluid movement of muscle and bone, he might have been a blind man using his hands to describe an inner vision of ideal beauty.

The wind shook the world outside, in sympathy with the climaxes that shook Julie. And when Bobby could withhold himself no longer, when he cried out and emptied himself into her, the skirling wind cried, too, and a bird that had taken shelter in a nearby eave was blown from its perch with a rustle of wings and a spiraling shriek.

For a while they lay side by side in the blackness, their breath mingling, touching each other almost reverently. They did not want or need to speak; talk would have diminished the moment.

The aluminum-slat shutters vibrated softly in the huffing wind.

Gradually the afterglow of lovemaking gave way to a curious uneasiness, the source of which Bobby could not identify. The enveloping blackness began to seem oppressive, as if a continued absence of light was somehow contributing to a thickening of the air, until it would become as viscid and unbreathable as syrup.

Though he had just made love to her, he was stricken by the crazy notion that Julie was not actually there with him, that what he had coupled with was a dream, or the congealing darkness itself, and that she had been stolen from him in the night,

58

whisked away by some power he could not fathom, and that she was forever beyond his reach.

His childish fear made him feel foolish, but he rose onto one elbow and turned on one of the wall-mounted bedside lamps.

When he saw Julie lying beside him, smiling, her head raised on a pillow, the level of his inexplicable anxiety abruptly dropped. He let out a rush of breath, surprised to discover that he'd pent it up in the first place. But a peculiar tension remained in him, and the sight of Julie, safe and undamaged but for the scabbing spot on her forehead, was insufficient to completely relax him.

"What's wrong?" she asked, as perceptive as ever.

"Nothing," he lied.

"Bit of a headache from all that rum in the eggnog?"

What troubled him was not a hangover, but the queer, unshakable feeling that he was going to lose Julie, that something out there in a hostile world was coming to take her away. As the optimist in the family, he wasn't usually given to grim forebodings of doom; accordingly, this strange augural chill frightened him more than it would have if he had been regularly subject to such disturbances.

"Bobby?" she said, frowning.

"Headache," he assured her.

He leaned down and gently kissed her eyes, then again, forcing her to close them so she could not see his face and read the anxiety that he was unable to conceal.

♦   ♦   ♦

LATER, AFTER showering and dressing, they ate a hasty breakfast while standing at the kitchen counter: English muffins and raspberry jam, half a banana each, and black coffee. By mutual agreement, they were not going to the office. A brief call to Clint Karaghiosis confirmed that the wrap-up on the Decodyne case was nearly completed, and that no other business needed their urgent personal attention.

Their Suzuki Samurai waited in the garage, and Bobby's spirits rose at the sight of it. The Samurai was a small sports truck with four-wheel drive. He had justified its purchase by pitching its dual nature—utilitarian and recreational—to Julie, especially noting its comparatively reasonable price tag, but in fact he had wanted it because it was fun to drive. She had not been deceived, and she had gone for it because she, too, thought it was fun to drive. This time, she was willing to let him have the wheel when he suggested she drive.

"I did enough driving last night," she said as she buckled herself into her shoulder harness.

Dead leaves, twigs, a few scraps of paper, and less identifiable detritus whirled and tumbled along the windswept streets. Dust devils spun out of the east, as the Santa Anas—named for the mountains out of which they arose—poured down through the canyons and across the arid, scrub-stubbled hills that Orange County's industrious developers had not yet graded and covered with thousands of nearly identical wood-and-stucco pieces of the California dream. Trees bent to the surging oceans of air that moved in powerful and erratic tides toward the real sea in the west. The previous night's fog was gone, and the day was so clear that, from the hills, Catalina Island could be seen twenty-six miles off the Pacific's distant coast.

Julie popped an Artie Shaw CD into the player, and the smooth melody and softly bouncing rhythms of "Begin the Beguine" filled the car. The mellow saxophones of Les Robinson, Hank Freeman, Tony Pastor, and Ronnie Perry provided strange counterpoint to the chaos and dissonance of the Santa Ana winds.

From Orange, Bobby drove south and west toward the beach cities—Newport, Corona Del Mar, Laguna, Dana Point. He traveled as much as possible on those few of the urbanized county's blacktop byways that could still be called back roads. They even passed a couple of orange groves, with which the county had once been carpeted, but which had mostly fallen to the relentless advance of the tracts and malls.

Julie became more talkative and bubbly as the miles rolled up on the odometer, but Bobby knew that her spritely mood was not genuine. Each time they set out to visit her brother Thomas, she worked hard to inflate her spirits. Although she loved Thomas, every time that she was with him, her heart broke anew, so she had to fortify herself in advance with manufactured good humor.

"Not a cloud in the sky," she said, as they passed the old Irvine Ranch fruit-packing plant. "Isn't it a beautiful day, Bobby?"

"A wonderful day," he agreed.

"The wind must've pushed the clouds all the way to Japan, piled them up miles high over Tokyo."

"Yeah. Right now California litter is falling on the Ginza."

Hundreds of red bougainvillea blossoms, stripped from their vines by the wind, blew across the road, and for a moment the Samurai seemed to be caught in a crimson snowstorm. Maybe it was because they had just spoken of Japan, but there was something oriental about the whirl of petals. He would not have been surprised to glimpse a kimono-clad woman at the side of the road, dappled in sunshine and shadow.

"Even a windstorm is beautiful here," Julie said. "Aren't we lucky, Bobby? Aren't we lucky to be living in this special place?"

Shaw's "Frenesi" struck up, string-rich swing. Every time he heard the song, Bobby was almost able to imagine that he was in a movie from the 1930s or '40s, that he would turn a corner and encounter his old friend Jimmy Stewart or maybe Bing Crosby, and they'd go off to have lunch with Cary Grant and Jean Arthur and Katharine Hepburn, and screwball things would happen.

"What movie are you in?" Julie asked. She knew him too well.

"Haven't figured it yet. Maybe *The Philadelphia Story.*"

By the time they pulled into the parking lot of Cielo Vista Care Home, Julie had whipped herself into a state of high good humor. She got out of the Samurai, faced west, and grinned at the horizon, which was delineated by the marriage of sea and sky, as if she had never before encountered a sight to match it. In truth it was a stunning panorama, because Cielo Vista stood on a bluff half a mile from the Pacific, overlooking a long stretch of southern California's Gold Coast. Bobby admired it, too, shoulders hunched slightly and head tucked down in deference to the cool and blustery wind.

When Julie was ready, she took Bobby's hand and squeezed it hard, and they went inside.

Cielo Vista Care Home was a private facility, operated without government funds, and its architecture eschewed all of the standard institutional looks. Its two-story Spanish façade of pale peach stucco was accented by white marble cornerpieces, doorframes, and window lintels; white-painted French windows and doors were recessed in graceful arches, with deep sills. The sidewalks were shaded by lattice arbors draped with a mix of purple- and yellow-blooming bougainvillea, from which the wind drew a chorus of urgent whispers. Inside, the floors were gray vinyl tile, speckled with peach and turquoise, and the walls were peach with white base and crown molding, which lent the place a warm and airy ambience.

They paused in the foyer, just inside the front door, while Julie withdrew a comb from her purse and pulled the wind tangles from her hair. After stopping at the front desk in the cozy visitors' lobby, they followed the north hall to Thomas's first-floor room.

His was the second of the two beds, nearest the windows, but he was neither there nor in his armchair. When they stopped in his open doorway, he was sitting at the worktable that belonged to both him and his roommate, Derek. Bent over the table, using a pair of scissors to clip a photograph from a magazine, Thomas appeared curiously both hulking and fragile, thickset yet delicate; physically, he was solid but mentally and emotionally he was frail, and that inner weakness shone through to belie the outer image of strength. With his thick neck, heavy rounded shoulders, broad back, proportionally short arms, and stocky legs, Thomas had a gnomish look, but when he became aware of them and turned his head to see who was there, his face was not graced by the cute and beguiling features of a fairy-tale creature; it was instead a face of cruel genetic destiny and biological tragedy.

"Jules!" he said, dropping the scissors and magazine, nearly knocking over his chair in his haste to get up. He was wearing baggy jeans and a green-plaid flannel shirt. He seemed ten years younger than his true age. "Jules, Jules!"

Julie let go of Bobby's hand and stepped into the room, opening her arms to her brother. "Hi, honey."

Thomas hurried to her in that shuffling walk of his, as if his shoes were heeled and soled with enough iron to preclude his lifting them. Although he was twenty years old, ten years younger than Julie, he was four inches shorter than she, barely five feet. He had been born with Down's syndrome, a diagnosis that even a layman could read in his face: his brow was sloped and heavy; inner epicanthic folds gave his eyes an oriental cast; the bridge of his nose was flat; his ears were low-set on a head that was slightly too small to be in proportion to his body; the rest of his features had those soft, heavy contours often associated with mental retardation. Though it was a countenance shaped more for expressions of sadness and loneliness, it now defied its naturally downcast lines and formed itself into a wondrous smile, a warm grin of pure delight.

Julie always had that effect on Thomas.

Hell, she has that effect on *me*, Bobby thought.

Stooping only slightly, Julie threw her arms around her brother when he came to her, and for a while they hugged each other.

"How're you doing?" she asked.

"Good," Thomas said. "I'm good." His speech was thick but not at all difficult to understand, for his tongue was not as deformed as those of some victims of DS; it was a little larger than it should have been but not fissured or protruding. "I'm real good."

"Where's Derek?"

"Visiting. Down the hall. He'll be back. I'm real good. Are you good?"

"I'm fine, honey. Just great."

"I'm just great too. I love you, Jules," Thomas said happily, for with Julie he was always free of the shyness that colored his relations with everyone else. "I love you so much."

"I love you, too, Thomas."

"I was afraid . . . maybe you wouldn't come."

"Don't I always come?"

"Always," he said. At last he relaxed his grip on his sister and peeked around her. "Hi, Bobby."

"Hi, Thomas. You're lookin' good."

"Am I?"

"If I'm lyin', I'm dyin'."

Thomas laughed. To Julie, he said, "He's funny."

"Do I get a hug too?" Bobby asked. "Or do I have to stand here with my arms out until someone mistakes me for a hatrack?"

Hesitantly, Thomas let go of his sister. He and Bobby embraced. After all these years, Thomas was still not entirely comfortable with Bobby, not because they had bad chemistry between them or any bad feelings, but because Thomas didn't like change very much and adapted to it slowly. Even after more than seven years, his sister being married was a change, something that still felt new to him.

But he likes me, Bobby thought, maybe even as much as I like him.

Liking DS victims was not difficult, once you got past the pity that initially distanced you from them, because most of them had an innocence and guilelessness that was charming and refreshing. Except when inhibited by shyness or embarrassment about their differences, they were usually forthright, more truthful than other people, and incapable of the petty social games and scheming that marred so many relationships among "ordinary" people. The previous summer, at Cielo Vista's Fourth of July picnic, a mother of one of the other patients had said to Bobby, "Sometimes, watching them, I think there's something in them—a gentleness, a special kindness—that's closer to God than anything in us." Bobby felt the truth of that observation now, as he hugged Thomas and looked down into his sweet, lumpish face.

"Did we interrupt a poem?" Julie asked.

Thomas let go of Bobby and hurried to the worktable, where Julie was looking at the magazine from which he had been clipping a picture when they'd arrived. He opened his current scrapbook—fourteen others were filled with his creations and shelved in a corner bookcase near his bed—and pointed to a two-page spread of pasted-in clippings that were arranged in lines and quatrains, like poetry.

"This was yesterday. Finished yesterday," Thomas said. "Took me a looooong time, and it was hard, but now it was . . . *is* . . . right."

Four or five years ago, Thomas had decided that he wanted to be a poet like someone he had seen and admired on television. The degree of mental retardation among victims of Down's syndrome varied widely, from mild to severe; Thomas was somewhere just above the middle of the spectrum, but he did not possess the intellectual capacity to learn to write more than his name. That didn't stop him. He had asked for paper, glue, a scrapbook, and piles of old magazines. Since he rarely asked for anything, and since Julie would have moved a mountain on her back to get him whatever he wanted, the items on his list were soon in his possession. "All kinds of magazines," he'd said, "with different pretty pictures . . . but ugly too . . . all kinds." From *Time, Newsweek, Life, Hot Rod, Omni, Seventeen,* and dozens of other publications, he snipped whole pictures and parts of pictures, arranging them as if they were words, in a series of images that made a statement that was important to him. Some of his "poems" were only five images long, and some involved hundreds of clippings arranged in orderly stanzas or, more often, in loosely structured lines that resembled free verse.

Julie took the scrapbook from him and went to the armchair by the window, where she could concentrate on his newest composition. Thomas remained at the worktable, watching her anxiously.

His picture poems did not tell stories or have recognizable thematic narratives, but neither were they merely random jumbles of images. A church spire, a mouse, a beautiful woman in an emerald-green ball gown, a field of daisies, a can of Dole pineapple rings, a crescent moon, pancakes in a stack with syrup drizzling down, rubies gleaming on a black-velvet display cloth, a fish with mouth agape, a child laughing, a nun praying, a woman crying over the blasted body of a loved one in some Godforsaken war zone, a pack of Lifesavers, a puppy with floppy ears, black-clad nuns with starched white wimples—from those and thousands of other pictures in his treasured boxes of clippings, Thomas selected the elements of his compositions. From the beginning Bobby recognized an uncanny *rightness* to many of the poems, a symmetry too fundamental to be defined, juxtapositions that were both naive and profound, rhythms as real as they were elusive, a personal vision plain to see but too mysterious to comprehend to any significant degree. Over the years, Bobby had seen the poems become better, more satisfying, though he understood them so little that he could not explain how he could discern the improvement; he just knew that it was there.

Julie looked up from the two-page spread in the scrapbook and said, "This is wonderful, Thomas. It makes me want to . . . run outside in the grass . . . and stand under the sky and maybe even dance, just throw my head back and laugh. It makes me glad to be alive."

"Yes!" Thomas said, slurring the word, clapping his hands.

She passed the book to Bobby, and he sat on the edge of the bed to read it.

The most intriguing thing about Thomas's poems was the emotional response they invariably evoked. None left a reader untouched, as an array of randomly assembled images might have done. Sometimes, when looking at Thomas's work, Bobby laughed out loud, and sometimes he was so moved that he had to blink back tears, and sometimes he felt fear or sadness or regret or wonder. He did not know why he responded to any particular piece as he did; the effect always defied analysis. Thomas's compositions functioned on some primal level, eliciting reaction from a region of the mind far deeper than the subconscious.

The latest poem was no exception. Bobby felt what Julie had felt: that life was good; that the world was beautiful; elation in the very fact of existence.

He looked up from the scrapbook and saw that Thomas was awaiting his reaction as eagerly as he had awaited Julie's, perhaps a sign that Bobby's opinion was cherished as much as hers, even if he still didn't rate as long or as ardent a hug as Julie did. "Wow," he said softly. "Thomas, this one gives me such a warm, tingly feeling that . . . I think my toes are curling."

Thomas grinned.

Sometimes Bobby looked at his brother-in-law and felt that two Thomases shared that sadly deformed skull. Thomas number one was the moron, sweet but feebleminded. Thomas number two was just as smart as anyone, but he occupied only a small part of the damaged brain that he shared with Thomas number one, a chamber in the center, from which he had no direct communication with the outside world. All of Thomas number two's thoughts had to be filtered through Thomas number one's part of the brain, so they ended up sounding no different from Thomas number one's thoughts; therefore the world could not know that number two was in there, thinking and feeling and fully *alive*—except through the evidence of the picture poems, the essence of which survived even after being filtered through Thomas number one.

"You've got such a talent," Bobby said, and he meant it— almost envied it.

Thomas blushed and lowered his eyes. He rose and quickly shuffled to the softly humming refrigerator that stood beside the door to the bathroom. Meals were served in the communal dining room, where snacks and drinks were provided on request, but patients with sufficient mental capacity to keep their rooms neat were allowed to have their own refrigerators stocked with their favorite snacks and drinks, to encourage as much independence as possible. He withdrew three cans of Coke. He gave one to Bobby, one to Julie. With the third he returned to the chair at the worktable, sat down, and said, "You been catchin' bad guys?"

"Yeah, we're keeping the jails full," Bobby said.

"Tell me."

Julie leaned forward in the armchair, and Thomas scooted his straight-backed chair closer to her, until their knees touched, and she recounted the highlights of the events at Decodyne last night. She made Bobby more heroic than he'd really been, and she played down her own involvement a little, not only out of modesty but in order not to frighten Thomas with too clear a picture of the danger in which she had put herself. Thomas was tough in his own way; if he hadn't been, he would have curled up on his bed long ago, facing into the corner, and never gotten up again. But he was not tough enough to endure the loss of Julie. He would be devastated even to imagine that she was vulnerable. So she made her daredevil driving and the shoot-out sound funny, exciting but not really dangerous. Her revised version of events entertained Bobby nearly as much as it did Thomas.

After a while, as usual, Thomas became overwhelmed by what Julie was telling him, and the tale grew more confusing than entertaining. "I'm full up," he said, which meant he was still trying to process everything he had been told, and didn't have room for any more just now. He was fascinated by the world outside Cielo Vista, and he often longed to be a part of it, but at the same time he found it too loud and bright and colorful to be handled in more than small doses.

Bobby got one of the older scrapbooks from the shelves and sat on the bed, reading picture poems.

Thomas and Julie sat in their chairs, Cokes put aside, knees to knees, leaning forward and holding hands, sometimes looking at each other, sometimes not, just being together, close. Julie needed that as much as Thomas did.

Julie's mother had been killed when Julie was twelve. Her father had died eight years later, two years before Bobby and Julie had been married. She'd been only twenty at the time, working as a waitress to put herself through college and to pay her half of the rent on a studio apartment she shared with another student. Her parents had never been rich, and though they had kept Thomas at home, the expense of looking after him had depleted what little savings they'd ever had. When her dad died, Julie had been unable to afford an apartment for her and Thomas, to say nothing of the time required to help him cope in a civilian environment, so she'd been forced to commit him to a state institution for mentally disabled children. Though Thomas never held it against her, she viewed the commitment as a betrayal of him.

She had intended to get a degree in criminology, but she dropped out of school in her third year and applied to the sheriffs' academy. She had worked as a deputy for fourteen months by the time Bobby met and married her; she had been living on peanuts, her life-style hardly better than that of a bag lady, saving most of her salary in hope of putting together a nest egg that would allow her to buy a small house someday and take Thomas in with her. Shortly after they were married, when Dakota Investigations became Dakota & Dakota, they brought Thomas to live with them. But they worked irregular hours, and although some victims of Down's syndrome were capable of living to a degree on their own, Thomas needed someone nearby at all times. The cost of three daily shifts of qualified companions was even more than the cost of high-level care at a private institution like Cielo Vista; but they would have borne it if they could have found enough reliable help. When it became impossible to conduct their business, have a life of their own, and take care of Thomas, too, they brought him to Cielo Vista. It was as comfortable a care institution as existed, but Julie viewed it as her second betrayal of her brother. That he was happy at Cielo Vista, even thrived there, did not lighten her burden of guilt.

One part of The Dream, an important part, was to have the time and financial resources to bring Thomas home again.

Bobby looked up from the scrapbook just as Julie said, "Thomas, think you'd like to go out with us for a while?"

Thomas and Julie were still holding hands, and Bobby saw his brother-in-law's grip tighten at the suggestion of an excursion.

"We could just go for a drive," Julie said. "Down to the sea. Walk on the shore. Get an ice cream cone. What do you say?"

Thomas looked nervously at the nearest window, which framed a portion of clear blue sky, where white sea gulls periodically swooped and capered. "It's bad out."

"Just a little windy, honey."

"Don't mean the wind."

"We'll have fun."

"It's bad out," he repeated. He chewed on his lower lip.

At times he was eager to venture out into the world, but at other times he withdrew from the prospect as if the air beyond Cielo Vista was purest poison. Thomas could never be argued or cajoled out of that agoraphobic mood, and Julie knew not to push the issue.

"Maybe next time," she said.

"Maybe," Thomas said, looking at the floor. "But today's *really* bad. I . . . sort of feel it . . . the badness . . . cold all over my skin."

For a while Bobby and Julie tried various subjects, but Thomas was talked out. He said nothing, did not make eye contact, and gave no indication that he even heard them.

They sat together in silence, then, until after a few minutes Thomas said, "Don't go yet."

"We're not going," Bobby assured him.

"Just 'cause I can't talk . . . don't mean I want you gone."

"We know that, kiddo," Julie said.

"I . . . need you."

"I need you too," Julie said. She lifted one of her brother's thick-fingered hands and kissed his knuckles.

# 16

AFTER BUYING an electric razor at a drugstore, Frank Pollard shaved and washed as best he could in a service-station restroom. He stopped at a shopping mall and bought a suitcase, underwear, socks, a couple of shirts, another pair of jeans, and incidentals. In the mall parking lot, with the stolen Chevy rocking slightly in the gusting wind, he packed the other purchases in the suitcase. Then he drove to a motel in Irvine, where he checked in under the name of George Farris, using one of the sets of ID he possessed, making a cash deposit because he lacked a credit card. He had cash in abundance.

He could have stayed in the Laguna area; but he sensed that he should not remain in one place too long. Maybe his wariness was based on hard experience. Or maybe he had been on the run for so long that he had become a creature of motion who could never again be truly comfortable at rest.

The motel room was large, clean, and tastefully decorated. The designer had been swept up in the southwest craze: white-washed wood, rattan side chairs with cushions upholstered in peach and pale-blue patterns, seafoam-green drapes. Only the mottled-brown carpet, evidently chosen for its ability to conceal stains and wear, spoiled the effect; by contrast, the light-hued furnishings seemed not merely to stand on the dark carpet but to float above it, creating spatial illusions that were disconcerting, even slightly eerie.

For most of the afternoon Frank sat on the bed, using a pile of pillows as a backrest. The television was on, but he did not watch it. Instead, he probed at the black hole of his past. Hard as he tried, he could still not recall anything of his life prior to waking in the alleyway the previous night. Some strange and exceedingly malevolent shape loomed at the edge of recollection, however, and he wondered uneasily if forgetfulness actually might be a blessing.

He needed help. Given the cash in the flight bag and his two sets of ID, he suspected that he would be unwise to seek assistance from the authorities. He withdrew the Yellow Pages from one of the nightstands and studied the listings for private investigators. But a PI called to mind old Humphrey Bogart movies and seemed like an anachronism in this modern age. How could a guy in a trenchcoat and a snap-brimmed fedora help him recover his memory?

Eventually, with the wind singing threnodies at the window, Frank stretched out to get some of the sleep he had missed last night.

A few hours later, just an hour before dusk, he woke suddenly, whimpering, gasping for breath. His heart pounded furiously.

When he sat up and swung his legs over the side of the bed, he saw that his hands were wet and scarlet. His shirt and jeans were smeared with blood. Some, though surely not all of it, was his own blood, for both of his hands bore deep, oozing scratches. His face stung, and in the bathroom, the mirror revealed two long scratches on his right cheek, one on his left cheek, and a fourth on his chin.

He could not understand how this could have happened in his sleep. If he had torn at himself in some bizarre dream frenzy—

and he could recall no dream—or if someone else had clawed him while he slept, he would have awakened at once. Which meant that he had been awake when it had happened, then had stretched out on the bed again and gone back to sleep—and had forgotten the incident, just as he had forgotten his life prior to that alleyway last night.

He returned in panic to the bedroom and looked on the other side of the bed, then in the closet. He was not sure what he was looking for. Maybe a dead body. He found nothing.

The very thought of killing anyone made him sick. He knew he did not have the capacity to kill, except perhaps in self-defense. So who had scratched his face and hands? Whose blood was on him?

In the bathroom again, he stripped out of his stained clothes and rolled them into a tight bundle. He washed his face and hands. He had bought a styptic pencil along with other shaving gear; he used that to stop the scratches from bleeding.

When he met his own eyes in the mirror, they were so haunted that he had to look away.

Frank dressed in fresh clothes and snatched the car keys off the dresser. He was afraid of what he might find in the Chevy.

At the door, as he disengaged the dead bolt, he realized that neither the frame nor the door itself was smeared with blood. If he had left during the afternoon and returned, bleeding from his hands, he would not have had the presence of mind to wipe the door clean before climbing into bed. Anyway, he had seen no bloody washcloth or tissues with which a cleanup might have been accomplished.

Outside, the sky was clear; the westering sun was bright. The motel's palm trees shivered in a cool wind, and a constant susurration rose from them, punctuated by an occasional series of hard clacks as the thick spines of the fronds met like snapping, wooden teeth.

The concrete walkway outside his room was not spotted with blood. The interior of the car was free of blood. No blood marked the dirty rubber mat in the trunk, either.

He stood by the open trunk, blinking at the sun-washed motel and parking lot around him. Three doors down, a man and woman in their twenties were unloading luggage from their black Pontiac. Another couple and their grade-school-age daughter were hurrying along the covered walkway, apparently heading toward the motel restaurant. Frank realized that he could not have gone out and committed murder and returned, blood-soaked and in broad daylight, without being seen.

In his room again, he went to the bed and studied the rumpled sheets. They were crimson-spotted, but not a fraction as saturated as they would have been if the attack—whatever its nature—had happened there. Of course, if all the blood was his, it might have spilled mostly on the front of his shirt and jeans. But he still could not believe that he had clawed himself in his sleep—one hand ripping at the other, both hands tearing at his face—without waking.

Besides, he had been scratched by someone with sharp fingernails. His own nails were blunt, bitten down to the quick.

# 17

SOUTH OF Cielo Vista Care Home, between Corona Del Mar and Laguna, Bobby tucked the Samurai into a corner of a parking lot at a public beach. He and Julie walked down to the shore.

The sea was marbled blue and green, with thin veins of gray. The water was dark in the troughs, lighter and more colorful where the waves rose and were half pierced by the rays of the fat, low sun. In serried ranks the breakers moved toward the strand, big but not huge, wearing caps of foam that the wind snatched from them.

Surfers in black wetsuits paddled their boards out toward where the swell rose, seeking a last ride before twilight. Others, also in wetsuits, sat around a couple of big coolers, drinking hot beverages from thermos bottles or Coors from the can. The day was too cool for sunbathing, and except for the surfers, the beach was deserted.

Bobby and Julie walked south until they found a low knoll, far enough back from the water to escape the spray. They sat on the stiff grass that flourished in patches in the sandy, salt-tinged soil.

When at last she spoke, Julie said, "A place like this, with a view like this. Not a big place."

"Doesn't have to be. A living room, one bedroom for us and one for Thomas, maybe a cozy little den lined with books."

"We don't even need a dining room, but I'd like a big kitchen."

"Yeah. A kitchen you can really live in."

She sighed. "Music, books, real home-cooked meals instead of junk food grabbed on the fly, lots of time to sit on the porch and enjoy the view—and the three of us together."

That was the rest of The Dream: a place by the sea and—by otherwise living simply—enough financial security to retire twenty years early.

One of the things that had drawn Bobby to Julie—and Julie to him—was their shared awareness of the shortness of life. Everyone knew that life was too short, of course, but most people pushed that thought out of mind, living as if there were endless tomorrows. If most people weren't able to deceive themselves about death, they could not have cared so passionately about the outcome of a ball game, the plot of a soap opera, the blatherings of politicians, or a thousand other things that actually meant nothing when considered against the inevitable fall of the endless night that finally came to everyone. They could not have endured to waste a minute standing in a supermarket line and would not have suffered hours in the company of bores or fools. Maybe a world lay beyond this one, maybe even Heaven, but you couldn't count on it; you could count only on darkness. Self-deception in this case was a blessing. Neither Bobby nor Julie was a gloom-monger. She knew how to enjoy life as well as anyone, and so did he, even if neither of them could buy the fragile illusion of immortality that served most people as a defense against the unthinkable. Their awareness expressed itself not in anxiety or depression, but in a strong resolve not to spend their lives in a hurly-burly of meaningless activity, to find a way to finance long stretches of time together in their own serene little tide pool.

As her chestnut hair streamed in the wind, Julie squinted at the far horizon, which was filling up with honey-gold light as the sinking sun drizzled toward it. "What frightens Thomas about being out in the world is people, too many people. But he'd be happy in a little house by the sea, a quiet stretch of coast, few people. I'm sure he would."

"It'll happen," Bobby assured her.

"By the time we build the agency big enough to sell, the

southern coast will be too expensive. But north of Santa Barbara is pretty."

"It's a long coast," Bobby said, putting an arm around her. "We'll still be able to find a place in the south. And we'll have time to enjoy it. We're not going to live forever, but we're young. Our numbers aren't going to come up for years and years yet."

But he remembered the premonition that had shivered through him in bed that morning, after they had made love, the feeling that something malevolent was out there in the wind-swept world, coming to take Julie away from him.

The sun had touched the horizon and begun to melt into it. The golden light deepened swiftly to orange and then to bloody red. The grass and tall weeds behind them rustled in the wind, and Bobby looked over his shoulder at the spirals of airborne sand that swirled across the slope between the beach and the parking lot, like pale spirits that had fled a graveyard with the coming of twilight. From the east a wall of night was toppling over the world. The air had grown downright cold.

# 18

CANDY SLEPT all day in the front bedroom that had once been his mother's, breathing her special scent. Two or three times a week, he carefully shook a few drops of her favorite perfume—Chanel No. 5—onto a white, lace-trimmed handkerchief, which he kept on the dresser beside her silver comb-and-brush set, so each breath he took in the room reminded him of her. Occasionally he half woke from slumber to readjust the pillows or pull the covers more tightly around him, and the trace of perfume always lulled him as if it were a tranquilizer; each time he happily drifted back into his dreams.

He slept in sweatpants and a T-shirt, because he had a hard time finding pajamas large enough and because he was too modest to sleep in the nude or even in his underwear. Being unclothed embarrassed Candy, even when no one was around to see him.

All of that long Thursday afternoon, hard winter sun filled the world outside, but little got past the flower-patterned shades and rose-colored drapes that guarded the two windows. The few times he woke and blinked at the shadows, Candy saw only the pearl-gray glimmer of the dresser mirror and glints from the silver-framed photographs on the nightstand. Drugged by sleep and by the freshly applied perfume on the handkerchief, he could easily imagine that his beloved mother was in her rocking chair, watching over him, and he felt safe.

He came fully awake shortly before sunset and lay for a while with his hands folded behind his head, staring up at the underside of the canopy that arched over the four-poster; he could not see it, but he knew it was there, and in his mind he could conjure up a vivid image of the fabric's rosebud pattern. For a while he thought about his mother, about the best times of his life, now all gone, and then he thought about the girl, the boy, and the woman he had killed last night. He tried to recall the taste of their blood, but that memory was not as intense as those involving his mother.

After a while he switched on a bedside lamp and looked around at the comfortably familiar room: rosebud wallpaper; rosebud bedspread; rosebud blinds; rose-colored drapes and carpets; dark mahogany bed, dresser, and highboy. Two afghans—one green like the leaves of a rose, one the shade of the petals—were draped over the arms of the rocking chair.

He went into the adjoining bathroom, locked and tested the door. The only light came from the fluorescent panels in the soffit, over the sink, for he had long ago lathered black paint on the small high window.

He studied his face in the mirror for a moment because he liked the way he looked. He could see his mother in his face. He had her blond hair, so pale it was almost white, and her sea-blue eyes. His face was all hard planes and strong features, with none of her beauty or gentleness, though his full mouth was as generous as hers.

As he undressed, he avoided looking down at himself. He was proud of his powerful shoulders and arms, his broad chest, and his muscular legs, but even catching a glimpse of the sex thing made him feel dirty and mildly ill. He sat on the toilet to make water, so he wouldn't have to touch himself. During his shower, when he soaped his crotch, he first pulled on a mitten that he had sewn from a pair of washcloths, so the flesh of his hand would not have to touch the wicked flesh below.

When he had dried off and dressed—athletic socks, running shoes, dark gray cords, black shirt—he hesitantly left the reliable shelter of his mother's old room. Night had fallen, and the upstairs hall was poorly lit by two low-wattage bulbs in a ceiling fixture that was coated with gray dust and missing half its pendant crystals. To his left was the head of the staircase. To his right were his sisters' room, his old room, and the other bath, the doors to which stood open; no lights were on back there. The oak floor creaked, and the threadbare runner did little to soften his footsteps. He sometimes thought he should give the rest of the house a thorough cleaning, maybe even spring for some new carpeting and fresh paint; however, though he kept his mother's room spotless and in good repair, he was not motivated to spend time or money on the rest of the house, and his sisters had little interest in—or talent for—homemaking.

A flurry of soft footfalls alerted him to the approach of the cats, and he stopped short of the stairs, afraid of treading on one of their paws or tails as they poured into the upstairs hall. A moment later they streamed over the top step and swarmed around him: twenty-six of them, if his most recent count was not out of date. Eleven were black, several more were chocolate-brown or tobacco-brown or charcoal-gray, two were deep gold, and only one was white. Violet and Verbina, his sisters, preferred dark cats, the darker the better.

The animals milled around him, walking over his shoes, rubbing against his legs, curling their tails around his calves. Among them were two Angoras, an Abyssinian, a tailless Manx, a Maltese, and a tortoiseshell, but most were mongrel cats of no easily distinguished lineage. Some had green eyes, some yellow, some silver-gray, some blue, and they all regarded him with great interest. Not one of them purred or meowed; their inspection was conducted in absolute silence.

Candy did not particularly like cats, but he tolerated these not only because they belonged to his sisters but because, in a way, they were virtually an extension of Violet and Verbina. To have hurt them, to have spoken harshly to them, would have been the same as striking out at his sisters, which he could never do because his mother, on her deathbed, had admonished him to provide for the girls and protect them.

76

In less than a minute the cats had fulfilled their mission and, almost as one, turned from him. With much swishing of tails and flexing of feline muscles and rippling of fur, they flowed like a single beast to the head of the stairs and down.

By the time he reached the first step, they were at the landing, turning, slipping out of sight. He descended to the lower hall, and the cats were gone. He passed the lightless and musty-smelling parlor. The odor of mildew drifted out of the study, where shelves were filled with the moldering romance novels that his mother had liked so much, and when he passed through the dimly lit dining room, litter crunched under his shoes.

Violet and Verbina were in the kitchen. They were identical twins. They were equally blond, with the same fair and faultless skin, with the same china-blue eyes, smooth brows, high cheekbones, straight noses with delicately carved nostrils, lips that were naturally red without lipstick, and small even teeth as bone-white as those of their cats.

Candy tried to like his sisters, and failed. For his mother's sake he could not *dis*like them, so he remained neutral, sharing the house with them but not as a real family might share it. They were too thin, he thought, fragile-looking, almost frail, and too pale, like creatures that infrequently saw the sun—which in fact seldom warmed them, since they rarely went outside. Their slim hands were well manicured, for they groomed themselves as constantly as if they, too, were cats; but, to Candy, their fingers seemed excessively long, unnaturally flexible and nimble. Their mother had been robust, with strong features and good color, and Candy often wondered how such a vital woman could have spawned this pallid pair.

The twins had piled up cotton blankets, six thick, in one corner of the big kitchen, to make a large area where the cats could lie comfortably, though the padding was actually for Violet and Verbina, so they could sit on the floor among the cats for hours at a time. When Candy entered the room, they were on the blankets, with cats all around them and in their laps. Violet was filing Verbina's fingernails with an emery board. Neither of them looked up, though of course they had already greeted him through the cats. Verbina had never spoken a word within Candy's hearing, not in her entire twenty-five years—the twins were four years younger than he was—but he was not sure whether she was unable to talk, merely unwilling to talk, or shy of talking only when around him. Violet was nearly as silent as her sister, but she did speak when necessary; apparently, at the moment, she had nothing that needed to be said.

He stood by the refrigerator, watching them as they huddled over Verbina's pale right hand, grooming it, and he supposed that he was unfair in his judgment of them. Other men might find them attractive in a strange way. Though, to him, their limbs seemed too thin, other men might see them as supple and erotic, like the legs of dancers and the arms of acrobats. Their skin was clear as milk, and their breasts were full. Because he was blessedly free of any interest in sex, he was not qualified to judge their appeal.

They habitually wore as little as possible, as little as he would tolerate before ordering them to put on more clothes. They kept the house excessively warm in winter, and most often dressed—as now—in T-shirts and short shorts or panties, bare-foot and bare-limbed. Only his mother's room, which was now his, was kept cooler, because he had closed the vents up there. Without his presence to demand a degree of modesty, they would have roamed the house in the nude.

Lazily, lazily, Violet filed Verbina's thumbnail, and they both stared at it as intently as if the meaning of life was to be read in the curve of the half-moon or the arc of the nail itself.

Candy raided the refrigerator, removing a chunk of canned ham, a package of Swiss cheese, mustard, pickles, and a quart of milk. He got bread from one of the cupboards and sat in a railback chair at the age-yellowed table.

The table, chairs, cabinets, and woodwork had once been glossy white, but they had not been painted since before his mother died. They were yellow-white now, gray-white in the seams and corners, crackle-finished by time. The daisy-patterned wallpaper was soiled and, in a couple of places, peel-ing along the seams, and the chintz curtains hung limp with grease and dust.

Candy made and consumed two thick ham-and-cheese sand-wiches. He gulped the milk straight from the carton.

Suddenly all twenty-six cats, which had been sprawling lan-guidly around the twins, sprang up simultaneously, proceeded to the pet door in the bottom of the larger kitchen door, and went outside in orderly fashion. Time to make their toilet, evi-dently. Violet and Verbina didn't want the house smelling of litter boxes.

Candy closed his eyes and took a long swallow of milk. He would have preferred it at room temperature or even slightly warm. It tasted vaguely like blood, though not as pleasantly pungent; it would have been more like blood if it had not been chilled.

Within a couple of minutes the cats returned. Now Verbina was lying on her back, with her head propped on a pillow, eyes closed, lips moving as if talking to herself, though no sound issued from her. She extended her other slender hand so her sister could meticulously file those nails too. Her long legs were spread, and Candy could see between her smooth thighs. She was wearing only a T-shirt and flimsy peach-colored panties that defined rather than concealed the cleft of her womanhood. The silent cats swarmed to her, draped themselves over her, more concerned about propriety than she was, and they regarded Candy accusatorily, as if they knew that he'd been staring.

He lowered his eyes and studied the crumbs on the table.

Violet said, "Frankie was here."

At first he was more surprised by the fact that she had spoken than by what she had said. Then the meaning of those three words reverberated through him as if he were a brass gong struck by a mallet. He stood up so abruptly that he knocked over his chair. "He was here? In the house?"

Neither the cats nor Verbina twitched at the crash of the chair or the sharpness of his voice. They lay somnolent, indifferent.

"Outside," Violet said, still sitting on the floor beside her reclining sister, working on the other twin's nails. She had a low, almost whispery voice. "Watching the house from the Eugenia hedge."

Candy glanced at the night beyond the windows. "When?"

"Around four o'clock."

"Why didn't you wake me?"

"He wasn't here long. He's never here long. A minute or two, then he goes. He's afraid."

"You saw him?"

"I knew he was there."

"You didn't try to stop him from leaving?"

"How could I?" She sounded irritable now, but her voice was no less seductive than it had been. "The cats went after him, though."

"Did they hurt him?"

"A little. Not bad. But he killed Samantha."

"Who?"

"Our poor little puss. Samantha."

Candy did not know the cats' names. They had always seemed to be not just a pack of cats but a single creature, most often moving as one, apparently thinking as one.

"He killed Samantha. Smashed her head against one of the stone pilasters at the end of the walk." At last Violet looked up from her sister's hand. Her eyes seemed to be a paler blue than before, icy. "I want you to hurt him, Candy. I want you to hurt him real bad, the way he hurt our cat. I don't care if he is our brother—"

"He isn't our brother any more, not after what he did," Candy said furiously.

"I want you to do to him what he did to our poor Samantha. I want you to smash him, Candy, I want you to crush his head, crack his skull open until his brains ooze out." She continued to speak softly, but he was riveted by her words. Sometimes, like now, when her voice was even more sensuous than usual, it seemed not merely to play upon his ears but to slither into his head, where it lay gently on his brain, like a mist, a fog. "I want you to pound him, hit him and tear him until he's just splintered bones and ruptured guts, and I want you to rip out his eyes. I want him to be sorry he hurt Samantha."

Candy shook himself. "If I get my hands on him, I'll kill him, all right, but not because of what he did to your cat. Because of what he did to our *mother*. Don't you remember what he did to *her*? How can you worry about getting revenge for a cat when we still haven't made him pay for our mother, after seven long years?"

She looked stricken, turned her face from him, and fell silent.

The cats flowed off Verbina's recumbent form.

Violet stretched out half atop her sister, half beside her. She put her head on Verbina's breasts. Their bare legs were entwined.

Rising part of the way out of her trancelike state, Verbina stroked her sister's silken hair.

The cats returned and cuddled against both twins wherever there was a warm hollow to welcome them.

"Frank was here," Candy said aloud but largely to himself, and his hands curled into tight fists.

A fury grew in him, like a small turning wheel of wind far out on the sea but soon to whirl itself into a hurricane. However, rage was an emotion he dared not indulge; he must control himself. A storm of rage would water the seeds of his dark need. His mother would approve of killing Frank, for Frank had betrayed the family; his death would benefit the family. But if Candy let his anger at his brother swell into a rage, then was unable to find Frank, he would have to kill someone else, because the need would be too great to deny. His mother, in Heaven, would be ashamed of him, and for a while she would turn her face from him and deny that she had ever given birth to him.

Looking up at the ceiling, toward the unseen sky and the place at God's court where his mother dwelled, Candy said, "I'll be okay. I won't lose control. I won't."

He turned from his sisters and the cats, and he went outside to see if any trace of Frank remained near the Eugenia hedge or at the pilaster where he'd killed Samantha.

# 19

BOBBY AND JULIE ate dinner at Ozzie's, in Orange, then shifted to the adjoining bar. The music was provided by Eddie Day, who had a smooth, supple voice; he played contemporary stuff but also tunes from the fifties and early sixties. It wasn't Big Band, but some early rock-and-roll had a swing beat. They could swing to numbers like "Dream Lover," rumba to "La Bamba," and cha-cha to any disco ditty that crept into Eddie's repertoire, so they had a good time.

Whenever possible, Julie liked to go dancing after she visited Thomas at Cielo Vista. In the thrall of the music, keeping time to the beat, focused on the patterns of the dance, she was able to put everything else out of her mind—even guilt, even grief. Nothing else freed her so completely. Bobby liked to dance, too, especially swing. Tuck in, throw out, change places, sugarpush, do a tight whip, tuck in again, throw out, trade places with both hands linked, back to basic position . . . Music soothed, but dance had the power to fill the heart with joy and to numb those parts of it that were bruised.

During the musicians' break, Bobby and Julie sipped beer at a table near the edge of the parquet dance floor. They talked about everything except Thomas, and eventually they got around to The Dream—specifically, how to furnish the seaside bungalow if they ever bought it. Though they would not spend a fortune on furniture, they agreed that they could indulge themselves with two pieces from the swing era: maybe a bronze and marble Art Deco cabinet by Emile-Jacques Ruhlmann, and *definitely* a Wurlitzer jukebox.

"The model 950," Julie said. "It was gorgeous. Bubble tubes. Leaping gazelles on the front panels."

"Fewer than four thousand were made. Hitler's fault. Wurlitzer retooled for war production. The model 500 is pretty too—or the 700."

"Nice, but they're not the 950."

"Not as *expensive* as the 950, either."

"You're counting pennies when we're talking ultimate beauty?"

He said, "Ultimate beauty is the Wurlitzer 950?"

"That's right. What else?"

"To me, you're the ultimate beauty."

"Sweet," she said. "But I still want the 950."

"To you, aren't *I* the ultimate beauty?" He batted his eyelashes.

"To me, you're just a difficult man who won't let me have my Wurlitzer 950," she said, enjoying the game.

"What about a Seeburg? A Packard Pla-mor? Okay. A Rock-ola?"

"Rock-ola made some beautiful boxes," she agreed. "We'll buy one of those *and* the Wurlitzer 950."

"You'll spend our money like a drunken sailor."

"I was born to be rich. Stork got confused. Didn't deliver me to the Rockefellers."

"Wouldn't you like to get your hands on that stork now?"

"Got him years ago. Cooked him, ate him for Christmas dinner. He was delicious, but I'd still rather be a Rockefeller."

"Happy?" Bobby asked.

"Delirious. And it's not just the beer. I don't know why, but tonight I feel better than I've felt in ages. I think we're going to get where we want to go, Bobby. I think we're going to retire early and live a long happy life by the sea."

His smile faded as she talked. Now he was frowning.

She said, "What's wrong with you, Sourpuss?"

"Nothing."

"Don't kid me. You've been a little strange all day. You've tried to hide it, but something's on your mind."

He sipped his beer. Then: "Well, you've got this good feeling that everything's going to be fine, but I've got a bad feeling."

"You? Mr. Blue Skies?"

He was still frowning. "Maybe you should confine yourself to office work for a while, stay off the firing line."

"Why?"

"My bad feeling."

"Which is?"

"That I'm going to lose you."

"Just try."

# 20

WITH ITS invisible baton, the wind conducted a chorus of whispery voices in the hedgerow. The dense Eugenias formed a seven-foot-high wall around three sides of the two-acre property, and they would have been higher than the house itself if Candy had not used power trimmers to chop off the tops of them a couple of times each year.

He opened the waist-high, wrought-iron gate between the two stone pilasters, and stepped out onto the graveled shoulder of the county road. To his left, the two-lane blacktop wound up into the hills for another couple of miles. To his right, it dropped down toward the distant coast, past houses on lots that were more parsimoniously proportioned the nearer they were to the shore, until in town they were only a tenth as big as the Pollard place. As the land descended westward, lights were clustered in ever greater concentration—then stopped abruptly, several miles away, as if crowding against a black wall; that wall was the night sky and the lightless expanse of the deep, cold sea.

Candy moved along the high hedge, until he sensed that he had reached the place where Frank had stood. He held up both big hands, letting the wind-fluttered leaves tremble against his palms, as if the foliage might impart to him some psychic residue of his brother's brief visit. Nothing.

Parting the branches, he peered through the gap at the house, which looked larger at night than it really was, as if it had eighteen or twenty rooms instead of ten. The front windows were dark; along the side, toward the back, where the light was filtered through greasy chintz curtains, a kitchen window was filled with a yellow glow. But for that one light, the house might have appeared abandoned. Some of the Victorian gingerbread had warped and broken away from the eaves. The porch roof was sagging, and a few railing balusters were broken, and the front steps were swaybacked. Even by the meager light of the low crescent moon, he could see the house needed painting; bare wood, like glimpses of dark bone, showed in many places, and the remaining paint was either peeling or as translucent as an albino's skin.

Candy tried to put himself in Frank's mind, to imagine why Frank kept returning. Frank was afraid of Candy, and he had reason to be. He was afraid of his sisters, too, and of all the memories that the house held for him, so he should have stayed away. But he crept back with frequency, in search of something—perhaps something that even he did not understand.

Frustrated, Candy let the branches fall together, retraced his steps along the hedge, and stopped at one gatepost, then the other, searching for the spot where Frank had fended off the cats and smashed Samantha's skull. Though far milder now than it had been earlier, the wind nevertheless had dried the blood that had stained the stones, and darkness hid the residue. Still, Candy was sure he could find the killing place. He gingerly touched the pilaster high and low, on all four faces, as if he expected a portion of it to be hot enough to sear his skin. But though he patiently traced the outlines of the rough stones and the mortar seams, too much time had passed; even his exceptional talents could not extract his brother's lingering aura.

He hurried along the cracked and canted walkway, out of the chilly night and into the stiflingly warm house again, into the kitchen, where his sisters were sitting on the blankets in the cats' corner. Verbina was behind Violet, a comb in one hand and a brush in the other, grooming her sister's flaxen hair.

Candy said, "Where's Samantha?"

Tilting her head, looking up at him perplexedly, Violet said, "I told you. Dead."

"Where's the *body?*"

"Here," Violet said, making a sweeping gesture with both hands to indicate the quiescent felines sprawled and curled around her.

"Which one?" Candy asked. Half of the creatures were so still that any of them might have been the dead one.

"All," Violet said. "They're all Samantha now."

Candy had been afraid of that. Each time one of the cats died, the twins drew the rest of the pack into a circle, placed the corpse at the center, and without speaking commanded the living to partake of the dead.

"Damn," Candy said.

"Samantha still lives, she's still a part of us," Violet said. Her voice was as low and whispery as before, but dreamier than usual. "None of our pusses ever really leaves us. Part of him . . . or her . . . stays in each of us . . . and we're all stronger because of that, stronger and purer, and always together, always and forever."

Candy did not ask if his sisters had shared in the feast, for he already knew the answer. Violet licked the corner of her mouth, as if remembering the taste, and her moist lips glistened; a moment later Verbina's tongue slid across her lips too.

Sometimes Candy felt as if the twins were members of an entirely different species from him, for he could seldom fathom their attitudes and behavior. And when they looked at him— Verbina, in perpetual silence—their faces and eyes revealed nothing of their thoughts or feelings; they were as inscrutable as the cats.

He only dimly grasped the twins' bond with the cats. It was their blessed mother's gift to them just as his many talents were his mother's generous bequest to him, so he did not question the rightness or wholesomeness of it.

Still, he wanted to hit Violet because she hadn't saved the body for him. She had known Frank had touched it, that it could be of use to Candy, but she had not saved it until he'd awakened, had not come to wake him early. He wanted to smash her, but she was his sister, and he couldn't hurt his sisters; he had to provide for them, protect them. His mother was watching.

"The parts that couldn't be eaten?" he asked.

Violet gestured toward the kitchen door.

He switched on the outside light and stepped onto the back porch. Small knobs of bone and vertebrae were scattered like queerly shaped dice on the unpainted floorboards. Only two sides of the porch were open; the house angled around the other two flanks of it, and in the niche where the house walls met, Candy found a piece of Samantha's tail and scraps of fur, jammed there by the night wind. The half-crushed skull was on the top step. He snatched it up and moved down onto the unmown lawn.

The wind, which had been declining since late afternoon, suddenly stopped altogether. The cool air would have carried the faintest sound a great distance; but the night was hushed.

Usually Candy could touch an object and see who had recently handled it before him. Sometimes he could even see where some of those people had gone after putting the object down, and when he went looking for them, they were always to be found where his clairvoyance had led him. Frank had killed the cat, and Candy hoped that contact with the remains would spark an inner vision that would put him on his brother's trail again.

Every speck of flesh had been stripped from Samantha's broken pate, and its contents had been emptied as well. Picked clean, licked smooth, dried by the wind, it might have been a portion of a fossil from a distant age. Candy's mind was filled not with images of Frank but of the other cats and Verbina and Violet, and finally he threw down the damaged skull in disgust.

His frustration sharpened his anger. He felt the need rising in him. He dared not let the need bloom . . . but resisting it was infinitely harder than resisting the charms of women and other sins. He *hated* Frank. He hated him so much, so deeply, had hated him so constantly for seven years, that he could not bear the thought that he had slept through an opportunity to destroy him.

Need. . . .

He dropped to his knees on the weedy lawn. He fisted his hands and hunched his shoulders and clenched his teeth, trying to make a rock of himself, an unmovable mass that would not be swayed one inch by the most urgent need, not one hair's width by even the most dire necessity, the most demanding hunger, the most passionate craving. He prayed to his mother to give him strength. The wind began to pick up again, and he believed it was a devil wind that would blow him toward temptation, so he fell forward on the ground and dug his fingers into the yielding earth, and he repeated his mother's sacred name—Roselle—whispered her name furiously into the grass and dirt, again and again, desperate to quell the germination of his dark need. Then he wept. Then he got up. And went hunting.

# 21

FRANK WENT to a theater and sat through a movie but was unable to concentrate on the story. He ate dinner at El Torito, though he didn't really taste the food; he just pushed down the enchiladas and rice as if feeding fuel to a furnace. For a couple of hours he drove aimlessly back and forth across the middle and southern reaches of Orange County, staying on the move only because, for the time being, he felt safer when in motion. Finally he returned to the motel.

He kept probing at the dark wall in his mind, behind which his entire life was concealed. Diligently, he sought the tiniest chink through which he might glimpse a memory. If he could find one crack, he was sure that the entire façade of amnesia would come tumbling down. But the barrier was smooth and flawless.

When he switched off the lights, he could not sleep.

The Santa Anas had abated. He could not blame his insomnia on the noisy winds.

Although the amount of blood on the sheets had been minimal and though it had dried since he'd awakened from his nap earlier in the day, he decided that the thought of lying in blood-stained bedclothes was preventing him from nodding off. He snapped on a lamp, stripped the bed, turned up the heat, stretched out in the darkness again, and tried to sleep without covers. No good.

He told himself that his amnesia—and the resultant loneliness and sense of isolation—was keeping him awake. Although there was some truth in that, he knew that he was kidding himself.

The real reason he could not sleep was fear. Fear of where he might go while sleepwalking. Fear of what he might do. Fear of what he might find in his hands when he woke up.

# 22

DEREK SLEPT. In the other bed. Snoring softly.

Thomas couldn't sleep. He got up and stood by the window, looking out. The moon was gone. The dark was very big.

He didn't like the night. It scared him. He liked sunshine, and flowers all bright, and grass looking green, and blue sky all over so you felt like there was a lid on the world keeping everything down here on the ground and in place. At night all the colors were gone, and the world was empty, like somebody took the lid off and let in a lot of nothingness, and you looked up at all that nothingness and you felt you might just float away like the colors, float up and away and out of the world, and then in the morning when they put the lid back on, you wouldn't be here, you'd be out there somewhere, and you could never get back in again. Never.

He put his fingertips against the window. The glass was cool.

He wished he could sleep away the night. Usually he slept okay. Not tonight.

He was worried about Julie. He always worried about her a little. A brother was supposed to worry. But this wasn't a little worry. This was a lot.

It started just that morning. A funny feeling. Not funny ha-ha. Funny strange. Funny scary. Something real bad's going to happen to Julie, the feeling said. Thomas got so upset, he tried to warn her. He TVed a warning to her. They said the pictures and voices and music on the TV were sent through the air, which he first thought was a lie, that they were making fun of his being dumb, expecting him to believe *anything*, but then Julie said it was true, so sometimes he tried to TV his thoughts to her, because if you could send pictures and music and voices through the air, thoughts ought to be easy. *Be careful, Julie,* he TVed. *Look out, be careful, something bad's going to happen.*

Usually, when he felt things about someone, that someone was Julie. He knew when she was happy. Or sad. When she was sick, he sometimes curled up on his bed and put his hands on his own belly. He always knew when she was coming to visit.

He felt things about Bobby too. Not at first. When Julie first brought Bobby around, Thomas felt nothing. But slowly he felt more. Until now he felt almost as much about Bobby as about Julie.

He felt things about some other people too. Like Derek. Like Gina, another Down's kid at The Home. And like a couple of the aides, one of the visiting nurses. But he didn't feel half as much about them as he did about Bobby and Julie. He figured that maybe the more he loved somebody, the bigger he felt things— *knew* things—about them.

Sometimes when Julie was worried about him, Thomas wanted real bad to tell her that he knew how she felt, and that he was all right. Because just knowing he understood would make her happier. But he didn't have the words. He couldn't explain how or why he sometimes felt other people's feelings. And he didn't want to try to tell them about it because he was afraid of looking dumb.

He *was* dumb. He knew that. He wasn't as dumb as Derek, who was very nice, good to room with, but who was real slow. They sometimes said "slow" instead of "dumb" when they talked in front of you. Julie never did. Bobby never did. But some people said "slow" and thought you didn't get it. He got it. They had bigger words, too, and he really didn't understand those, but he sure understood "slow." He didn't *want* to be dumb, nobody gave him a choice, and sometimes he TVed a message to God, asking God to make him not dumb any more, but either God wanted him to stay dumb always and forever— but why?—or God just didn't get the messages.

Julie didn't get the messages either. Thomas always knew when he got through to someone with a TVed thought. He never got to Julie.

But he could sometimes get through to Bobby, which was funny. Not ha-ha funny. Strange funny. Interesting funny. When Thomas TVed a thought to Julie, Bobby sometimes got it instead. Like this morning. When he'd TVed a warning to Julie—

*—Something bad's going to happen, Julie, something real bad is coming—*

—Bobby had picked it up. Maybe because Thomas and Bobby both loved Julie. Thomas didn't know. He couldn't figure. But it sure happened. Bobby tuned in.

Now Thomas stood at the window, in his pajamas, and looked out at the scary night, and he felt the Bad Thing out there, felt it like a ripple in his blood, like a tingle in his bones. The Bad Thing was far away, not anywhere near Julie, but coming.

Today, during Julie's visit, Thomas wanted to tell her about the Bad Thing coming. But he couldn't find a way to say it and make sense, and he was scared of sounding dumb. Julie and Bobby knew he was dumb, sure, but he hated to sound dumb in front of them, to *remind* them how dumb he was. Every time he almost started to tell her about the Bad Thing, he just forgot how to use words. He had the words in his head, all lined up in a row, ready to say, but then suddenly they were mixed up, and he couldn't make them get back in the right order, so he couldn't say the words because they'd be just words without meaning anything, and he'd look really, really dumb.

Besides, he didn't know what to tell her the Bad Thing was. He thought maybe it was a person, a real terrible person out there, going to do something to Julie, but it didn't exactly feel like a person. Partly a person, but something else. Something that made Thomas feel cold not just on his outside but on his inside, too, like standing in a winter wind and eating ice cream at the same time.

He shivered.

He didn't want to get these ugly feelings about whatever was out there, but he couldn't just go back to bed and tune out, either, because the more he felt about the far-away Bad Thing, the better he could warn Julie and Bobby when the thing wasn't so far away any more.

Behind him, Derek murmured in a dream.

The Home was real quiet. All the dumb people were deep asleep. Except Thomas. Sometimes he liked to be awake when everyone else wasn't. Sometimes that made him feel smarter than all of them put together, seeing things they couldn't see and knowing things they couldn't know because they were asleep and he wasn't.

He stared at the nothingness of night.

He put his forehead against the glass.

For Julie's sake, he reached. Into the nothingness. Toward the far-away.

He opened himself. To the feelings. To the ripple-tingle.

A big ugly-nasty hit him. Like a wave. It came out of the night and hit him, and he stumbled back from the window and fell on his butt beside the bed, and then he couldn't feel the Bad Thing at all, it was gone, but what he had felt was so big and so ugly that his heart was pounding and he could hardly breathe, and right away he TVed to Bobby:

*Run, go, get away, save Julie, the Bad Thing's coming, the Bad Thing, run, run.*

# 23

THE DREAM was filled with the music of Glenn Miller's "Moonlight Serenade," though like everything in dreams, the song was indefinably different from the real tune. Bobby was in a house that was at once familiar yet totally strange, and somehow he knew it was the seaside bungalow to which he and Julie were going to retire young. He drifted into the living room, over a dark Persian carpet, past comfortable-looking upholstered chairs, a huge old chesterfield with rounded back and thick cushions, a Ruhlmann cabinet with bronze panels, an Art Deco lamp, and overflowing bookshelves. The music was coming from outside, so he went out there. He enjoyed the easy transitions of the dream, moving through a door without opening it, crossing a wide porch and descending wooden stairs without ever quite lifting a foot. The sea rumbled to one side, and the phosphorescent foam of the breakers glowed faintly in the night. Under a palm tree, in the sand, with a scattering of shells around it, stood a Wurlitzer 950, ablaze with gold and red light, bubble tubes percolating, gazelles perpetually leaping, figures of Pan perpetually piping, record-changing mechanism gleaming like real silver, and a large black platter spinning on the turntable. Bobby felt as if "Moonlight Serenade" would go on forever, which would have been fine with him, because he had never been more mellow, more at peace, and he sensed that Julie had come out of the house behind him, that she was waiting on the damp sand near the water's edge, and that she wanted to dance with him, so he turned, and there she was, exotically illuminated by the Wurlitzer, and he took a step toward her—

*Run, go, get away, save Julie, the Bad Thing's coming, the Bad Thing, run, run!*

The indigo ocean suddenly leapt as if under the lash of a storm, and spume exploded into the night air.

Hurricane winds shook the palms.

*The Bad Thing! Run! Run!*

The world tilted. Bobby stumbled toward Julie. The sea surged up around her. It wanted her; it was going to seize her; it was water with a will, a thinking sea with a malevolent consciousness gleaming darkly in its depths.

*The Bad Thing!*

The Glenn Miller tune speeded up, whirling at double time.

*The Bad Thing!*

The soft, romantic light from the Wurlitzer flamed brighter, stung his eyes, yet did not drive back the night. It was radiating light as if the door to Hell had opened, but the darkness around them only intensified, yielding nothing to that supernatural blaze.

*THE BAD THING! THE BAD THING!*

The world tilted again. Heaved and rolled.

Bobby staggered across the carnival-ride beach, toward Julie, who seemed unable to move. She was being swallowed by the churning oil-black sea.

*THE BAD THING THE BAD THING THE BAD THING!*

With the hard crack of riven stone, the sky split above them, but no lightning stabbed out of that crumbling vault.

Geysers of sand erupted around Bobby. Inky water exploded out of sudden gaping holes in the beach.

He looked back. The bungalow was gone. The sea rose on all sides. The beach was dissolving under his feet.

Screaming, Julie disappeared under the water.

*BADTHINGBADTHINGBADTHINGBADTHING!*

A twenty-foot wave loomed over Bobby. It broke. He was swept away. He tried to swim. The flesh on his arms and hands bubbled and blistered and began to peel off, revealing glints of ice-white bone. The midnight seawater was an acid. His head went under. He gasped, broke the surface, but the corrosive sea had already kissed away his lips, and he felt his gums receding from his teeth, and his tongue turned to rancid mush in the salty rush of caustic brine that he had swallowed. Even the spray-filled air was erosive, eating away his lungs in an instant, so when he tried to breathe he could not. He went down, flailing at the waves with arms and hands that were only bone, caught in an undertow, sucked into everlasting darkness, dissolution, oblivion.

*BADTHING!*

Bobby sat straight up in bed.

He was screaming, but no cry issued from him. When he realized he had been dreaming, he stopped trying to scream, and finally a low and miserable sound escaped him.

He had thrown off the sheets. He sat on the edge of the bed, feet on the floor, both hands on the mattress, steadying himself as if he was still on that heaving beach or struggling to swim in those roiling tides.

The green numbers of the projection clock glowed faintly on the ceiling: 2:43.

For a while the drum-loud thud of his own heart filled him with sound from within, and he was deaf to the outer world. But after a few seconds he heard Julie breathing steadily, rhythmically, and he was surprised that he had not awakened her. Evidently he had not been thrashing in his sleep.

The panic that infused the dream had not entirely left him. His anxiety began to swell again, partly because the room was as lightless as that devouring sea. Afraid of waking Julie, he did not switch on the bedside lamp.

As soon as he was able to stand, he got up and circled the bed in the perfect blackness. The bathroom was on her side, but a clear path was provided, and he found his way as he had on countless other nights, without difficulty, guided both by experience and instinct.

He eased the door shut behind him and switched on the lights. For a moment the fluorescent brilliance prevented him from looking into the glary surface of the mirror above the double sinks. When at last he regarded his reflection, he saw that his flesh had not been eaten away. The dream had been frighteningly vivid, unlike anything he'd known before; in some strange way it had been even more real than waking life, with intense colors and sounds that pulsed through his slumbering mind with the fulgurate dazzle of light along the filament of an incandescent bulb. Though aware that it had been a dream, he had half feared that the nightmare ocean had left its corrosive mark on him even after he woke.

Shuddering, he leaned against the counter. He turned on the cold water, bent forward, and splashed his face. Dripping, he looked at his reflection again and met his eyes. He whispered to himself: "What the hell was *that?*"

# 24

CANDY PROWLED.

The eastern end of the Pollard family's two-acre property dropped into a canyon. The walls were steep, composed mostly of dry crumbling soil veined in places by pink and gray shale. Only the expansive root systems of the hardy, desert vegetation—chapparal, thick clumps of bunchgrass, pampas grass, scattered mesquite—kept the slopes from eroding extensively in every heavy rain. A few eucalyptuses, laurels, and melaleucas grew on the walls of the canyon, and where the floor was broad enough, melaleucas and California live oaks sank roots deep into the earth along the runoff channel. That channel was only a dry streambed now, but during a heavy rain it overflowed.

Fleet and silent in spite of his size, Candy followed the canyon eastward, moving upslope, until he came to a junction with another declivity that was too narrow to be called a canyon. There, he turned north. The land continued to climb, though not as steeply as before. Sheer walls soared on both sides of him, and in places the passage was nearly pinched off, narrowing to only a couple of feet. Brittle tumbleweeds, blown into the ravine by the wind, had collected in mounds at some of those choke points, and they scratched Candy as he pushed through them.

Without even a fragment moon, the night was unusually dark at the bottom of that fissure in the land, but he seldom stumbled and never hesitated. His gifts did not include superhuman vision; he was as blinded by lightlessness as anyone. However, even in the blackest night, he knew when obstacles lay before him, sensed the contours of the land so well that he could proceed with surefooted confidence. He did not know how this sixth sense served him, and he did nothing to engage it; he simply had an uncanny awareness of his relationship with his surroundings, knew his place at all times, much as the best high-wire walkers, though blindfolded, could proceed with self-assurance along a taut line above the upturned faces of a circus crowd.

This was another gift from his mother.

All of her children were gifted. But Candy's talents exceeded those of Violet, Verbina, and Frank.

The narrow passage opened into another canyon, and Candy turned east again, along a rocky runoff channel, hurrying now as his need grew. Though ever more widely separated, houses were still perched high above, on the canyon rim; their bright windows were too far away to illuminate the ground before him, but now and then he glanced up longingly because within those homes was the blood he needed.

God had given Candy a taste for blood, made him a predator, and therefore God was responsible for whatever Candy did; his mother had explained all of that long ago. God wanted him to be selective in his killing; but when Candy was unable to restrain himself, the ultimate blame was God's, for He had instilled the blood lust in Candy but had not provided him with the strength to control it.

Like that of all predators, Candy's mission was to thin the sick and the weak from the herd. In his case, morally degenerate members of the human herd were the intended prey: thieves, liars, cheats, adulterers. Unfortunately he did not always recognize sinners when he met them. Fulfilling his mission had been far easier when his mother had been alive, for she had no trouble spotting the blighted souls for him.

Tonight he would try as best he could to confine his killing to wild animals. Slaughtering people—especially close to home—was chancy; it might bring him under the eye of the police. He could risk killing locals only when they had crossed the family in some way and simply could not be allowed to live.

If he was unable to satisfy his need with animals, he would go somewhere, anywhere, and kill people. His mother, up there in Heaven, would be angry with him and disappointed by his lack of control, but God would not be able to blame him. After all, he was only what God had made him.

With the lights of the last house well behind him, he stopped in a grove of melaleucas. The day's strong winds had drained out of the high hills, down through the canyons, and out to sea; currently the air seemed utterly still. Drooping trailers hung from the branches of the melaleucas, and every long, blade-sleek leaf was motionless.

His eyes had adapted to the darkness. The trees were silver in the dim starlight, and their cascading trailers contributed to an illusion that he was surrounded by a silent waterfall or frozen in a paperweight blizzard. He could even make out the ragged scrolls of bark that curled away from the trunks and limbs in the perpetual peeling process that lent a unique beauty to the species.

He could not see any prey.

He could hear no furtive movement of wildlife in the brush.

However, he knew that many small creatures, filled with warm blood, were huddled nearby in burrows, in secret nests, in drifts of old leaves, and in the sheltered niches of rocks. The very thought of them made him half mad with hunger.

He held his arms out in front of him, palms facing away from him, fingers spread. Blue light, the shade of pale sapphire, faint as the glow of a quarter-moon, perhaps a second in duration, pulsed from his hands. The leaves trembled, and the sparse bunchgrass stirred, then all was still as darkness reclaimed the canyon floor.

Again, blue light shone forth from his hands, as if they were hooded lanterns from which the shutters had been briefly lifted. This time the light was twice as bright as before, a deeper blue, and it lasted perhaps two seconds. The leaves rustled, and a few of the drooping trailers swayed, and the grass shivered for thirty or forty feet in front of him.

Disturbed by those queer vibrations, something scurried toward Candy, started past him. With that special sense of his surroundings that did not rely on sight or sound or smell, he reached to his left and snatched at the unseen darting creature. His reflexes were as uncanny as anything else about him, and he seized his prey. A field mouse. For an instant it froze in terror. Then it squirmed in his grasp, but he held fast to it.

His power had no effect on living things. He could not stun his prey with the telekinetic energy that radiated from his open palms. He could not draw them forth or call them to him, only frighten them out of hiding. He could have shattered one of the melaleucas or sent geysers of dirt and stones into the air, but no matter how hard he strained, he could not have stirred one hair on the mouse by using just his mind. He didn't know why he was hampered by that limitation. Violet and Verbina, whose gifts were not half as impressive as his, seemed to have power *only* over living things, smaller animals like the cats. Plants bent to Candy's will, of course, and sometimes insects, but nothing with a mind, not even something with a mind as weak as that of a mouse.

Kneeling under the silvery trees, he was swaddled in gloom so deep that he could see nothing of the mouse except its dimly gleaming eyes. He brought the fist-wrapped creature to his mouth.

It made a thin, terrified sound, more of a peep than a squeal.

He bit off its head, spat it out, and fastened his lips upon the torn neck. The blood was sweet, but there was too little of it.

He cast the dead rodent aside and raised his arms again, palms out, fingers spread. This time the splash of spectral light was an intense, electric, sapphire blue. Although it was of no longer duration than before, its effect was startlingly greater. A half dozen waves of vibrations, each a fraction of a second apart, slammed up the inclined floor of the canyon. The tall trees shook, and the hundreds of drooping trailers lashed the air, and the leaves thrashed with a sound like swarms of bees. Pebbles and smaller stones were flung up from the ground, and loose rocks rattled against one another. Every blade of bunchgrass stood up stiff and straight, like hair on a frightened man's nape, and a few clumps tore out of the soil and tumbled away into the night, along with showers of dead leaves, as if a wind had captured them. But no wind disturbed the night—only the brief burst of sapphire light and the powerful vibrations that accompanied it.

Wildlife erupted from concealment, and some of the animals streamed toward him, heading down the canyon. He had learned long ago that they never recognized his scent as that of a human being. They were as likely to flee toward him as away from him. Either he had no scent that they could detect . . . or they smelled something wild in him, something more like themselves than like a human being, and in their panic they did not realize that he was a predator.

They were visible, at best, as shapeless dark forms, streaking past him, like shadows flung off by a spinning lamp. But he also sensed them with his psychic gift. Coyotes loped by, and a panicked raccoon brushed against his leg; he did not reach out for those, because he wanted to avoid being badly clawed or bitten. At least a double score of mice streamed within reach, as well, but he wanted something more full of life, heavy with blood.

He snatched at what he thought was a squirrel, missed, but a moment later seized a rabbit by its hind legs. It shrieked. It thrashed with its less formidable forepaws, but he got hold of those, too, not only immobilizing the creature but paralyzing it with fear.

He held it up to his face.

Its fur had a dusty, musky smell.

Its red eyes glistened with terror.

He could hear its thunderous heart.

He bit into its throat. The fur, hide, and muscle resisted his teeth, but blood flowed.

The rabbit twitched, not in an attempt to escape but as if to express its resignation to its fate; they were slow spasms, strangely sensuous, as if the creature almost welcomed death. Over the years Candy had seen this behavior in countless small animals, especially in rabbits, and he always thrilled to it, for it gave him a heady sense of power, made him feel as one with the fox and the wolf.

The spasms ceased, and the rabbit went limp in his hands. Though it was still alive, it had acknowledged the imminence of death and had entered a trancelike state in which it evidently felt no pain. This seemed to be a grace that God bestowed on small prey.

Candy bit into its throat again, harder this time, deeper, then bit again, deeper still, and the life of the rabbit spurted and bubbled into his greedy mouth.

Far away in another canyon, a coyote howled. It was answered by others in its pack. A chorus of eerie voices rose and fell and rose again, as if the coyotes were aware that they were not the only hunters in the night, as if they smelled the fresh kill.

When he had supped, Candy cast the drained corpse aside.

His need was still great. He would have to break open the blood reservoirs within more rabbits or squirrels before his thirst was slaked.

He got to his feet and headed farther up into the canyon, where the wildlife had not been disturbed by his first use of the power, where creatures of many kinds waited in their burrows and hidey-holes to be harvested. The night was deep and bountiful.

# 25

MAYBE IT WAS just Monday morning blues. Maybe it was the bruised sky and the promise of rain that formed her mood. Or maybe she was tense and sour because the violent events at Decodyne were only four days in the past and therefore still too fresh. But for some reason, Julie did not want to take on this Frank Pollard's case. Or any other new case, for that matter. They had a few ongoing security contracts with firms they had served for years, and she wanted to stick to that comfortable, familiar business. Most of the work they did was about as risky as going to the supermarket for a quart of milk, but danger was a potential of the job, and the degree of danger in each new case was unknown. If a frail, elderly lady had come to them that Monday morning, seeking help in finding a lost cat, Julie probably would have regarded her as a menace on a par with an ax-wielding psychopath. She was edgy. After all, if luck had not been with them last week, Bobby would now be *four days dead.*

Sitting forward in her chair, leaning over her sturdy metal-and-Formica desk, arms crossed on the green-felt blotter, Julie studied Pollard. He could not meet her eyes, and that evasion aroused her suspicion in spite of his harmless—even appealing—appearance.

He looked as if he ought to have a Vegas comedian's name—Shecky, Buddy, something like that. He was about thirty years old, five ten, maybe a hundred and eighty pounds, which on him was thirty pounds too much; however, it was his face that was most suited for a career in comedy. Except for a couple of curious scratches that were mostly healed, it was a pleasant mug: open, kind, round enough to be jolly, deeply dimpled. A permanent flush tinted his cheeks, as if he had been standing in an arctic wind for most of his life. His nose was reddish, too, apparently not from too great a fondness for booze, but from having been broken a few times; it was lumpish enough to be amusing, but not sufficiently squashed to make him look like a thug.

Shoulders slumped, he sat in one of the two leather-and-chrome chairs in front of Julie's desk. His voice was soft and pleasant, almost musical. "I need help. I don't know where else to go for it."

In spite of his comedic looks, his manner was bleak. Though it was mellifluous, his voice was heavy with despair and weariness. With one hand he periodically wiped his face, as if pulling off cobwebs, then peered at his hand with puzzlement each time it came away empty.

The backs of his hands were marked with scabbed-over scratches, too, a couple of which were slightly swollen and enflamed.

"But frankly," he said, "seeking help from private detectives seems ridiculous, as if this isn't real life but a TV show."

"I've got heartburn, so it's real life, all right," Bobby said. He was standing at one of the big sixth-floor windows that faced out toward the mist-obscured sea and down on the nearby buildings of Fashion Island, the Newport Beach shopping center adjacent to the office tower in which Dakota & Dakota leased a seven-room suite. He turned from the view, leaned against the sill, and extracted a roll of Rolaids from the pocket of his Ultrasuede jacket. "TV detectives never suffer heartburn, dandruff, or the heartbreak of psoriasis."

"Mr. Pollard," Julie said, "I'm sure Mr. Karaghiosis has explained to you that strictly speaking we aren't private detectives."

"Yes."

"We're security consultants. We primarily work with corporations and private institutions. We have eleven employees with sophisticated skills and years of security experience, which is a lot different from the one-man PI fantasies on TV. We don't shadow men's wives to see if they're being unfaithful, and we don't do divorce work or any of the other things that people usually come to private detectives for."

"Mr. Karaghiosis explained that to me," Pollard said, looking down at his hands, which were clenched on his thighs.

From the sofa to the left of the desk, Clint Karaghiosis said, "Frank told me his story, and I really think you ought to hear why he needs us."

Julie noted that Clint had used the would-be client's first name, which he had never done before during six years with Dakota & Dakota. Clint was solidly built—five foot eight, a hundred and sixty pounds. He looked as though he had once been an inanimate assemblage of chunks of granite and slabs of marble, flint and fieldstone, slate and iron and lodestone, which some alchemist had transmuted into living flesh. His broad countenance, though handsome enough, also looked as if it had been chiseled from rock. In a search for a sign of weakness in his face, one could say only that, though strong, some features were not as strong as others. He had a rocklike personality too: steady, reliable, imperturbable. Few people impressed Clint, and fewer still pierced his reserve and elicited more than a polite, businesslike response from him. His use of the client's first name seemed to be a subtle expression of sympathy for Pollard and a vote of confidence in the truthfulness of whatever tale the man had to tell.

"If Clint thinks this is something for us, that's good enough for me," Bobby said. "What's your problem, Frank?"

Julie was not impressed that Bobby had used the client's first name so immediately, casually. Bobby liked everyone he met, at least until they emphatically proved themselves unworthy of being liked. In fact, you had to stab him in the back repeatedly, virtually giggling with malice, before he would finally and regretfully consider the possibility that maybe he *shouldn't* like you. Sometimes she thought she had married a big puppy that was pretending to be human.

Before Pollard could begin, Julie said, "One thing, first. If we decide to accept your case—and I stress the *if*—we aren't cheap."

"That's no problem," Pollard said. He lifted a leather flight bag from the floor at his feet. It was one of two he'd brought with him. He put it on his lap and unzipped it. He withdrew a couple of packs of currency and put them on the desk. Twenties and hundreds.

As Julie took the money to inspect it, Bobby pushed away from the windowsill and went to Pollard's side. He looked down into the flight bag and said, "It's crammed full."

"One hundred and forty thousand dollars," Pollard said.

Upon quick inspection, the money on the desk did not appear to be counterfeit. Julie pushed it aside and said, "Mr. Pollard, are you in the habit of carrying so much cash?"

"I don't know," Pollard said.

"You don't know?"

"I don't know," he repeated miserably.

"He literally doesn't know," Clint said. "Hear him out."

In a voice at once subdued yet heavy with emotion, Pollard said, "You've got to help me find out where I go at night. What in God's name am I doing when I should be sleeping?"

"Hey, this sounds interesting," Bobby said, sitting down on one corner of Julie's desk.

Bobby's boyish enthusiasm made Julie nervous. He might commit them to Pollard before they knew enough to be sure that it was wise to take the case. She also didn't like him sitting on her desk. It just didn't seem businesslike. She felt that it gave the prospective client an impression of amateurism.

From the sofa, Clint said, "Should I start the tape?"

"Definitely," Bobby said.

Clint was holding a compact, battery-powered tape recorder. He flicked the switch and set the recorder on the coffee table in front of the sofa, with the built-in microphone aimed at Pollard, Julie, and Bobby.

The slightly chubby, round-faced man looked up at them. The rings of bluish skin around his eyes, the watery redness of the eyes themselves, and the paleness of his lips belied any image of robust health to which his ruddy cheeks might have lent credence. A hesitant smile flickered across his mouth. He met Julie's eyes for no more than a second, looked down at his hands again. He seemed frightened, beaten, altogether pitiable. In spite of herself she felt a pang of sympathy for him.

As Pollard began to speak, Julie sighed and slumped back in her chair. Two minutes later, she was leaning forward again, listening intently to Pollard's soft voice. She did not want to be fascinated, but she was. Even phlegmatic Clint Karaghiosis, hearing the story for the second time, was obviously captivated by it.

If Pollard was not a liar or a raving lunatic—and most likely he was both—then he was caught up in events of an almost supernatural nature. Julie did not believe in the supernatural.

She tried to remain skeptical, but Pollard's demeanor and evident conviction persuaded her against her will.

Bobby began making holy-jeez-gosh-wow sounds and slapping the desk in astonishment at the revelation of each new twist in the tale. When the client— No. Pollard. Not "the client." He wasn't their client yet. Pollard. When Pollard told them about waking in a motel room Thursday afternoon, with blood on his hands, Bobby blurted, "We'll take the case!"

"Bobby, wait," Julie said. "We haven't heard everything Mr. Pollard came here to tell us. We shouldn't—"

"Yeah, Frank," Bobby said, "what the hell happened *then?*"

Julie said, "What I mean is, we have to hear his whole story before we can possibly know whether or not we can help him."

"Oh, we can help him, all right," Bobby said. "We—"

"Bobby," she said firmly, "could I see you alone for a moment?" She got up, crossed the office, opened the door to the adjoining bathroom, and turned on the light in there.

Bobby said, "Be right back, Frank." He followed Julie into the bathroom, closing the door behind them.

She switched on the ceiling exhaust fan to help muffle their voices, and spoke in a whisper. "What's wrong with you?"

"Well, I have flat feet, no arches at all, and I've got that ugly mole in the middle of my back."

"You're impossible."

"Flat feet and a mole are too many faults for you to handle? You're a hard woman."

The room was small. They were standing between the sink and the toilet, almost nose to nose. He kissed her forehead.

"Bobby, for God's sake, you just told Pollard we'll take his case. Maybe we won't."

"Why wouldn't we? It's *fascinating.*"

"For one thing, he sounds like a nut."

"No, he doesn't."

"He says some strange power caused that car to disintegrate, blew out streetlights. Strange flute music, mysterious blue lights . . . This guy's been reading the *National Enquirer* too long."

"But that's just it. A true nut would already be able to explain what happened to him. He'd claim he'd met God or Martians. This guy is baffled, looking for answers. That strikes me as a sane response."

"Besides, we're in business, Bobby. Business. Not for fun. For money. We're not a couple of damned hobbyists."

"He's got money. You saw it."

"What if it's hot money?"

"Frank's no thief."

"You know him less than an hour and you're sure he's no thief? You're so trusting, Bobby."

"Thank you."

"It wasn't a compliment. How can you do the kind of work you do, and be so trusting?"

He grinned. "I trusted you, and that turned out okay."

She refused to be charmed. "He says he doesn't know where he got the money, and just for the sake of the argument, let's say we buy that part of the story. And let's also say you're right about him not being a thief. So maybe he's a drug dealer. Or something else. There's a thousand ways it could be hot money without being stolen. And if we find out that it's hot, we can't keep what he pays us. We'll have to turn it over to the cops. We'll have wasted our time and energy. Besides . . . it's going to be messy."

"Why do you say that?" he asked.

"Why do I say that? He just told you about waking up in a motel room with blood all over his hands!"

"Keep your voice down. You might hurt his feelings."

"God forbid!"

"Remember, there was no body. It must've been his own blood."

Frustrated, she said, "How do we know there was no body? Because he says there wasn't? He might be such a nutcase that he wouldn't even notice the body if he stepped in its steaming bowels and stumbled over its decapitated head."

"What a vivid image."

"Bobby, he says maybe he clawed at himself, but that's not very damned likely. Probably some poor woman, some innocent girl, maybe even a child, a helpless schoolgirl, was attacked by that man, dragged into his car, raped and beaten and raped again, forced to perform every humiliating act a perverse mind could imagine, then driven to some lonely desert canyon, maybe tortured with needles and knives and God knows what, then clubbed to death, and pitched naked into a dry wash, where coyotes are even now chewing on the softer parts of her, with flies crawling in and out of her open mouth."

"Julie, you're forgetting something."

"What?"

*"I'm* the one with the overactive imagination."

She laughed. She couldn't help it. She wanted to thump his skull hard enough to knock some sense into him, but she laughed instead and shook her head.

He kissed her cheek, then reached for the doorknob.

She put her hand on his. "Promise we won't take the case until we've heard his whole story and have time to think about it."

"All right."

They returned to the office.

Beyond the windows, the sky resembled a sheet of steel that had been scorched black in places, with a few scattered incrustations of mustard-yellow corrosion. Rain had not begun to fall, but the air seemed tense in expectation of it.

The only lights in the room were two brass lamps on tables that flanked the sofa, and a silk-shaded brass floorlamp in one corner. The overhead fluorescents were not on, because Bobby hated the glare and believed that an office should be as cozily lighted as a den in a private home. Julie thought an office should look and feel like an office. But she humored Bobby and usually left the fluorescents off. Now as the oncoming storm darkened the day, she wanted to switch on the overheads and chase away the shadows that had begun to gather in those corners untouched by the amber glow of the lamps.

Frank Pollard was still in his chair, staring at the framed posters of Donald Duck, Mickey Mouse, and Uncle Scrooge that adorned the walls. They were another burden under which Julie labored. She was a fan of Warner Brothers cartoons, because they had a harder edge than Disney's creations, and she owned videotape collections of them, plus a couple of animation cels of Daffy Duck, but she kept that stuff at home. Bobby brought the Disney cartoon characters into the office because (he said) they relaxed him, made him feel good, and helped him think. No clients ever questioned their professional abilities merely because of the unconventional artwork on their walls, but she still worried about what they might think.

She went behind her desk again, and again Bobby perched on it.

After winking at Julie, Bobby said, "Frank, I was premature

in accepting the case. We really can't make that decision until we've heard your whole story."

"Sure," Frank said, looking quickly at Bobby, at Julie, then down at his scratched hands, which were now clutching the open flight bag. "That's perfectly understandable."

"Of course it is," Julie said.

Clint switched on the tape recorder again.

Exchanging the flight bag on his lap for the one on the floor, Pollard said, "I should give you these." He unzipped the second satchel and withdrew a plastic bag that contained a small portion of the handsful of black sand he'd been clutching when he had awakened after his brief sleep Thursday morning. He also withdrew the bloody shirt he had been wearing when he had arisen from his even shorter nap later that same day. "I saved them because . . . well, they seemed like evidence. Clues. Maybe they'll help you figure out what's going on, what I've done."

Bobby accepted the shirt and the sand, examined them briefly, then put them on the desk beside him.

Julie noted that the shirt had been thoroughly saturated with blood, not merely spotted. Now the dry brownish stains made the material stiff.

"So you were in the motel Thursday afternoon," Bobby prompted.

Pollard nodded. "Nothing much happened that night. I went to a movie, couldn't get interested in it. Drove around a while. I was tired, real tired, in spite of the nap, but I couldn't sleep at all. I was afraid to sleep. Next morning I moved to another motel."

"When did you finally sleep again?" Julie asked.

"The next evening."

"Friday evening that was?"

"Yeah. I tried to stay awake with lots of coffee. Sat at the counter in the little restaurant attached to the motel, and drank coffee until I started to float off the stool. Stomach got so acidic, I had to stop. Went back to my room. Every time I started nodding off, I went out for a walk. But it was pointless. I couldn't stay awake forever. I was coming apart at the seams. Had to get some rest. So I went to bed shortly past eight that evening, fell asleep instantly, and didn't wake up until half past five in the morning."

"Saturday morning."

"Yeah."

"And everything was okay?" Bobby asked.

"At least there was no blood. But there was something else."

They waited.

Pollard licked his lips, nodded as if confirming to himself his willingness to continue. "See, I'd gone to bed in my boxer shorts . . . but when I woke up I was fully clothed."

"So you were sleepwalking, and you dressed in your sleep," Julie said.

"But the clothes I was wearing weren't any I'd seen before."

Julie blinked. "Excuse me?"

"They weren't the clothes I was wearing when I came to in that alleyway two nights before, and they weren't the clothes I bought at the mall on Thursday morning."

"Whose clothes were they?" Bobby asked.

"Oh, they must be mine," Pollard said, "because they fit me too well to belong to anyone else. They fit perfectly. Even the shoes fit perfectly. I couldn't have lifted that outfit from someone else and been lucky enough to have it all fit so well."

Bobby slipped off the desk and began to pace. "So what are you saying? That you left that motel in your underwear, went out to some store, bought clothes, and nobody objected to your immodesty or even questioned you about it?"

Shaking his head, Pollard said, "I don't know."

Clint Karaghiosis said, "He could've dressed in his room, while sleepwalking, then went out, bought other clothes, changed into them."

"But why would he do that?" Julie asked.

Clint shrugged. "I'm just offering a possible explanation."

"Mr. Pollard," Bobby said, "why would you have done something like that?"

"I don't know." Pollard had used those three words so often that he was wearing them out; each time he repeated them, his voice seemed softer and fuzzier than before. "I don't think I did. It doesn't feel right—as an explanation, I mean. Besides, I didn't fall asleep in the motel until after eight o'clock. I probably couldn't have gotten up again, gone out, and bought the clothes before the stores closed."

"Some places are open until ten o'clock," Clint said.

"There was a narrow window of opportunity," Bobby agreed.

"I don't think I would've broken into a store after hours," Pollard said. "Or stolen the clothes. I don't think I'm a thief."

"We know you're not a thief," Bobby said.

"We don't know any such thing," Julie said sharply.

Bobby and Clint looked at her, but Pollard continued to stare at his hands, too shy or confused to defend himself.

She felt like a bully for having questioned his honesty. Which was nuts. They knew nothing about him. Hell, if he was telling the truth, he knew nothing about himself.

Julie said, "Listen, whether he bought or stole the clothes is not the point here. I can't accept either. At least not with our current scenario. It's just too outrageous—the man going to a mall or K Mart or someplace in his underwear, outfitting himself, while he's sleepwalking. Could he do all that and not wake up—and appear to be awake to other people? I don't think so. I don't know anything about sleepwalking, but if we research it, I don't think we'll find such a thing is possible."

"Of course, it wasn't just the clothes," Clint said.

"No, not just the clothes," Pollard said. "When I woke up, there was a large paper bag on the bed beside me, like one of those you get at a supermarket if you don't want plastic. I looked inside, and it was full of . . . money. More cash."

"How much?" Bobby asked.

"I don't know. A lot."

"You didn't count it?"

"It's back at the motel where I'm staying now, the new place. I keep moving. I feel safer that way. Anyway, you can count it later if you want. I tried to count it, but I've lost my ability to do even simple arithmetic. Yeah, that sounds screwy, but it's what happened. Couldn't add the numbers. I keep trying but . . . numbers just don't mean much to me any more." He lowered his head, put his face in his hands. "First I lost my memory. Now I'm losing essential skills, like math. I feel as if . . . as if I'm coming apart . . . dissolving . . . until there's going to be none of me left, just a body, no mind at all . . . gone."

"That won't happen, Frank," Bobby said. "We won't let it. We'll find out who you are and what all this means."

"Bobby," Julie said warningly.

"Hmmm?" He smiled obtusely.

She got up from her desk and went into the bathroom.

"Ah, Jeez." Bobby followed her, closed the door, and turned on the fan. "Julie, we *have* to help the poor guy."

*108*

"The man is obviously experiencing psychotic fugues. He's doing these things in a blacked-out condition. He gets up in the middle of the night, yeah, but he's not sleepwalking. He's awake, alert, but in a fugue state. He could steal, kill—and not remember any of it."

"Julie, I'll bet you that was his own blood on his hands. He may be having blackouts, fugues, whatever you want to call them, but he's not a killer. How much you want to bet?"

"And you still say he's not a thief? On a regular basis he wakes up with a bagful of money, doesn't know where he got it, but he's not a thief? You think maybe he counterfeits money during these amnesiac spells? No, I'm sure you think he's too nice to be a counterfeiter."

"Listen," he said, "we've got to go with gut feelings sometimes, and my gut feeling is that Frank is a good guy. Even Clint thinks he's a good guy."

"Greeks are notoriously gregarious. They like everybody."

"You telling me Clint is your typical Greek social animal? Are we talking about the same Clint? Last name—Karaghiosis? Guy who looks as if he was cast from concrete, and smiles about as often as a cigar store Indian?"

The light in the bathroom was too bright. It bounced off the mirror, white sink, white walls, and white ceramic tile. Thanks to the glare and Bobby's good-natured if iron-willed determination to help Pollard, Julie was getting a headache.

She closed her eyes. "Pollard's pathetic," she admitted.

"Want to go back in there and hear him out?"

"All right. But, dammit, don't tell him we'll help him until we've heard everything. All right?"

They returned to the office.

The sky no longer looked like cold, scorched metal. It was darker than before, and churning, molten. Though only the mildest breeze stirred at ground level, strong winds apparently were at work in higher altitudes, for dense black thunderheads were being harried inland from the sea.

Like metal filings drawn to magnets, shadows had piled up in some corners. Julie reached for the switch to snap on the overhead fluorescents. Then she saw Bobby looking around with obvious pleasure at the softly lustrous, burnished brass surfaces of the lamps, at the way the polished oak end tables and coffee table glimmered in the fall of warm buttery light, and she left the switch unflicked.

She sat behind her desk again. Bobby perched on the edge of it, legs dangling.

Clint clicked on the tape recorder, and Julie said, "Frank . . . Mr. Pollard, before you continue your story, I'd like you to answer a few important questions for me. In spite of the blood on your hands, and the scratches, you believe you're incapable of hurting anyone?"

"Yeah. Except maybe in self-defense."

"And you don't think you're a thief?"

"No. I can't . . . I don't see myself as a thief, no."

"Then why haven't you gone to the police for help?"

He was silent. He clutched the open flight bag on his lap and peered into it, as if Julie was speaking to him from its interior.

She said, "Because if you *really* feel certain you're an innocent man in all regards, the police are best equipped to help you find out who you are and who's pursuing you. You know what I think? I think you're not as certain of your innocence as you pretend. You know how to hot-wire a car, and although any man with reasonable knowledge of automobiles could perform that trick, it's at least an indication of criminal experience. And then there's the money, all that money, bagsful of it. You don't remember committing any crimes, but in your heart you're convinced you have, so you're afraid to go to the cops."

"That's part of it," he acknowledged.

She said, "You do understand, I hope, that if we take your case, and if we turn up evidence that you've committed a criminal act, we'll have to convey that information to the police."

"Of course. But I figure if I went to the cops first, they wouldn't even look for the truth. They'd make up their minds that I was guilty of something even before I finished telling my story."

"And of course *we* wouldn't do that," Bobby said, turning his head to favor Julie with a meaningful look.

Pollard said, "Instead of helping me, they'd look around for some recent crimes to pin on me."

"The police don't work that way," Julie assured him.

"Of course they do," Bobby said mischievously. He slid off the desk and began to pace back and forth from the Uncle Scrooge poster to one of Mickey Mouse. "Haven't we seen 'em do that a thousand times on TV shows? Haven't we all read Hammett and Chandler?"

"Mr. Pollard," Julie said, "I was a police officer once—"

"Proves my point," Bobby said. "Frank, if you'd gone to the cops, you'd no doubt already have been booked, tried, convicted, and sentenced to a thousand years."

"There's a more important reason I can't go to the cops. That would be like going public. Maybe the press would hear about me, and be real eager to do a story about this poor guy with amnesia and bags of cash. Then he would know where to find me. I can't risk that."

Bobby said, "Who is 'he,' Frank?"

"The man who was chasing me the other night."

"The way you said it, I thought you'd remembered his name, had a specific person in mind."

"No. I don't know who he is. I'm not even entirely sure *what* he is. But I know he'll come for me again if he learns where I am. So I've got to keep my head down."

From the sofa, Clint said, "I better flip the tape over."

They waited while he popped the cassette out of the recorder.

Although it was only three o'clock, the day was in the grip of a false twilight indistinguishable from the real one. The breeze at ground level was striving to match the wind that drove the clouds at higher altitudes; a thin fog poured in from the west, exhibiting none of the lazy motion with which fogs usually advanced, swirling and churning, a molten flux that seemed to be trying to solder the earth to the thunderheads above.

When Clint had the recorder going again, Julie said, "Frank, is that the end of it? When you woke Saturday morning, wearing new clothes, with the paper bag full of money on the bed beside you?"

"No. Not the end." He raised his head, but he didn't look at her. He stared past her at the dreary day beyond the windows, though he seemed to be gazing at something much farther away than Newport Beach. "Maybe it's never going to end."

From the second flight bag out of which he had earlier withdrawn the bloody shirt and the sample of black sand, he produced a one-pint mason jar of the type used to store home-canned fruits and vegetables, with a sturdy, hinged glass lid that clamped on a rubber gasket. The jar was filled with what appeared to be rough, uncut, dully gleaming gems. Some were more polished than others; they sparkled, flared.

Frank released the lid, tipped the jar, and poured some of the contents onto the imitation blond-wood Formica desktop.

Julie leaned forward.

Bobby stepped in for a closer look.

The less irregular gems were round, oval, teardrop, or lozenge-shaped; some aspects of each stone were smoothly curved, and some were naturally beveled with lots of sharp edges. Other gems were lumpy, jagged, pocked. Several were as large as fat grapes, others as small as peas. They were all red, though they varied in their degree of coloration. They vigorously refracted the light, a pool of scarlet glitter on the pale surface of the desk; the gems marshaled the diffuse glow of the lamps through their prisms, and cast shimmering spears of crimson toward the ceiling and one wall, where the acoustic tiles and Sheetrock appeared to be marked by luminous wounds.

"Rubies?" Bobby asked.

"They don't look quite like rubies," Julie said. "What are they, Frank?"

"I don't know. They might not even be valuable."

"Where'd you get them?"

"Saturday night I couldn't sleep much at all. Just minutes at a time. I kept tossing and turning, popping awake again as soon as I dozed off. Afraid to sleep. And I didn't nap Sunday afternoon. But by yesterday evening, I was so exhausted, I couldn't keep my eyes open any more. I slept in my clothes, and when I got up this morning, my pants pockets were full of these things."

Julie plucked one of the more polished stones from the pile and held it to her right eye, looking through it toward the nearest lamp. Even in its raw state, the gem's color and clarity were exceptional. They might, as Frank implied, be only semiprecious, but she suspected that they were, in fact, of considerable value.

Bobby said, "Why're you keeping them in a mason jar?"

"Because I had to go buy one anyway to keep *this,*" Frank said.

From the flight bag he produced a larger, quart-size jar and placed it on the desk.

Julie turned to look at it and was so startled that she dropped the gem she had been examining. An insect, nearly as large as her hand, lay in that glass container. Though it had a dorsal shell like a beetle—midnight black with blood-red markings around the entire rim—the thing within that carapace more closely resembled a spider than a beetle. It had the eight, sturdy, hairy legs of a tarantula.

"What the hell?" Bobby grimaced. He was mildly entomo-phobic. When he encountered any insect more formidable than a housefly, he called upon Julie to capture or kill it, while he watched from a distance.

"Is it alive?" Julie asked.

"Not now," Frank said.

Two forearms, like miniature lobster claws, extended from under the front of the thing's shell, one on each side of the head, though they differed from the appendages of a lobster in that the pincers were far more highly articulated than those of any common crustacean. They somewhat resembled hands, with four curved, chitinous segments, each jointed at the base; the edges were wickedly serrated.

"If that thing got hold of your finger," Bobby said, "I bet it could snip it off. You say it was alive, Frank?"

"When I woke up this morning, it was crawling on my chest."

"Good God!" Bobby paled visibly.

"It was sluggish."

"Yeah? Well, it sure looks quick as a damned cockroach."

"I think it was dying already," Frank said. "I screamed, brushed it off. It just lay there on its back, on the floor, kicking kinda feebly for a few seconds, then it was still. I stripped the case off one of the bed pillows, scooped the thing into it, knotted the top so it wouldn't crawl away if it was still alive. Then I discovered the gems in my pockets, so I bought two mason jars, one for the bug, and it hasn't moved since I put it in there, so I figure it's dead. You ever see anything like it?"

"No," Julie said.

"Thank God, no," Bobby agreed. He was not leaning over the jar for a closer look, as Julie was. In fact he had taken a step back from the desk, as if he thought the creepy-crawler might be able, in a wink, to cut its way through the glass.

Julie picked up the jar and turned it so she could look at the bug face-on. Its satin-black head was almost as big as a plum and half hidden under the carapace. Multifaceted, muddy yellow eyes were set high on the sides of the face, and under each of them was what appeared to be another eye, a third smaller than the one above it and reddish-blue. Queer patterns of tiny holes, half a dozen thornlike extrusions, and three clusters of silky-looking hairs marked the otherwise smooth, shiny surface of that hideous countenance. Its small mouth, open now, was a circular orifice in which she saw what appeared to be rings of tiny but sharp teeth.

Staring at the occupant of the jar, Frank said, "Whatever the hell I'm mixed up in, it's a bad thing. It's a real bad thing, and I'm afraid."

Bobby twitched. In a thoughtful voice, speaking more to himself than to them, Bobby said, "Bad thing. . . ."

Putting the jar down, Julie said, "Frank, we'll take the case."

"All right!" Clint said, and switched off the recorder.

Turning away from the desk, heading toward the bathroom, Bobby said, "Julie, I need to see you alone for a moment."

For the third time they stepped into the bathroom together, closed the door behind them, and switched on the fan.

Bobby's face was grayish, like a highly detailed portrait done in pencil; even his freckles were colorless. His customarily merry blue eyes were not merry now.

He said, "Are you crazy? You told him we'll take the case."

Julie blinked in surprise. "Isn't that what you wanted?"

"No."

"Ah. Then I guess I heard you wrong. Must be too much wax in my ears. Solid as cement."

"He's probably a lunatic, dangerous."

"I'd better go to a doctor, have my ears professionally cleaned."

"This wild story he's made up is just—"

She held up one hand, halting him in midsentence. "Get real, Bobby. He didn't imagine that bug. What is that thing? I've never even seen pictures of anything like it."

"What about the money? He must've stolen it."

"Frank's no thief."

"What—did God tell you that? Because there's no other way you could know. You only met Pollard little more than an hour ago."

"You're right," she said. "God told me. And I always listen to God because if you don't listen to Him, then He's likely to visit a plague of teeming locusts on you or maybe set your hair on fire with a lightning bolt. Listen, Frank's so lost, adrift, I feel sorry for him. Okay?"

He stared at her, chewing on his pale lower lip for a moment, then finally said, "We work good together because we complement each other. You're strong where I'm weak, and I'm strong where you're weak. In many ways we're not at all alike, but we belong together because we fit like pieces of a puzzle."

"What's your point?"

"One way we're different but complementary is our motivation. This line of work suits me because I get a kick out of helping people who're in trouble through no fault of their own. I like to see good triumph. Sounds like a comic-book hero, but it's the way I feel. You, on the other hand, are primarily motivated by a desire to stomp the bad guys. Yeah, sure, I like to see the bad guys all crumpled and whimpering, too, but it's not as important to me as it is to you. And, of course, you're happy to help innocent people, but with you that's secondary to the stomping and crushing. Probably because you're still working out your rage over the murder of your mother."

"Bobby, if I want psychoanalysis, I'll get it in a room where the primary piece of furniture is a couch—not a toilet."

Her mother had been taken hostage in a bank holdup when Julie was twelve. The two perpetrators had been high on amphetamines and low on common sense and compassion. Before it was all over, five of the six hostages were dead, and Julie's mother was not the lucky one.

Turning to the mirror, Bobby looked at her reflection, as if he was uncomfortable meeting her eyes directly. "My point is—suddenly you're acting like me, and that's no good, that destroys our balance, disrupts the harmony of this relationship, and it's the harmony that has always kept us alive, successful and alive. You want to take this case because you're fascinated, it excites your imagination, and because you'd like to help Frank, he's so pitiful. Where's your usual outrage? I'll tell you where it is. You don't have any because, at this moment anyway, there's no one to elicit it, no bad guy. Okay, there's the guy he says chased him that night, but we don't even know if he's real or just a figment of Frank's fantasy. Without an obvious bad guy to focus your anger, I should have to drag you into this every step of the way, and that's what I was doing, but now you're doing the dragging, and that worries me. It doesn't feel right."

She let him ramble on, with their gazes locked in the mirror, and when at last he finished, she said, "No, that's not your point."

"What do you mean?"

"I mean, everything you just said is smoke. What's really bothering you, Robert?"

His reflection tried to stare down her reflection.

She smiled. "Come on. Tell me. We never keep secrets."

Bobby-in-the-mirror looked like some bad imitation of the real Bobby Dakota. The real Bobby, her Bobby, was full of fun and life and energy. Bobby-in-the-mirror was gray-faced, almost grim; his vitality had been sapped by worry.

"Robert?" she prodded.

"You remember last Thursday when we woke?" he said. "The Santa Anas were blowing. We made love."

"I remember."

"And right after we'd made love . . . I had the strange, terrible feeling that I was going to lose you, that something out there in the wind was . . . coming to get you."

"You told me about it later that night, at Ozzie's, when we were talking about jukeboxes. But the windstorm ended, and nothing got me. Here I am."

"That same night, Thursday night, I had a nightmare, the most vivid damn dream you can imagine." He told her about the little house on the beach, the jukebox standing in the sand, the thunderous inner voice—THE BAD THING IS COMING, THE BAD THING, BAD THING!—and about the corrosive sea that had swallowed both of them, dissolving their flesh and dragging their bones into lightless depths. "It rocked me. You can't conceive of how *real* it seemed. Sounds crazy but . . . that dream was almost more real than real life. I woke up, scared as bad as I've ever been. You were sleeping, and I didn't wake you. Didn't tell you about it later because I didn't see the point of worrying you and because . . . well, it seems childish to put much stock in a dream. I haven't had the nightmare again. But since then—Friday, Saturday, yesterday—I've had moments when a strange anxiety sort of shivers through me, and I think maybe some bad thing is coming to get you. And now, out there in the office, Frank said he was mixed up in a bad thing, a real bad thing, that's how he put it, and right away I made the connection. Julie, maybe this case is the bad thing I dreamed about. Maybe we shouldn't take it."

She stared at Bobby-in-the-mirror for a moment, wondering how to reassure him. Finally she decided that, because their roles had reversed, she should deal with him as Bobby would deal with her in a similar situation. Bobby would not resort to logic and reason—which were her tools—but would charm and humor her out of a funk.

Instead of responding directly to his concerns, she said, "As long as we're getting things off our chests, you know what bothers me? The way you sit on my desk sometimes when we're talking to a prospective client. With some clients, it might make sense for *me* to sit on the desk, wearing a short skirt, showing some leg, 'cause I have good legs, even if I say so myself. But you never wear skirts, short or otherwise, and you don't have the gams for it, anyway."

"Who's talking about desks?"

"I am," she said, turning away from the mirror and looking at him directly. "We leased a seven-room suite instead of eight, to save money, and by the time the rest of the staff was set up, we had only one office for ourselves, which seemed okay. There's plenty of room in there for two desks, but you say you don't want one. Desks are too formal for you. All you need is a couch to lie on while making calls, you say, yet when clients come in, you sit on my desk."

"Julie—"

"Formica is a hard, nearly impervious surface, but sooner or later you'll have spent so much time sitting on my desk, it'll be marked by a permanent imprint of your ass."

Because she wouldn't look at the mirror, he had to turn away from it, too, and face her. "Didn't you hear what I said about the dream?"

"Now, don't get me wrong. You've got a cute ass, Bobby, but I don't want the imprint on my desktop. Pencils will keep rolling into the depression. Dust will collect in it."

"What's going on here?"

"I want to warn you that I'm thinking of having the top of my desk wired, so I can electrify it with a flick of a switch. You sit on it then, and you'll know what a fly feels like when it settles on one of those electronic bug zappers."

"You're being difficult, Julie. Why're you being difficult?"

"Frustration. I haven't gotten to stomp or crush any bad guys lately. Makes me irritable."

He said, "Hey, wait a minute. You're not being difficult."

"Of course I'm not."

"You're being *me!*"

"Exactly." She kissed his right cheek and patted his left. "Now, let's go back out there and take the case."

She opened the door and stepped out of the bathroom.

With some amusement, Bobby said, "I'll be damned," and followed her into the office.

Frank Pollard was talking quietly with Clint, but he fell silent and looked up hopefully as they entered.

Shadows clung to the corners like monks to their cloisters, and for some reason the amber glow from the three lamps reminded her of the scintillant and mysterious light of serried votive candles in a church.

The puddle of scarlet gems still glimmered on the desk.

The bug was still in a death crouch in the mason jar.

"Did Clint explain our fee schedule?" she asked Pollard.

"Yes."

"Okay. In addition, we'll need ten thousand dollars as an advance against expenses."

Outside, lightning scarred the bellies of the clouds. The bruised sky ruptured, and cold rain spattered against the windows.

# 26

VIOLET HAD BEEN awake for more than an hour, and during most of that time she had been a hawk, swooping high on the wind, darting down now and then to make a swift kill. The open sky was nearly as real to her as it was to the bird that she had invaded. She glided on thermal currents, the air offering little resistance to the sleek fore edges of her wings, with only the lowering gray clouds above, and the whole huddled world below.

She was also aware of the shadowy bedroom in which her body and a portion of her mind remained. Violet and Verbina usually slept during the day, for to sleep away the night was to waste the best of times. They shared a room on the second floor, one king-size bed, never more than an arm's reach from each other, though usually entwined. That Monday afternoon, Verbina was still asleep, naked, on her belly, with her head turned away from her sister, occasionally mumbling wordlessly into her pillow. Her warm flank pressed against Violet. Even while Violet was with the hawk, she was aware of her twin's body heat, smooth skin, slow rhythmic breathing, sleepy murmurings, and distinct scent. She smelled the dust in the room, too, and the stale odor of the long unwashed sheets—and the cats, of course.

She not only smelled the cats, which slept upon the bed and the surrounding floor or lay lazily licking themselves, but lived in each of them. While a part of her consciousness remained in her own pale flesh and a part soared with the feathered predator, other aspects of her held tenancy in each of the cats, twenty-five of them now that poor Samantha was gone. Simultaneously Violet experienced the world through her own senses, through those of the hawk, and through the fifty eyes and twenty-five noses and fifty ears and hundred paws and twenty-five tongues of the pack. She could smell her own body odor not merely through her own nose but through the noses of all the cats: the faint soapy residue of last night's bath; the pleasantly lingering tang of lemon-scented shampoo; the staleness that always followed sleep; halitosis ripe with the vapor ghosts of the raw eggs and onions and raw liver that she had eaten that morning before going to bed with the rising sun. Each member of the pack had a sharper olfactory sense than she did, and each perceived her scent differently from the way she did; they found her natural fragrance strange yet comforting, intriguing yet familiar.

She could smell, see, hear, and feel herself through her sister's senses, as well, for she was always inextricably linked with Verbina. At will, she could swiftly enter or disengage from the minds of other lifeforms, but Verbina was the only other *person* with whom she could join in that way. It was a permanent link, which they had shared since birth, and though Violet could disengage from the hawk or the cats whenever she wished, she could never disengage from her twin. Likewise, she could control the minds of animals as well as inhabit them, but she was not able to control her sister. Their link was not that of puppet-master and puppet, but special and sacred.

All of her life, Violet had lived at the confluence of many rivers of sensation, bathed in great churning currents of sound and scent and sight and taste and touch, experiencing the world not only through her own senses but those of countless surrogates. For part of her childhood, she had been autistic, so overwhelmed by sensory input that she could not cope; she had turned inward, to her secret world of rich, varied, and profound experience, until she had learned to control the incoming flood, harnessing it instead of being swept away. Only then had she chosen to relate to the people around her, abandoning autism, and she had not learned to talk until she was six years old. She had never risen out of those deep, fast currents of extraordinary sensation to stand on the comparatively dry bank of life on which other people existed, but at least she had learned to interact with her mother, Candy, and others to a limited degree.

Verbina had never coped half as well as Violet, and evidently never would. Having chosen a life almost exclusively defined by sensation, she exhibited little or no concern for the exercise and development of her intellect. She had never learned to talk, showed only the vaguest interest in anyone but her sister, and immersed herself with joyous abandonment in the ocean of sensory stimuli that surged around her. Running as a squirrel, flying as a hawk or gull, rutting as a cat, loping and killing as a coyote, drinking cool water from a stream through the mouth of a raccoon or field mouse, entering the mind of a bitch in heat as other dogs mounted her, simultaneously sharing the terror of the cornered rabbit and the savage excitement of the predatory fox, Verbina enjoyed a breadth of life that no one else but Violet could ever know. And she preferred the constant thrill of immersion in the wildness of the world to the comparatively mundane existence of other people.

Now, although Verbina still slept, a part of her was with Violet in the soaring hawk, for even sleep did not necessitate the complete disconnection of their links to other minds. The continuous sensory input of the lesser species was not only the primary fabric from which their lives were cut, but the stuff of which their dreams were formed, as well.

Under storm clouds that grew darker by the minute, the hawk glided high over the canyon behind the Pollard property. It was hunting.

Far below, among pieces of dried and broken tumbleweed, between spiny clumps of gorse, a fat mouse broke cover. It scurried along the canyon floor, alert for signs of enemies at ground level but oblivious to the feathered death that observed it from far above.

Instinctively aware that the mouse could hear the flapping of wings from a great distance and would scramble into the nearest haven at the first sound of them, the hawk silently tucked its wings back, half folding them against its body, and dived steeply, angling toward the rodent. Though she had shared this experience countless times before, Violet held her breath as they plummeted twelve hundred feet, dropping past ground level and farther down into the ravine; and though she actually was safely on her back in bed, her stomach seemed to turn within her, and a primal terror swelled within her breast even as she let out a thin squeal of pleasurable excitement.

On the bed beside Violet, her sister also softly cried out.

On the canyon floor the mouse froze, sensing onrushing doom but not certain from which quarter it was coming.

The hawk deployed its wings as foils at the last moment; abruptly the true substance of the air became apparent and provided a welcome braking resistance. Letting its hindquarters precede it, extending its legs, opening its claws, the hawk seized the mouse even as the creature reacted to the sudden spread of wings and tried to flee.

Though remaining with the hawk, Violet entered the mind of the mouse an instant before the predator had taken it. She felt the icy satisfaction of the hunter and the hot fear of the prey. From the perspective of the hawk, she felt the plump mouse's flesh puncture and split under the sharp and powerful assault of her talons, and from the perspective of the mouse, she was wracked by searing pain and was aware of a dreadful rupturing within. The bird peered down at the squealing rodent in its grasp, and shivered with a wild sense of dominance and power, with a realization that hunger would again be sated. It loosed a caw of triumph that echoed along the canyon. Feeling small and helpless in the grip of its winged assailant, in the thrall of excruciating fear so intense as to be strangely akin to the most exquisite of sensory pleasures, the mouse looked up into the steely, merciless eyes and ceased to struggle, went limp, resigned itself to death. It saw the fierce beak descending, was aware of being rended, but no longer felt pain, only numb resignation, then a brief moment of shattering bliss, then nothing, nothing. The hawk tipped back its head and let bloody ribbons and warm knots of flesh fall down its gullet.

On the bed Violet turned on her side to face her sister. Having been shaken from sleep by the power of the experience with the hawk, Verbina came into Violet's arms. Naked, pelvis to pelvis, belly to belly, breasts to breasts, the twins held each other and shuddered uncontrollably. Violet gasped against Verbina's tender throat, and through her link with Verbina's mind, she felt that hot flood of her own breath and the warmth it brought to her sister's skin. They made wordless sounds and clung to each other, and their frantic breathing did not begin to subside until the hawk tore the last red sliver of nourishing meat from the mouse's hide and, with a flurry of wings, threw itself into the sky again.

Below was the Pollard property: the Eugenia hedge; the gabled, slate-roofed, weathered-looking house; the twenty-year-old Buick that had belonged to their mother and that Candy sometimes drove; clusters of primrose burning with red and yellow and purple blooms in a narrow and untended flowerbed that extended the length of the decrepit back porch. Violet also saw Candy far below, at the northeast corner of the sprawling property.

Still holding fast to her sister, gracing Verbina's throat and cheek and temple with a lace of gentle kisses, Violet simultaneously directed the hawk to circle above her brother. Through the bird, she watched him as he stood, head bowed, at their mother's grave, mourning her as he had mourned her every day, without exception, since her death those many years ago.

Violet did not mourn. Her mother had been as much a stranger to her as anyone in the world, and she had felt nothing special at the woman's passing. Indeed, because Candy was gifted, too, Violet felt closer to him than she had to her mother, which was not saying much because she did not really know him or care a great deal about him. How could she be close to anyone if she could not enter his mind and live with him, through him? That incredible intimacy was what welded her to Verbina, and it marked the myriad relationships she enjoyed with all the fowl and fauna that populated nature's world. She simply did not know how to relate to anyone without that intense, innermost connection, and if she could not love, she could not mourn.

Far below the wheeling hawk, Candy dropped to his knees beside the grave.

# 27

MONDAY AFTERNOON. Thomas sat at his worktable. Making a picture poem.

Derek helped. Or thought he did. He sorted through a box of magazine clippings. He chose pictures, gave them to Thomas. If the picture was right, Thomas trimmed it, pasted it on the page. Most of the time it wasn't right, so he put it aside and asked for another picture and another until Derek gave him something he could use.

He didn't tell Derek the awful truth. The awful truth was that he wanted to make the poem by himself. But he couldn't hurt Derek's feelings. Derek was hurt enough. Too much. Being dumb really hurt, and Derek was dumber than Thomas. Derek was dumber-looking, too, which was more hurt. His forehead sloped more than Thomas's. His nose was flatter, and his head had a squashy shape. Awful truth.

Later, tired of making the picture poem, Thomas and Derek went to the wreck room, and that was where it happened. Derek got hurt. He got hurt so much he cried. A girl did it. Mary. In the wreck room.

Some people were playing a game of marbles in one corner. Some were watching TV. Thomas and Derek were sitting on a couch near some windows, Being Sociable when anyone came around. The aides always wanted people at The Home to Be Sociable. It was good for you to Be Sociable. When no one came around to Be Sociable with them, Thomas and Derek were watching hummingbirds at a feeder that hung outside the windows. Hummingbirds didn't really hum, but they zipped around and were a lot of fun to watch. Mary, who was new at The Home, didn't zip around and wasn't fun to watch, but she hummed a lot. No, she buzzed. Buzz, buzz, buzz, all the time.

Mary knew about eye cues. She said they really mattered, eye cues, and maybe they did, though Thomas had never heard of them and didn't understand what they were, but then a lot of things he didn't understand were important. He knew what eyes were, of course. He knew a cue was a stick you hit balls with because they had a pool table right there in the wreck room, near where he and Derek were sitting, though nobody used it much. He figured it would be a bad thing, real bad, if you stuck yourself in the eye with a cue, but this Mary said eye cues were good and she had a big one for a Down's kid.

"I'm a high-end moron," she said, real happy with herself, you could tell.

Thomas didn't know what a moron was, but he couldn't see a high end to Mary anywhere, she was fat and mostly droopy all over.

"You're probably a moron, too, Thomas, but you ain't high-end like me. I'm almost normal, and you ain't as close normal as me."

All this only confused Thomas.

It confused Derek even more, you could tell, and in his thick and sometimes hard to understand voice, Derek said, "Me? No moron." He shook his head. "Cowboy." He smiled. "Cowboy."

Mary laughed at him. "You ain't no cowboy or ever going to be. What you are is you're an imbecile."

They had to ask her to say it a few times before they got it, but even then they didn't really get it. They could say it but didn't know what it was any more than they knew what one of these eye cues looked like.

"You've got your normal people," Mary said, "then morons under them, then imbeciles, who're dumber than morons, and then you got idiots, who're dumber than even imbeciles. Me, I'm a high-end moron, and I ain't going to be here forever, I'm going to be good, behave, work hard to be normal, and someday go back to the halfway house."

"Halfway where?" Derek asked, which was what Thomas wondered too.

Mary laughed at him. "Halfway to being normal, which is more than you'll ever be, you poor damn imbecile."

This time Derek realized she was looking down on him, making fun, and he tried not to cry, but he did. He got red in the face and cried, and Mary grinned sort of wild, she was all puffed up, excited, like she'd won some big prize. She'd used a bad word—damn—and should be ashamed, but she wasn't, you could tell. She said the other word again, which Thomas now saw was a bad word, too, "imbecile," and she kept saying it, until poor Derek got up and ran, and even then she shouted it after him.

Thomas went back to their room, looking for Derek, and Derek was in the closet with the door shut, bawling. Some of the aides came, and they talked to Derek real nice, but he didn't want to come out of the closet. They had to talk to him a long time to get him to come out of there, but even then he couldn't stop crying, and so after a while they had to Give Him Something. Once in a while when you were sick, like with the flew, the aides asked you to Take Something, which meant a pill of one shape or another, one color or another, big or little. But when they had to Give You Something, it always meant a needle, which was a bad thing. They never had to Give Something to Thomas because he was always good. But sometimes Derek, nice as he was, got to feeling so bad about himself that he couldn't stop crying, and sometimes he hit himself, just hit himself in the face, until he broke himself open and got blood on himself, and even then he wouldn't stop, so they had to Give Him Something For His Own Good. Derek never hit anyone else, he was nice, but For His Own Good he sometimes had to be made to relax or sometimes even made to sleep, which was what happened the day Mary the high-end moron called him an imbecile.

After Derek was made to sleep, one of the aides sat beside Thomas at the worktable. It was Cathy. Thomas liked Cathy. She was older than Julie but not as old as somebody's mother. She was pretty. Not as pretty as Julie but pretty, with a nice voice and eyes you weren't afraid to look into. She took one of Thomas's hands in both of hers, and she asked if he was okay. He said he was, but he really wasn't, and she knew it. They talked a while. That helped. Being Sociable.

She told him about Mary, so he'd understand, and that helped too. "She's so frustrated, Thomas. She was out there in the world for a while, at a halfway house, and she even had a part-time job, making a little money of her own. She was trying so hard, but it didn't work, she had too many problems, so she had to be institutionalized again. I think she regrets what she did to Derek. She's just so disappointed that she needed to feel superior to someone."

"I am . . . *was* . . . was out there in the world once," Thomas said.

"I know you were, honey."

"With my dad. Then with my sister. And Bobby."

"Did you like it out there?"

"Some of it . . . scared me. But when I was with Julie and Bobby . . . I liked that part."

On his bed, Derek was snoring now.

The afternoon was half gone. The sky was getting ugly-stormy. The room had shadows everywhere. Only the desk lamp was on. Cathy's face looked pretty in the lampglow. Her skin was like peach-colored satin. He knew what satin was like. Julie once had a dress of satin.

For a while he and Cathy were quiet.

Then he said, "Sometimes it's hard."

She put her hand on his head. Smoothed his hair. "Yeah, I know, Thomas. I know."

She was so nice. He didn't know why he started to cry when she was so nice, but he did. Maybe it was because she *was* so nice.

Cathy scooted her chair closer to his. He leaned against her. She put her arms around him. He cried and cried. Not hard terrible crying like Derek. Soft. But he couldn't stop. He tried not to cry because crying made him feel dumb, and he hated feeling dumb.

Through his tears, he said, "I *hate* feeling dumb."

"You're not dumb, honey."

"Yeah, I am. Hate it. But I can't be nothing else. I try not to think about being dumb, but you can't not think about it when it's what you are, and when other people aren't, and they go out in the world every day and they live, but you don't go out in the world and don't even want to but, oh, you *want* to, even when you say you don't." That was a lot for him to say, and he was surprised that he had said it all, surprised but also frustrated because he wanted so bad to tell her how it felt, being dumb, being afraid of going out in the world, and he'd failed, hadn't been able to find the right words, so the feeling was still all bottled up in him. "Time. There's lots of time, see, when you're dumb and can't go out in the world, lots of time to fill up, but then there really ain't *enough* time, not enough for learning how to be not afraid of things, and I've got to learn how not to be afraid so I can go back and be with Julie and Bobby, which I want to do real bad, before all the time runs out. There's too big amounts of time and not enough, and that sounds dumb, don't it?"

"No, Thomas. It doesn't sound dumb."

He didn't move out of her arms. He wanted to be hugged.

Cathy said, "You know, sometimes life is hard for everyone. Even for smart people. Even for the smartest of them all."

With one hand he wiped at his damp eyes. "It is? Sometimes is it hard for you?"

"Sometimes. But I believe there's a God, Thomas, and that he put us here for a reason, and that every hardship we have to face is a test, and that we're better for enduring them."

He raised his head to look at her. Such nice eyes. Good eyes. They were eyes that loved you. Like Julie's eyes or Bobby's.

Thomas said, "God made me dumb to test me?"

"You're not dumb, Thomas. Not in some ways. I don't like to hear you call yourself dumb. You're not as smart as some, but that's not your fault. You're different, that's all. Being . . . different is your hardship, and you're coping with it well."

"I am?"

"Beautifully. Look at you. You're not bitter. You're not sullen. You reach out to people."

"Being Sociable."

She smiled, pulled a tissue from the box of Kleenex on the worktable, and wiped the tears from his face. "Of all the smart people in the world, Thomas, not a one of them handles hardship better than you do, and most not as well."

He knew she meant what she said, and her words made him happy, even if he didn't quite believe life was ever hard for smart people.

She stayed a while. Made sure he was okay. Then she left.

Derek was still snoring.

Thomas sat at the worktable. Tried to make more poem.

After a while he went to the window. Rain was coming down now. It trickled on the glass. The afternoon was almost gone. Night was soon coming down on top of the rain.

He put his hands against the glass. He reached into the rain, into the gray day, into the nothingness of the night that was slowly sneaking up on them.

The Bad Thing was still out there. He could feel it. A man but not a man. Something more than a man. Very bad. Ugly-nasty. He'd felt it for days, but he hadn't TVed a warning to Bobby since last week because the Bad Thing wasn't coming any closer. It was far away, right now Julie was safe, and if he TVed too many warnings to Bobby, then Bobby would stop paying attention to them, and when the Bad Thing finally showed up, Bobby wouldn't believe in it any more, and then it would get to Julie because Bobby wouldn't be paying attention.

What Thomas most feared was that the Bad Thing would take Julie to the Bad Place. Their mother went to the Bad Place when Thomas was two years old, so he'd never known her. Then their dad went to the Bad Place later, leaving Thomas with just Julie.

He didn't mean Hell. He knew about Heaven and Hell. Heaven was God's. The devil owned Hell. If there was a Heaven, he was sure his mom and dad went there. You wanted to go up to Heaven if you could. Things were better there. In Hell, the aides weren't nice.

But, to Thomas, the Bad Place wasn't just Hell. It was Death. Hell was *a* bad place, but Death was *the* Bad Place. Death was a word you couldn't picture. Death meant everything stopped, went away, all your time ran out, over, done, kaput. How could you picture that? A thing wasn't real if you couldn't picture it. He couldn't *see* Death, couldn't get a picture of it in his head, not if he thought about it the way other people seemed to think about it. He was just too dumb, so he had to picture it in his head as a *place*. They said Death came to take you, and it had come to take his father one night, his heart had attacked him, but if it came to take you, then it had to take you to some *place*. And that was the Bad Place. It's where you were taken and never allowed to come back. Thomas didn't know what happened to a person there. Maybe nothing nasty. Except you weren't allowed to come back and see people you loved, which made it nasty enough, no matter if the food was good over there. Maybe some people went on to Heaven, some to Hell, but you couldn't come back from either one, so both were part of the Bad Place, just different rooms. And he wasn't sure Heaven and Hell were real, so maybe all there was in the Bad Place was darkness and cold and so much empty space that when you went over there you couldn't even find the people who'd gone ahead of you.

That scared him most of all. Not just losing Julie to the Bad Place, but not being able to find her when he went over there himself.

He was already afraid of the night. All that big empty. The lid off the world. So if just the night itself was so scary, the Bad Place would be lots worse. It was sure to be bigger than the night, and daylight never came in the Bad Place.

Outside, the sky got darker.

Wind blew the palms.

Rain ran down the glass.

The Bad Thing was far away.

But it would come closer. Soon.

# 28

CANDY WAS having one of those days when he could not accept that his mother was dead. Every time he crossed a threshold or turned a corner, he expected to see her. He thought he heard her rocking in the parlor, humming softly to herself as she knitted a new afghan, but when he went in there to look, the rocking chair was filmed with dust and draped with a shawl of cobwebs. Once, he hurried into the kitchen, expecting to find her in a brightly flowered housedress overlaid with a ruffle-trimmed white apron, dropping neat spoonsful of cookie batter on baking sheets or perhaps mixing a cake, but, of course, she was not there. In a moment of acute emotional turmoil, Candy raced upstairs, certain that he would find his mother in bed, but when he burst into her room, he remembered that it was *his* room now, and that she was gone.

Eventually, to jar himself out of that strange and troubling mood, he went into the backyard and stood by her lonely grave in the northeast corner of the large property. He had buried her there, seven years ago, under a solemn winter sky similar to the one that currently hid the sun, with a hawk circling above just as one circled now. He had dug her grave, wrapped her in sheets scented with Chanel No. 5, and lowered her into the ground secretly, because interment on private property, not designated as a gravesite, was against the law. If he had allowed her to be buried elsewhere, he would have had to go live there with her, for he could not have endured being separated from her mortal remains for any great length of time.

Candy dropped to his knees.

Over the years the original mound of earth had settled, until her grave was marked by a shallow concavity. The grass was sparser there, the blades coarse, wiry, different from the rest of the lawn, though he did not know why; even in the months following her burial, the grass above her had not flourished. No headstone memorialized her passing; although the backyard was sheltered by the high hedge, he could not risk calling attention to her illegal resting place.

Staring at the ground before him, Candy wondered if a headstone would help him accept her death. If every day he saw her name and the date of her death deeply cut into a slab of marble, that sight should slowly but permanently engrave the loss upon his heart, sparing him days like this, when he was disturbed by a queer forgetfulness and by a hope that could never be fulfilled.

He stretched out on the grave, his head turned to one side with an ear against the earth, as if he half expected to hear her speaking to him from her subterranean bed. Pressing his body hard into the unyielding ground, he longed to feel the vitality that she had once radiated, the singular energy that had flowed from her like heat from the open door of a furnace, but he felt nothing. Though his mother had been a special woman, Candy knew it was absurd to expect her corpse, after seven years, to radiate even a ghost of the love that she had lavished upon him when she was alive; nevertheless, he was grievously disappointed when not even the faintest aura shimmered upward through the dirt from her sacred bones.

Hot tears burned in his eyes, and he tried to hold them back. But a faint rumble of thunder passed through the sky, and a few fat droplets of rain began to fall, and neither the storm nor his tears could be restrained.

She lay only five or six feet beneath him, and he was overcome by an urge to claw his way down to her. He knew her flesh would have deteriorated, that he would find only bones cradled in a vile muck of unthinkable origin, but he wanted to hold her and be held, even if he had to arrange her skeletal arms around himself in a staged embrace. He actually ripped at the grass and tore up a few handsful of topsoil. Soon, however, he was wracked by powerful sobs that swiftly exhausted him and left him too weak to struggle with reality any longer.

She was dead.

Gone.

Forever.

As the cold rain fell in greater volume, pounding on Candy's back, it seemed to leech his hot grief from him and fill him, instead, with icy hatred. Frank had killed their mother; he *must* pay for that crime with his own life. Lying on a muddy grave and weeping like a child would not bring Candy one step closer to vengeance. Finally he got up and stood with his hands fisted at his sides, letting the storm sluice some of the mud and grief from him.

He promised his mother that he would be more relentless and diligent in his pursuit of her killer. The next time he got a lead on Frank, he would not lose him.

Looking up at the cloud-choked and streaming sky, addressing his mother in Heaven, he said, "I'll find Frankie, kill him, crush him, I will. I'll smash his skull open and cut his hateful brain into pieces and flush it down a toilet."

The rain seemed to penetrate him, driving a chill deep into his marrow, and he shuddered.

"If I find anyone who lifted a hand to help him, I'll cut their hands off. I'll tear out the eyes of anyone who looked at Frankie with sympathy. I swear I will. And I'll cut out the tongues of any bastards who spoke kind words to him."

Suddenly the rain fell with greater force than before, hammering the grass flat, crackling through the leaves of a nearby oak, stirring a chorus of whispers from the Eugenias. It snapped against his face, making him squint, but he did not lower his eyes from Heaven.

"If he's found anyone to care about, anyone at all, I'll take them away from him like he took you from me. I'll break them open, get the blood out of them, and throw them away like garbage."

He had made these same promises many times during the past seven years, but he made them now with no less passion than he had before.

"Like garbage," he repeated through clenched teeth.

His need for vengeance was no less fierce now than it had been on the day of her murder seven years ago. His hatred of Frank was, if anything, harder and sharper than ever.

*"Like garbage."*

An ax of lightning cleaved the contusive sky. Briefly a long, jagged laceration gaped open in the dark clouds, which for a moment seemed to him not like clouds at all but like the infinitely strange and throbbing body of some godlike being, and through the lightning-rent flesh he thought he glimpsed the shining mystery beyond.

# 29

CLINT DREADED the rainy season in southern California. Most of the year was dry, and in the on-again-off-again drought of the past decade, some winters were marked by only a few storms. When rain finally fell, the natives seemed to have forgotten how to drive in it. As gutters overflowed, the streets clogged with traffic. The freeways were worse; they looked like infinitely long car washes in which the conveyors had broken down.

While the gray light slowly faded out of that Monday afternoon, he drove first to Palomar Laboratories in Costa Mesa. It was a large, single-story concrete-block building one block west of Bristol Avenue. Their medical-lab division analyzed blood samples, Pap smears, and biopsies, among other things, but they also performed industrial- and geological-sample analyses of all kinds.

He parked his Chevy in the adjoining lot. Carrying a plastic bag from Von's supermarket, he sloshed through the deep puddles, head bent against the driving rain, and went into the small reception lounge, dripping copiously.

An attractive young blonde sat on a stool behind the counter at the reception window. She was wearing a white uniform and a purple cardigan. She said, "You should have an umbrella."

Clint nodded, put the supermarket bag on the counter, and began to untie the knot in the straps, to open it.

"At least a raincoat," she said.

From an inside jacket pocket, he withdrew a Dakota & Dakota card, passed it to her.

"Is this who you want billed?" she asked.

"Yeah."

"Have you used our service before?"

"Yeah."

"You have an account?"

"Yeah."

"I haven't seen you in here before."

"No."

"My name's Lisa. I've only been here about a week. Never had a private eye come in before, least since I've started."

From the large white sack he withdrew three smaller, clear, Ziploc bags and lined them up side by side.

"You got a name?" she asked, cocking her head, smiling at him.

"Clint."

"You go around without an umbrella or raincoat in this weather, Clint, you'll catch your death, even as sturdy as you look."

"First, the shirt," Clint said, pushing that bag forward. "We want the bloodstains analyzed. Not just typed. We want the whole nine yards. A complete genetic workup too. Take samples from four different parts of the shirt, because there might be more than one person's blood on it. If so, do a workup on both."

Lisa frowned at Clint, then at the shirt in the bag. She began filling out an analysis order.

"Same program on this one," he said, pushing forward the second bag. It contained a folded sheet of Dakota & Dakota stationery that was mottled with several spots of blood. Back at the office, Julie had sterilized a pin in a match flame, stuck Frank Pollard's thumb, and squeezed the crimson samples onto the paper. "We want to know if any of the blood on the shirt matches what's on this stationery."

The third bag contained the black sand.

"Is this a biological substance?" Lisa asked.

"I don't know. Looks like sand."

"Because if it's a biological substance, it should go to our medical division, but if it's not biological it should go to the industrial lab."

"Send a little to both. And put a rush on it."

"Costs more."

"Whatever."

As she filled out the third form, she said, "There's a few beaches in Hawaii with black sand, you ever been there?"

"No."

"Kaimu. That's the name of one of the black beaches. Comes from a volcano, somehow. The sand, I mean. You like beaches?"

"Yeah."

She looked up, her pen poised over the form, and gave him a big smile. Her lips were full. Her teeth were very white. "I *love* the beach. Nothing I like better than putting on a bikini and soaking up some sun, really just *baking* in the sun, and I don't care what they say about a tan being bad for you. Life's short anyway, you know? Might as well look good while we're here. Besides, being in the sun makes me feel . . . oh, not lazy exactly, because I don't mean it saps my energy, just the opposite, it makes me feel full of energy, but a lazy energy, sort of the way a lioness walks—you know?—strong-looking but easy. The sun makes me feel like a lioness."

He said nothing.

She said, "It's erotic, the sun. I guess that's what I'm trying to say. You lay out in the sun enough, on a nice beach, and all your inhibitions sort of melt away."

He just stared at her.

After she finished filling out the analysis orders, gave him copies, and attached each order to the correct sample, Lisa said, "Listen, Clint, we're living in a modern world, right?"

He didn't know what she meant.

She said, "We're all liberated these days, am I right? So if a girl finds a guy attractive, she doesn't have to wait for him to make the move."

Oh, Clint thought.

Leaning back on her stool, maybe to let him see how her full breasts filled out her white uniform blouse, she smiled and said, "Would you be interested in a dinner, movie?"

"No."

Her smile froze.

"Sorry," he said.

He folded the copies of the work orders and put them in the same jacket pocket from which earlier he had withdrawn a business card.

She was glaring at him, and he realized he'd hurt her feelings.

Searching for something to say, all he could come up with was, "I'm gay."

She blinked and shook her head as if recovering from a stunning blow. Like sun piercing clouds, her smile broke through the gloom on her face. "Had to be to resist this package, I guess."

"Sorry."

"Hey, it's not your fault. We are what we are, huh?"

He went into the rain again. It was getting colder. The sky looked like the ruins of a burned-out building to which the fire department had arrived too late: wet ashes, dripping cinders.

# 30

AS NIGHT FELL on that rainy Monday, Bobby Dakota stood at the hospital window and said, "Not much of a view, Frank. Unless you're keen on parking lots." He turned and surveyed the small, white room. Hospitals always gave him the creeps, but he did not express his true feelings to Frank. "The decor sure won't be featured in *Architectural Digest* anytime soon, but it's comfy enough. You've got TV, magazines, and three meals a day in bed. I noticed some of the nurses are real lookers, too, but please try to keep your hands off the nuns, okay?"

Frank was paler than ever. The dark circles around his eyes had grown like spreading inkblots. He not only looked as if he belonged in a hospital but as if he had been there for weeks already. He used the power controls to tilt the bed up. "Are these tests really necessary?"

"Your amnesia might have a physical cause," Julie said. "You heard Dr. Freeborn. They'll look for cerebral abscesses, neoplasms, cysts, clots, all kinds of things."

"I'm not sure about this Freeborn," Frank said worriedly.

Sanford Freeborn was Bobby and Julie's friend, as well as their physician. A few years ago they had helped him get his brother out of deep trouble.

"Why? What's wrong with Sandy?"

Frank said, "I don't know him."

"You don't know anybody," Bobby said. "That's your problem. Remember? You're an amnesiac."

After accepting Frank as a client, they had taken him directly to Sandy Freeborn's office for a preliminary examination. All Sandy knew was that Frank could remember nothing but his name. They had not told him about the bags of money, the blood, black sand, red gems, weird insect, or any of the rest of it. Sandy didn't ask why Frank had come to them instead of the police or why they had accepted a case so far outside their usual purview; one of the things that made him a good friend was his reliable discretion.

Nervously adjusting the sheets, Frank said, "You think a private room is really necessary?"

Julie nodded. "You also want us to find out what you do at night, where you go, which means monitoring you, tight security."

"A private room's expensive," Frank said.

"You can afford the finest care," Bobby said.

"The money in those bags might not be mine."

Bobby shrugged. "Then you'll have to work off your hospital bill—change a few hundred beds, empty a few thousand bedpans, perform some brain surgery free of charge. You might *be* a brain surgeon. Who knows? With amnesia, it's just as likely you've forgotten that you're a surgeon as that you're a used-car salesman. Worth a try. Get a bone saw, cut off the top of some guy's head, have a peek in there, see if anything looks familiar."

Leaning against the bed rail, Julie said, "When you're not in radiology or some other department, undergoing tests, we'll have a man with you, watching over you. Tonight it's Hal."

Hal Yamataka had already taken his station in an uncomfortable-looking, upholstered chair provided for visitors. He was to one side of the bed, between Frank and the door, in a position to watch both his charge and, if Frank was in the mood, the wall-mounted television. Hal resembled a Japanese version of Clint Karaghiosis: about five foot seven or eight, broad in the shoulders and chest, as solid-looking as if he had been built by a mason who knew how to fit stones tight together and hide the mortar. In case nothing worth watching was on television and his charge proved to be a lousy conversationalist, he had brought a John D. MacDonald novel.

Looking at the rain-washed window, Frank said, "I guess I'm just . . . scared."

"No need to be scared," Bobby said. "Hal's not as dangerous as he looks. He's never killed anyone he liked."

"Only once," Hal said.

Bobby said, "You once killed someone you liked? Over what?"

"He asked to borrow my comb."

"There you go, Frank," Bobby said. "Just don't ask to borrow his comb, and you're safe."

Frank was in no mood to be kidded. "I can't stop thinking about waking up with blood on my hands. I'm afraid maybe I've already hurt someone. I don't want to hurt anyone else."

"Oh, you can't hurt Hal," Bobby said. "He's an impenetrable oriental."

"Inscrutable," Hal said. "I'm an *inscrutable* oriental."

"I don't want to hear about your sex problems, Hal. Anyway, if you didn't eat so much sushi and didn't have raw-fish breath, you'd get scruted as often as anyone."

Reaching over the bed railing, Julie took one of Frank's hands.

He smiled weakly. "Your husband always like this, Mrs. Dakota?"

"Call me Julie. Do you mean, does he always act like a wiseass or a child? Not always, but most of the time, I'm afraid."

"You hear that, Hal?" Bobby said. "Women and amnesiacs—they have no sense of humor."

To Frank, Julie said, "My husband believes everything in life should be fun, even car accidents, even funerals—"

"Even dental hygiene," Bobby said.

"—and he'd probably be making jokes about fallout in the middle of a nuclear war. That's just the way he is. He can't be cured—"

"She's tried," Bobby said. "She sent me to a happiness detox center. They promised to knock some gloom into me. Couldn't."

"You'll be safe here," Julie said, squeezing Frank's hand before letting go of it. "Hal will look after you."

# 31

THE ENTOMOLOGIST'S house was in the Turtle Rock development in Irvine, within easy driving distance of the university. Low, black, mushroom-shaped Malibu lamps threw circles of light on the rain-puddled walkway that led to the softly gleaming oak doors.

Carrying one of Frank Pollard's leather flight bags, Clint stepped onto the small covered porch and rang the bell.

A man spoke to him through an intercom set just below the bell push. "Who is it, please?"

"Dr. Dyson Manfred? I'm Clint Karaghiosis. From Dakota and Dakota."

Half a minute later, Manfred opened the door. He was at least ten inches taller than Clint, six feet five or six, and thin. He was wearing black slacks, a white shirt, and a green necktie; the top button of the shirt was undone, and the tie hung loose.

"Good God, man, you're soaked."

"Just damp."

Manfred moved back, opening the door wide, and Clint stepped into the tile-floored foyer.

As he closed the door, Manfred said, "Ought to have a raincoat or umbrella on a night like this."

"It's invigorating."

"What is?"

"Bad weather," Clint said.

Manfred looked at him as if he was strange, but in Clint's view it was Manfred himself who was strange. The guy was too thin, all bones. He could not fill his clothes; his trousers hung shapelessly on his knobby hips, and his shoulders poked at the fabric of his shirt as if only bare, sharp bones lay under there. Angular and graceless, he looked as if he had been assembled from a pile of dry sticks by an apprentice god. His face was long and narrow, with a high brow and a lantern jaw, and his well-tanned, leathery skin seemed to be stretched so tight over his cheekbones that it might split. He had peculiar amber eyes that regarded Clint with an expression of cool curiosity no doubt familiar to the thousands of bugs he had pinned to specimen boards.

Manfred's gaze traveled down Clint to the floor, where water was puddling around his running shoes.

"Sorry," Clint said.

"It'll dry. I was in my study. Come along."

Glancing into the living room, to his right, Clint noted fleur-de-lis wallpaper, a thick Chinese rug, too many overstuffed chairs and sofas, antique English furniture, wine-red velour drapes, and tables cluttered with bibelots that glimmered in the lamplight. It was a very Victorian room, not in harmony with the California lines and layout of the house itself.

He followed the entomologist past the living room, along a short hall to the study. Manfred had a singular, stilting gait. Tall and sticklike as he was, with shoulders hunched and head thrust forward slightly, he seemed as unevolved and prehistoric as a praying mantis.

Clint had expected a university professor's study to be crammed full of books, but only forty or fifty volumes were shelved in one case to the left of the desk. There were cabinets with wide, shallow drawers that probably were filled with creepy-crawlies, and on the walls were insects in specimen boxes, framed under glass.

When he saw Clint staring at one collection in particular, Manfred said, "Cockroaches. Beautiful creatures."

Clint did not reply.

"The simplicity of their design and function, I mean. Few would find them beautiful in appearance, of course."

Clint couldn't shake the feeling that the bugs were really alive.

Manfred said, "What do you think of that big fellow in the corner of the collection?"

"He's big, sir."

"Madagascar hissing roach. The scientific name's *Grompha-dorrhina portentosa*. That one's over eight and a half centimeters long, about three and a half inches. Absolutely beautiful, isn't he?"

Clint said nothing.

Settling into the chair behind his desk, Manfred somehow folded his long bony arms and legs into that compact space, the way a large spider could scrunch itself into a tiny ball.

Clint did not sit down. Having put in a long day, he was eager to go home.

Manfred said, "I received a call from the university chancellor. He asked me to cooperate with your Mr. Dakota in any way I could."

UCI—the University of California at Irvine—had long been striving to become one of the country's premier universities. The current chancellor and the one before him had sought to attain that status by offering enormous salaries and generous fringe benefits to world-class professors and researchers at other institutions. Before committing substantial resources in the form of a well-upholstered job offer, however, the university hired Dakota & Dakota to conduct a background investigation on the prospective faculty member. Even a brilliant physicist or biologist could have too great a thirst for whiskey, a nose for cocaine, or an unfortunate attraction to underage girls. UCI wanted to buy brainpower, respectability, and academic glory, not scandal; Dakota & Dakota served them well.

Manfred propped his elbows on the arms of his chair and steepled his fingers, which were so long that they looked as if they must have at least one extra knuckle each. "What's the problem?" he asked.

Clint opened the leather flight bag and removed the quart-size, wide-mouth mason jar. He put it on the entomologist's desk.

The bug in the jar was at least twice as big as the Madagascar hissing roach on the wall.

For a moment Dr. Dyson Manfred seemed to have been quick-frozen. He didn't move a finger; his eyes didn't blink. He stared intently at the creature in the jar. At last he said, "What is this—a hoax?"

"It's real."

Manfred leaned forward, hunching over the desk and lowering his head until his nose almost touched the thick glass behind which the insect crouched. "Alive?"

"Dead."

"Where did you find this—not here in southern California?"

"Yes."

"Impossible."

"What is it?" Clint asked.

Manfred looked up at him, scowling. "I've never seen anything like it. And if *I* haven't seen anything like it, neither has anyone else. It's of the phylum *Arthropoda,* I'm sure, which includes such things as spiders and scorpions, but whether it can be classed an insect, I can't say, not until I've examined it. If it *is* an insect, it's of a new species. Where, exactly, did you find it, and why on earth would it be of interest to private detectives?"

"I'm sorry, sir, but I can't tell you anything about the case. I have to protect the client's privacy."

Manfred carefully turned the jar around in his hands, studying the resident from every side. "Just incredible. I must have it." He looked up, and his amber eyes were no longer cool and appraising, but gleaming with excitement. "I must have this specimen."

"Well, I intended to leave it with you for examination," Clint said. "But as to whether you can have permanent possession—"

"Yes. Permanent."

"That's up to my boss and the client. Meanwhile we want to know what it is, where it comes from, everything you can tell us about it."

With exaggerated care, as if handling the finest crystal instead of ordinary glass, Manfred put the jar on the blotter. "I'll make a complete photographic and videotape record of the specimen from every angle and in extreme close-up. Then it'll be necessary to dissect it, though that'll be done with utmost care, I assure you."

"Whatever."

"Mr. Karaghiosis, you seem terribly blasé about this. Do you fully understand what I've said? This would appear to be an entirely new species, which would be extraordinary. Because how could any such species, producing individuals of this size, be overlooked for so long? This is going to be big news in the world of entomology, Mr. Karaghiosis, very big news."

Clint looked at the bug in the bottle.

He said, "Yeah, I figured."

# 32

FROM THE HOSPITAL, Bobby and Julie drove a company Toyota into the county's western flatlands to Garden Grove, looking for 884 Serape Way, the address on the driver's license that Frank held in the name of George Farris.

Julie peered through the rain-dappled side windows and forward between the thumping windshield wipers, checking house numbers.

The street was lined with bright sodium-vapor lamps and

thirty-year-old, single-story homes. They had been built in two basic, boxy models, but an illusion of individuality was provided by a variety of trim. This one was stucco with brick accents. That one was stucco with cedar-shingle panels—or Bouquet Canyon stone or desert bark or volcanic rock.

California was not all Beverly Hills, Bel Air, and Newport Beach, not all mansions and seaside villas, which was the television image. Economies of home design had made the California dream accessible to the waves of immigrants that for decades had flooded in from back east, and now from farther shores—as was evident from Vietnamese- and Korean-language bumper stickers on some cars parked along Serape.

"Next block," Julie said. "My side."

Some people said such neighborhoods were a blot on the land, but to Bobby they were the essence of democracy. He had been raised on a street like Serape Way, north in Anaheim instead of Garden Grove, and it had never seemed ugly. He remembered playing with other kids on long summer evenings, when the sun set with orange and crimson flares, and the feathery silhouettes of the backlit palms were as black as ink drawings against the sky; at twilight the air sometimes smelled of star jasmine and echoed with the cry of a lingering sea gull far to the west. He remembered what it meant to be a kid with a bicycle in California—the vistas for exploration, the grand possibilities for adventure; every street of stucco homes, seen for the first time and from the seat of a Schwinn, had seemed exotic.

Two coral trees dominated the yard at 884 Serape. The white blooms of the azalea bushes were softly radiant in the bleak night.

Tinted by the sodium-vapor streetlamps, the falling rain looked like molten gold. But as Bobby hurried along the walkway behind Julie, the rain was almost as cold as sleet on his face and hands. He was wearing a warmly lined, nylon jacket with a hood, but he shivered.

Julie rang the doorbell. The porch light came on, and Bobby sensed someone looking them over through the fisheye lens in the front door. He pushed back his hood and smiled.

The door opened on a security chain, and an Asian man peered out. He was in his forties, short, slender, with black hair fading to gray at the temples. "Yes?"

Julie showed him her private investigator's license and explained that they were looking for someone named George Farris.

"Police?" The man frowned. "Nothing wrong, no need for police."

"No, see, we're private investigators," Bobby explained.

The man's eyes narrowed. He looked as if he would close the door in their faces, but abruptly he brightened, smiled. "Oh, you're PI! Like on TV." He took the chain off the door and let them in.

Actually he didn't just let them in, he welcomed them as if they were honored guests. Within three minutes flat, they learned his name was Tuong Tran Phan (the order of his names having been rearranged to accommodate the western custom of putting the surname last), that he and his wife, Chinh, were among the boat people who fled Vietnam two years after the fall of Saigon, that they had worked in laundries and dry cleaners, and eventually opened two dry-cleaning stores of their own. Tuong insisted on taking their coats. Chinh—a petite woman with delicate features, dressed in baggy black slacks and a yellow silk blouse—said she would provide refreshments, even though Bobby explained that only a few minutes of their time was required.

Bobby knew first-generation Vietnamese-Americans were sometimes suspicious of policemen, even to the extent of being reluctant to call for help when they were victims of crime. The South Vietnamese police often had been corrupt, and the North Vietnamese overlords, who seized the South after the U.S. withdrawal, had been murderous. Even after fifteen years or longer in the States, many Vietnamese remained at least somewhat distrustful of all authorities.

In the case of Tuong and Chinh Phan, however, that suspicion did not extend to private investigators. Evidently they had seen so many heroic television gumshoes, they believed all PIs were champions of the underdog, knights with blazing .38s instead of lances. In their roles as liberators of the oppressed, Bobby and Julie were conducted, with some ceremony, to the sofa, which was the newest and best piece of furniture in the living room.

The Phans marshaled their exceptionally good-looking children in the living room for introductions: thirteen-year-old Rocky, ten-year-old Sylvester, twelve-year-old Sissy, and six-year-old Meryl. They were obviously born-and-raised Americans, except that they were refreshingly more courteous and well-mannered than many of their contemporaries. When introductions had been made, the kids returned to the kitchen, where they had been doing their schoolwork.

In spite of their polite protestations, Bobby and Julie were swiftly served coffee laced with condensed milk and exquisite little Vietnamese pastries. The Phans had coffee as well.

Tuong and Chinh sat in worn armchairs that were visibly less comfortable than the sofa. Most of their furniture was in simple contemporary styles and neutral colors. A small Buddhist shrine stood in one corner; fresh fruit lay on the red altar, and several sticks of incense bristled from ceramic holders. Only one stick was lit, and a pale-blue ribbon of fragrant smoke curled upward. The only other Asian elements were black-lacquered tables.

"We're looking for a man who might once have lived at this address," Julie said, selecting one of the petits fours from the tray on which Mrs. Phan had served them. "His name's George Farris."

"Yes. He lived here," Tuong said, and his wife nodded.

Bobby was surprised. He had been certain that the Farris name and the address had been randomly matched by a document forger, that Frank had never lived here. Frank had been equally certain that Pollard, not Farris, was his real name.

"You bought this house from George Farris?" Julie asked.

Tuong said, "No, he was dead."

"Dead?" Bobby asked.

"Five or six years ago," Tuong said. "Terrible cancer."

Then Frank Pollard *wasn't* Farris and hadn't lived here. The ID was entirely fake.

"We bought house just a few months ago from widow," Tuong said. His English was good, though occasionally he dropped the article before the noun. "No, what I mean to say—from widow's estate."

Julie said, "So Mrs. Farris is dead too."

Tuong turned to his wife, and a meaningful look passed between them. He said, "It is very sad. Where do such men come from?"

Julie said, "What man are you speaking of, Mr. Phan?"

"The one who killed Mrs. Farris, her brother, two daughters."

Something seemed to slither and coil in Bobby's stomach. He instinctively liked Frank Pollard and was certain of his innocence, but suddenly a worm of doubt bored into the fine, polished apple of his conviction. Could it be just a coincidence that Frank was carrying the ID of a man whose family had been slaughtered—or was Frank responsible? He was chewing a bite of cream-filled pastry, and though it was tasty, he had trouble swallowing it.

"It was late July," Chinh said. "During the heat wave, which you may remember." She blew on her coffee to cool it. Bobby noticed that most of the time Chinh spoke perfect English, and he suspected that her occasional infelicities of language were conscious mistakes that she inserted in order not to seem more well-spoken than her husband, a subtle and thoroughly Asian courtesy. "We buy house last October."

"They never catch the killer," Tuong Phan said.

"Do they have a description of him?" Julie asked.

"I don't think so."

Reluctantly Bobby glanced at Julie. She appeared to be as shaken as he was, but she did not give him an I-told-you-so look.

She said, "How were they murdered? Shot? Strangled?"

"Knife, I think. Come. I show you where bodies were found."

The house had three bedrooms and two bathrooms, but one bath was being remodeled. The tile had been torn off the walls, floor, and counter. The cabinets were being rebuilt with quality oak.

Julie followed Tuong into the bathroom, and Bobby stayed at the doorway with Mrs. Phan.

The rattle-hiss of the rain echoed down through the ceiling vent.

Tuong said, "Body of youngest Farris daughter was here, on the floor. She was thirteen. Terrible thing. Much blood. The grout between tiles was permanently stained, all had to come out."

He led them into the bedroom his daughters shared. Twin beds, nightstands, and two small desks left little room for anything else. But Sissy and Meryl had squeezed in a lot of books.

Tuong Phan said, "Mrs. Farris's brother, staying with her for a week, was killed here. In his bed. Blood was on walls, carpet."

"We saw the house before it was listed with a real-estate agent, before the carpet was replaced and the walls repainted," Chinh Phan said. "This room was the worst. It gave me bad dreams for a while."

They proceeded to the sparely furnished master bedroom: a queen-size bed, nightstands, two ginger-jar lamps, but no bureau or chest of drawers. The clothes that would not fit in the closet were arranged along one wall, in cardboard storage boxes with clear plastic lids.

Their frugality struck Bobby as similar to his and Julie's. Perhaps they, too, had a dream for which they were working and saving.

Tuong said, "Mrs. Farris was found in this room, in her bed. Terrible things were done to her. She was bitten, but they never wrote about that in newspapers."

"Bitten?" Julie asked. "By what?"

"Probably by killer. On the face, throat . . . other places."

"If they didn't write about it in the papers," Bobby said, "how do you know about the bites?"

"Neighbor who found bodies still lives next door. She says that both older daughter and Mrs. Farris were bitten."

Mrs. Phan said, "She's not the kind to imagine such things."

"Where was the second daughter found?" Julie asked.

"Please follow me." Tuong led them back the way they had come, through the living room and dining room, into the kitchen.

The four Phan children were sitting around a breakfast table. Three of them were diligently reading textbooks and taking notes. No television or radio provided distraction, and they appeared to be enjoying their studies. Even Meryl, who was a first-grader and probably had no homework to speak of, was reading a children's book.

Bobby noticed two colorful charts posted on the wall near the refrigerator. The first displayed each kid's grades and major test results since the start of the school year in September. The other was a list of household chores for which each child was responsible.

Throughout the country, universities were in a bind, because an inordinately large percentage of the best applicants for admission were of Asian extraction. Blacks and Hispanics complained about being aced out by another minority, and whites shouted reverse racism when denied admission in favor of an Asian student. Some attributed Asian-Americans' success to a conspiracy, but Bobby saw the simple explanation for their achievements everywhere in the Phan house: They tried harder. They embraced the ideals upon which the country had been based—including hard work, honesty, goal-oriented self-denial, and the freedom to be whatever one wanted to be. Ironically, their great success was partly due to the fact that so many born Americans had become cynical about those same ideals.

The kitchen was open to a family room that was furnished as humbly as the rest of the house.

Tuong said, "Oldest Farris girl found here by sofa. Seventeen."

"Very pretty girl," Chinh said sadly.

"She, like mother, was bitten. So our neighbor says."

Julie said, "What about the other victims, the younger daughter and Mrs. Farris's brother—were they bitten too?"

"Don't know," Tuong said.

"The neighbor didn't see their bodies," Chinh said.

They were silent for a moment, looking at the floor where the dead girl had been found, as if the enormity of this crime was such that the stain of it should somehow have reappeared on this brand-new carpet. Rain droned on the roof.

Bobby said, "Doesn't it sometimes bother you to live here? Not because murders took place in these rooms, but because the killer was never found. Don't you worry about him coming back some night?"

Chinh nodded.

Tuong said, "Everywhere is danger. Life itself is danger. Less risky never being born." A faint smile flickered across his face and was gone. "Leaving Vietnam in tiny boat was more danger than this."

Glancing at the table in the adjoining kitchen, Bobby saw the four kids still deeply involved with their studies. The prospect of a murderer returning to the scene of this crime did not faze them.

"In addition to dry-cleaning," Chinh said, "we remodel houses, sell them. This is fourth. We will live here maybe another year, remodeling room by room, then sell, take a profit."

Tuong said, "Because of murders, some people would not consider moving here after the Farrises. But danger is also opportunity."

"When we finish with the house," Chinh said, "it won't just be remodeled. It will be clean, spiritually clean. Do you understand? The innocence of the house will be restored. We will have chased out the evil that the killer brought here, and we'll have left our own spiritual imprint on these rooms."

Nodding, Tuong said, "That is a satisfaction."

Removing the forged driver's license from his pocket, Bobby held it so his fingers covered the name and address, leaving the photograph visible. "Do you recognize this man?"

"No," Tuong said, and Chinh agreed.

As Bobby put the license away, Julie said, "Do you know what George Farris looked like?"

"No," Tuong said. "As I told you, he died of cancer, many years before his family was killed."

"I thought maybe you'd seen a photo of him here in the house, before the Farrises' belongings were removed."

"No. Sorry."

Bobby said, "You mentioned earlier that you didn't buy the house through a realtor. You worked with the estate?"

"Yes. Mrs. Farris's other brother inherited everything."

"Do you happen to have his name and address?" Bobby asked. "I think we'll need to talk to him."

# 33

DINNERTIME CAME. Derek woke up. He was groggy but hungry too. He leaned on Thomas when they walked to the dining room. Food got eaten. Spaghetti. Meatballs. Salad. Good bread. Chocolate cake. Cold milk.

Back in their room, they watched TV. Derek fell asleep again. It was a bad night on TV. Thomas sighed with disgust. After an hour or so, he stopped the set. None of the shows was smart enough to care about. They were too stupid-silly even for a moron, which Mary said he was. Maybe imbeciles would like them. Probably not.

He used the bathroom. Brushed his teeth. Washed his face. He didn't look in the mirror. He didn't like mirrors because they showed him what he was.

After changing into pajamas, he got in bed and made the lamp go dark, even though it was only eight-thirty. He turned on his side, with his head propped on two pillows, and studied the night sky framed by the nearest window. No stars. Clouds. Rain. He liked rain. When a storm came down, it was like a lid on the night, and you didn't feel like you might float up in all that darkness and just disappear.

He listened to the rain. It whispered. It cried tears on the window.

Far away, the Bad Thing was loose. Ugly-nasty waves spread out from it the way ripples spread across a pond when you dropped a stone in the water. The Bad Thing was like a big stone dropped into the night, a thing that didn't belong in this world, and with a little effort Thomas could sense the waves from it breaking over him.

He reached out. Felt it. A throbbing thing. Cold and full of anger. Mean. He wanted to get closer. Learn what it was.

He tried TVing questions at it. What are you? Where are you? What do you want? Why are you going to hurt Julie?

Suddenly, like a big magnet, the Bad Thing began pulling him. He'd never felt anything like that before. When he tried to TV his thoughts to Bobby or Julie, they didn't grab him and pull at him the way this Bad Thing did.

A part of his mind seemed to unravel like a ball of string, and the loose end sailed through the window and way up into the night, through the darkness, until it found the Bad Thing. Suddenly Thomas was very close to the Bad Thing, too close. It was all around him, big ugly and so strange that Thomas felt like he'd dropped into a swimming pool full of ice and razor blades. He didn't know if it was a man, couldn't see its shape, only feel it; it might be pretty on the outside, but on the inside it was throbbing and dark and deep nasty. He sensed the Bad Thing was eating. The food was still alive and squirming. Thomas was scared big, and right away he tried to pull back, but for a moment the ugly mind held him tight, and he could get away only by picturing the mind-string rewinding itself onto the ball.

When the mind-string was all wound up again, Thomas turned away from the window, onto his stomach. He was breathing real fast. He listened to his heart boom.

He had a sick-making taste in his mouth. The same taste he got sometimes when he bit his tongue, not meaning to, and the same taste as when the dentist yanked one of his teeth, meaning to. Blood.

Sick and scared, he sat up in bed and made the lamp come

on right away. He took a tissue from the box on the nightstand. He spit into it and looked to see if there was blood. There wasn't. Just spit.

He tried again. No blood.

He knew what that meant. He'd been too close to the Bad Thing. Maybe even *inside* the bad thing, just for a blink. The ugly taste in his mouth was the same taste the Bad Thing tasted, tearing with its teeth at some living, squirming food. Thomas didn't have blood in his mouth, he just had a memory of blood in his mouth. But that was bad enough; this time wasn't at all like biting his tongue or getting a tooth yanked, because this time what he tasted wasn't his own blood.

Though enough warm was in the room, he started shivering and couldn't stop.

♦ ♦ ♦

CANDY PROWLED the canyons, in the grip of urgent need, rattling wild animals out of burrows and nests. He was kneeling in the mud beside a huge oak, pummeled by rain, sucking blood from the ravished throat of a rabbit, when he felt someone place a hand atop his head.

He threw down the rabbit and sprang to his feet, turning around as he did so. Nobody was there. Two of his sisters' blackest cats were twenty feet behind him, visible only because their eyes were luminous in the gloom; they had been following him since he'd left the house. Otherwise he was alone.

For a second or two, he still felt the hand on his head, though no hand was there. Then the queer sensation passed.

He studied the shadows on all sides and listened to the rain snapping through the oak leaves.

Finally, shrugging off the episode, driven by his fierce need, he proceeded farther east, moving upslope. A two-foot-wide stream had formed on the canyon floor, six or eight inches deep, not large enough to hamper his progress.

The drenched cats followed. He did not want them with him, but he knew from experience that he would not be able to chase them away. They did not always accompany him, but when they chose to follow in his tracks, they could not be dissuaded.

After he had gone about a hundred yards, he dropped to his knees again, held his hands in front of him, and allowed the power to erupt once more. Shimmering sapphire light swept through the night. Brush shook, trees stirred, and rocks clattered against one another. In the wake of the light, clouds of dust flew up, ghostly silver columns that rippled like wind-stirred shrouds, then vanished into the darkness.

A bevy of animals burst from cover, and some raced toward Candy. He snatched at a rabbit, missed, but seized a squirrel. It tried to bite him, but he swung it hard by one leg, bashing its head against the muddy ground, stunning it.

♦ ♦ ♦

VIOLET WAS with Verbina in the kitchen. They were sitting on the layered blankets with twenty-three of their twenty-five cats.

Parts of her mind—and parts of her sister's—were in Cinders and Lamia, the black cats through which they were accompanying their brother. Watching Candy seize and destroy his prey, Cinders and Lamia were excited, and Violet was excited too. Electrified.

The wet January night was deep, illumined only by the ambient light from the communities to the west, which was reflected off the bellies of the low clouds. In that wilderness, Candy was the wildest creature of them all, a fierce and powerful and merciless predator who crept swiftly and silently through the rugged canyons, taking what he needed and wanted. He was so strong and limber that he appeared to flow up the canyon, over rocks and fallen timber, around prickly brush, as if he were not a man of flesh and blood, but the rippled moonshadow of some flying creature soaring high above the earth.

When Candy seized the squirrel and bashed its head against the ground, Violet divided the part of her mind that was in Lamia and Cinders, and also entered the squirrel. It was stunned by the blow. It struggled feebly and looked at Candy with unalloyed terror.

Candy's big, strong hands were on the squirrel, but it seemed to Violet that they were on her, as well, moving over her bare legs, hips, belly, and breasts.

Candy snapped its spine against his bent knee.

Violet shuddered. Verbina whimpered and clung to her sister.

The squirrel no longer had any feeling in its extremities.

With a low growl, Candy bit the animal's throat. He tore at its hide, chewing open the blood-rich vessels.

Violet felt the hot blood spurting out of the squirrel, felt Candy's mouth fastened hungrily to the wound. It almost seemed as though no surrogate lay between them, as if his lips were pressed firmly to Violet's throat and as if her own blood was flooding into his mouth. She wished that she could enter Candy's mind and be on both the giving and receiving end of the blood, but she could only meld with animals.

She no longer had the strength to sit up. She settled back onto the blankets, only half aware that she was softly chanting a monotonous litany: *"Yea, yes, yes, yes, yes. . . ."*

Verbina rolled atop her sister.

Around them the cats tumbled together in a roiling mass of fur and tails and whiskered faces.

♦   ♦   ♦

THOMAS TRIED again. For Julie's sake. He reached out toward the cold, glowing mind of the Bad Thing. Right away the Bad Thing drew him toward it. He let his mind unwind like a big ball of string. It pierced the window, zoomed into the night, made contact.

He TVed questions: What are you? Where are you? What do you want? Why are you going to hurt Julie?

♦   ♦   ♦

JUST AS CANDY threw aside the dead squirrel and got to his feet, he felt the hand on his head again. He twitched, turned, and flailed at the darkness with both fists.

No one was behind him. With radiant amber eyes, the two cats watched him from about twenty feet away, dark blots on the pale silt. All the wildlife in the immediate vicinity had fled. If someone was spying on him, the intruder was concealed in the brush farther back along the canyon or in a niche on one of the canyon walls, certainly not near enough to have touched him.

Besides, he still felt the hand. He rubbed at the top of his head, half expecting to find leaves stuck in his wet hair. Nothing.

But the pressure of a hand remained, even increased, and was so well defined that he could feel the outlines of four fingers, a thumb, and the curve of a palm against his skull.

*What . . . where . . . what . . . why . . . ?*

Those words echoed inside his head. No voice had broken through the drizzling sounds of the rain.

*What . . . where . . . what . . . why . . . ?*

Candy turned in a full circle, angry and confused.

A crawling sensation arose in his head, different from anything he had ever known before. As if something was burrowing in his brain.

"Who are you?" he said aloud.

*What . . . where . . . what . . . why . . . ?*

"Who are you?"

◆ ◆ ◆

THE BAD THING was a man. Thomas knew that now. An ugly-inside man and something else, too, but still at least partly a man.

The Bad Thing's mind was like a whirlpool, blacker than black, swirling real fast, sucking Thomas down, down, wanting to gobble him alive. He tried to break loose. Swim away. Wasn't easy. The Bad Thing was going to pull him into the Bad Place, and he'd never be able to come back. He thought he was a goner. But his fear of the Bad Place, of going where Julie and Bobby would never find him and where he'd be alone, was so big he finally tore free and rewound himself into his room at Cielo Vista.

He slid down on the mattress and drew the covers over his head, so he couldn't see the night beyond the window, and so nothing out there in the night could see him.

# 34

WALTER HAVALOW, Mrs. George Farris's surviving brother and heir to her modest estate, lived in a richer neighborhood than the Phans, but he was poorer in courtesy and good manners. His English Tudor house in Villa Park had beveled-glass windows filled with a light that Julie found warm and beckoning, but Havalow stood in the doorway and did not invite them inside even after he had studied their PI license and returned it to her.

"What do you want?"

Havalow was tall, potbellied, with thinning blond hair and a thick mustache that was part blond and part red. His penetrating hazel eyes marked him as a man of intelligence, but they were cold, watchful, and calculating—the eyes of a Mafia accountant.

"As I explained," Julie said, "the Phans told us you could help. We need a photograph of your late brother-in-law, George Farris."

"Why?"

"Well, as I said, there's a man going around pretending to be Mr. Farris, and he's a player in a case we're working on."

"Can't be my brother-in-law. He's dead."

"Yes, we know. But this imposter's ID is very good, and it would help us to have a photo of the real George Farris. I'm sorry I can't tell you anything more. I'd be violating our client's privacy."

Havalow turned away and closed the door in their faces.

Bobby looked at Julie and said, "Mr. Conviviality."

Julie rang the bell again.

After a moment, Havalow opened the door. "What?"

"I know we arrived unannounced," Julie said, struggling to remain cordial, "and I apologize for the intrusion, but a photo of your—"

"I was just going to get the picture," he said impatiently. "I'd have it in hand by now if you hadn't rung the bell again." He turned away from them and closed the door a second time.

"Is it our body odor?" Bobby wondered.

"What a jerk."

"You think he's really coming back?"

"He doesn't, I'll break the door down."

Behind them, rain dripped off the overhang that sheltered the last ten feet of the walkway, and water gurgled hollowly through a downspout—cold sounds.

Havalow returned with a shoe box full of snapshots. "My time is valuable. If you want my cooperation, you'll keep that in mind."

154

Julie resisted her worst instincts. Rudeness irritated the hell out of her. She fantasized knocking the box out of his grasp, seizing one of his hands, and bending the index finger as far back as it would go, thus straining the digital nerve on the front of his hand while simultaneously pinching the radial and median nerves on the back, forcing him to kneel. Then a knee driven into the underside of his chin, a swift chop to the back of his neck, a well-placed kick to his soft, protruding belly . . .

Havalow rummaged through the box and extracted a Polaroid of a man and a woman sitting at a redwood picnic table on a sunny day. "That's George and Irene."

Even in the yellowish light of the porch lamp, Julie could see that George Farris had been a rangy man with a long narrow face, the exact physical opposite of Frank Pollard.

"Why would someone be claiming he's George?" Havalow asked.

"We're dealing with a possible criminal who uses multiple fake IDs," Julie said. "George Farris is just one of his identities. No doubt your brother-in-law's name was probably chosen at random by the document forger this guy used. Forgers sometimes use the names and addresses of the deceased."

Havalow frowned. "You think it's possible this man using George's name is the same guy who killed Irene, my brother, my two nieces?"

"No," Julie said immediately. "We're not dealing with a killer here. Just a confidence man, a swindler."

"Besides," Bobby said, "no killer would link himself to murders he'd committed by getting ID in the name of his victim's husband."

Making eye contact with Julie, clearly trying to determine how much they were snowing him, Havalow said, "This guy your client?"

"No," Julie lied. "He ripped off our client, and we've been hired to track him down, so he can be forced to make restitution."

Bobby said, "Can we borrow this photo, sir?"

Havalow hesitated. He was still making eye contact with Julie.

Bobby handed Havalow a Dakota & Dakota business card. "We'll get the picture back to you. There's our address, phone number. I understand your reluctance to part with a family photo, especially since your sister and brother-in-law are no longer alive, but if—"

Apparently deciding that they were not lying, Havalow said, "Hell, take it. I'm not sentimental about George. Never could stand him. Always thought my sister was a fool for marrying him."

"Thank you," Bobby said. "We—"

Havalow stepped back and closed the door.

Julie rang the bell.

Bobby said, "Please don't kill him."

Scowling with impatience, Havalow opened the door.

Stepping between Julie and Havalow, Bobby held out the forged driver's license bearing George Farris's name and Frank's picture. "One more thing, sir, and we'll get out of your hair."

"I live to a very tight schedule," Havalow said.

"Have you seen this man before?"

Irritated, Havalow took the driver's license and inspected it. "Doughy face, bland features. There're a million like him within a hundred miles of here—wouldn't you say?"

"And you've never seen him?"

"Are you slow-witted? Do I have to put it in short, simple sentences? No. I have never seen him."

Retrieving the license, Bobby said, "Thanks for your time and—"

Havalow closed the door. Hard.

Julie reached for the bell.

Bobby stayed her hand. "We've got everything we came for."

"I want—"

"I know what you want," Bobby said, "but torturing a man to death is against the law in California."

He hustled her away from the house, into the rain.

In the car again, she said, "That rude, self-important bastard!"

Bobby started the engine and switched on the windshield wipers. "We'll stop at the mall, buy you one of those giant teddy bears, paint Havalow's name on it, let you tear the guts out of it. Okay?"

"Who the hell does he think he is?"

While Julie glowered back at the house, Bobby drove away from it. "He's Walter Havalow, babe, and he's got to be himself until he dies, which is a worse punishment than anything you could do to him."

A few minutes later, when they were out of Villa Park, Bobby drove into the lot at a Ralph's supermarket and tucked the Toyota into a parking space. He doused the headlights, switched off the wipers, but left the engine running so they would have heat.

Only a few cars were in front of the market. Puddles as large as swimming pools reflected the store lights.

Bobby said, "What've we learned?"

"That we *loathe* Walter Havalow."

"Yes, but what have we learned that's germane to the case? Is it just a coincidence that Frank's been using George Farris's name and Farris's family was slaughtered?"

"I don't believe in coincidence."

"Neither do I. But I still don't think Frank is a killer."

"Neither do I, though anything's possible. But what you said to Havalow was true—surely Frank wouldn't kill Irene Farris and everyone else in the house, then carry around fake ID that links him to them."

Rain began to fall harder than before, drumming noisily on the Toyota. The heavy curtain of water blurred the supermarket.

Bobby said, "You want to know what I think? I think Frank was using Farris's name, and whoever's after him found out about it."

"Mr. Blue Light, you mean. The guy who supposedly can make a car fall apart around you and magically induce streetlights to blow out."

"Yeah, him," Bobby said.

"If he exists."

"Mr. Blue Light discovered Frank was using the Farris name, and went to that address, hoping to find him. But Frank had never been there. It was just a name and address his document forger picked at random. So when Mr. Blue didn't find Frank, he killed everyone in the house, maybe because he thought they were lying to him and hiding Frank, or maybe just because he was in a rage."

"*He'd* have known how to deal with Havalow."

"So you think I'm right, I'm on to something?"

She thought about it. "Could be."

He grinned at her. "Isn't it fun being a detective?"

"Fun?" she said incredulously.

"Well, I meant 'interesting.' "

"We're either representing a man who killed four people, or we're representing a man who's been targeted by a brutal murderer, and that strikes you as fun?"

"Not as much fun as sex, but more fun than bowling."

"Bobby, sometimes you make me nuts. But I love you."

He took her hand. "If we're going to pursue the investigation, I'm damned well going to enjoy it as much as I can. But I'll drop the case in a minute if you want."

"Why? Because of your dream? Because of the Bad Thing?" She shook her head. "No. We start letting a weird dream spook us, pretty soon *anything* will spook us. We'll lose our confidence, and you can't do this kind of work without confidence."

Even in the dim backsplash from the dashboard lights, she could see the anxiety in his eyes.

Finally he said, "Yeah, that's what I knew you'd say. So let's get to the bottom of it as fast as we can. According to his other driver's license, he's James Roman, and he lives in El Toro."

"It's almost eight-thirty."

"We can be there, find the house . . . maybe forty-five minutes. That's not too late."

"All right."

Instead of putting the car in gear, he slid his seat back and stripped out of his down-lined, nylon jacket. "Unlock the glovebox and give me my gun. From now on I'm wearing it everywhere."

Each of them had a license to carry a concealed weapon. Julie struggled out of her own jacket, then retrieved two shoulder holsters from under her seat. She took both revolvers out of the glovebox: two snub-nosed Smith & Wesson .38 Chief's Specials, reliable and compact guns that could be carried inconspicuously beneath ordinary clothing with little or no help from a tailor.

◆ ◆ ◆

THE HOUSE was gone. If anyone named James Roman had lived there, he had new lodgings now. A bare concrete slab lay in the middle of the lot, surrounded by grass, shrubbery, and several trees, as if the structure had been snared from above by intergalactic moving men and neatly spirited away.

Bobby parked in the driveway, and they got out of the Toyota to have a closer look at the property. Even in the slashing rain, a nearby streetlamp cast enough light to reveal that the lawn was trampled, gouged by tires, and bare in spots; it was also littered with splinters of wood, pale bits of Sheetrock, crumbled stucco, and a few fragments of glass that sparkled darkly.

The strongest clue to the fate of the house was to be found in the condition of the shrubbery and trees. Those bushes closest to the slab were all either dead or badly damaged, and on closer inspection appeared to be scorched. The nearest tree was leafless, and its stark black limbs lent an anachronistic feeling of Halloween to the drizzly January night.

"Fire," Julie said. "Then they tore down what was left."

"Let's talk to a neighbor."

The empty lot was flanked by houses. But lights glowed only at the house on the north side.

The man who answered the doorbell was about fifty-five, six feet two, solidly built, with gray hair and a neatly trimmed gray mustache. His name was Park Hampstead, and he had the air of a retired military man. He invited them in, with the proviso that they leave their sodden shoes on the front porch. In their socks, they followed him to a breakfast nook off the kitchen, where the yellow vinyl dinette upholstery was safe from their damp clothing; even so, Hampstead made them wait while he draped thick peach-colored beach towels over two of the chairs.

"Sorry," he said, "but I'm something of a fussbudget."

The house had bleached-oak floors and modern furniture, and Bobby noticed that it was spotless in every corner.

"Thirty years in the Marine Corps left me with an abiding respect for routine, order, and neatness," Hampstead explained. "In fact, when Sharon died three years ago—she was my wife—I think maybe I got a little crazy about neatness. The first six or eight months after her funeral, I cleaned the place top to bottom at least twice a week, because as long as I was cleaning, my heart didn't hurt so bad. Spent a fortune on Windex, paper towels, Fantastik, and sweeper bags. Let me tell you, no military pension can support the Endust habit I developed! I got over that stage. I'm still a fussbudget but not *obsessed* with neatness."

He had just brewed a fresh pot of coffee, so he poured for them as well. The cups, saucers, and spoons were all spotless. Hampstead provided each of them with two crisply folded paper napkins, then sat across the table from them.

"Sure," he said, after they raised the issue, "I knew Jim Roman. Good neighbor. He was a chopper jockey out of the El Toro Air Base. That was my last station before retirement. Jim was a hell of a nice guy, the kind who'd give you the shirt off his back, then ask if you needed money to buy a matching tie."

"Was?" Julie asked.

"He die in the fire?" Bobby asked, remembering the scorched shrubbery and soot-blackened concrete slab next door.

Hampstead frowned. "No. He died about six months after Sharon. Make it . . . two and a half years ago. His chopper crashed on maneuvers. He was only forty-one, eleven years younger than me. Left a wife, Maralee. A fourteen-year-old daughter named Valerie. Twelve-year-old son, Mike. Real nice kids. Terrible thing. They were a close family, and Jim's accident devastated them. They had some relatives back in Nebraska, but no one they could really turn to." Hampstead stared past Bobby, at the softly humming refrigerator, and his eyes swam out of focus. "So I tried to step in, help out, advise Maralee on finances, give a shoulder to lean on and an ear to listen when the kids needed that. Took 'em to Disneyland and Knott's from time to time, you know, that sort of thing. Maralee told me lots of times what a godsend I was, but it was really me who needed them more than the other way around, because doing things for them was what finally began to take my mind off losing Sharon."

Julie said, "So the fire happened more recently?"

Hampstead did not respond. He got up, went to the sink, opened the cupboard door below, returned with a spray bottle of Windex and a dish towel, and began to wipe the refrigerator door, which already appeared to be as clean as the antiseptic surfaces in a hospital surgery. "Valerie and Mike were terrific kids. After a year or so it almost got to seem like they were *my* kids, the ones me and Sharon never had. Maralee grieved for Jim a long time, almost two years, before she began to remember she was a woman in her prime. Maybe what started to happen between her and me would've upset Jim, but I don't think so; I think he'd have been happy for us, even if I was eleven years older than her."

When he finished wiping the refrigerator, Hampstead inspected the door from the side, at an angle to the light, apparently searching for a fingerprint or smudge. As if he had just heard the question that Julie had asked a minute ago, he suddenly said, "The fire was two months ago. I woke up in the middle of the night, heard sirens, saw an orange glow at the window, got up, looked out. . . ."

He turned away from the refrigerator, studied the kitchen for a moment, then went to the nearest tile-topped counter and began to spritz and wipe that gleaming surface.

Julie looked at Bobby. He shook his head. Neither of them said anything.

After a moment Hampstead continued: "Got over to their house just ahead of the firemen. Went in through the front door. Made it into the foyer, then to the foot of the steps, but couldn't get up to the bedroom, the heat was too intense, and the smoke. I called their names, nobody answered. If I'd heard an answer maybe I would've found the strength to go up there somehow in spite of the flames. I guess I must've blacked out for a few seconds and been carried out by firemen, 'cause I woke up on the front lawn, coughing, choking, a paramedic bent over me, giving me oxygen."

"All three of them died?" Bobby asked.

"Yeah," Hampstead said.

"What caused the fire?"

"I'm not sure they ever figured that out. I might've heard something about a short in the wiring, but I'm not sure. I think they even suspected arson for a while, but that never led anywhere. Doesn't much matter, does it?"

"Why not?"

"Whatever caused it, they're all three dead."

"I'm sorry," Bobby said softly.

"Their lot's been sold. Construction starts on a new house sometime this spring. More coffee?"

"No, thank you," Julie said.

Hampstead surveyed the kitchen, then moved to the stainless-steel range hood, which he began to clean in spite of the fact that it was spotless. "I apologize for the mess. Don't know how the place gets like this when it's just me living here. Sometimes I think there must be gremlins sneaking behind my back, messing things up to torment me."

"No need for gremlins," Julie said. "Life itself gives us all the torment we can handle."

Hampstead turned away from the range hood. For the first time since he had gotten up from the table and begun his cleaning ritual, he made eye contact with them. "No gremlins," he agreed. "Nothing as simple and easy to handle as gremlins." He was a big man and obviously tough from years of military training and discipline, but the shimmering, watery evidence of grief brimmed in his eyes, and at the moment he seemed as lost and helpless as a child.

♦   ♦   ♦

IN THE CAR again, staring through the rain-spattered windshield at the vacant lot where the Roman house had once stood, Bobby said, "Frank finds out that Mr. Blue Light knows about the Farris ID, so he gets new ID in the name of James Roman. But Mr. Blue eventually learns about that, too, and he goes looking for Frank at the Roman address, where he discovers only the widow and the kids. He kills them, same way he killed the Farris family, but this time he sets fire to the house to cover the crime. Is that the way it looks to you?"

"Could be," Julie said.

"He burns the bodies because he bites them, like the Phans told us, and the bite marks help the police tie his crimes together, so he wants to throw the cops off the trail."

Julie said, "Then why doesn't he burn them every time?"

"Because that would be just as much of a giveaway as the bite marks. Sometimes he burns the bodies, sometimes he doesn't, and maybe sometimes he disposes of them so they're never even found."

They were both silent for a moment. Then she said, "So we're dealing with a mass murderer, a serial killer, who's evidently a raving psychotic."

"Or a vampire," Bobby said.

"Why's he after Frank?"

"I don't know. Maybe Frank once tried to drive a wooden stake through his heart."

"Not funny."

"I agree," Bobby said. "Right now, nothing seems funny."

162

# 35

FROM DYSON MANFRED'S house full of insect specimens in Irvine, Clint Karaghiosis drove through the chilly rain to his own house in Placentia. It was a homey two-bedroom bungalow with a rolled-shingle roof, a deep front porch in the California Craftsman style, and French windows full of warm amber light. By the time he got there, the car heater had pretty much dried his rain-soaked clothes.

Felina was in the kitchen when Clint entered by way of the connecting door from the garage. She hugged him, kissed him, held fast to him for a moment, as if surprised to see him alive again.

She believed that his job was fraught with danger every day, though he had often explained that he did mostly boring leg-work. He chased facts instead of culprits, pursued a trail of paper rather than blood.

He understood his wife's concern, however, because he worried unreasonably about her too. For one thing, she was an attractive woman with black hair, an olive complexion, and startlingly beautiful gray eyes; in this age of lenient judges, with a surfeit of merciless sociopaths on the streets, a good-looking woman was regarded by some as fair game. Furthermore, though the office where Felina worked as a data processor was only three blocks from their house, an easy walk even in bad weather, Clint nevertheless worried about the danger she faced at the busiest of the intersections that she had to cross; in an emergency, a warning cry or blaring horn would not alert her to onrushing death.

He could not let her know how much he worried, for she was justly proud that she was so independent in spite of her deafness. He did not want to diminish her self-respect by indicating in any way that he was not entirely confident of her ability to deal with every rotten tomato that fate threw at her. So he daily reminded himself that she had lived twenty-nine years without coming to serious harm, and he resisted the urge to be overly protective.

While Clint washed his hands at the sink, Felina set the kitchen table for a late dinner. An enormous pot of homemade vegetable soup was heating on the stove, and together they ladled out two large bowls of it. He got a shaker of Parmesan cheese from the refrigerator, and she unwrapped a loaf of crusty Italian bread.

He was hungry, and the soup was excellent—thick with vegetables and chunks of lean beef—but by the time Felina had finished her first bowlful, Clint had eaten less than half of his, because he repeatedly paused to talk to her. She could not read his lips well when he tried to converse and eat at the same time, and for the moment his hunger was less compelling than his need to tell her about his day. She refilled her bowl and refreshed his.

Beyond the walls of his own small home, he was only slightly more talkative than a stone, but in Felina's company he was as loquacious as a talk-show host. He didn't just prattle, either, but settled with surprising ease into the role of a polished raconteur. He had learned how to deliver an anecdote in such a way as to sharpen its impact and maximize Felina's response, for he loved to elicit a laugh from her or watch her eyes widen with surprise. In all of Clint's life, she was the first person whose opinion of him truly mattered, and he wanted her to think of him as smart, clever, witty, and fun.

Early in their relationship he had wondered if her deafness had anything to do with his ability to open up to her. Deaf since birth, she had never heard the spoken word and therefore had not learned to speak clearly. She responded to Clint—and would later tell him about her own day—by way of sign language, which he had studied in order to understand her nimble-fingered speech. Initially he had thought that the main encouragement to intimacy was her disability, which ensured that his innermost feelings and secrets, once revealed to her, would go no further; a conversation with Felina was nearly as private as a conversation with himself. In time, however, he finally understood that he opened up to her in spite of her deafness, not because of it, and that he wanted her to share his every thought and experience—and to share hers in return—simply because he loved her.

When he told Felina how Bobby and Julie had adjourned to the bathroom for three private chats during Frank Pollard's appointment, she laughed delightedly. He loved that sound; it was so warm and singularly melodious, as if the great joy in life that she could not express in spoken words was entirely channeled into her laughter.

"They're some pair, the Dakotas," he said. "When you first meet them, they seem so dissimilar in some ways, you figure they can't possibly work well together. But then you get to know them, you see how they fit like two pieces of a puzzle, and you realize they've got a nearly perfect relationship."

Felina put down her soup spoon and signed: *So do we.*

"We sure do."

*We fit better than puzzle pieces. We fit like a plug and socket.*

"We sure do," he agreed, smiling. Then he picked up on the sly sexual connotation of what she'd said, and he laughed. "You're a filthy-minded wench, aren't you?"

She grinned and nodded.

"Plug and socket, huh?"

*Big plug, tight socket, good fit.*

"Later on, I'll check your wiring."

*I am in desperate need of a first-rate electrician. But tell me more about this new client.*

Thunder cracked and clattered across the night outside, and a sudden gust of wind rattled the rain against the window. The sounds of the storm made the warm and aromatic kitchen even more inviting by comparison. Clint sighed with contentment, then was touched by a brief sadness when he realized that the deeply satisfying sense of shelter, induced by the sounds of thunder and rain, was a specific pleasure that Felina could never experience or share with him.

From his pants pocket he withdrew one of the red gems that Frank Pollard had brought to the office. "I borrowed this one 'cause I wanted you to see it. The guy had a jarful of them."

She pinched the grape-sized stone between thumb and index finger and held it up to the light. *Beautiful,* she signed with her free hand. She put the gem beside her soup bowl, on the cream-white Formica surface of the kitchen table. *Is it very valuable?*

"We don't know yet," he said. "We'll get an opinion from a gemologist tomorrow."

*I think it's valuable. When you take it back to the office, make sure there's no hole in your pocket. I have a hunch you'd have to work a long time to pay for it if you lost it.*

The stone took in the kitchen light, bounced it from prism to prism, and cast it back with a bright tint, painting Felina's face with luminous crimson spots and smears. She seemed to be spattered with blood.

A queer foreboding overtook Clint.

She signed, *What're you frowning about?*

He didn't know what to say. His uneasiness was out of proportion to the cause of it. A cold prickling swiftly progressed from the base of his spine all the way to the back of his neck, as if dominoes of ice were falling in a row. He reached out and moved the gem a few inches, so the blood-red reflections fell on the wall beside Felina instead of on her face.

# 36

BY ONE-THIRTY in the morning, Hal Yamataka was thoroughly hooked by the John D. MacDonald novel, *The Last One Left*. The room's only chair wasn't the most comfortable seat he'd ever parked his butt in, and the antiseptic smell of the hospital always made him a bit queasy, and the chile rellenos he'd eaten for dinner were still coming back on him, but the book was so involving that eventually he forgot all of those minor discomforts.

He even forgot Frank Pollard for a while, until he heard a brief hiss, like air escaping under pressure, and felt a sudden draft. He looked away from the book, expecting to see Pollard sitting up in the bed or trying to get out of it, but Pollard was not there.

Startled, Hal sprang up, dropping the book.

The bed was empty. Pollard had been there all night, asleep for the last hour, but now he was gone. The place was not brightly lighted because the fluorescents behind the bed were turned off, but the shadows beyond the reading lamp were too shallow to conceal a man. The sheets were not tossed aside but were draped neatly across the mattress, and both of the side railings were locked in place, as if Frank Pollard had evaporated like a figure carved from Dry Ice.

Hal was certain that he would have heard Pollard lower one of the railings, get out of bed, then lift the railing into place again. Surely he would have heard Pollard climbing *over* it too.

The window was closed. Rain washed down the glass, glimmering with silvery reflections of the room's light. They were on the sixth floor, and Pollard could not escape by the window, yet Hal checked it, noting that it was not merely closed but locked.

Stepping to the door of the adjoining bathroom, he said, "Frank?" When no one answered, he entered. The bath was deserted.

Only the narrow closet remained as a viable hiding place. Hal opened it and found two hangers that held the clothes Pollard had been wearing when he'd checked into the hospital. The man's shoes were there, too, with his socks neatly rolled and tucked into them.

"He can't have gotten past me and into the hall," Hal said, as if giving voice to that contention would magically make it true.

He pulled open the heavy door and rushed into the corridor. No one was in sight in either direction.

He turned to the left, hurried to the emergency exit at the end of the hall, and opened the door. Standing on the sixth-floor landing, he listened for footsteps rising or descending, heard none, peered over the iron railing, down into the well, then up. He was alone.

Retracing his steps, he returned to Pollard's room and glanced inside at the empty bed. Still disbelieving, he proceeded to the junction of corridors, where he turned right and went to the glass-walled nurses' station.

None of the five night-shift nurses had seen Pollard on the move. Since the elevators were directly opposite the nurses' station, where Pollard would have had to wait in full view of the people on duty, it seemed unlikely that he had left the hospital by that route.

"I thought you were watching over him," said Grace Fulgham, the gray-haired supervisor of the sixth-floor night staff. Her solid build, indomitable manner, and life-worn but kind face would have made her perfect for the female lead if Hollywood ever started remaking the old Tugboat Annie or Ma and Pa Kettle movies. "Wasn't that your job?"

"I never left the room, but—"

"Then how did he get past you?"

"I don't know," Hal said, chagrined. "But the important thing is . . . he's suffering from partial amnesia, somewhat confused. He might wander off anywhere, out of the hospital, God knows where. I can't figure how he got past me, but we have to find him."

Mrs. Fulgham and a younger nurse named Janet Soto began a swift and quiet inspection of all the rooms along Pollard's corridor.

Hal accompanied Nurse Fulgham. As they were checking out 604, where two elderly men snored softly, he heard eerie music, barely audible. As he turned, seeking the source, the notes faded away.

If Nurse Fulgham heard the music, she did not remark on it. A moment later in the next room, 606, when those strains arose once more, marginally louder than before, she whispered, "What *is* that?"

To Hal it sounded like a flute. The unseen flautist produced no discernible melody, but the flow of notes was haunting nonetheless.

They reentered the hall as the music stopped again, and just as a draft swept along the corridor.

"Someone's left a window open—or probably a stairway door," the nurse said quietly but pointedly.

"Not me," Hal assured her.

Janet Soto stepped out of the room across the hall just as the blustery draft abruptly died. She frowned at them, shrugged, then headed toward the next room on her side.

The flute warbled softly. The draft struck up again, stronger than before, and beneath the astringent odors of the hospital, Hal thought he detected a faint scent of smoke.

Leaving Grace Fulgham to her search, Hal hurried toward the far end of the corridor. He intended to check the door at the head of the emergency stairs, to make sure that he hadn't left it open.

From the corner of his eye, he saw the door to Pollard's room beginning to swing shut, and he realized that the draft must be coming from in there. He pushed through the door before it could close, and saw Frank sitting up in bed, looking confused and frightened.

The draft and flute had given way to stillness, silence.

"Where did you go?" Hal asked, approaching the bed.

"Fireflies," Pollard said, apparently dazed. His hair was spiked and tangled, and his round face was pale.

"Fireflies?"

"Fireflies in a windstorm," Pollard said.

Then he vanished. One second he was sitting in bed, as real and solid as anyone Hal had ever known, and the next second he was gone as inexplicably and neatly as a ghost abandoning a haunt. A brief hiss, like air escaping from a punctured tire, accompanied his departure.

Hal swayed as if he had been stricken. For a moment his heart seemed to seize up, and he was paralyzed by surprise.

Nurse Fulgham stepped into the doorway. "No sign of him in any of the rooms off this corridor. He might've gone up or down another floor—don't you think?"

"Uh. . . ."

"Before we check out the rest of this level, maybe I'd better call security and get them moving on a search of the entire hospital. Mr. Yamataka?"

Hal glanced at her, then back at the empty bed. "Uh . . . yeah. Yeah, that's a good idea. He might wander off to . . . God knows where."

Nurse Fulgham hurried away.

Weak-kneed, Hal went to the door, closed it, put his back against it, and stared at the bed across the room. After a while he said, "Are you there, Frank?"

He received no answer. He had not expected one. Frank Pollard had not turned invisible; he had *gone* somewhere, somehow.

Not sure why he was less wonderstruck than frightened by what he had seen, Hal hesitantly crossed the room to the bed. He gingerly touched the stainless-steel railing, as if he thought that Pollard's vanishing act had tapped some elemental force, leaving a deadly residual current in the bed. But no sparks crackled under his fingertips; the metal was cool and smooth.

He waited, wondering how soon Pollard would reappear, wondering if he ought to call Bobby now or wait until Pollard materialized, wondering if the man *would* materialize again or disappear forever. For the first time in memory, Hal Yamataka was gripped by indecision; he was ordinarily a quick thinker, and quick to act, but he had never come face to face with the supernatural before.

The only thing he knew for sure was that he must not let

Fulgham or Soto or anyone else in the hospital know what had really happened. Pollard was caught up in a phenomenon so strange that word of it would spread quickly from the hospital staff to the press. Protecting a client's privacy was always one of Dakota & Dakota's prime objectives, but in this case it was even more important than usual. Bobby and Julie had said that someone was hunting for Pollard, evidently with violent intentions; therefore, keeping the press out of the case might be essential if the client was to survive.

The door opened, and Hal jumped as if he'd been stuck with a hatpin.

In the doorway stood Grace Fulgham, looking as if she had just either guided a tugboat through stormy seas or chopped and carried a couple of cords of firewood that Pa had been too lazy to deal with. "Security's putting a man at every exit to stop him if he tries to leave, and we're mobilizing the nursing staff on each floor to look for him. Do you intend to join the search?"

"Uh, well, I've got to call the office, my boss. . . ."

"If we find him, where will we find you?"

"Here. Right here. I'll be here, making some calls."

She nodded and went away. The door eased shut after her.

A privacy curtain hung from a ceiling track that described an arc around three sides of the bed. It was bunched against the wall, but Hal Yamataka drew it to the foot of the bed, blocking the view from the doorway, in case Pollard materialized just as someone stepped in from the corridor.

His hands were shaking, so he jammed them in his pockets. Then he took his left hand out to look at his wristwatch: 1:48.

Pollard had been missing for perhaps eighteen minutes—except, of course, for the few seconds during which he had flickered into existence and talked about fireflies in a windstorm. Hal decided to wait until two o'clock to call Bobby and Julie.

He stood at the foot of the bed, clutching the railing with one hand, listening to the night wind crying at the window and the rain snapping against the glass. The minutes crawled past like snails on an incline, but at least the wait gave him time to calm down and think about how he would tell Bobby what had happened.

As the hands on his watch lined up at two o'clock, he went the rest of the way around the bed and was reaching for the phone on the nightstand when he heard the eerie ululation of a distant flute. The half-drawn bed-curtain fluttered in a sudden draft.

He returned to the foot of the bed and looked past the end of the curtain to the hallway door. It was closed. That was not the source of the draft.

The flute died. The air in the room grew still, leaden.

Abruptly the curtain shivered and rippled, gently rattling the bearings in the overhead track, and a breath of cool air swept around the room, ruffling his hair. The atonal, ghostly music rose again.

With the door shut and the window closed tight, the only possible source of the draft was the ventilation grille in the wall above the nightstand. But when Hal stood on his toes and raised his right hand in front of that outlet, he felt nothing issuing from it. The chilly currents of air appeared to have sprung up within the room itself.

He turned in a circle, moved this way and that, trying to get a fix on the flute. Actually, it didn't sound like a flute when he listened closely; it was more like a fluctuant wind whistling through a lot of pipes at the same time, big ones and little ones, threading together many vague but separate sounds into a loosely woven keening that was simultaneously eerie and melancholy, mournful yet somehow . . . threatening. It faded, then returned a third time. To his surprise and bewilderment, the tuneless notes seemed to be issuing from the empty air above the bed.

Hal wondered if anyone else in the hospital could hear the flute this time. Probably not. Though the music was louder now than when it had begun, it remained faint; in fact, if he had been asleep, the mysterious serenade would not have been loud enough to wake him.

Before Hal's eyes, the air over the bed shimmered. For a moment he could not breathe, as if the room had become a temporary vacuum chamber. He felt his ears pop the way they did during a too-rapid altitude change.

The strange warbling and the draft died together, and Frank Pollard reappeared as abruptly as he had vanished. He was lying on his side, with his knees drawn up in the fetal position. For a few seconds he was disoriented; when he realized where he was, he clutched the bed railing and pulled himself into a sitting position. The skin around his eyes was puffy and dark, but other-

*171*

wise he was dreadfully pale. His face had a greasy sheen to it, as if it wasn't perspiration pouring from him but clear beads of oil. His blue cotton pajamas were rumpled, darkly mottled with sweat, and caked with dirt in places.

He said, "Stop me."

"What the hell's going on here?" Hal asked, his voice cracking.

"Out of control."

"Where did you go?"

"For God's sake, help me." Pollard was still clutching the bed rail with his right hand, but he reached entreatingly toward Hal with his left. "Please, please . . ."

Stepping closer to the bed, Hal reached out—

—and Pollard vanished, this time not only with a hissing sound, as before, but with a shriek and sharp crack of tortured metal. The stainless-steel railing, which he had been gripping so fiercely, had torn loose of the bed and vanished with him.

Hal Yamataka stared in astonishment at the hinges to which the adjustable railing had been fixed. They were twisted and torn, as if made of cardboard. A force of incredible power had pulled Pollard out of that room, snapping quarter-inch steel.

Staring at his own outstretched hand, Hal wondered what would have happened to him if he had been gripping Pollard. Would he have disappeared with the man? To where? Not someplace he would want to be: he was sure of that.

Or maybe only part of him would have gone with Pollard. Maybe he would have come apart at a joint, just as the bed railing had done. Maybe his arm would have ripped out of his shoulder socket with a crack almost as sharp as that with which the steel hinges had separated, and maybe he would have been left screaming in pain, with blood squirting from snapped vessels.

He snatched his hand back, as if afraid Pollard might suddenly reappear and seize it.

As he rounded the bed to the phone, he thought that his legs were going to fail him. His hands were shaking so badly, he almost dropped the receiver and had difficulty dialing the Dakotas' home number.

# 37

BOBBY AND JULIE left for the hospital at 2:45. The night looked deeper than usual; streetlamps and headlights did not fully penetrate the gloom. Shatters of rain fell with such force, they appeared to bounce off the blacktop streets, as if they were hard fragments of a disintegrating vault that arced through the night above.

Julie drove because Bobby was only three-quarters awake. His eyes were heavy, and he couldn't stop yawning, and his thoughts were fuzzy at the edges. They had gone to bed only three hours before Hal Yamataka had awakened them. If Julie had to get by on only that much sleep, she could do it, but Bobby needed at least six—preferably eight—hours in the sack in order to function well.

That was a minor difference between them, no big deal. But because of several such minor differences, Bobby suspected that Julie was tougher overall than he was, even if he could whip her ten times out of ten in an arm-wrestling competition.

He chuckled softly.

She said, "What?"

She braked for a traffic light as it phased to red. Its bloody image was reflected in distorted patterns by the black, mirror-like surface of the rain-slick street.

"I'm crazy to give you an advantage by admitting this, but I was thinking that in some ways you're tougher than me."

She said, "That's no revelation. I've always known I'm tougher."

"Oh, yeah? If we arm wrestle, I'll whip you every time."

"How sad." She shook her head. "Do you really think beating up someone smaller than you, and a woman to boot, makes you a macho man?"

"I could beat up a lot of women *bigger* than me," Bobby assured her. "And if they're old enough, I could take them on two or three or four at a time. In fact, you throw half a dozen big grandmothers at me, and I'll take them all on with one hand tied behind my back!"

The traffic light turned green, and she drove on.

"I'm talking *big* grandmothers," he said. "Not frail little old ladies. Big, fat, solid grandmothers, six at a time."

"That is impressive."

"Damn right. Though it'd help if I had a tire iron."

She laughed, and he grinned. But they could not forget where they were going or why, and their smiles faded to a pair of matching frowns. They drove in silence. The thump of the windshield wipers, which ought to have lulled Bobby to sleep, kept him awake instead.

Finally Julie said, "You think Frank actually vanished in front of Hal's eyes, the way he says?"

"I've never known Hal to lie or give in to hysteria."

"Me neither."

She turned left at the next corner. A few blocks ahead, beyond billowing curtains of rain, the lights of the hospital appeared to pulse and flicker and stream like an iridescent liquid, which made it look every bit as miragelike as a phantom oasis shimmering behind veils of heat rising from desert sands.

♦ ♦ ♦

WHEN THEY entered the room, Hal was standing at the foot of the bed, which was largely concealed by the privacy curtain. He looked like a guy who had not only seen a ghost, but had embraced it and kissed it on its cold, damp, putrescent lips.

"Thank God, you're here." He looked past them, into the hall. "The head nurse wants to call the cops, file a missing person—"

"We've dealt with that," Bobby said. "Dr. Freeborn talked to her by phone, and we've signed a release absolving the hospital."

"Good." Gesturing toward the open door, Hal said, "We'll want to keep this as private as we can."

After closing the door, Julie joined them at the foot of the bed.

Bobby noted the missing railing and broken hinges. "What's this?"

Hal swallowed hard. "He was holding the railing when he vanished . . . and it went with him. I didn't mention it on the phone, 'cause I figured you already thought I was nuts, and this would confirm it."

"Tell us now," Julie said quietly. They were all talking softly, for otherwise Nurse Fulgham was certain to stop by and remind them that most of the patients on the floor were sleeping.

When Hal finished his story, Bobby said, "The flute, the peculiar breeze . . . that's what Frank told us *he* heard shortly after he regained consciousness that night in the alleyway, and somehow he knew it meant someone was coming."

Some of the dirt that Hal had observed on Frank's pajamas, after his second reappearance, was on the bed sheets. Julie plucked up a pinch of it. "Not dirt exactly."

Bobby examined the grains on her fingertips. "Black sand."

To Hal, Julie said, "Frank hasn't reappeared since he vanished with the railing?"

"No."

"And when was that?"

"A couple of minutes after two o'clock. Maybe two-oh-two, two-oh-three, something like that."

"About an hour and twenty minutes ago," Bobby said.

They stood in silence, staring at the mountings from which the bed railing had been torn. Outside, a squall of wind threw rain against the window with sufficient force to make it sound like out-of-season Halloween pranksters pitching handsful of dried corn.

Finally Bobby looked at Julie. "What do we do now?"

She blinked. "Don't ask me. This is the first case I've ever worked on that involves witchcraft."

"Witchcraft?" Hal said nervously.

"Just a figure of speech," Julie assured him.

Maybe, Bobby thought. He said, "We've got to assume he'll come back before morning, perhaps a couple of times, and sooner or later he'll stay put. This must be what happens every night when he sleeps; this is the traveling he doesn't remember when he wakes up."

"Traveling," Julie said. Under the circumstances, that ordinary word seemed as exotic and full of mystery as any in the language.

♦　♦　♦

CAREFUL NOT to wake the patients, they borrowed two additional chairs from other rooms along the corridor. Hal sat tensely just inside the closed door of room 638, in a position to prevent any of the hospital staff from walking in unimpeded. Julie sat at the foot of the bed, and Bobby stationed himself at the side of it nearest the window, where the railing was still in place.

They waited.

From her chair, Julie only had to turn her head slightly to look across the room at Hal. When she glanced the other way she could see Bobby. But because of the privacy curtain that was drawn along the side of the bed with the missing railing, Hal and Bobby were not in each other's line of sight.

She wondered if Hal would have been astonished to see how quickly Bobby went to sleep. Hal was still pumped up by what had happened, and Julie, only having heard about Frank's sorcerous disappearance second-hand, was nonetheless eagerly— and nervously—anticipating the chance to witness the same bit of magic herself. Bobby was a man of considerable imaginative powers, with a childlike sense of wonder, so he was probably more excited about these events than either she or Hal was; furthermore, because of his premonition of trouble, he suspected that the case was going to be full of surprises, some nasty, and these events no doubt alarmed him. Yet he could slump against the inadequately padded arm of his chair, let his chin drop against his chest, and doze off. He would never be felled by stress. At times his sense of proportion, his ability to put *anything* in a manageable perspective, seemed superhuman. When Bobby McFerrin's song "Don't Worry, Be Happy" had been a hit a couple of years ago, she had not been surprised that her own Bobby had been enamoured of it; the tune was essentially his personal anthem. Apparently by an act of will, he could readily achieve serenity, and she admired that.

By 4:40, when Bobby had been slumbering contentedly for nearly an hour, she watched him doze with admiration that rapidly escalated to unhealthy envy. She had the urge to give his chair a kick, toppling him out of it. She restrained herself only because she suspected that he would merely yawn, curl up on his side, and sleep even more comfortably on the floor, at which point her envy would become so all-consuming that she would simply have to kill him where he lay. She imagined herself in court: *I know murder is wrong, Judge, but he was just too laid-back to live.*

A cascade of soft, almost melancholy notes fell out of the air in front of her.

"The flute!" Hal said, leaving his chair with the suddenness of a popcorn kernel bursting off a heated pan.

Simultaneously, a breath of cool air stirred through the room, without apparent source.

Getting to her feet, Julie whispered, "Bobby!"

She shook him by the shoulder, and he came awake just as the atonal music faded and the air turned crypt-still.

Bobby rubbed his eyes with his palms, and yawned. "What's wrong?"

Even as he spoke, the haunting music swelled again, faint but louder than before. Not music, actually, just noise. And Hal was right: listening closely, you could also tell it was not a flute.

She stepped toward the bed.

Hal had left his station by the door. He put a hand on her shoulder, halting her. "Be careful."

Frank had reported three—maybe four—separate trillings of the faux flute, and as many agitations of the air, before Mr. Blue Light had appeared on his trail that night in Anaheim, and Hal had noticed that three episodes had preceded each of Frank's own reappearances. However, those accompanying phenomena evidently could not be expected in an immutable pattern, for when the second rivulet of unharmonious notes finished spilling out of the ether, the air immediately above the bed shimmered, as if a double handful of pale tarnished sequins had been swept up and set aflutter in rising currents of heat, and suddenly Frank Pollard winked into existence atop the rumpled sheets.

Julie's ears popped.

"Holy cow!" Bobby said, which was just what Julie would have expected him to say.

She, on the other hand, was unable to speak.

Gasping, Frank Pollard sat up in bed. His face was bloodless. Around his rheumy eyes, the skin looked bruised. Sour perspiration glistened on his face and beaded in his beard stubble.

He was holding a pillowcase half filled with something. The end was twisted and held shut with a length of cord. He let go of it, and it fell off the side of the bed where the railing was missing, striking the floor with a soft *plop.*

When he spoke, his voice was hoarse and strange. "Where am I?"

"You're in the hospital, Frank," Bobby said. "It's all right. You're where you belong now."

"Hospital . . . ," Frank said, savoring the word as if he had just heard it—and was now pronouncing it—for the first time. He looked around, obviously bewildered; he still didn't know where he was. "Don't let me slip—"

He vanished midsentence. A brief hiss accompanied his abrupt departure, as if the air in the room was escaping through a puncture in the skin of reality.

"Damn!" Julie said.

"Where were his pajamas?" Hal said.

"What?"

"He was wearing shoes, khaki pants, a shirt and sweater," Hal said, "but the last time I saw him, a couple of hours ago, he still had on his pajamas."

At the far end of the room, the door began to open but bumped against Hal's empty chair. Nurse Fulgham poked her head through the gap. She looked down at the chair, then across the room at Hal and Julie, then at Bobby, who stepped to the foot of the bed to peer past his two associates and the half-drawn privacy curtain.

Their astonishment at Frank's vanishing act must have been ill concealed, for the woman frowned and said, "What's wrong?"

Julie quickly crossed the room as Grace Fulgham slid the chair aside and opened the door all the way. "Everything's fine. We just spoke by phone with our man heading up the search, and he says they've found someone who saw Mr. Pollard earlier tonight. We know which way he was heading, so now it's only a matter of time until we find him."

"We didn't expect you'd be here so long," Fulgham said, frowning past Julie at the curtained bed.

Even through the heavy door, maybe she had heard the faint warble of the flute that wasn't a flute.

"Well," Julie said, "this is the easiest place from which to coordinate the search."

By standing just inside the door, with Hal's empty chair between them, Julie was trying to block the nurse's advance without appearing to do so. If Fulgham got past the curtain, she might notice the missing railing, the black sand in the bed, and the pillowcase that was filled with God-knew-what. Questions about any of those things might be difficult to answer convincingly, and if the nurse remained in the room too long, she might be there when Frank returned.

Julie said, "I'm sure we haven't disturbed any of the other patients. We've been very quiet."

"No, no," Nurse Fulgham said, "you haven't disturbed anyone. We just wondered if you might like some coffee to help keep you awake."

"Oh." Julie turned to look at Hal and Bobby. "Coffee?"

"No," the two men said simultaneously. Then, speaking over each other, Hal said, "No, thank you," and Bobby said, "Very kind of you."

"I'm wide awake," Julie said, frantic to be rid of the woman, but trying to sound casual, "and Hal doesn't drink coffee, and Bobby, my husband, can't handle caffeine because of prostate problems." I'm babbling, she thought. "Anyway, we'll be leaving soon now, I'm sure."

"Well," the nurse said, "if you change your mind. . . ."

After Fulgham left, letting the door close behind her, Bobby whispered, "Prostate trouble?"

Julie said, "Too much caffeine causes prostate trouble. Seemed like a convincing detail to explain why, with all your yawning, you didn't want coffee."

"But I don't have a prostate problem. Makes me sound like an old fart."

"I have it," Hal said. "And I'm not an old fart."

"What is this?" Julie said. "We're *all* babbling."

She pushed the chair in front of the door and returned to the bed, where she picked up the pillowcase-bag that Frank Pollard had brought from . . . from wherever he had been.

"Careful," Bobby said. "Last time Frank mentioned a pillowcase, it was the one he trapped that insect in."

Julie gingerly set the bag on a chair and watched it closely. "Doesn't seem to be anything squirming around in it." She started to untie the knotted cord from the neck of the sack.

Grimacing, Bobby said, "If you let out something big as a house cat, with a lot of legs and feelers, I'm going straight to a divorce lawyer."

The cord slipped free. She pulled open the pillowcase, and looked inside. "Oh, God."

Bobby took a couple of steps backward.

"No, not that," she assured him. "No bugs. Just more cash." She reached into the sack and withdrew a couple of bundles of hundred-dollar bills. "If it's all hundreds, there could be as much as a quarter of a million in here."

"What's Frank doing?" Bobby wondered. "Laundering money for the mob in the Twilight Zone?"

Hollow, lonely, tuneless piping pierced the air again, and like a needle pulling thread, the sound brought with it a draft that rustled the curtain.

Shivering, Julie turned to look at the bed.

The flutelike notes faded with the draft, then soon rose again, faded, rose, and faded a fourth time as Frank Pollard reappeared. He was on his side, arms against his chest, hands fisted, grimacing, his eyes squeezed shut, as if he were preparing himself to receive the killing blow of an ax.

Julie stepped toward the bed, and again Hal stopped her.

Frank sucked in a deep breath, shuddered, made a low anguished mewling, opened his eyes—and vanished. Within two or three seconds, he appeared yet again, still shuddering. But immediately he vanished, reappeared, vanished, reappeared, vanished, as if he were an image flickering on a television set with poor signal reception. At last he stuck fast to the fabric of reality and lay on the bed, moaning.

After rolling off his side, onto his back, he gazed at the ceiling. He raised his fists from his chest, uncurled them, and stared at his hands, baffled, as if he had never seen fingers before.

"Frank?" Julie said.

He did not respond to her. With his fingertips he explored the contours of his face, as if a Braille reading of his features would recall to him the forgotten specifics of his appearance.

Julie's heart was racing, and every muscle in her body felt as if it had been twisted up as tight as an overwound clock spring. She was not afraid, really. It was not a tension engendered by fear but by the sheer *strangeness* of what had happened. "Frank, are you okay?"

Blinking through the interstices of his fingers, he said, "Oh. It's you, Mrs. Dakota. Yeah . . . Dakota. What's happened? Where am I?"

"You're in the hospital now," Bobby said. "Listen, the important question isn't where you are, but where the hell have you *been?*"

"Been? Well . . . what do you mean?"

Frank tried to sit up in bed, but he seemed temporarily to lack the strength to get off his back.

Picking up the bed controls, Bobby elevated the upper half

of the mattress. "You weren't in this room during most of the last few hours. It's almost five in the morning, and you've been jumping in and out of here like . . . like . . . like a crew member of the Starship *Enterprise* who keeps beaming back up to the mothership!"

"*Enterprise?* Beaming up? What're you talking about?"

Bobby looked at Julie. "Whoever this guy is, wherever he comes from, we now know for sure that he's been living out past the edge of modern culture, on the fringe. You ever known a modern American who hasn't at least *heard* of *Star Trek?*"

To Bobby, Julie said, "Thanks for your analysis, Mr. Spock."

"Mr. Spock?" Frank said.

"See!" Bobby said.

"We can question Frank later," Julie said. "He's confused right now, anyway. We've got to get him out of here. If that nurse comes back and sees him, how do we explain his reappearance? Is she really going to believe he wandered back *into* the hospital, past security and the nursing staff, up six floors, with nobody spotting him?"

"Yeah," Hal said, "and though he seems to be back for good, what if he pops away again, in front of her eyes?"

"Okay, so we'll get him out of bed and sneak him down those stairs at the end of the hall," Julie said, "out to the car."

As they talked about him, Frank turned his head back and forth, following the conversation. He appeared to be watching a tennis match for the first time, unable to comprehend the rules of the game.

Bobby said, "Once we've gotten him out of here, we can tell Fulgham he's been found just a few blocks away and that we're meeting with him to determine whether he wants—or even needs—to be returned to the hospital. He's our client, after all, not our ward, and we have to respect his wishes."

Without having to wait for tests to be conducted, they now knew that Frank was not suffering strictly from physical ailments like cerebral abscesses, clots, aneurysms, cysts, or neoplasms. His amnesia did not spring from brain tumors, but from something far stranger and more exotic than that. No malignancy, regardless of how singular its nature, would invest its victim with the power to step into the fourth dimension—or to wherever Frank was stepping when he vanished.

"Hal," Julie said, "get Frank's other clothes from the closet, bundle them up, and stuff them in the pillowcase with the money."

"Will do."

"Bobby, help me get Frank out of bed, see if he can stand on his own feet. He looks awful weak."

The remaining bed railing stuck for a moment when Bobby tried to lower it, but he struggled with it because they could not take Frank out of bed on the other side without drawing back the privacy curtain and exposing him to anyone who might push open the door.

"You could've done me a big favor and packed this rail off to Oz with the other one," Bobby told Frank, and Frank said, "Oz?"

When the railing finally folded down, out of the way, Julie found that she was hesitant to touch Frank, for fear of what might happen to her—or parts of her—if he pulled another disappearing act. She had seen the shattered hinges of the bed railing; she was also keenly aware that Frank had not brought the railing back with him, but had abandoned it in the other-where or otherwhen to which he traveled.

Bobby hesitated, too, but overcame his apprehension, grabbing the man's legs and swinging them over the edge of the bed, taking hold of his arm and helping him into a sitting position. In some ways she might be tougher than Bobby, but when it came to encounters with the unknown, he was clearly more flexible and quick to adapt than she was.

Finally she quelled her fear, and together she and Bobby assisted Frank off the bed and onto his feet. His legs buckled under him, and they had to support him. He complained of weakness and dizziness.

Stuffing the other set of clothes in the pillowcase, Hal said, "If we have to, Bobby and I can carry him."

"I'm sorry to be so much trouble," Frank said.

To Julie, he had never sounded or looked more pathetic, and she felt a flush of guilt about her reluctance to touch him.

Flanking Frank, their arms around him to provide support, Julie and Bobby walked him back and forth, past the rain-washed window, giving him a chance to recover the use of his legs. Gradually his strength and balance returned.

"But my pants keep trying to fall down," Frank said.

They propped him against the bed, and he leaned on Julie

while Bobby lifted the blue cotton sweater to see if the belt needed to be cinched in one notch. The tongue end of the belt was weakened by scores of small holes, as if industrious insects had been boring at it. But what insects ate leather? When Bobby touched the tarnished brass buckle, it crumbled as though made of flaky pastry dough.

Gaping at the glittering crumbs of metal on his fingers, Bobby said, "Where do you shop for clothes, Frank? In a dumpster?"

In spite of Bobby's light tone, Julie knew he was unnerved. What substance or circumstances could so profoundly alter the composition of brass? When he brushed his fingers against the bed sheets to wipe off the curious residue, she flinched, half expecting his flesh to have been contaminated by the contact with the brass, and to crumble as the buckle had done.

◆   ◆   ◆

AFTER CINCHING Frank's pants with the belt that he had worn when he'd checked into the hospital, Hal helped Bobby slip their client out of the room. With Julie scouting the way, they went quickly and quietly along the hall and through the fire door at the head of the emergency stairs. Frank's skin remained cold to the touch, and he was still clammy with perspiration; but the effort brought a flush to his cheeks, which made him look less like a walking corpse.

Julie hurried to the bottom of the stairwell to see what lay beyond the lower door. With the thump and scrape of their footsteps echoing hollowly off the bare concrete walls, the three men went down four flights without much difficulty. At the fourth-floor landing, however, they had to pause to let Frank catch his breath.

"Are you always this weak when you wake up and don't remember where you've been?" Bobby asked.

Frank shook his head. His words issued in a thin wheeze: "No. Always frightened . . . tired, but not as bad . . . as this. I feel like . . . whatever I'm doing . . . wherever I'm going . . . it's taking a bigger and bigger toll. I'm not . . . not going to survive . . . a lot more of this."

As Frank was talking, Bobby noticed something peculiar about the man's blue cotton sweater. The pattern of the cable knit was wildly irregular in places, as if the knitting machine had briefly gone berserk. And on the back, near his right shoulderblade, a patch of fibers was missing; the hole was the size of a block of four postage stamps, though with irregular rather than straight edges. But it wasn't just a hole. A piece of what appeared to be khaki filled the gap, not merely sewn on but woven tightly into the surrounding cotton yarn, as if at the garment factory itself. Khaki of the same shade and hard finish as the pants that Frank was wearing.

A shiver of dread pierced Bobby, although he was not sure why. His subconscious mind seemed to understand how the patch had come to be and what it meant, and grasped some hideous consequence not yet fulfilled, while his conscious mind was baffled.

He saw that Hal, on the other side of Frank, had noticed the patch, too, and was frowning.

Julie ascended the stairs while Bobby was staring in puzzlement at the khaki swatch. "We're in luck," she said. "There're two doors at the bottom. One leads into a hallway off the lobby, where we'd probably run into a security man, even though they aren't looking for Frank any more. But the other door leads into the parking garage, the same level our car's on. How you doing, Frank? You going to be okay?"

"Getting my . . . second wind," he said less wheezily than before.

"Look at this," Bobby said, calling Julie's attention to the khaki woven into the blue cotton sweater.

While Julie studied the peculiar patch, Bobby let go of Frank and, on a hunch, stooped down to examine the legs of his client's pants. He found a corresponding irregularity: blue cotton yarn from the sweater was woven into the slacks. It was not one spot of the same size and shape as that in the sweater, but a series of three smaller holes near the cuff on the right leg; however, he was sure that more accurate measurements would confirm what he knew from a quick look—that the total amount of blue yarn in those three holes would just about fill the hole in the shoulder of the sweater.

"What's wrong?" Frank asked.

Bobby didn't respond but took hold of the somewhat baggy leg of the pants and pulled it taut, so he could get a better look at the three patches. Actually, "patches" was an inaccurate word because these abnormalities in the fabric did not look like repairs; they were too well blended with the material around them to be handwork.

Julie squatted beside him and said, "First, we've got to get Frank out of here, back to the office."

"Yeah, but this is real strange," Bobby said, indicating the irregularities in the pants. "Strange and . . . important somehow."

"What's wrong?" Frank repeated.

"Where'd you get these clothes?" Bobby asked him.

"Well . . . I don't know."

Julie pointed to the white athletic sock on Frank's right foot, and Bobby saw at once what had caught her attention: several blue threads, precisely the color of the sweater. They were not loose, clinging to the sock. They were woven into the very fabric of it.

Then he noticed Frank's left shoe. It was a dark brown hiking shoe, but a few thin, squiggly white lines marred the leather on the toe. When he studied them closely, he saw that the lines appeared to be coarse threads like those in the athletic socks; scraping at them with one fingernail, he discovered they were not stuck to the shoe, but were an integral part of the surface of the leather.

The missing yarn of the sweater had somehow become a part of both the khaki pants and one of the socks; the displaced threads of the sock had become part of the shoe on the other foot.

"What's wrong?" Frank repeated, more fearfully than before.

Bobby hesitated to look up, expecting to see that the filaments of displaced shoe leather were embedded in Frank's face, and that the displaced flesh was magically entwined with the cable knit of the sweater. He stood and forced himself to confront his client.

Aside from the dark and puffy rings around his eyes, the sickly pallor relieved only by the flush on his upper cheeks, and the fear and confusion that gave him a tormented look, nothing was wrong with his face. No leather ornamentation. No khaki stitched into his lips. No filaments of blue yarn or plastic shoelace tips or button fragments bristling from his eyeballs.

Silently castigating himself for his overactive imagination, Bobby patted Frank's shoulder. "It's okay. It's all right. We'll figure it out later. Come on, let's get you out of here."

# 38

IN THE EMBRACE of darkness, enwrapped by the scent of Chanel No. 5, under the very blankets and sheets that had once warmed his mother and that he had so carefully preserved, Candy dozed and awakened repeatedly with a start, though he could not remember any nightmares.

Between periods of fitful sleep, he dwelt on the incident in the canyon, earlier that night, when he had been hunting and had felt an unseen presence put a hand on his head. He'd never before experienced anything like that. He was disturbed by the encounter, unsure whether it was threatening or benign, and anxious to understand it.

He first wondered if it had been his mother's angelic presence, hovering above him. But he quickly dismissed that explanation. If his mother had stepped through the veil between this world and the next, he would have recognized her spirit, her singular aura of love, warmth, and compassion. He would have fallen to his knees under the weight of her ghostly hand and wept with joy at her visitation.

Briefly he had considered that one or both of his inscrutable sisters possessed a heretofore unrevealed talent for psychic contact and reached out to him for unknown reasons. After all, somehow they controlled their cats and appeared to have equal influence over other small animals. Maybe they could enter human minds as well. He didn't want that pale, cold-eyed pair invading his privacy. At times he looked at them and thought of snakes—sinuous albino snakes, silent and watchful—with desires as alien as any that motivated reptiles. The possibility that they could intrude into his mind was chilling, even if they could not control him.

But between bouts of sleep, he abandoned that idea. If Violet and Verbina possessed such abilities, they would have enslaved him long ago, as thoroughly as they had enslaved the cats. They would have forced him to do degrading, obscene things; they did not possess his self-control in matters of the flesh and would live, if they could, in constant violation of God's most fundamental commandments.

He could not understand why his mother had sworn him to keep and protect them, any more than he could understand how she could love them. Of course her compassion for those miscreant offspring was only one more example of her saintly nature. Forgiveness and understanding flowed from her like clear, cool water from an artesian well.

For a while he dozed. When he woke with a start again, he turned on his side and watched the faint light of dawn appear along the edges of the drawn blinds.

He considered the possibility that the presence in the canyon had been his brother Frank. But that was also unlikely. If Frank had possessed telepathic abilities, he would have found a way to employ them to destroy Candy a long, long time ago. Frank was less talented than his sisters and much less talented than his brother Candy.

Then who had approached him twice in the canyon, insistently pressing into his mind? Who sent the disconnected words that echoed in his head: *What . . . where . . . what . . . why . . . what . . . where . . . what . . . why . . . ?*

Last night, he'd tried to get a mental grip on the presence. When it hastily withdrew from him, he had tried to let part of his consciousness soar up into the night with it, but he had been unable to sustain a pursuit on that psychic plane. He sensed, however, that he might be able to develop that ability.

If the unwelcome presence ever returned, he would try to knot a filament of his mind to it and trace it to its source. In his twenty-nine years, his own siblings were the only people he had encountered with what might be called psychic abilities. If someone out there in the world was also gifted, he must learn who it was. Such a person, not born of his sainted mother, was a rival, a threat, an enemy.

Though the sun beyond the blinded windows had not fully risen, he knew that he would not be able to doze again. He threw back the covers, crossed the dark and furniture-crowded room with the assurance of a blind man in a familiar place, and went into the adjoining bath. After locking the door, he undressed without glancing in the mirror. He peed forcefully without looking down at his hateful organ. When he showered, he soaped and rinsed the sex thing only with the washcloth mitten that he'd made and that protected his innocent hand from being corrupted by the monstrous, wicked flesh below.

# 39

FROM THE HOSPITAL in Orange, they went directly to their offices in Newport Beach. They had a lot of work to do on Frank's behalf, and his worsening plight evoked in them a greater sense of urgency than ever. Frank rode with Hal, and Julie followed in order to be able to offer assistance if unforeseen developments occurred during the trip. The entire case seemed to be a *series* of unforeseen developments.

By the time they reached their deserted offices—the Dakota & Dakota staff would not arrive for a couple of hours yet—the sun was fully risen behind the clouds in the east. A thin strip of blue sky, like a crack under the door of the storm, was visible over the ocean to the west. As the four of them passed through the reception lounge into their inner sanctum, the rain halted abruptly, as if a godly hand had turned a celestial lever; the water on the big windows stopped flowing in shimmering sheets, and coalesced into hundreds of small beads that glimmered with a mercury-gray sheen in the cloud-dulled morning light.

Bobby indicated the bulging pillowcase that Hal was carrying. "Take Frank into the bathroom, help him change into the clothes he was wearing when we checked him into the hospital. Then we'll have a real close look at the clothes he's wearing now."

Frank had recovered his balance and most of his strength. He did not need Hal's assistance. But Julie knew Bobby wouldn't let Frank go anywhere unchaperoned from now on. They needed to keep an eye on him constantly, in order not to miss any clues that might lead to an explanation of his sudden vanishments and reappearances.

Before attending to Frank, Hal removed the rumpled clothes

from the pillowcase. He left the rest of its contents on Julie's desk.

"Coffee?" Bobby asked.

"Desperately," Julie said.

He went out to the pantry that opened off the lounge, to start up one of their two Mr. Coffee machines.

Sitting at her desk, Julie emptied the pillowcase. It contained thirty bundles of hundred-dollar bills in packs bound by rubber bands. She fanned the edges of the bills in ten bundles to ascertain if lower denominations were included; they were all hundreds. She chose two packets at random and counted them. Each contained one hundred bills. Ten thousand in each. By the time Bobby returned with mugs, spoons, cream, sugar, and a pot of hot coffee, all on a tray, Julie had concluded that this was the largest of Frank's three hauls to date.

"Three hundred K," she said, as Bobby put the tray on her desk.

He whistled softly. "What's that bring the total to?"

"With this, we'll be holding six hundred thousand for him."

"Soon have to get a bigger office safe."

♦ ♦ ♦

HAL YAMATAKA put Frank's other set of clothes on the coffee table. "Something's wrong with the zipper in the pants. I don't mean just that it doesn't work, which it doesn't. I mean, something's very *wrong* with it."

Hal, Frank, and Julie pulled up chairs around the low glass-topped table, and drank strong black coffee while Bobby sat on the couch and carefully inspected the garments. In addition to the oddities he had noticed at the hospital, he discovered that most of the teeth in the pants zipper were metal, as they should have been, while about forty others, interspersed at random, appeared to be hard black rubber; in fact, the slide was jammed on a couple of the rubber ones.

Bobby stared in puzzlement at the anomalous zipper, slowly moving a finger up and down one of the notched tracks, until he was suddenly struck by inspiration. He picked up one of the shoes Frank had been wearing and examined the heel. It looked perfectly normal, but in the heel of the second shoe, thirty or forty tiny, brass-bright bits of metal were embedded in the rubber, flush with the surface of it.

"Anybody have a penknife?" Bobby asked.

Hal withdrew one from his pocket. Bobby used it to pry loose a couple of the shiny rectangles, which appeared to have been set in the rubber when it was still molten. Zipper teeth. They fell onto the glass table: *tink . . . tink.* At a glance he estimated that the amount of rubber displaced by those teeth was equal to what he had found in the zipper.

◆　◆　◆

SITTING IN the Dakotas' Disney-embellished office, Frank Pollard was overwhelmed by a weariness that was cartoonish in its extremity, the degree of utter exhaustion sufficient to render Donald Duck so limp that he might slip off a chair and pour onto the floor in a puddle of mallard flesh and feathers. It had been seeping into him day by day, hour by hour, since he had awakened in that alleyway last week; but now it suddenly poured through him as if a dike had broken. This surging flood of weariness had a density not of water but of liquid lead, and he felt enormously heavy; he could lift a foot or move a limb only with effort, and even keeping his head up was a strain on his neck. Virtually every joint in his body ached dully, even his elbow and wrist and finger joints, but especially his knees, hips, and shoulders. He felt feverish, not acutely ill, but as if his strength had been steadily sapped by a low-grade viral infection from which he had been suffering his entire life. Weariness had not dulled his senses; on the contrary, it abraded his nerve endings as surely as a fine-grade sandpaper might have done. Loud sounds made him cringe, bright light made him squint in pain, and he was exquisitely sensitive to heat and cold and the textures of everything he touched.

His exhaustion seemed only in part a result of his inability to sleep more than a couple of hours a night. If Hal Yamataka and the Dakotas could be believed—and Frank saw no reason for them to lie to him—he performed an incredible vanishing act several times during the night, though upon returning to his bed and staying put there, he could recall nothing of what he had done. Whatever the cause of those disappearances, no matter where he had gone or how or why, the very act of vanishing seemed likely to require an expenditure of energy as surely as walking or running or lifting heavy weights or any other physical act; therefore, perhaps his weakness and profound weariness were largely the result of his mysterious night journeys.

Bobby Dakota had pried only a couple of the brass teeth from the heel of the shoe. After studying them for a moment, he put down the penknife, leaned back against the sofa, and looked thoughtfully at the gloomy but rainless sky beyond the office's big windows. They were all silent, waiting to hear what he deduced from the condition of those clothes and shoes.

Even exhausted, preoccupied with his own fears, and after only a one-day association with the Dakotas, Frank realized that Bobby was the more imaginative and mentally nimble of the two. Julie was probably smarter than her husband; but she was also a more methodical thinker than he was, far less likely than he was to make sudden leaps of logic to arrive at insightful deductions and imaginative solutions. Julie would more often be right than Bobby was, but on those occasions when the firm resolved a client's problems *quickly*, the resolution would usually be attributable to Bobby. They made a good pair, and Frank was relying on their complementary natures to save him.

Turning to Frank again, Bobby said, "What if, somehow, you can teleport yourself, send yourself from here to there in a wink?"

"But that's . . . magic," Frank said. "I don't believe in magic."

"Oh, I do," Bobby said. "Not witches and spells and genies in bottles, but I believe in the possibility of fantastic things. The very fact that the world exists, that we're alive, that we can laugh and sing and feel the sun on our skin . . . that seems like a kind of magic to me."

"Teleport myself? If I can. I don't *know* I can. Evidently I have to fall asleep first. Which means teleportation must be a function of my subconscious mind, essentially involuntary."

"You weren't asleep when you reappeared in the hospital room or any of the other times you vanished," Hal said. "Maybe the first time, but not later. Your eyes were open. You spoke to me."

"But I don't remember it," Frank said frustratedly. "I only

remember going to sleep, then suddenly I was lying awake in bed, in a lot of distress, confused, and you were all there."

Julie sighed. "Teleportation. How can that be possible?"

"You saw it." Bobby shrugged. He picked up his coffee and took a sip, more relaxed than anyone in the room, as though having a client with an astonishing psychic power was, if not an ordinary occurrence, at least a situation that all of them should have realized was simply inevitable, given enough years in the private security business.

"I saw him disappear," Julie agreed, "but I'm not sure that proves he . . . teleported."

"When he disappeared," Bobby said, "he went *somewhere.* Right?"

"Well . . . yes."

"And going from one place to another, instantaneously, as an act of sheer willpower . . . as far as I'm concerned, that's teleportation."

"But how?" Julie asked.

Bobby shrugged again. "Right now, it doesn't matter how. Just accept the assumption of teleportation as a place to start."

"As a theory," Hal said.

"Okay," Julie agreed. "Theoretically, let's assume Frank can teleport himself."

To Frank, who was sealed off from his own experience by amnesia, that was like assuming iron was lighter than air in order to allow an argument for the possibility of steel-plated blimps. But he was willing to go along with it.

Bobby said, "Good, all right, then that assumption explains the condition of these clothes."

"How?" Frank asked.

"It'll take a while to get to the clothes. Stay with me. First, consider that maybe teleporting yourself requires that the atoms of your body temporarily disassociate themselves from one another, then come together again an instant later at another place. Same thing goes for the clothes you're wearing and for anything on which you've got a firm grip, like the bed railing."

"Like the teleportation pod in that movie," Hal said. *"The Fly."*

"Yeah," Bobby said, clearly getting excited now. He put down his coffee and slid forward on the edge of the sofa, gesticulating as he spoke. "Sort of like that. Except the power to do this is maybe all in Frank's mind, not in a futuristic machine. He just sort of *thinks* himself somewhere else, disassembles himself in a fraction of a second—*poof!*—and reassembles himself at his destination. Of course, I'm also assuming the mind remains intact even during the time the body is dispersed in disconnected atoms, because it would have to be the sheer power of the mind that transports those billions of particles and keeps them together like a shepherd collie herding sheep, then welds them to one another again in the right configurations at the far end."

Though his weariness was sufficient to have resulted from an impossibly complex and strenuous task like the one Bobby had just described, Frank was unconvinced. "Well, gee, I don't know. . . . This isn't something you go to school to learn. UCLA doesn't have a course in teleportation. So it's . . . instinct? Even supposing I instinctively know how to break my body down into a stream of atomic particles and send it somewhere else, then put it together again . . . how can any human mind, even the greatest genius ever born, be powerful enough to keep track of those billions of particles and get them all back exactly as they belong? It'd take a hundred geniuses, a thousand, and I'm not even *one*. I'm no dummy, but I'm no brighter than the average guy."

"You've answered your own question," Bobby said. "You don't need superhuman intelligence for this, 'cause teleportation isn't primarily a function of intelligence. It's not instinct, either. It's just . . . well, an ability programmed into your genes, like vision or hearing or the sense of smell. Think of it this way: Any scene you look at is composed of billions of separate points of color and light and shade and texture, yet your eyes instantly order those billions of bits of input into a coherent scene. You don't have to *think* about seeing. You just see, it's automatic. You understand what I meant about magic? Vision is almost magical. With teleportation, there's probably a trigger mechanism you have to pull—like *wishing* yourself to be elsewhere— but thereafter the process is pretty much automatic; the mind makes it happen the way it makes instantaneous sense of all the data coming in through your eyes."

Frank closed his eyes tight and concentrated on wishing himself into the reception lounge. When he opened his eyes and was still in the inner office, he said, "It doesn't work. It's not that easy. I can't do it at will."

Hal said, "Bobby, are you saying all of us have this ability, and only Frank has figured out how to use it?"

"No, no. This is probably a scrap of genetic material unique to Frank, maybe even a talent that sprung from genetic *damage.*"

They were all silent, absorbing what Bobby had conjectured.

Outside, the layer of clouds was cracking, peeling, and the old blue paint of the sky was showing through in more places every minute. But the brightening day did not lift Frank's spirits.

Finally Hal Yamataka indicated the pile of garments on the coffee table. "How does all this explain the condition of those clothes?"

Bobby picked up the blue cotton sweater and held it so they could see the khaki swatch on the back. "Okay, let's suppose the mind can automatically shepherd all the molecules of its own body through the teleportation process without a single error. It can also deal with other things Frank wants to take with him, like his clothes—"

"And bags full of money," Julie said.

"But why the bed railing?" Hal asked. "No reason for him to want to take that with him."

To Frank, Bobby said, "You can't remember it now, but you clearly knew what was happening while you were caught up in that series of teleportations. You were trying to stop, you asked Hal to help you stop, and you seized the railing to stop yourself, to anchor yourself to the hospital room. You were *concentrating* on your grip on that railing, so when you went, you took it with you. As for the clothes getting scrambled the way they are . . . Maybe your mind concentrates first on getting your body back together in the proper order because error-free physical re-creation is crucial to your survival, but then sometimes you might not have the energy left to do as good a job on secondary things like clothes."

"Well," Frank said, "I can't remember prior to last week, but this is the first time anything like this has happened since then, even though I've apparently been . . . traveling more nights than not. Then again, even if my clothes have come through okay, *I* seem to be getting more weary, weaker, and more confused day by day. . . ."

He did not have to finish the thought, because the worry in their eyes and faces made clear their understanding. If he was teleporting, and if it was a strenuous act that bled him of strength that could not be restored by rest, he was gradually going to get less meticulous about the reconstitution of his clothes and whatever other items he tried to carry with him. But more important—he might begin to have difficulty reconstituting his body, as well. He might return from one of his late-night rambles and find fragments of his sweater woven into the back of his hand, and the skin replaced by that cotton might turn up as a pale patch in the dark leather of his shoe, and the displaced leather from the shoe might appear as an integral part of his tongue . . . or as strands of alien cells twisted through his brain tissue.

Fear, never far away and circling like a shark in the depths of Frank's mind, abruptly shot to the surface, called forth by the worry and pity that he saw in the faces of those on whom he was depending for salvation. He closed his eyes, but that was a rotten idea because he had a vision of his own face when he shut out theirs, his face as it might look after a disastrous reconstitution at the end of a future telekinetic journey: eight or ten misplaced teeth sprouting from his right eye socket; the evicted eye staring lidlessly from the middle of the cheek below; his nose smeared in hideous lumps of flesh and gristle across the side of his face. In the vision he opened his misshapen mouth, perhaps to scream, and within were two fingers and a portion of his hand, rooted where the tongue should have been.

He opened his eyes as a low cry of terror and misery escaped him.

He was shuddering. He couldn't stop.

◆　◆　◆

HAVING FRESHENED everyone's coffee and, at Bobby's suggestion, having laced Frank's mug with bourbon in spite of the early hour, Hal went to the nook off the reception lounge to brew another pot.

After Frank had been fortified with a few sips of the spiked coffee, Julie showed the photograph to him and watched his reaction carefully. "You recognize either of the people in this?"

"No. They're strangers to me."

"The man," Bobby said, "is George Farris. The *real* George Farris. We got the picture from his brother-in-law."

Frank studied the photograph with renewed interest. "Maybe I knew him, and that's why I borrowed his name—but I can't recall ever seeing him before."

"He's dead," Julie said, and thought that Frank's surprise was genuine. She explained how Farris had died, years ago . . . and then how his family had been slaughtered far more recently. She told him about James Roman, too, and how Roman's family died in a fire in November.

With what appeared to be sincere dismay and confusion, Frank said, "Why all these deaths? Is it coincidence?"

Julie leaned forward. "We think Mr. Blue killed them."

"Who?"

"Mr. Blue Light. The man you said pursued you that night in Anaheim, the man you think is hunting you for some reason. We believe he discovered you were traveling under the names Farris and Roman, so he went to the addresses he got for them, and when he didn't find you there, he killed everyone, either while trying to squeeze information out of them or . . . just for the hell of it."

Frank looked stricken. His pale face grew even paler, as if it were an image doing a slow fade on a movie screen. The bleak look in his eyes intensified. "If I hadn't been using that fake ID, he never would've gone to those people. It's because of me they died."

Feeling sorry for the guy, ashamed of the suspicion that had driven her to approach the issue in this manner, Julie said, "Don't let it eat you, Frank. Most likely, the paper artist who forged your documents took the names at random from a list of recent deaths. If he'd used another approach, the Farris and Roman families would never have come to Mr. Blue's attention. But it's not your fault the forger used the quick and lazy method."

Frank shook his head, tried to speak, could not.

"You *can't* blame yourself," Hal said from the doorway, where he had evidently been standing long enough to have gotten the gist of the photo's importance. He seemed genuinely distressed to see Frank so anguished. Like Clint, Hal had been won over by Frank's gentle voice, self-effacing manner, and cherubic demeanor.

Frank cleared his throat, and finally the words broke loose:

196

"No, no, it's on me, my God, all those people dead because of me."

♦   ♦   ♦

IN DAKOTA & DAKOTA'S computer center, Bobby and Frank sat in two spring-backed, typist chairs with rubber wheels, and Bobby switched on one of the three state-of-the-art IBM PCs, each of which was outlinked to the world through its own modem and phone line. Though bright enough to work by, the overhead lights were soft and diffuse to prevent glare on the terminal screens, and the room's one window was covered with blackout drapes for the same reason.

Like policemen in the silicon age, modern private detectives and security consultants relied on the computer to make their work easier and to compile a breadth and depth of information that could never be acquired by the old-fashioned gumshoe methods of Sam Spade and Philip Marlowe. Pounding the pavement, interviewing witnesses and potential suspects, and conducting surveillances were still aspects of their job, of course, but without the computer they would be as ineffective as a blacksmith trying to fix a flat tire with a hammer and anvil and other tools of his trade. As the twentieth century progressed through its last decade, private investigators who were ignorant of the microchip revolution existed only in television dramas and the curiously dated world of most PI novels.

Lee Chen, who had designed and now operated their electronic data-gathering system, would not arrive in the office until around nine o'clock. Bobby did not want to wait nearly an hour to start putting the computer to work on Frank's case. He was not a primo hacker, as Lee was, but he knew all the hardware, had the ability to learn new software quickly when he needed to, and was almost as comfortable tracking down information in cyberspace as he was pouring through files of age-yellowed newspapers.

Using Lee's code book, which he removed from a locked desk drawer, Bobby first entered a Social Security Administration data network that contained files to which broad public access was legal. Other files in the same system were restricted and supposedly inaccessible behind walls of security codes required by various right-to-privacy laws.

From the open files, he inquired as to the number of men

named Frank Pollard in the Administration's records, and within seconds the response appeared on the screen: counting variations of Frank, such as Franklin and Frankie and Franco— plus names like Francis, for which Frank might be a diminutive—there were six hundred and nine Frank Pollards in possession of Social Security numbers.

"Bobby," Frank said anxiously, "does that stuff on the screen make sense to you? Are those words, real words, or jumbled letters?"

"Huh? Of course they're words."

"Not to me. They don't look like anything to me. Gibberish."

Bobby picked up a copy of *Byte* magazine that was lying between two of the computers, opened it to an article, and said, "Read that."

Frank accepted the magazine, stared at it, flipped ahead a couple of pages, then a couple more. His hands began to shake. The magazine rattled in his grip. "I can't. Jesus, I've lost that too. Yesterday, I lost the ability to do math, and now I can't read any more, and I get more confused, foggy in the head, and I ache in every joint, every muscle. This teleporting's wearing me down, killing me. I'm falling apart, Bobby, mentally and physically, faster all the time."

"It's going to be all right," Bobby said, though his confidence was largely feigned. He was pretty sure they would get to the bottom of this, would learn who Frank was and where he went at night and how and why; however, he could see that Frank was declining fast, and he would not have bet money that they'd find all the answers while Frank was still alive, sane, and able to benefit from their discoveries. Nevertheless, he put his hand on Frank's shoulder and gave it a gentle reassuring squeeze. "Hang in there, buddy. Everything's going to be okay. I really think it is. I really do."

Frank took a deep breath and nodded.

Turning to the display terminal again, feeling guilty about the lie he'd just told, Bobby said, "You remember how old you are, Frank?"

"No."

"You look about thirty-two, thirty-three."

"I feel older."

Softly whistling Duke Ellington's "Satin Doll," Bobby thought a moment, then asked the SSA computer to eliminate those

Frank Pollards younger than twenty-eight and older than thirty-eight. That left seventy-two of them.

"Frank, do you think you've ever lived anywhere else, or are you a died-in-the-wool Californian?"

"I don't know."

"Let's assume you're a son of the sunshine state."

He asked the SSA computer to whittle down the remaining Frank Pollards to those who applied for their Social Security numbers while living in California (fifteen), then to those whose current addresses on file were in California (six).

The public-access portion of the Social Security Administration's data network was forbidden by law to reveal Social Security numbers to casual researchers. Bobby referred to the instructions in Lee Chen's code book and entered the restricted files through a complicated series of maneuvers that circumvented SSA security.

He was unhappy about breaking the law, but it was a fact of high-tech life that you never got the maximum benefit from your data-gathering system if you played strictly by the rules. Computers were instruments of freedom, and governments were to one degree or another instruments of repression; the two could not always exist in harmony.

He obtained the six numbers and addresses for the Frank Pollards living in California.

"Now what?" Frank wondered.

"Now," Bobby said, "I use these numbers and addresses to cross reference with the California Department of Motor Vehicles, all of the armed forces, state police, major city police, and other government agencies to get descriptions of these six Frank Pollards. As we learn their height, weight, hair color, color of their eyes, race . . . we'll gradually eliminate them one by one. Better yet, if one of them is you, and if you've ever served in the military or been arrested for a crime, we might even be able to turn up a picture of you in one of those files and confirm your identity with a photo match."

♦ ♦ ♦

SITTING AT the desk, catercorner from each other, Julie and Hal removed the rubber bands from more than half of the packets of cash. They sorted through the hundred-dollar bills, trying to determine if some of them had consecutive serial numbers that might indicate they were stolen from a bank, savings and loan, or other institution.

Suddenly Hal looked up and said, "Why do those flutelike sounds and drafts precede Frank when he teleports himself?"

"Who knows?" Julie said. "Maybe it's displaced air following him down some tunnel in another dimension, from the place he left to the place he's going."

"I was just thinking. . . . If this Mr. Blue is real, and if he's searching for Frank, and if Frank heard those flutes and felt those gusts in that alleyway . . . then Mr. Blue is also able to teleport."

"Yeah. So?"

"So Frank's not unique. Whatever he is, there's another one like him. Maybe even more than one."

"Here's something else to think about," Julie said. "If Mr. Blue can teleport himself, and if he finds out where Frank is, we won't be able to defend a hiding place from him. He'll be able to pop up among us. And what if he arrived with a submachine gun, spraying bullets as he materialized?"

After a moment of silence, Hal said, "You know, gardening has always seemed like a pleasant profession. You need a lawn-mower, a weed whacker, a few simple tools. There's not much overhead, and you hardly ever get shot at."

♦　♦　♦

BOBBY FOLLOWED Frank into the office, where Julie and Hal were examining the money. Putting a sheet of paper on the desk, he said, "Move over, Sherlock Holmes. The world now has a greater detective."

Julie angled the page so she and Hal could read it together. It was a laser-printed copy of the information that Frank had filed with the California Department of Motor Vehicles when he had last applied for an extension of his driver's license.

"The physical statistics match," she said. "Is your first name really Francis and your middle name Ezekiel?"

Frank nodded. "I didn't remember until I saw it. But it's me, all right. Ezekiel."

Tapping the printout, she said, "This address in El Encanto Heights—does it ring a bell?"

"No. I can't even tell you where El Encanto is."

"It's adjacent to Santa Barbara," Julie said.

"So Bobby tells me. But I don't remember being there. Except . . ."

"What?"

Frank went to the window and looked out toward the distant sea, above which the sky was now entirely blue. A few early gulls swooped in arcs so huge and smoothly described that their exuberance was thrilling to watch. Clearly, Frank was neither thrilled by the birds nor charmed by the view.

Finally, still facing the window, he said, "I don't recall being in El Encanto Heights . . . except that every time I hear the name, my stomach sort of sinks, you know, like I'm on a roller coaster that's just taken a plunge. And when I try to think about El Encanto, strain to remember it, my heart pounds, and my mouth goes dry, and it's a little harder to get my breath. So I think I must be repressing any memories I have of the place, maybe because something happened to me there, something bad . . . something I'm too scared to remember."

Bobby said, "His driver's license expired seven years ago, and according to the DMV's records, he never tried to renew it. In fact, sometime this year he'd have been weeded out of even their dead files, so we were lucky to find this before they expunged it." He laid two more printouts on the desk. "Move over, Holmes *and* Sam Spade."

"What're these?"

"Arrest reports. Frank was stopped for traffic violations, once in San Francisco a little more than six years ago. The second time was on Highway 101, north of Ventura, five years ago. He didn't have a valid driver's license either time and, because of odd behavior, was taken into custody."

The photographs that were a part of both arrest records showed a slightly younger, even pudgier man who was without a doubt their current client.

Bobby pushed aside some of the money and sat on the edge of her desk. "He escaped from jail both times, so they're looking for him even after all these years, though probably not too hard, since he wasn't arrested for a major crime."

Frank said, "I draw a blank on that too."

"Neither report indicates *how* he escaped," Bobby said, "but I suspect he didn't saw his way through the bars or dig a tunnel or whittle a gun out of a bar of soap or use any of the long-accepted, traditional methods of jailbreak. Oh, no, not our Frank."

"He teleported," Hal guessed. "Vanished when no one was looking."

"I'd bet on it," Bobby agreed. "And after that he began to carry false ID good enough to satisfy any cop who pulled him over."

Looking at the papers before her, Julie said, "Well, Frank, at least we know this is your real name, and we've nailed down a real address for you up there in Santa Barbara County, not just another motel room. We're beginning to make headway."

Bobby said, "Move over, Holmes, Spade, *and* Miss Marple."

Unable to embrace their optimism, Frank returned to the chair in which he'd been sitting earlier. "Headway. But not enough. And not fast enough." He leaned forward with his arms on his thighs, hands clasped between his spread knees, and stared morosely at the floor. "Something unpleasant just occurred to me. What if I'm not only making mistakes with my clothes when I reconstitute myself? What if I've *already* begun to make mistakes with my own biology too? Nothing major. Nothing visible. Hundreds or thousands of tiny mistakes on a cellular level. That would explain why I feel so lousy, so tired and sore. And if my brain tissue isn't coming back together right . . . that would explain why I'm confused, fuzzy-headed, unable to read or do math."

Julie looked at Hal, at Bobby, and knew that both men wanted to allay Frank's fear but were unable to do so because the scenario that he had outlined was not only possible but likely.

Frank said, "The brass buckle looked perfectly normal until Bobby touched it . . . then it turned to dust."

# 40

ALL NIGHT LONG, when sleep made Thomas's head empty, ugly dreams filled it up. Dreams of eating small live things. Dreams of drinking blood. Dreams of being the Bad Thing.

He finished sleeping all of a sudden, sitting up in bed, trying to scream but unable to find any sounds in himself. For a while he sat there, shaking, being afraid, breathing so hard and fast his chest ached.

The sun was back, and the night was gone away, and that made him feel better. Getting out of bed, he stepped into his slippers. His pajamas were cold with sweat. He shivered. He pulled on a robe. He went to the window, looked out and up, liking the blue sky very much. Leftover rain made the green lawn look soggy, the sidewalks darker than usual, and the dirt in the flowerbeds almost black, and in the puddles you could see the blue sky again like a face in a mirror. He liked all of that, too, because the whole world looked clean and new after all the rain emptied out of the sky.

He wondered if the Bad Thing was still far away, or closer, but he didn't reach out to it. Because last night it tried to hold him. Because it was so strong he almost couldn't get away from it. And because even when he *did* get away, it tried to follow him. He'd felt it hanging on, coming back across the night with him, and he'd shaken it off real quick like, but maybe next time he wouldn't be so lucky, and maybe it would come all the way, right into his room with him, not just its mind but the Bad Thing itself. He didn't understand how that could happen, but somehow he knew it might. And if the Bad Thing came to The Home, being awake would be like being asleep with a nightmare filling up your head. Terrible things would happen, and there would be no hope.

Turning away from the window, starting toward the closed door to the bathroom, Thomas glanced at Derek's bed and saw Derek dead. He was on his back. His face was bashed, bruised, swollen. His eyes were open big, you could see them shine in the light from the window and the low light from the lamp beside the bed. His mouth was open, too, like he was shouting, but all the sound was out of him like air out of a popped balloon, and he would not have any more sound in him ever again, you could tell. Blood was let out of him, too, lots of it, and a pair of scissors were stuck in his belly, deep in, with not much more than the handles showing, the same scissors Thomas used to clip pictures from magazines for his poems.

He felt a big twist of pain in his heart, like maybe somebody was sticking scissors in him too. But it wasn't hurt-pain so much as what he called "feel-pain," because it was losing Derek that he was feeling, not real hurt. It was as bad as real hurt, though, because Derek was his friend, he liked Derek. He was scared, too, because he somehow knew the Bad Thing had let the life out of Derek, the Bad Thing was here at The Home. Then he realized this could happen just the way things sometimes happened in TV stories, with the cops coming and believing that Thomas killed Derek, blaming Thomas, and everyone hating Thomas for what he'd done, but he hadn't done it, and all the while the Bad Thing was still loose to do more killing, maybe even doing to Julie what it'd done to Derek.

The hurt, the fear for himself, the fear for Julie—all of it was too much. Thomas gripped the footboard of his own bed and closed his eyes and tried to get air into himself. It wouldn't come. His chest was tight. Then the air came in, and so did an ugly-nasty smell, which in a while he realized was the stink of Derek's blood, so he gagged and almost puked.

He knew he had to Get Control of Himself. The aides didn't like it when you Lost Control of Yourself, so they Gave You Something For Your Own Good. He'd never Lost Control before and didn't want to lose it now.

He tried not to smell the blood. Took long deep breaths. Made himself open his eyes to look at the dead body. He figured looking at it the second time wouldn't be as bad as the first. He knew it was going to be there this time, so it wouldn't be such a big surprise.

The surprise was—the body was gone.

Thomas closed his eyes, put one hand to his face, looked again between spread fingers. The body still wasn't there.

He started shaking because what he thought, first, was that this was like some other TV stories he'd seen where nasty-dead bodies were walking around like live bodies, rotting and getting wormy, with bones showing in places, killing people for no reason and even sometimes eating them. He could never watch much of one of those stories. He sure didn't want to *be* in one.

He was so scared he almost TVed to Bobby—*Dead people, look out, look out, dead people hungry and mean and walking around*—but stopped himself when he saw there wasn't blood on Derek's blankets and sheets. The bed wasn't rumpled, either. Neatly made. No walking dead person was quick enough to get out of bed, change sheets and blankets, make everything right just in the few little seconds while Thomas's eyes were closed.

Then he heard the shower pouring down on the floor of the stall in the bathroom, and he heard Derek singing soft the way he always did when he washed himself. For just a moment, in his head, Thomas had a picture of a dead person taking a shower, trying to be neat, but rotten chunks were falling off with the dirt, showing more bones, clogging the drain. Then he realized Derek was never really dead. Thomas hadn't really seen a body on the bed. What he'd seen was something else he'd learned from TV stories—he'd seen a vision. A sidekick vision. He was a sidekick.

Derek hadn't been killed. What Thomas saw, just for a moment, was Derek being dead tomorrow or some other day after tomorrow. It might be something that would happen no matter what Thomas did to stop it, or it might be something that would happen only if he let it happen, but at least it wasn't something that *already* happened.

He let go of the footboard and went to his worktable. His legs were shaky. He was glad to sit down. He opened the top drawer of the cabinet that stood beside the table. He saw his scissors in there, where they should be, with his colored pencils and pens and paper clips and Scotch tape and stapler—and a half-eaten Hershey's bar in an open wrapper, which *shouldn't* be in there because it would Draw Bugs. He took the candy out of the drawer and stuffed it in a pocket of his robe, reminding himself to put it in the refrigerator later.

For a while he stared at the scissors, listened to Derek sing in the shower, and thought how the scissors were jammed in Derek's belly, letting all the music and other sounds out of him forever, sending him to the Bad Place. Finally he touched the black plastic handles. They felt all right, so he touched the metal blades, but that was bad, real bad, as if leftover lightning from a storm was in the blades and jumped into him when he touched them. Sizzling, crackling white light flashed through him. He snatched his hand back. His fingers tingled. He closed the drawer and hurried back to bed and sat there with the covers pulled around his shoulders the way TV Indians wrapped themselves in blankets when they sat at TV campfires.

The shower stopped. So did the singing. After a while Derek came out of the bathroom, followed by a cloud of damp, soapy-smelling air. He was dressed for the day. His wet hair was combed back from his forehead.

He was not a rotting dead person. He was all alive, every part of him, at least every part you could see, and no bones poked out anywhere.

"Good morning," Derek said, the words slurred and muffled by his crooked mouth and too-big tongue. He smiled.

"Good morning."

"You sleep good?"

"Yeah," Thomas said.

"Breakfast soon."

"Yeah."

"Maybe sticky buns."

"Maybe."

"I like sticky buns."

"Derek?"

"Huh?"

"If I ever tell you . . ."

Derek waited, smiling.

Thomas thought out what he wanted to say, then continued: "If I ever tell you the Bad Thing's coming, and I tell you to run, don't just stand around like a dumb person. You just *run.*"

Derek stared at him, thinking about it, still smiling, then after a while he said, "Sure, okay."

"Promise?"

"Promise. But what's a bad thing?"

"I don't know really, for sure, but I'll feel when it's coming, I think, and tell you, and you'll run."

"Where?"

"Anywhere. Down the hall. Find some aides, stay with them."

"Sure. You better wash. Breakfast soon. Maybe sticky buns."

Thomas unwrapped himself from the blanket and got out of bed. He stepped into his slippers again and walked to the bathroom.

Just as Thomas was opening the bathroom door, Derek said, "You mean at breakfast?"

Thomas turned. "Huh?"

"You mean a bad thing might come at breakfast?"

"Might," Thomas said.

"Could it be . . . poached eggs?"

"Huh?"

"The bad thing—could it be poached eggs? I don't like poached eggs, all slimy, yuck, that'd be real bad, not good at all like cereal and bananas and sticky buns."

"No, no," Thomas said. "The bad thing isn't poached eggs. It's a person, some funny-weird person. I'll feel when it's coming, and tell you, and you'll run."

"Oh. Yeah, sure. A person."

Thomas went into the bathroom, closed the door. He didn't have much beard. He had an electric razor, but he only used it a couple-few times a month, and today he didn't need it. He brushed his teeth, though. And he peed. He made the water start in the shower. Only then did he let himself laugh, because enough time had passed so Derek wouldn't even wonder if Thomas was laughing at him.

Poached eggs!

Though Thomas usually didn't like seeing himself, seeing how lumpy and wrong and dumb his face was, he peeked at the steam-streaked mirror. One time long ago, past when he could remember, he'd been laughing when he'd happened to see himself in a mirror, and for once—surprise!—he hadn't felt so bad about how he looked. When he laughed he looked more like a normal person. Just pretending to laugh didn't make him look more normal, it had to be real laughing, and smiling didn't do it, either, because a smile wasn't enough of a laugh to change his face. In fact, a smile could sometimes look so sad, he couldn't stand seeing himself at all.

Poached eggs.

Thomas shook his head, and when his laughter finished he turned from the mirror.

To Derek the most worst bad thing he could think of was poached eggs and no sticky buns, which was very funny ha-ha. You try to tell Derek about walking dead people and scissors sticking out of bellies and something that eats little live animals, and old Derek would look at you and smile and nod and not get it at all.

For as long as he could remember, Thomas had wished he was a normal person, not dumb, and many times he thanked God for at least making him not as dumb as poor Derek. But now he half wished he was dumber, so he could get those ugly-nasty vision-pictures out of his mind, so he could forget about Derek going to die and the Bad Thing coming and Julie being in danger, so he'd have nothing to worry about except poached eggs, which wouldn't be much of a worry at all, since he sort of *liked* poached eggs.

# 41

WHEN CLINT KARAGHIOSIS arrived at Dakota & Dakota shortly before nine o'clock, Bobby took him by the shoulder, turned him around, and went back to the elevators with him. "You drive, and I'll fill you in on what's happened during the night. I know you've got other cases to tend to, but the Pollard thing is getting hotter by the minute."

"Where're we going?"

"First, Palomar Labs. They called. Test results are ready."

Only a few clouds remained in the sky, and they were all far off toward the mountains, moving away like the billowing sails of great galleons on an eastward journey. It was a quintessential southern California day: blue, pleasantly warm, everything green and fresh, and rush-hour traffic so hideously snarled that it could transform an ordinary citizen into a foaming-at-the-mouth sociopath with a yearning to pull the trigger of a semiautomatic weapon.

Clint avoided freeways, but even surface streets were clogged. By the time Bobby recounted everything that had transpired since they had seen each other yesterday afternoon, they were still ten minutes from Palomar in spite of the questions occasioned by Clint's amazement—subdued like all of his reactions, but amazement nonetheless—over the discovery that Frank was evidently able to teleport himself.

Finally Bobby changed the subject because talking too much about psychic phenomena to a phlegmatic guy like Clint made him feel like an airhead, as if he had lost his grip on reality. While they inched along Bristol Avenue, he said, "I can remember when you could go anywhere in Orange County and *never* get caught in traffic."

"Not so long ago."

"I remember when you didn't have to sign a developer's waiting list to buy a house. Demand wasn't five times supply."

"Yeah."

"And I remember when orange groves were all over Orange County."

"Me too."

Bobby sighed. "Hell, listen to me, like an old geezer, babbling about the good old days. Pretty soon, I'll be talking about how nice it was when there were still dinosaurs around."

"Dreams," Clint said. "Everyone's got a dream, and the one more people have than any other is the California dream, so they never stop coming, even though so many have come now that the dream isn't really quite attainable any more, not the original dream that started it all. Of course, maybe a dream should be unattainable, or at least at the outer limits of your reach. If it's too easy, it's meaningless."

Bobby was surprised by the long burst of words from Clint, but more surprised to hear the man talking about something as intangible as dreams. "You're already a Californian, so what's your dream?"

After a brief hesitation, Clint said, "That Felina will be able to hear someday. There're so many medical advancements these days, new discoveries and treatments and techniques all the time."

As Clint turned left off Bristol, onto the side street where Palomar Laboratories stood, Bobby decided that was a good dream, a damned fine dream, maybe even better than his and Julie's dream about buying time and getting a chance to bring Thomas out of Cielo Vista and into a remade family.

They parked in the lot beside the huge concrete-block building in which Palomar Laboratories was housed. As they were walking toward the front door, Clint said, "Oh, by the way, the receptionist here thinks I'm gay, which is fine with me."

"What?"

Clint went inside without saying more, and Bobby followed him to the reception window. An attractive blonde sat at the counter.

"Hi, Lisa," Clint said.

"Hi!" She punctuated her response by cracking her chewing gum.

"Dakota and Dakota."

"I remember," she said. "Your stuff's ready. I'll get it."

She glanced at Bobby and smiled, and he smiled, too, though her expression seemed a little peculiar to him.

When she returned with two large, sealed manila envelopes—one labeled SAMPLES, the other ANALYSES—Clint handed the second one to Bobby. They stepped to one side of the lounge, away from the counter.

Bobby tore open the envelope and skimmed the documents inside. "Cat's blood."

"You serious?"

"Yeah. When Frank woke up in that motel, he was covered with cat's blood."

"I knew he was no killer."

Bobby said, "The cat may have an opinion about that."

"The other stuff is?"

"Well . . . bunch of technical terms here . . . but what it comes down to is that it's what it looks like. Black sand."

Stepping back to the reception counter, Clint said, "Lisa, you remember we talked about a black-sand beach in Hawaii?"

"Kaimu," she said. "It's a dynamite place."

"Yeah, Kaimu. Is it the only one?"

"Black-sand beach, you mean? No. There's Punaluu, which is a real sweet place too. Those are on the big island. I guess there must be more on the other islands, 'cause there's volcanoes all over the place, aren't there?"

Bobby joined them at the counter. "What do volcanoes have to do with it?"

Lisa took her chewing gum out of her mouth and put it aside on a piece of paper. "Well, the way I heard it, really hot lava flows into the sea, and when it meets the water, there're these huge explosions, which throw off zillions and zillions of these really teeny-tiny beads of black glass, and then over a long period of time the waves rub all the beads together until they're ground down into sand."

"They have these beaches anywhere but Hawaii?" Bobby wondered.

She shrugged. "Probably. Clint, is this fella your . . . friend?"

"Yeah," Clint said.

"I mean, you know, your *good* friend?"

"Yeah," Clint said, without looking at Bobby.

Lisa winked at Bobby. "Listen, you make Clint take you to Kaimu, 'cause I'll tell you something—it's really terrific to go out on a black beach at night, make love under the stars, because it's soft, for one thing, but mainly because black sand doesn't reflect moonlight like regular sand. It seems like you're floating in space, darkness all around, it really sharpens your senses, if you know what I mean."

"Sounds terrific," Clint said. "Take care, Lisa." He headed for the door.

As Bobby turned to follow Clint, Lisa said, "You make him take you to Kaimu, you hear? You'll have a good time."

Outside, Bobby said, "Clint, you've got some explaining to do."

"Didn't you hear her? These little beads of black glass—"

"That's not what I'm talking about. Hey, look at you, you're grinning. I don't think I've ever seen you grinning. I don't think I *like* you grinning."

# 42

BY NINE O'CLOCK, Lee Chen had arrived at the offices, opened a bottle of orange-flavored seltzer, and settled in the computer room midst his beloved hardware, where Julie was waiting for him. He was five six, slender but wiry, with a warm brass complexion and jet-black hair that bristled in a modified punk style. He wore red tennis shoes and socks, baggy black cotton pants with a white belt, a black and charcoal-gray shirt with a subtle leaf pattern, and a black jacket with narrow lapels and big shoulder pads. He was the most stylishly dressed employee at Dakota & Dakota, even compared to Cassie Hanley, their receptionist, who was an unashamed clotheshorse.

While Lee sat in front of his computers, sipping seltzer, Julie filled him in on what had happened at the hospital and showed him the printouts of the information Bobby had acquired earlier that morning. Frank Pollard sat with them, in the third chair, where Julie could keep an eye on him. Throughout their conversation, Lee exhibited no surprise at what he was being told, as if his computers had bestowed on him such enormous wisdom and foresight that nothing—not even a man capable of teleportation—could surprise him. Julie knew that Lee, as well as everyone else in the Dakota & Dakota family, would never leak a word of any client's business to anyone; but she didn't know how much of his supercool demeanor was real and how much was a conscious image that he put on every morning with his ultra-voguish clothes.

Though his unshakable nonchalance might be partly feigned, his talent for computers was unquestionably real. When Julie had finished her condensed version of recent events, Lee said, "Okay, what do you need from me now?" There was no doubt on either his part or hers that eventually he could provide whatever she required.

She gave him a steno pad. Double rows of currency serial numbers filled the first ten pages. "Those are random samplings of the bills in each of the bags of cash we're holding for Frank. Can you find out if it's hot money—stolen, maybe an extortion or ransom payment?"

Lee quickly paged through the lists. "No consecutive numbers? That makes it harder. Usually cops don't have a record of the serial numbers of stolen money unless it was brand-new bills, which are still bound in packets, consecutively numbered, right off the press."

"Most of this cash is fairly well circulated."

"There's an outside chance it might still be from a ransom or extortion payoff, like you said. The cops would've taken down all the numbers before they let the victim make the drop, just in case the perp made a clean getaway. It looks bleak, but I'll try. What else?"

Julie said, "An entire family in Garden Grove, last name Farris, was murdered last year."

"Because of me," Frank said.

Lee propped his elbows on the arms of his chair, leaned back, and steepled his fingers. He looked like a wise Zen master who had been forced to don the clothes of an avant-garde artist after getting the wrong suitcase at the airport. "No one really dies, Mr. Pollard. They just go on from here. Grief is good, but guilt is pointless."

Though she knew too few computer fanatics to be certain, Julie suspected that not many found a way to combine the hard realities of science and technology with religion. But in fact, Lee had arrived at a belief in God through his work with computers and his interest in modern physics. He once explained to her why a profound understanding of the dimensionless space inside a computer network, combined with a modern physicist's view of the universe, led inevitably to faith in a Creator, but she hadn't followed a thing he'd said.

She gave Lee Chen the dates and details of the Farris and

Roman murders. "We think they were all killed by the same man. I haven't got a clue to his real name, so I call him Mr. Blue. Considering the savagery of the murders, we suspect he's a serial killer with a long list of victims. If we're right, the murders have been so widely spread or Mr. Blue has covered his tracks so well that the press has never made connections between the crimes."

"Otherwise," Frank said, "they'd have sensationalized it on their front pages. Especially if this guy regularly bites his victims."

"But since most police agencies are computer-linked these days," Julie said, "they might've made connections across jurisdictions, saw what the press didn't. There might be one or more quiet, ongoing investigations between local, state, and federal authorities. We need to know if any police in California—or the FBI nationally—are on to Mr. Blue, and we need to know anything they've learned about him, no matter how trivial."

Lee smiled. In the middle of his brass-hued face, his teeth were like pegs of highly polished ivory. "That means going past the public-access files in their computers. I'll have to break their security, one agency after another, all the way into the FBI."

"Difficult?"

"Very. But I'm not without experience." He pushed his jacket sleeves farther up on his arms, flexed his fingers, and turned to the terminal keyboard as if he were a concert pianist about to interpret Mozart. He hesitated and glanced sideways at Julie. "I'll work into their systems indirectly to discourage tracebacks. I won't damage any data or breach national security, so I probably won't even be noticed. But if someone spots me snooping and puts a tracer on me that I don't see or can't shake, they might pull your PI license for this."

"I'll sacrifice myself, take the blame. Bobby's license won't be pulled, too, so the agency won't go down. How long will this take?"

"Four or five hours, maybe more, maybe a lot more. Can somebody bring me lunch at noon? I'd rather eat here and not take a break."

"Sure. What would you like?"

"Big Mac, double order of fries, vanilla shake."

Julie grimaced. "How come a high-tech guy like you never heard of cholesterol?"

"Heard of it. Don't care. If we never really die, cholesterol can't kill me. It can only move me out of this life a little sooner."

# 43

ARCHER VAN CORVAIRE cracked open the Levolor blind and peered through the thick bulletproof glass in the front door of his Newport Beach shop. He squinted suspiciously at Bobby and Clint, though he knew and expected them. At last he unlocked the door and let them in.

Van Corvaire was about fifty-five but invested a lot of time and money in the maintenance of a youthful appearance. To thwart time, he'd undergone dermabrasion, face-lifts, and liposuction; to improve on nature, he'd had a nose job, cheek implants, and chin restructuring. He wore a toupee of such exquisite craftsmanship, it would have passed for his own dyed-black hair—except that he sabotaged the illusion by insisting on not merely a replacement but a lush, unnatural pompadour. If he ever got into a swimming pool wearing that toupee, it would look like the conning tower of a submarine.

After reengaging both dead bolts, he turned to Bobby. "I never do business in the morning. I take only afternoon appointments."

"We appreciate the exception you've made for us," Bobby said.

Van Corvaire sighed elaborately. "Well, what is it?"

"I have a stone I'd like you to appraise for me."

He squinted, which wasn't appealing, since his eyes were already as narrow as those of a ferret. Before his name change thirty years ago, he'd been Jim Bob Spleener, and a friend would have told him that when he squinted suspiciously he looked very much like a Spleener and not at all like a van Corvaire. "An appraisal? That's all you want?"

He led them through the small but plush salesroom: hand-textured plaster ceiling; bleached suede walls; whitewashed oak floors; custom area carpet by Patterson, Flynn & Martin in shades of peach, pale blue and sandstone; a modern white sofa flanked by pickled-finish, burlwood tables by Bau; four elegant rattan chairs encircling a round table with a glass top thick enough to survive a blow from a sledgehammer.

One small merchandise display case stood off to the left. Van Corvaire's business was conducted entirely by appointment; his jewelry was custom designed for the very rich and tasteless, people who would find it necessary to buy hundred-thousand-dollar necklaces to wear to a thousand-dollar-a-plate charity dinner, and never grasp the irony.

The back wall was mirrored, and van Corvaire watched himself with obvious pleasure all the way across the room. He hardly took his eyes off his reflection until he passed through the door into the workroom.

Bobby wondered if the guy ever got so entranced by his image that he walked smack into it. He didn't like Jim Bob van Corvaire, but the narcissistic creep's knowledge of gems and jewelry was often useful.

Years ago, when Dakota & Dakota Investigations was just Dakota Investigations, without the ampersand and the redundancy (better never put it that way around Julie, who would appreciate the clever wordplay but would make him eat the "redundancy" part), Bobby had helped van Corvaire recover a fortune in unmounted diamonds stolen by a lover. Old Jim Bob desperately wanted his gems but didn't want the woman sent to prison, so he went to Bobby instead of to the police. That was the only soft spot Bobby had ever seen in van Corvaire; in the intervening years the jeweler no doubt had grown a callus over it too.

Bobby fished one of the marble-size red stones from his pocket. He saw the jeweler's eyes widen.

With Clint standing to one side of him, with Bobby behind him and looking over his shoulder, van Corvaire sat on a high stool at a workbench and examined the rough-cut stone through a loupe. Then he put it on the lighted glass table of a microscope and studied it with that more powerful instrument.

"Well?" Bobby asked.

The jeweler did not respond. He rose, elbowing them out of the way, and went to another stool, farther along the work-bench. There, he used one scale to weigh the stone and another to determine if its specific gravity matched that of any known gems.

Finally, he moved to a third stool that was positioned in front of a vise. From a drawer he withdrew a ring box in which three large, cut gems lay on a square of blue velvet.

"Junk diamonds," he said.

"They look nice to me," Bobby said.

"Too many flaws."

He selected one of those stones and fixed it in the vise with a couple of turns of the crank. Gripping the red beauty in a small pair of pliers, he used one of its sharper edges to attempt to score the polished facet of the diamond in the vise, pressing with considerable effort. Then he put the pliers and red gem aside, picked up another jeweler's loupe, leaned forward, and studied the junk diamond.

"A faint scratch," he said. "Diamond cuts diamond." He held the red stone between thumb and forefinger, staring at it with obvious fascination—and greed. "Where did you get this?"

"Can't tell you," Bobby said. "So it's just a red diamond?"

"*Just?* The red diamond may be the rarest precious stone in the world! You must let me market it for you. I have clients who'd pay anything to have this as the centerstone of a necklace or pendant. It'll probably be too big for a ring even after final cut. It's huge!"

"What's it worth?" Clint asked.

"Impossible to say until it's finish-cut. Millions, certainly."

"Millions?" Bobby said doubtfully. "It's big but not *that* big."

Van Corvaire finally tore his gaze from the stone and looked up at Bobby. "You don't understand. Until now, there were only seven known red diamonds in the world. This is the eighth. And when it's cut and polished, it'll be one of the two largest. This comes as close to priceless as anything gets."

♦　♦　♦

OUTSIDE Archer van Corvaire's small shop, where heavy traffic roared past on Pacific Coast Highway, with disco-frenetic flares of sunlight flashing off the chrome and glass, it was hard to believe that the tranquility of Newport Harbor and its burden of beautiful yachts were just beyond the buildings on the far side of the street. In a sudden moment of enlightenment, Bobby realized that his entire life (and perhaps nearly everyone else's) was like this street at this precise point in time: all bustle and noise, glare and movement, a desperate rush to break out of the herd, to achieve something and transcend the frantic whirl of commerce, thereby earning respite for reflection and a shot at serenity—when all the time serenity was only a few steps away, on the far side of the street, just out of sight.

That realization contributed to a heretofore subtle feeling that the Pollard case was somehow a trap—or, more accurately, a squirrel cage that spun faster and faster even as he scampered frantically to get a footing on its rotating floor. He stood for a few seconds by the open door of the car, feeling ensnared, caged. At that moment he was not sure why, in spite of the obvious dangers, he had been so eager to take on Frank's problems and put all that he cared about at risk. He knew now that the reasons he had quoted to Julie and to himself—sympathy for Frank, curiosity, the excitement of a wildly different kind of job—were merely justifications, not reasons, and that his true motivation was something he did not yet understand.

Unnerved, he got in the car and pulled the door shut as Clint started the engine.

"Bobby, how many red diamonds would you say are in the mason jar? A hundred?"

"More. A couple hundred."

"Worth what—hundreds of millions?"

"Maybe a billion or more."

They stared at each other, and for a while neither of them spoke. It wasn't that no words were adequate to the situation; instead, there was *too much* to say and no easy way to determine where to begin.

At last Bobby said, "But you couldn't convert the stones to cash, not quickly anyway. You'd have to dribble them onto the market over a lot of years to prevent a sudden dilution of their rarity and value, but also to avoid causing a sensation, drawing unwanted attention, and maybe having to answer some unanswerable questions."

"After they've mined diamonds for hundreds of years, all over the world, and only found seven red ones . . . where the hell did Frank come up with a jarful?"

Bobby shook his head and said nothing.

Clint reached into his pants pocket and withdrew one of the diamonds, smaller than the specimen that Bobby had brought for Archer van Corvaire's appraisal. "I took this home to show it to Felina. I was going to return it to the jar when I got to the office, but you hustled me out before I had a chance. Now that I know what it is, I don't want it in my possession a minute longer."

Bobby took the stone and put it in his pocket with the larger diamond. "Thank you, Clint."

♦  ♦  ♦

DR. DYSON MANFRED'S study, in his house in Turtle Rock, was the most uncomfortable place Bobby had ever been. He had been happier last week, flattened on the floor of his van, trying to avoid being chopped to bits by automatic weapons fire than he was among Manfred's collection of many-legged, carapaced, antenna-bristled, mandibled, and thoroughly repulsive exotic bugs.

Repeatedly, in his peripheral vision, Bobby saw something move in one of the many glass-covered boxes on the wall, but every time he turned to ascertain which hideous creature was about to slip out from under the frame, his fear proved unfounded. All of the nightmarish specimens were pinned and motionless, lined up neatly beside one another, none missing. He also would have sworn that he heard things skittering and slithering inside the shallow drawers of the many cases that he knew contained more insects, but he supposed that those sounds were every bit as imaginary as the phantom movement glimpsed from the corners of his eyes.

Though he knew Clint to be a born stoic, Bobby was impressed by the apparent ease with which the guy endured the creepy-crawly decor. This was an employee he must never lose. He decided on the spot to give Clint a significant raise in salary before the day was out.

Bobby found Dr. Manfred nearly as disquieting as his collection. The tall, thin, long-limbed entomologist seemed to be the offspring of a professional basketball player and one of those African stick insects that you saw in nature films and hoped never to encounter in real life.

Manfred stood behind his desk, his chair pushed out of the way, and they stood in front of it. Their attention was directed upon a two-foot-long, one-foot-wide, white-enamel, inch-deep lab tray which occupied the center of the desktop and over which was draped a small white towel.

"I have had no sleep since Mr. Karaghiosis brought this to me last night," Manfred said, "and I won't sleep much tonight, either, just turning over all the remaining questions in my mind. This dissection was the most fascinating of my career, and I doubt that I'll ever again experience anything in my life to equal it."

The intensity with which Manfred spoke—and the implication that neither good food nor good sex, neither a beautiful sunset nor a fine wine, could be a fraction as satisfying as insect dismemberment—gave Bobby a queasy stomach.

He glanced at the fourth man in the room, if only to divert his attention briefly from their bugophile host. The guy was in his late forties, as round as Manfred was angular, as pink as Manfred was pale, with red-gold hair, blue eyes, and freckles. He sat on a chair in the corner, straining the seams of his gray jogging suit, with his hands fisted on his heavy thighs, looking like a good Boston Irish fellow who had been trying to eat his way into a career as a Sumo wrestler. The entomologist hadn't introduced or even referred to the well-padded observer. Bobby figured that introductions would be made when Manfred was ready. He decided not to force the issue—if only because the round man silently regarded them with a mixture of wonder, suspicion, fear, and intense curiosity that encouraged Bobby to believe they would not be pleased to hear what he had to tell them when, at last, he spoke.

With long-fingered, spidery hands—which Bobby might have sprayed with Raid if he'd had any—Dyson Manfred removed the towel from the white-enamel tray, revealing the remains of Frank's insect. The head, a couple of the legs, one of the highly articulated pincers, and a few other unidentifiable parts had been cut off and put aside. Each grisly piece rested on a soft pad of what appeared to be cotton cloth, almost as a jeweler might present a fine gem on velvet to a prospective buyer. Bobby stared at the plum-size head with its small reddish-blue eye, then at its two large muddy-yellow eyes that were too similar in color to Dyson Manfred's. He shivered. The main part of the bug was in the middle of the tray, on its back. The exposed underside had been slit open, the outer layers of tissue removed or folded back, and the inner workings revealed.

Using the gleaming point of a slender scalpel, which he handled with grace and precision, the entomologist began by showing them the respiratory, ingestive, digestive, and excretory systems of the bug. Manfred kept referring to the "great art" of the biological design, but Bobby saw nothing that equaled a painting by Matisse; in fact, the guts of the thing were even more repellent than its exterior. One term—"polishing chamber"—struck him as odd, but when he asked for a further explanation, Manfred only said, "in time, in time," and went on with his lecture.

When the entomologist finished, Bobby said, "Okay, we know how the thing ticks, so what does that tell us about it that we might want to know? For instance, where does it come from?"

Manfred stared at him, unresponding.

Bobby said, "The South American jungles?"

Manfred's peculiar amber eyes were hard to read, and his silence puzzling.

"Africa?" Bobby said. The entomologist's stare was beginning to make him twitchier than he already was.

"Mr. Dakota," Manfred said finally, "you're asking the wrong question. Let me ask the interesting ones for you. What does this creature eat? Well, to put it in the simplest terms that any layman can understand—it eats a broad spectrum of minerals, rock, and soil. What does it ex—"

"It eats dirt?" Clint asked.

"That's an even simpler way to express it," Manfred said. "Not precise, mind you, but simpler. We don't yet understand how it breaks down those substances or how it obtains energy from them. There are aspects of its biology that we can see perfectly clearly but that still remain mysterious."

"I thought insects ate plants or each other or . . . dead meat," Bobby said.

"They do," the entomologist confirmed. "This thing is not an insect—or any other class of the phylum *Arthropoda*, for that matter."

"Sure looks like an insect to me," Bobby said, glancing down at the partly dismantled bug and grimacing involuntarily.

"No," Manfred said, *"this* is a creature that evidently bores through soil and stone, capable of ingesting that material in chunks as large as fat grapes. And the next question is, 'If that's what it eats, what does it excrete?' And the answer, Mr. Dakota, is that it excretes diamonds."

Bobby jerked as if the entomologist had hit him.

He glanced at Clint, who looked as surprised as Bobby felt. The Pollard case had induced several changes in the Greek, and now it had robbed him of his poker face.

In a tone of voice that suggested Manfred was playing them for fools, Clint said, "You're telling us it turns dirt into diamonds?"

"No, no," Manfred said. "It methodically eats through veins of diamond-bearing carbon and other material, until it finds the gems. Then it swallows them in their encrusted jackets of minerals, *digests* those minerals, passes the rough diamond into the polishing chamber, where any remaining extraneous matter is worn away by vigorous contact with these hundreds of fine, wirelike bristles that line the chamber." With the scalpel he pointed to the feature of the bug that he had just described. "Then it squirts the raw diamond out the other end."

The entomologist opened the center drawer of his desk, removed a white handkerchief, unfolded it, and revealed three red diamonds, all considerably smaller than the one Bobby had taken to van Corvaire, but probably worth hundreds of thousands, maybe millions, apiece.

"I found these at various points in the creature's system."

The largest of the three was still partially encased in a mottled brown-black-gray mineral crust.

"They're diamonds?" Bobby said, playing ignorant. "I've never seen red diamonds."

"Neither had I. So I went to another professor, a geologist who happens to be a gemologist as well, got him out of bed at midnight to show these to him."

Bobby glanced at the would-be Irish Sumo wrestler, but the man did not rise from his chair or speak, so he evidently was not the geologist.

Manfred explained what Bobby and Clint already knew— that these scarlet diamonds were among the rarest things on earth—while they pretended that it was all news to them. "This discovery strengthened my suspicions about the creature, so I went straight to Dr. Gavenall's house and woke *him* shortly before two o'clock this morning. He threw on sweats and sneakers, and we came right back here, and we've been here ever since, working this out together, unable to believe our own eyes."

At last the round man rose and stepped to the side of the desk.

"Roger Gavenall," Manfred said, by way of introduction. "Roger is a geneticist, a specialist in recombinant DNA, and widely known for his creative projections of macroscale genetic engineering that might conceivably progress from current knowledge."

"Sorry," Bobby said, "I lost you at 'Roger is . . .' We'll need some more of that layman's language, I'm afraid."

"I'm a geneticist and futurist," Gavenall said. His voice was unexpectedly melodic, like that of a television game-show host. "Most genetic engineering, for the foreseeable future, will take place on a *micro*scopic scale—creating new and useful bacteria, repairing flawed genes in the cells of human beings to correct inherited weaknesses and prevent inherited disease. But eventually we'll be able to create whole new species of animals and insects, *macro*scale engineering—useful things like voracious mosquito eaters that will eliminate the need to spray Malathion in tropical regions like Florida. Cows that are maybe half the size of today's cows and a lot more metabolically efficient, so they require less food, yet produce twice as much milk."

Bobby wanted to suggest that Gavenall consider combining the two biological inventions to produce a small cow that ate only enormous quantities of mosquitoes and produced *three* times as much milk. But he kept his mouth shut, certain that neither of the scientists would appreciate his humor. Anyway, he had to admit that his compulsion to make a joke of this was an attempt to deal with his own deep-seated fear of the ever-increasing weirdness of the Pollard case.

"This thing," Gavenall said, indicating the deconstructed bug in the lab tray, "isn't anything that nature created. It's clearly an engineered lifeform, so astonishingly task-specific in every aspect of its biology that it's essentially a biological machine. A diamond scavenger."

Using a pair of forceps and the scalpel, Dyson Manfred gently turned over the insect that wasn't an insect, so they could see its midnight-black shell rimmed with red markings.

Bobby thought he heard whispery movement in many parts of the study, and he wished Manfred would let some sunlight into the room. The windows were covered with interior wood shutters, and the slats were tightly shut. Bugs liked darkness and shadows, and the lamps here seemed insufficiently bright to dissuade them from scurrying out of the shallow drawers, over Bobby's shoes, up his socks, and under the legs of his pants.

Hanging his pendulous belly over the desk, indicating the crimson edging on the carapace, Gavenall said, "On a hunch Dyson and I shared, we showed a representation of this pattern to an associate in the mathematics department, and he confirmed that it's an obvious binary code."

"Like the universal product code that's on everything you buy at the grocery store," the entomologist explained.

Clint said, "You mean the red marks are the bug's *number?*"

"Yes."

"Like . . . well, like a license plate?"

"More or less," Manfred said. "We haven't taken a chip of the red material for analysis yet, but we suspect it'll prove to be a ceramic material, painted onto the shell or spray-bonded in some fashion."

Gavenall said, "Somewhere there are a lot of these things, industriously digging for diamonds, red diamonds, and each of them carries a coded serial number that identifies it to whomever created it and set it to work."

Bobby grappled with that concept for a moment, trying to find a way to see it as a part of the world in which he lived, but it simply did not fit. "Okay, Dr. Gavenall, you're able to envision engineered creatures like this—"

"I couldn't have envisioned this," Gavenall said adamantly. "It never would've occurred to me. I could only recognize it for what it was, for what it must be."

"All right, but nevertheless you recognized what it must be, which is something neither Clint nor I could've done. So now tell me—who could make something like this damned thing?"

Manfred and Gavenall exchanged a meaningful look and were both silent for a long moment, as if they knew the answer to his question but were reluctant to reveal it. Finally, lowering his game-show-host voice to an even more mellifluous note, Gavenall said, "The genetic knowledge and engineering skill required to produce this thing do not yet exist. We're not even close to being able to . . . to . . . not even *close.*"

Bobby said, "How long until science advances far enough to make this thing possible?"

"No way of arriving at a precise answer," Manfred said.

"Guess."

"Decades?" Gavenall said. "A century? Who knows?"

Clint said, "Wait a minute. What're you telling us? That this thing comes from the future, that it came through some . . . some time warp from the next century?"

"Either that," Gavenall said, "or . . . it doesn't come from this world at all."

Stunned, Bobby looked down at the bug with no less revulsion but with considerably more wonder and respect than he'd had a moment ago. "You really think this might be a biological machine created by people from another world? An alien artifact?"

Manfred worked his mouth but produced no sound, as if rendered speechless by the prospect of what he was about to say.

"Yes," Gavenall said, "an alien artifact. Seems more likely to me than the possibility that it came tumbling back to us through some hole in time."

Even as Gavenall spoke, Dyson Manfred continued to work his mouth in a frustrated attempt to break the silence that gripped him, and his lantern jaw gave him the look of a praying mantis masticating a grisly lunch. When words at last issued from him, they came in a rush: "We want you to understand, we will not, flatly will not, return this specimen. We'd be derelict as scientists to allow this incredible thing to reside in the hands of laymen, we must preserve and protect it, and we will, even if we have to do so by force."

A flush of defiance lent a glow of health to the entomologist's pale, angular face for the first time since Bobby had met him.

"Even if by force," he repeated.

Bobby had no doubt that he and Clint could beat the crap out of the human stick bug and his rotund colleague, but there was no reason to do so. He didn't care if they kept the thing in the lab tray—as long as they agreed to some ground rules about how and when they would go public with it.

All he wanted right now was to get out of that bughouse, into warm sunlight and fresh air. The whispery sounds from the specimen drawers, though certainly imaginary, grew louder and more frenzied by the minute. His entomophobia would soon kick him off the ledge of reason and send him screaming from the room; he wondered if his anxiety was apparent or if he was sufficiently self-controlled to conceal it. He felt a bead of sweat slip down his left temple, and had the answer.

"Let's be absolutely frank," Gavenall said. "It's not only our obligation to science that requires us to maintain possession of this specimen. Revelation of this find will *make* us, academically and financially. Neither one of us is a slouch in his field, but this will catapult us to the top, the very top, and we're willing to do whatever is necessary to protect our interests here." His blue eyes had narrowed, and his open Irish face had closed up into a hard mask of determination. "I'm not saying I'd kill to keep that specimen . . . but I'm not saying I wouldn't, either."

Bobby sighed. "I've done a lot of research for UCI into the backgrounds of prospective faculty members, so I know the academic world can be as competitive and vicious and dirty— dirtier—than either politics or show business. I'm not going to fight you on this. But we've got to reach an agreement about when you can go public with it. I don't want you doing anything that would bring my client to the attention of the press until we've resolved his case and are sure he's . . . out of danger."

"And when will that be?" Manfred asked.

Bobby shrugged. "A day or two. Maybe a week. I doubt it'll drag on much longer than that."

The entomologist and geneticist beamed at each other, obviously delighted. Manfred said, "That's no problem at all. We'll need much longer than that to finish studying the specimen, prepare our first paper for publication, and devise a strategy to deal with both the scientific community and the media."

Bobby imagined that he heard one of the shallow drawers sliding open in the case behind him, forced outward by the weight of a vile torrent of giant, squirming Madagascar roaches.

"But I'll take the three diamonds with me," he said. "They're quite valuable, and they belong to my client."

Manfred and Gavenall hesitated, made a token protest, but quickly agreed. Clint took the stones and rewrapped them in the handkerchief. The scientists' capitulation convinced Bobby there had been more than three diamonds in the bug, probably at least five, leaving them with two stones to support their thesis regarding the bug's origins and purpose.

"We'll want to meet your client, interview him," Gavenall said.

"That's up to him," Bobby said.

"It's essential. We *must* interview him."

"That's his decision," Bobby said. "You've gotten most of what you wanted. Eventually he may agree, and then you'll have everything you're after. But don't push it now."

The round man nodded. "Fair enough. But tell me . . . where *did* he find the thing?"

"He doesn't remember. He has amnesia." The drawer behind him was open now. He could hear the shells of the huge roaches clicking and scraping together as they poured out of confinement and down the front of the cabinet, swarming toward him. "We really have to go," he said. "We don't have another minute to spare." He left the study quickly, trying not to look as if he was bolting for his life.

Clint followed him, as did the two scientists, and at the front door, Manfred said, "I'm going to sound as if I ought to be writing stories for some sensational tabloid, but if this *is* an alien artifact that came into your client's hands, do you think he could've gotten it inside a . . . well, a spaceship? Those people who claim to have been abducted and forced to undergo examinations aboard spaceships . . . they always seem to go through a period of amnesia first, before learning the truth."

"Those people are crackpots or frauds," Gavenall said sharply. "We can't let ourselves be associated with that sort of thing." He frowned, and the frown deepened into a scowl, and he said, "Unless in this case it's true."

Looking back at them from the stoop, grateful to be outside, Bobby said, "Maybe it is. I'm at a point where I'll believe anything till it's disproved. But I'll tell you this . . . my feeling is that whatever is happening to my client is something a lot stranger than alien abduction."

"A lot," Clint agreed.

Without further elaboration, they went down the front walkway to the car. Bobby opened his door and stood for a moment, reluctant to get into Clint's Chevy. The mild breeze washing down the Irvine hills felt so *clean* after the stale air in Manfred's study.

He put one hand in his pocket, felt the three red diamonds, and said softly, "Bug shit."

When he finally got into the car and slammed the door, he barely resisted the urge to reach under his shirt to determine if the things he still felt crawling on him were real.

Manfred and Gavenall stood on the front stoop, watching Bobby and Clint, as if half expecting their car to tip back on its rear bumper and shoot straight into the sky to rendezvous with some great glowing craft out of a Spielberg movie.

Clint drove two blocks, turned at the corner, and pulled to the curb as soon as they were out of sight. "Bobby, where in the hell *did* Frank get that thing?"

Bobby could only answer him with another question: "How many different places does he go when he teleports? The money, the red diamonds and the bug, the black sand—and how far away are some of those places? Really *far* away?"

"And who is he?" Clint asked.

"Frank Pollard from El Encanto Heights."

"But I mean, who is that?" Clint thumped one fist against the steering wheel. "Who the hell *is* Frank Pollard from El Encanto?"

"I think what you really want to know is not who he is. More important . . . *what* is he?"

# 44

By SURPRISE Bobby came to visit.

Lunch was eaten before Bobby came. Dessert was still in Thomas's mind. Not the taste of it. The memory. Vanilla ice cream, fresh strawberries. The way dessert made you feel.

He was alone in his room, sitting in his armchair, thinking about making a picture poem that would have the feeling of eating ice cream and strawberries, not the taste but the good feeling, so some day when you didn't have any ice cream or strawberries, you could just look at the poem and get that same good feeling even without eating anything. Of course, you couldn't use pictures of ice cream or strawberries in the poem, because that wouldn't be a poem, that would be only *saying* how good ice cream and strawberries made you feel. A poem didn't just say, it showed you and made you feel.

Then Bobby came through the door, and Thomas was so happy he forgot the poem, and they hugged. Somebody was with Bobby, but it wasn't Julie, so Thomas was disappointed. He was embarrassed, too, because it turned out he'd met the person with Bobby a couple times before, over the years, but he didn't remember him right away, which made him feel dumb. It was Clint. Thomas said the name to himself, over and over, so maybe he'd remember next time: *Clint, Clint, Clint, Clint, Clint.*

"Julie couldn't come," Bobby said, "she's babysitting a client."

Thomas wondered why a baby would ever need a private eye, but he didn't ask. In TV only grownups needed private eyes, which were called private *eyes* because they looked out for you, though he wasn't sure why they were called private. He also wondered how a baby could pay for a private eye, because he knew eyes like Bobby and Julie worked for money like everyone else, but babies didn't work, they were too little to do anything. So where'd this one get the money to pay Bobby and Julie? He hoped they didn't get cheated out of their money, they worked hard for it.

Bobby said, "She told me to tell you she loves you even more than she did yesterday, and she'll love you even more tomorrow."

They hugged again because this time Thomas was giving the hug to Bobby for Julie.

Clint asked if he could see the latest scrapbook of poems. He took it across the room and sat in Derek's armchair, which was okay because Derek wasn't in it, he was in the wreck room.

Bobby moved the chair from the worktable, putting it closer to the armchair that belonged to Thomas. He sat, and they talked about what a big blue day it was and how nice the flowers looked where they were all bright outside Thomas's window.

For a while they talked about lots of things, and Bobby was funny—except when they talked about Julie, he changed. He was worried for Julie, you could tell. When he talked about her, he was like a good picture poem—he didn't say his worry, but he showed it and made you feel it.

Thomas was already worried for Julie, so Bobby's worry made him feel even worse, made him scared for her.

"We've got our hands full with the current case," Bobby said, "so neither one of us might be able to visit again until this weekend or the first of the week."

"Okay, sure," Thomas said, and a big coldness rushed in from somewhere and filled him up. Each time Bobby mentioned the new case, the one with the baby, his picture poem of worry was even easier to read.

Thomas wondered if this was the case where they were going to meet up with the Bad Thing. He was pretty sure it was. He thought he should tell Bobby about the Bad Thing, but he couldn't find a way. No matter how he told it, he'd sound like the dumbest dumb person who ever lived at The Home. It was better to wait until the danger was coming a lot nearer, then TV to Bobby a real hard warning that'd scare him into looking out for the Bad Thing and shooting it when he saw it. Bobby would pay attention to a TVed warning because he wouldn't know where it came from, that it came from just a dumb person.

And Bobby could shoot, too, all private eyes could shoot because most days it was bad out there in the world, and you knew you were going to meet up with somebody who was going to shoot at you first or try to run you down with a car or stab you or strangle you or, once in a while, try to throw you off a building, or even Try To Make It Look Like Suicide, and since most good guys didn't carry guns around with them, private eyes who watched over them had to be good shooters.

After a while Bobby had to go. Not to the bathroom but back to work. So they hugged again. And then Bobby and Clint were gone, and Thomas was alone.

He went to the window. Looked out. The day was good, better than night. But even with the sun pushing most darkness out past the edge of the world, and even with the rest of the darkness hiding from the sun behind trees and buildings, there was badness in the day. The Bad Thing hadn't gone out past the edge of the world with the night. It was still there, somewhere in the day, you could tell.

Last night, when he got too close to the Bad Thing and it tried to grab him, he was so afraid, he pulled away quick like. He had a feeling the Bad Thing was trying to find out who he was and where he was, and then was going to come to The Home and eat him like it ate the little animals. So he pretty much made up his mind not to get real close to it again, stay far away, but now he couldn't do that because of Julie and the baby. If Bobby, who never worried, was so worried for Julie, then Thomas needed to be even more worried for her than he was. And if Julie and Bobby thought the baby should be watched over, then Thomas had to worry about the baby, too, because what was important to Julie was important to him.

He reached out into the day.

It was there. Far away yet.

He didn't get close.

He was scared.

But for Julie, for Bobby, for the baby, he'd have to stop being scared, get closer, and be sure he knew all the time where the Bad Thing was and whether it was coming this way.

# 45

JACKIE JAXX did not arrive at the offices of Dakota & Dakota until ten past four that Tuesday afternoon, a full hour after Bobby and Clint returned, and to Julie's annoyance he spent half an hour creating an atmosphere that he found conducive to his work. He felt the room was too bright, so he closed the blinds on the large windows, though the approaching winter twilight and an incoming bank of clouds over the Pacific had already robbed the day of much of its light. He tried different arrangements with the three brass lamps, each of which was equipped with a three-way bulb, giving him what seemed an infinite number of combinations; he finally left one of them at seventy watts, one at thirty, and one off completely. He asked Frank to move from the sofa to one of the chairs, decided that wasn't going to work, moved Julie's big chair out from behind the desk and put him in that, then arranged four other chairs in a semicircle in front of it.

Julie suspected that Jackie could have worked effectively with the blinds open and all of the lamps on. He was a performer, however, even when off the stage, and he could not resist being theatrical.

In recent years magicians had forsaken fake show-biz monikers like The Great Blackwell and Harry Houdini in favor of names that at least seemed like real ones, but Jackie was a throwback. Just as Houdini's real name was Erich Weiss, so Jackie had been baptized David Carver. Because he performed comic magic, he had avoided mysterious-sounding names. And because, since puberty, he had yearned to be part of the night-club and Vegas scene, he had chosen a new identity that, to him and those in his social circle, sounded like Nevada royalty. While other kids thought about being teachers, doctors, real-estate salesmen or auto mechanics, young Davey Carver had dreamed of being someone like Jackie Jaxx; now, God help him, he was living his dream.

Although he was currently between a one-week engagement in Reno and a stint as the opening act for Sammy Davis in Vegas, Jackie showed up not in blue jeans or an ordinary suit, but in an outfit he could have worn during performances: a black leisure suit with emerald-green piping on the lapels and cuffs of the jacket, a matching green shirt, and black patent-leather shoes. He was thirty-six years old, five feet eight, thin, cancerously tanned, with hair that he dyed ink-black and teeth that were unnaturally, *ferociously* white, thanks to the modern miracle of dental bonding.

Three years ago Dakota & Dakota had been hired by the Las Vegas hotel with which Jackie had a long-term contract, and charged with the sticky task of uncovering the identity of a blackmailer who was trying to extort most of the magician's income. The case had many unexpected twists and turns, but by the time they reached the end, the thing that most surprised Julie was that she had gotten over her initial distaste for the magician and had come to sort of like him. Sort of.

Finally Jackie settled on the chair directly in front of Frank. "Julie, you and Clint sit to my right. Bobby, to my left, please."

Julie saw no good reason why she couldn't sit in whichever of the three chairs she chose, but she played along.

Half of Jackie's Vegas act involved the hypnotizing and comic exploitation of audience members. His knowledge of hypnotic technique was so extensive, and his understanding of the functioning of the mind in a trance state was so profound, that he was frequently invited to participate in medical conferences with physicians, psychologists, and psychiatrists who were exploring practical uses of hypnosis. Perhaps they could have persuaded a psychiatrist to help them pierce Frank's amnesia with hypnotic regression therapy. But it was doubtful that any doctor was as qualified for the task as Jackie Jaxx.

Besides, no matter what fantastic things Jackie learned about Frank, he could be counted on to keep his mouth shut. He owed a lot to Bobby and Julie, and in spite of his faults, he was a man who paid his debts and had at least a vestigial sense of loyalty that was rare in the me-me-me culture of show business.

In the moody amber light of the two brass lamps, with the world darkening rapidly beyond the drawn blinds, Jackie's smooth and well-projected voice, full of low rounded tones and an occasional dramatic vibrato, commanded not just Frank's attention but everyone else's as well. He used a beveled teardrop crystal on a gold chain to focus Frank's attention, after suggesting that the others look at Frank's face rather than at the bauble, to avoid unwanted entrancement.

"Frank, please watch the light winking in the crystal, a very soft and lovely light fluttering from one facet to another, one facet to another, a very warm and appealing light, warm, fluttering. . . ."

After a while, lulled somewhat herself by Jackie's calculated patter, Julie noticed Frank's eyes glaze over.

Beside her, Clint switched on the small tape recorder that he had used when Frank had told them his story yesterday afternoon.

Still twisting the chain back and forth between his thumb and forefinger to make the crystal spin on the end of it, Jackie said, "All right, Frank, you are now slipping into a very relaxed state, a deeply relaxed state, where you will hear only my voice, no other, and will respond only to my voice, no other. . . ."

When he had conveyed Frank into a deep trance and finished giving him instructions related to the interrogation ahead, Jackie told him to close his eyes. Frank obliged.

Jackie put the crystal down. He said, "What is your name?"

"Frank Pollard."

"Where do you live?"

"I don't know."

Having been briefed on the phone by Julie earlier in the day, aware of the information they were seeking from their client, Jackie said, "Have you ever lived in El Encanto?"

A hesitation. Then: "Yes."

Frank's voice was strangely flat. His face was so haggard and deathly pale that he seemed almost like an exhumed corpse that had been sorcerously revitalized for the purpose of serving as a bridge between the members of a séance and those to whom they wished to speak in the land of the dead.

"Do you recall your address in El Encanto?"

"No."

"Was your address 1458 Pacific Hill Road?"

A frown flickered across Frank's face and was gone almost as soon as it came. "Yes. That's what . . . Bobby found . . . with the computer."

"But do you actually remember that place?"

"No."

Jackie adjusted his Rolex watch, then used both hands to smooth back his thick, black hair. "When did you live in El Encanto, Frank?"

"I don't know."

"You must tell me the truth."

"Yeah."

"You cannot lie to me, Frank, or hide anything from me. That is impossible in your current state. When did you live there?"

"I don't know."

"Did you live there alone?"

"I don't know."

"Do you remember being in the hospital last night, Frank?"

"Yeah."

"And you . . . disappeared?"

"They say I did."

"Where did you disappear to, Frank?"

Silence.

"Frank, where did you disappear to?"

"I . . . I'm afraid."

"Why?"

"I . . . don't know. I can't think."

"Frank, do you remember waking up in your car last Thursday morning, parked along a street in Laguna Beach?"

"Yeah."

"Your hands were full of black sand."

"Yeah." Frank wiped his hands on his thighs, as if he could feel the black grains clinging to his sweaty palms.

"Where did you get that sand, Frank?"

"I don't know."

"Take your time. Think about it."

"I don't know."

"Do you remember checking into a motel later . . . napping . . . then waking up with blood all over yourself?"

"I remember," Frank said, and he shuddered.

"Where did that blood come from, Frank?"

"I don't know," he said miserably.

"It was cat blood, Frank. Did you know it was cat blood?"

"No." His eyelids fluttered, but he did not open his eyes. "Just cat blood? Really?"

"Do you remember encountering a cat that day?"

"No."

Clearly, a more aggressive technique would be required to get the answers they needed. Jackie began to talk Frank backward in time, gradually regressing him to his admission to the hospital yesterday evening, then farther back toward the moment he had awakened in that Anaheim alleyway in the earliest hours of Thursday morning, knowing nothing but his name. Beyond that point might lie his memory, if he could be induced to step through the veil of amnesia and recover his past.

Julie leaned slightly forward in her chair and looked past Jackie Jaxx, wondering how Bobby was enjoying the show. She figured the spinning crystal and other hocus-pocus would appeal to his boyish spirit of adventure, and that he would be smiling and bright-eyed.

Instead he was somber. His teeth must have been clenched, for his jaw muscles bulged. He had told her what they learned at Dyson Manfred's house, and she had been as astonished and shaken as he and Clint. But that didn't seem to explain his current mood. Maybe he was still unnerved by the memory of the bugs in the entomologist's study. Or maybe he continued to be troubled by that dream he'd had last week: *the bad thing is coming, the bad thing. . . .*

She had dismissed his dream as unimportant. Now she wondered if it had been genuinely prophetic. After all the weirdness that Frank had brought into their lives, she was more willing to give credence to such things as omens, visions, and prescient dreams.

*The bad thing is coming, the bad thing. . . .*

Maybe the bad thing was Mr. Blue.

Jackie regressed Frank to the alleyway, to the very moment

234

when he had first awakened in a strange place, disoriented and confused. "Now go back further, Frank, just a little further, back just a few more seconds, and a few more, back, back, beyond the total darkness in your mind, beyond that black wall in your mind. . . ."

Since the questioning had begun, Frank had appeared to dwindle in Julie's desk chair, as if made of wax and subjected to a flame. He had grown paler, too, if that was possible, as white as candle paraffin. But now, as he was forced backward through the darkness in his mind, toward the light of memory on the other side, he sat up straighter, put his hands on the arms of the chair and clutched the vinyl almost tightly enough to cause the upholstery to split. He seemed to be growing, returning to his former size, as if he had drunk one of the magic elixirs that Alice had consumed in her adventures at the far end of the rabbit hole.

"Where are you now?" Jackie asked.

Frank's eyes twitched beneath his closed lids. An inarticulate, strangled sound issued from him. "Uh . . . uh . . ."

"Where are you now?" Jackie insisted gently but firmly.

"Fireflies," Frank said shakily. "Fireflies in a windstorm!" He began to breathe rapidly, raggedly, as if he were having trouble drawing air into his lungs.

"What do you mean by that, Frank?"

"Fireflies . . ."

"Where are you, Frank?"

"Everywhere. Nowhere."

"We don't have fireflies in southern California, Frank, so you must be somewhere else. Think, Frank. Look around yourself now and tell me where you are."

"Nowhere."

Jackie made a few more attempts to get Frank to describe his surroundings and be more specific as to the nature of the fireflies, all to no avail.

"Move him on from there," Bobby said. "Farther back."

Julie glanced at the recorder in Clint's hand and saw the spools turning behind the plastic window in the tapedeck.

With his melodic and vibrant voice, in seductively rhythmic cadences, Jackie ordered Frank to regress past the firefly-speckled darkness.

Suddenly Frank said, "What am I doing here?" He was not

referring to the offices of Dakota & Dakota, but to the place that Jackie Jaxx had drawn him to in his memory. "Why here?"

"Where are you, Frank?"

"The house. What in the hell am I doing here, why did I come here? This is crazy, I shouldn't be here."

"Whose house is it, Frank?" Bobby asked.

Because he had been instructed to hear only the hypnotist's voice, Frank did not respond until Jackie repeated the question. Then: "Her house. It's *her* house. She's dead, of course, been dead seven years, but it's still her house, always will be, the bitch will haunt the place, you can't destroy that kind of evil, not entirely, part of it lingers in the rooms where she lived, in everything she touched."

"Who was she, Frank?"

"Mother."

"Your mother? What was her name?"

"Roselle. Roselle Pollard."

"This is the house on Pacific Hill Road?"

"Yeah. Look at it, my God, what a place, what a dark place, what a bad place. Can't people see what a bad place it is? Can't they see that something terrible lives in there?" He was crying. Tears glimmered in his eyes, then streamed down his cheeks. Anguish twisted his voice. "Can't they see what's in there, what lives there, what hides there and *breeds* in that bad place? Are people blind? Or do they just not *want* to see?"

Julie was riveted by Frank's tortured voice and by the agony that had wrenched his face into an approximation of the pained countenance of a lost and frightened child. But she turned away from him and peered past the hypnotist to see if Bobby had reacted to the words "bad place."

He was looking at her. The expression of distress that darkened his blue eyes was proof enough that the reference had not escaped him.

At the other end of the room, carrying a sheaf of printouts, Lee Chen entered from the reception lounge. He closed the door quietly. Julie put a finger to her lips, then motioned him to the sofa.

Jackie spoke soothingly to Frank, trying to allay the fear that had electrified him.

Suddenly Frank let out a sharp cry of fear. He sounded more like a frightened animal than like a man. He sat up even straighter. He was trembling. He opened his eyes, but obviously did not see anything in the room; he was still in a trance. "Oh, my God, he's coming, he's coming now, the twins must've told him I'm here, he's coming!"

Frank's unalloyed terror was so pure and intense that some of it was communicated to Julie. Her heartbeat speeded up, and she began to breathe more rapidly, shallowly.

Trying to keep his subject relaxed enough to be cooperative, Jackie said, "Calm down, Frank. Relax and be calm. Nobody can hurt you. Nothing unpleasant will happen. Be calm, relaxed, calm. . . ."

Frank shook his head. "No. No, he's coming, he's coming, he's going to get me this time. Dammit, why did I come back here? Why did I come back and give him a chance at me?"

"Relax now—"

"He's there!" Frank tried to rise to his feet, seemed unable to find the strength, and dug his fingers even deeper into the vinyl padding on the arms of the chair. "He's right *there,* and he sees me, he sees me."

Bobby said, "Who is he, Frank?" and Jackie repeated the question.

"Candy. It's Candy!" When he was asked again for the name of this person he feared, he repeated: "Candy."

"His name is Candy?"

"He *sees* me!"

In a more forceful and commanding voice than before, Jackie said, "You will relax, Frank. You *will* be calm and relaxed."

But Frank only grew more agitated. He had broken into a sweat. Fixed on something in a far place and time, his eyes were wild. His terror seemed to be sweeping him into a heart-bursting panic.

"I don't have much control of him," Jackie said worriedly. "I'm going to have to bring him out of it."

Bobby slid forward to the edge of his chair. "No, not yet. In a minute but not yet. Ask him about this Candy. Who is the guy?"

Jackie repeated the question.

Frank said, "He's death."

Frowning, Jackie said, "That's not a clear answer, Frank."

"He's death walking, he's death living, he's my brother, *her* child, her favorite child, her *spawn,* and I hate him, he wants to kill me, here he comes!"

With a wretched bleat of terror, Frank started to push up from the chair.

Jackie ordered him to stay where he was.

Frank sat down reluctantly, but his terror only grew, because he could still see Candy coming toward him.

Jackie tried to bring him out of that place in the past, forward to the present, and out of his trance, but to no avail.

"Got to get away now, now, *now,"* Frank said desperately.

Julie was frightened for him. She'd never seen anyone look more pathetic or vulnerable. He was drenched in sweat, shaking violently. His hair had fallen over his forehead, into his eyes, but it did not interfere with the vision of terror that he had called up from his past. He clutched the arms of the chair so fiercely that a fingernail on his right hand finally punctured the vinyl upholstery.

"I've got to get out of here," Frank repeated urgently.

Jackie told him to stay put.

"No, I've got to get away from him!"

To Bobby, Jackie Jaxx said, "This has never happened to me, I've lost control of him. Jesus, look at him, I'm afraid the guy's going to have a heart attack."

"Come on, Jackie, you've got to help him," Bobby said sharply. He got off his chair, squatted beside Frank, putting his hand on Frank's in a gesture of comfort and reassurance.

"Bobby, don't," Clint said, standing up so fast that he dropped the tape recorder he'd been balancing on his thigh.

Bobby didn't respond to Clint, for he was too focused on Frank, who seemed to be shaking himself to pieces in front of them. The guy was like a boiler with a jammed release valve, filled to the bursting point not with steam pressure but with manic terror. Bobby was trying to calm him, where Jackie had failed.

For an instant Julie didn't understand what had made Clint shoot to his feet. But she realized that Bobby had seen something the rest of them had missed: fresh blood on Frank's right hand. Bobby hadn't put his hand over Frank's merely to offer comfort; he was trying, as gently as possible, to loosen Frank's grip on the arm of the chair, because Frank had torn open the vinyl and cut himself, perhaps repeatedly, on an exposed staple or upholstery tack.

"He's coming, got to get away!" Frank let go of the chair, grabbed Bobby's hand, and got to his feet, pulling Bobby up with him.

Suddenly Julie understood what Clint feared, and she stood up so fast that she knocked her chair over. "Bobby, no!"

Thrown into a panic by the vision of his murderous brother, Frank screamed. With a hiss like steam escaping from a locomotive engine, he vanished. And took Bobby with him.

# 46

FIREFLIES IN A WINDSTORM.

Bobby seemed to be floating in space, for he had no sense of his body's position, couldn't tell if he was lying or sitting or standing, right side up or upside down, as if weightless in an immense void. He had no sense of smell or taste. He could hear nothing. He could feel neither heat nor cold nor texture nor weight. The only thing he could see was limitless blackness that seemed to stretch to the ends of the universe—and millions upon millions of tiny fireflies, ephemeral as sparks, that swarmed around him. Actually, he was not sure he saw them at all, because he was not aware of having eyes with which to look at them; it was more as if he was . . . *aware* of them, not through any of the usual senses but through some inner sight, the mind's eye.

At first he panicked. The extreme sensory deprivation convinced him that he was paralyzed, without feeling in any limb or inch of skin, felled by a massive cerebral hemorrhage, deafened and blinded and trapped forever in a damaged brain that had severed all its connections to the outside world.

Then he became aware that he was in motion, not drifting in the blackness as he had first thought, but speeding through it, *rocketing* at a tremendous, frightening speed. He became aware of being drawn forward as if he were a bit of lint flying toward some vacuum cleaner of cosmic power, and all around him the fireflies swirled and tumbled. It was like being on an amusement park ride so huge and fast that only God could have designed it for His own pleasure, though there was no pleasure whatsoever in it for Bobby as he roller-coastered through pitch blackness, trying to scream.

He hit the forest floor on his feet, swayed, and almost fell against Frank, in front of whom he was standing. Frank still had a painfully tight grip on his hand.

Bobby was desperate for air. His chest ached; his lungs seemed to have shriveled up. He sucked in a deep breath, another, exhaling explosively.

He saw the blood, which was on both of their hands now. An image of torn upholstery flashed through his mind. Jackie Jaxx. Bobby remembered.

When Bobby tried to pull loose of his client, Frank held him fast and said, "Not here. No, I can't risk this. Too dangerous. Why am I here?"

Steeped in the scent of pines, Bobby surveyed the surrounding primeval forest, which was thick with shadows as dusk introduced night to the world. The air was frigid, and the bristling boughs of the giant evergreens drooped under a weight of snow, but he saw nothing frightening in that scene.

Then he realized that Frank was staring past him. He turned to discover they were on the edge of the forest. A snow-covered meadow sloped up gently behind them. At the top was a log cabin, not a rustic shack but an elaborate structure that clearly showed the input of an architect, a vacation retreat for someone with plenty of disposable income. A mantle of snow was draped over the main roof, another over the porch roof, each decorated with a fringe of icicles that glittered in the last beams of cold sunlight. No lights glowed at the windows. No smoke curled up from any of the three chimneys. The place appeared to be deserted.

"He knows about this," Frank said, still panicked. "I bought it under another name, but he found out about it, and he came here, almost killed me here, and he's probably keeping tabs on it, checking in regularly, hoping to catch me again."

Bobby was numbed less by the subzero cold than by the realization that he had teleported out of their office and onto this slope in the Sierras or some other mountains. He finally found his voice and said, "Frank, what—"

Darkness.

Fireflies.

Velocity.

He hit the floor rolling, slammed into a coffee table, and felt Frank let go of his hand. The table crashed over, spilling a vase and other decorative—and breakable—items onto a hardwood floor.

He'd sustained a solid knock to the head. When he pushed onto his knees and tried to stand, he was too dizzy to get up.

Frank was already on his feet, looking around, breathing hard. "San Diego. This was my apartment once. He found out about it. Had to get out fast."

When Frank reached down to help Bobby get up, Bobby unthinkingly accepted his hand, the uninjured one.

"Someone else lives here now," Frank said. "Must be off at work, we're lucky."

Darkness.

Fireflies.

Velocity.

Bobby found himself standing at a rusted iron gate between two stone pilasters, looking at a Victorian-style house with a sagging porch roof, broken balusters, and swaybacked steps. The sidewalk was cracked and canted, and weeds flourished in an unmown lawn. In the gloaming it looked like every kid's conception of a seriously haunted house, and he suspected it would look even worse in broad daylight.

Frank gasped. "Jesus, no, not here!"

Darkness.

Fireflies.

Velocity.

Papers fluttered to the floor from a massive mahogany desk, as if a wind had swept through the room, though the air was still now. They were in a book-lined study with French windows. An old man had risen from a wing-backed leather chair. He was wearing gray flannel slacks, a white shirt, a blue cardigan, and a look of surprise.

Frank said, "Doc," and with his free hand reached toward the startled elder.

Darkness.

Bobby had figured out that all was lightless and featureless because, for the moment, he did not exist as a coherent physical entity; he had no eyes, no ears, no nerve endings with which to feel. But understanding brought no diminishment of his fear.

Fireflies.

---

The millions of tiny, whirling points of light were probably the atomic particles of which his flesh was constructed, being shepherded along sheerly by the power of Frank's mind.

Velocity.

They were teleporting, and the process was probably just about instantaneous, requiring only microseconds from physical dissolution to reconstitution, though subjectively it seemed longer.

The decrepit house again. It must be the place in the hills north of Santa Barbara. They were upslope from the gate, along the Eugenia hedge that encircled the property.

Frank let out a low cry of terror the instant that he saw where he was.

Bobby was afraid of running into Candy just as much as Frank was, but also afraid of Frank, and of teleporting—

Darkness.

Fireflies.

Velocity.

This time they didn't materialize with the balance and stability of their arrival in the old man's study or at the peeling house with the rusted gate, but with the clumsiness of their intrusion into that apartment in San Diego. Bobby stumbled a few steps up a slope, still in Frank's grip as firmly as if they had been handcuffed, and they both fell to their knees on the plush, well-cropped grass.

Frantically Bobby tried to wrench loose of Frank. But Frank held fast with superhuman strength and pointed to a gravestone only a few feet in front of them. Bobby looked around and saw that they were alone in a cemetery, where massive coral trees and palms loomed eerily in the purple-gray twilight.

"He was our neighbor," Frank said.

Gasping for breath, unable to speak, still twisting his hand in an attempt to escape Frank's iron grip, Bobby saw the name NORBERT JAMES KOLREEN in the granite headstone.

"She had him killed," Frank said, "had her precious Candy kill him just because she felt he'd been rude to her. *Rude* to her! The crazy bitch."

Darkness.

Fireflies.

Velocity.

The book-lined study. The old man in the doorway now, looking into the room at them.

Bobby felt as if he had been on a corkscrew roller coaster for hours, turning upside down at high speed, again and again, until he couldn't be sure any more if he was actually moving . . . or standing still while the rest of the world spun and looped around him.

"I shouldn't have come here, Dr. Fogarty," Frank said worriedly. Blood dripped off his injured hand, spotting a pale-green section of the Chinese carpet. "Candy might've seen me at the house, might be trying to follow. Don't want to lead him to you."

Fogarty said, "Frank, wait—"

Darkness.

Fireflies.

Velocity.

They were in the backyard of the decaying house, thirty or forty feet from steps and a porch that were as spavined and dilapidated as those at the front of the place. Lights shone in the first-floor windows.

"I want to go, I want to be out of here," Frank said.

Bobby expected to teleport at once, and steeled himself for it, but nothing happened.

"I want *out* of here," Frank said again. When they did not pop from that place to another, Frank cursed in frustration.

Suddenly the kitchen door opened, and a woman stepped into sight. She stopped on the threshold and stared at them. The fading, muddy purple twilight barely exposed her, and the light from the kitchen silhouetted her but did not reveal any details of her face. Whether it was a trick of the strange illumination or an accurate revelation of her form, Bobby could not know, but when starkly outlined, she presented a powerfully erotic picture: sylphlike, gracefully thin yet clearly and lushly feminine, a smoky phantom that seemed either thinly clad or nude, and that issued a call of desire without making a sound. There was a powerful lubricity in this mysterious woman that made her the equal of any siren that had ever induced sailors to run their ships onto hull-gouging rocks.

"My sister Violet," Frank said with obvious dread and disgust.

Bobby noticed movement around her feet, a swarming of shadows. They poured down the steps, onto the lawn, and he saw they were cats. Their eyes were iridescent in the gloom.

He was gripping Frank every bit as hard as Frank was gripping him, for now he feared release as much as he had previously feared continued captivity. "Frank, get us out of here."

"I can't. I don't have control of this, of myself."

There were a dozen cats, two dozen, still more. As they rushed off the porch and across the first few yards of unmown grass, they were silent. Then, simultaneously, they cried out, as if they were a single creature. Their wail of anger and hunger instantly cured Bobby of his nausea and made his stomach quiver, instead, with terror.

"Frank!"

He wished he hadn't taken off his shoulder holster back at the office. His gun was back there on Julie's desk, of no use to him, but as he glimpsed the bared teeth of the oncoming horde, he figured the revolver wouldn't stop them anyway, at least not enough of them.

The nearest of the cats leaped—

♦　♦　♦

JULIE WAS standing by her office chair, where it had been moved into the center of the room for the session of hypnotic therapy. She was unable to step away from it because she had last seen Bobby when he had been next to that chair, and it was where she felt closest to him. "How long now?"

Clint was standing at her side. He looked at his watch. "Less than six minutes."

Jackie Jaxx was in the bathroom, splashing his face with cold water. Still on the sofa with a sheaf of printouts, Lee Chen was not as relaxed as he had been six and a half minutes ago. His Zen calm had been shattered. He was holding those papers in both hands, as if afraid they would vanish from his grasp, and his eyes were as wide now as they had been the moment that Bobby and Frank disappeared.

Julie was lightheaded with fear, but she was determined not to lose control of herself. Though there seemed to be nothing that she could do to help Bobby, an opportunity for action might arise when she least expected it, and she wanted to be calm and ready. "Last night, Hal said that Frank returned the first time about eighteen minutes after he'd left."

Clint nodded. "Then we've twelve minutes to go."

"After his second disappearance, he didn't return for hours."

"Listen," Clint said, "if they don't show up here again in twelve minutes or an hour or three hours, that doesn't mean anything terrible has happened to Bobby. It's not going to be the same every time."

"I know. What I'm more worried about is . . . the damn bed railing."

Clint said nothing.

Unable to keep her voice even, she said, "Frank never did bring it back. What happened to it?"

"He'll bring Bobby back," Clint said. "He won't let Bobby out there . . . wherever he goes."

She wished she felt confident about that.

♦  ♦  ♦

DARKNESS.

Fireflies.

Velocity.

Rain poured straight down in warm torrents, as if Bobby and Frank had materialized under a waterfall. It pasted their clothes to them in an instant. There was no wind whatsoever, as if the tremendous weight and ferocity of the rainfall had drowned the wind as it would a fire; the air was steamy-humid. They had traveled far enough around the globe to have left twilight behind; the sun was up there somewhere behind the steely plating of gray clouds.

They were on their sides this time, facing each other like two inebriates who had been arm wrestling and had fallen drunkenly off their stools onto the floor of the barroom, where they still lay with their hands locked in competition. They were not in a bar, however, but in lush tropical foliage: ferns; dark green plants with rubbery, deeply crenulated foliage; ground-hugging succulent vines with leaves as plump as gum candies and berries the same shade as the flesh of a Mandarin orange.

Bobby pulled away from Frank, and this time his client let him go without a struggle. He scrambled to his feet and pushed through the slick, spongy, clinging flora.

He didn't know where he was going and didn't care. He just had to put a little space between himself and Frank, distance himself from the danger that Frank now represented to him. He was overwhelmed by what had happened, overloaded with new experiences that he needed to consider and to which he had to adapt before he could go on.

Within half a dozen steps he broke out of the tropical brush and onto a dark expanse of land, the nature of which at first eluded him. The rain came down not in droplets and not in sheets, but in roaring, silver-gray cascades that dramatically reduced visibility; it swept his hair over his eyes, too, which didn't help. He supposed some people, sitting by windows in dry rooms, might even have seen beauty in the storm, but there was just too damned much rain, a flood; it met the earth and the greenery with a cacophonous roar that threatened to deafen him. The rain not only exhausted him but made him wildly and irrationally angry, as if he was being pelted not by rain but by spittle, great gobs of phlegmy spit, and as if the roar was actually the combined voices of thousands of onlookers showering him with insults and other abuse. He stumbled forward through the peculiarly mushy soil—not muddy, but mushy—looking for someone to blame for the rain, someone to shout at and shake and maybe even punch. In six or eight steps, however, he saw the breakers rolling ashore in a tumult of white foam, and he knew he was standing on a black-sand beach. That realization stopped him cold.

"Frank!" he shouted, and when he turned to look back the way he had come, he saw that Frank was following him, a few steps behind and round-backed, as if he were an old man unable to stand up to the force of the rain, or as if his spine had been warped by all the moisture. "Frank, dammit, where are we?"

Frank stopped, unbent his back slightly, lifted his head, and blinked stupidly. "What?"

Raising his voice even further, Bobby shouted above the tumult: "Where are we!"

Pointing to Bobby's left, Frank indicated an enigmatic, rain-shrouded structure that stood like the ancient shrine of a long-dead religion, perhaps a hundred feet farther down the black beach. "Lifeguard station!" He pointed the other direction, up the beach, indicating a large wooden building considerably farther from them but less mysterious because its size made it easier to see. "Restaurant. One of the most popular on the island."

"What island?"

"The big island."

"What big island?"

"Hawaii. We're standing on Punaluu Beach."

"This was where *Clint* was supposed to take me," Bobby said. He laughed, but it was a strange, wild laugh that spooked him, so he stopped.

Frank said, "The house I bought and abandoned is back there." He indicated the direction from which they had come. "Overlooking a golf course. I loved the place. I was happy there for eight months. Then *he* found me. Bobby, we have to get out of here."

Frank took a few steps toward Bobby, out of the mushy area and onto that section of the beach where the sand was better compacted.

"That's far enough," Bobby ordered when Frank was six or eight feet from him. "Don't come any closer."

"Bobby, we have to go now, right away. I can't teleport exactly when I want. That'll happen when it happens, but at least we have to get away from this part of the island. He knows I lived here. He's familiar with this area. And he may be following us."

The fiery anger in Bobby was not quenched by the rain; it grew hotter than ever. "You lying bastard."

"It's true, really," Frank said, obviously surprised by Bobby's vehemence. They were close enough to converse without shouting now, but Frank still spoke louder than usual to be heard over the crackle-hiss-patter-rumble of the deluge. "Candy came here after me, and he was worse than I'd ever seen him, more horrible, more evil. He came into my house with a baby, an infant he'd picked up somewhere, only months old, he'd probably killed its parents. He bit into that poor baby's throat, Bobby, then laughed and offered me its blood, taunted me with it. He drinks blood, you know, *she* taught him to drink blood, and he relishes it now, thrives on it. And when I wouldn't join him at the baby's throat, he threw it aside the way you'd discard an empty beer can, and he came for me, but I . . . traveled."

"I didn't mean you were lying about him." A wave broke closer to shore than the others, washing around Bobby's feet and leaving short-lived, lacelike traceries of foam on the black sand. "I mean you lied to us about your amnesia. You remember everything. You know exactly who you are."

"No, no." Frank shook his head and made negating gestures with his hands. "I didn't know. It *was* a blank. And maybe it'll be a blank again when I stop traveling and stay put someplace."

"Lying shit!" Bobby said.

He stooped, scooped up handsful of wet black sand and threw it at Frank in a blind fury, two more sopping handsful, then two more. He began to realize that he was behaving like a child throwing a tantrum.

Frank flinched from the wet sand but waited patiently for Bobby to stop. "This isn't like you," he said, when at last Bobby relented.

"To hell with you."

"Your rage is all out of proportion to anything you imagine I've done to you."

Bobby knew that was true. As he wiped his wet sand-covered hands on his shirt and tried to catch his breath, he began to understand that he was not angry at Frank but at what Frank represented to him. Chaos. Teleportation was a funhouse ride in which the monsters and dangers were not illusory, in which the constant threat of death was to be taken seriously, in which there were no rules, no verities that could be relied upon, where up was down and in was out. Chaos. They had ridden the back of a bull named Chaos, and Bobby had been flat-out terrified.

"You okay?" Frank asked.

Bobby nodded.

More than fear was involved. On a level deeper than intellect or even instinct, perhaps as deep as the soul itself, Bobby had been *offended* by that chaos. Until now he had not realized what a powerful need he had for stability and order. He'd always thought of himself as a free spirit who thrived on change and the unexpected. But now he saw that he had limits and that, in fact, beneath the devil-may-care attitude he sometimes struck, beat the steady heart of a stability-loving traditionalist. He suddenly understood that his passion for swing music had roots of which he'd never been aware: the elegant and complex rhythms and melodies of big-band jazz appealed to his bebop surface *and* to the secret seeker of order who dwelt in his heart. No wonder he liked Disney cartoons, in which Donald Duck might run wild and Mickey might get in a tangled mess with Pluto, but in which order triumphed in the end. Not for him the chaotic universe of Warner Brothers' Looney Tunes, in which reason and logic seldom won more than a temporary victory.

"Sorry, Frank," he said at last. "Give me a second. This sure isn't the place for it, but I'm having an epiphany."

"Listen, Bobby, please, I'm telling the truth. Evidently I can remember everything when I travel. The very fact of traveling tears down the wall blocking my memory, but as soon as I stop traveling, the wall goes up again. It's part of the degeneration I'm undergoing, I guess. Or maybe it's just a desperate need to forget what's happened to me in the past, what's happening now, and what will sure as hell happen to me in the days to come."

Though no wind had risen, some of the breakers were larger now, washing deep onto the beach. They battered the backs of Bobby's legs and, on retreating, buried his feet in coaly sand.

Struggling to explain himself, Frank said, "See, traveling isn't easy for me, like it is for Candy. He can control where he wants to go, and when. He can travel just by deciding to do it, virtually by wishing himself someplace, like you suggested I might be able to do. But I can't. My talent for teleportation isn't really a talent, it's a curse." His voice grew shaky. "I didn't even know I could do it until seven years ago, the day that bitch died. All of us who came from her womb are cursed, we can't escape it. I thought I could escape somehow by killing her, but that didn't release me."

After the events of the past hour, Bobby thought nothing could surprise him, but he was startled by the confession Frank had made. This pathetic, sad-eyed, dimpled, comic-faced, pudgy man seemed an unlikely perpetrator of matricide. "You killed your own mother?"

"Never mind about her. We haven't time for her." Frank looked back toward the brush out of which they had come, and both ways along the beach, but they were still alone in the downpour. "If you'd known her, if you'd suffered under her hand," Frank said, his voice shaking with anger, "if you'd known the atrocities she's capable of, you'd have picked up an ax and chopped at her too."

"You took an ax and gave your mother forty whacks?" That crazy sound burst from Bobby again, a laugh as wet as the rain but not as warm, and again he was spooked by himself.

"I discovered I could teleport when Candy had me backed into a corner, going to kill me for having killed her. And that's the only time I can travel—when it's a matter of survival."

"Nobody was threatening you last night in the hospital."

"Well, see, when I start traveling in my sleep, I think maybe I'm trying to escape from Candy in a dream, which triggers teleportation. Traveling always wakes me, but then I can't stop, I keep popping from place to place, sometimes staying a few seconds, sometimes an hour or more, and it's beyond my control, like I'm being bounced around inside a goddamn cosmic pinball machine. It exhausts me. It's killing me. You can *see* how it's killing me."

Frank's earnest persistence and the numbing, relentless roar of the rain had washed away Bobby's rage. He was still somewhat afraid of Frank, of the potential for chaos that Frank represented, but he was no longer angry.

"Years ago," Frank said, "dreams started me traveling maybe one night a month, but gradually the frequency increased, until the last few weeks it happens almost every time I go to sleep. And when we finally wind up in your office or wherever this episode is going to come to an end, you'll remember everything that's happened to us, but I won't. And not only because I *want* to forget, but because what you suspected is true—I'm not always putting myself back together without mistakes."

"Your mental confusion, loss of intellectual skills, amnesia—they're symptoms of those mistakes."

"Yeah. I'm sure there's sloppy reconstruction and cell damage every time I travel, nothing dramatic in any one trip, but the effect is incremental . . . and accelerating. Sooner or later it's going to go critical, and I'll either die or experience some weird biological meltdown. Coming to you for help was pointless, no matter how good you are at what you do, because nobody can help me. Nobody."

Bobby had already reached that conclusion, but he was still curious. "What is it with your family, Frank? Your brother has the power to make that car disintegrate around you, the power to blow out those streetlamps, and he can teleport. And what was that business with the cats?"

"My sisters, the twins, they have this thing with animals."

"How come all of you possess these . . . abilities? Who *was* your mother, your father?"

"We don't have time for that now, Bobby. Later. I'll try to explain later." He held out his cut hand, which had either stopped bleeding or was sluiced free of blood by the rain. "I could pop out of here any moment, and you'd be stranded."

"No thanks," Bobby said, shunning his client's hand. "Call me an old fuddy-duddy, but I'd prefer an airliner." He patted his hip pocket. "Got my wallet, credit cards. I can be back in Orange County tomorrow, and I don't have to take a chance that I'll arrive there with my left ear where my nose should be."

"But Candy's probably going to follow us, Bobby. If you're here when he shows up, he'll kill you."

Bobby turned to his right and started to walk toward the distant restaurant. "I'm not afraid of anyone named Candy."

"You better be," Frank said, grabbing his arm and halting him.

Jerking away as if making contact with his client was tantamount to contracting the bubonic plague, Bobby said, "How could he follow us anyway?"

When Frank worriedly surveyed the beach again, Bobby realized that because of the pounding rain and the underlying crash of the surf, they might not hear the telltale flutelike sounds that would warn them of Candy's imminent arrival.

Frank said, "Sometimes, when he touches something you recently touched, he sees an image of you in his mind, and sometimes he can see where you went after you put the object down, and he can follow you."

"But I didn't touch anything back there at the house."

"You stood on the back lawn."

"So?"

"If he can find the place where the grass is trampled, find where we stood, he might be able to put his fingers to the grass and see us, see this place, and come after us."

"For God's sake, Frank, you make this guy sound supernatural."

"He's the next thing to it."

Bobby almost said he would take his chances with brother Candy, regardless of his godlike powers. Then he remembered what the Phans had told him about the savage murders of the Farris family. He also remembered the Roman family, their brutalized bodies torched to cover the ragged gashes that Candy's teeth had torn in their throats. He recalled what Frank had said about Candy offering him the fresh blood of a living baby, factored in the unmitigated terror in Frank's eyes at that very moment, and thought of the inexplicable prophetic dream he'd had about the "bad thing." At last said, "All right, okay, if he shows up, and if you're able to pop out of here before he kills us both, then I'd be better off with you. I'll take your hand, but only until we walk up to that restaurant, call a cab, and are on our way to the airport." He gripped Frank's hand reluctantly. "As soon as we're out of this area, I let go."

"All right. Good enough," Frank said.

Squinting as the rain battered their faces, they headed toward the restaurant. The structure, which stood perhaps a hundred and fifty yards away, appeared to be made of gray, weathered wood and lots of glass. Bobby thought he saw dim lights in the place, but he could not be sure; the large windows were no doubt tinted, which filtered out what fraction of the lampglow was not already hidden by the veils of rain.

Every third or fourth incoming wave was now much larger than the others, reached farther onto the beach, and sloshed around their legs with enough force to unbalance them. They moved toward the higher end of the strand, away from the breakers, but the sand was far softer there; it sucked at their shoes and made progress more laborious.

Bobby thought of Lisa, the blond receptionist at Palomar Labs. He pictured her coming along the beach right now, taking a crazy-romantic walk in the warm rain with some guy who'd brought her to the islands, pictured her face when she saw him strolling the black-sand beach hand-in-hand with another man, cheating on Clint.

This time his laughter didn't have a scary edge.

Frank said, "What?"

Before Bobby could even start to explain, he saw that some-one actually was heading in their general direction through the obscuring rain. It was a dark figure, not Lisa, a man, and he was only about thirty yards away.

He hadn't been there a moment ago.

"It's him," Frank said.

Even at a distance the guy looked big. He spotted them and turned directly toward them.

Bobby said, "Get us out of here, Frank."

"I can't do it on demand. You know that."

"Then let's run," he urged, and he tried to pull Frank along the beach, toward the abandoned lifeguard tower and whatever lay beyond.

But after floundering a few steps through the sand, Frank stopped and said, "No, I can't, I'm worn out. I'm going to have to pray that I pop out of here in time."

He looked worse than worn out. He looked half dead.

Bobby turned toward Candy again, and saw the dark brother slogging through the soft, wet sand much faster than they had managed but still with some difficulty. "Why doesn't he just teleport from there to here in a flash, overwhelm us?"

Frank's horror at the sight of his oncoming nemesis was so complete that he didn't appear capable of speech. Yet the words came with the shallow breaths that rasped out of him: "Short hops, under a few hundred feet, aren't possible. Don't know why."

Maybe if the trip was too short, the mind had a fraction of a second less than the minimum time required to deconstruct and fully reconstruct the body. It didn't matter what the reason was. Even if he couldn't teleport across the remaining stretch of sand, Candy was going to reach them in seconds.

He was only thirty feet away and closing, a massive juggernaut of a man, with a neck thick enough to support a car balanced on his head, and arms that would give him an advantage in a wrestling match with a four-ton industrial robot. His blond hair was almost white. His face was broad and sharp-featured and hard—and as cruel as the face of one of those pre-psychotic young boys who liked to set ants on fire with matches and test the effects of full-strength lye on neighborhood dogs. Charging through the storm, kicking up gouts of wet black sand with each step, he looked less like a man than like a demon with a fierce hunger for human souls.

Holding fast to his client's hand, Bobby said, "Frank, for God's sake, let's get out of here."

When Candy was close enough for Bobby to see blue eyes as wild and vicious as those of a rattlesnake on Benzedrine, he let out a wordless roar of triumph. He flung himself at them.

Darkness.

Fireflies.

Velocity.

Pale morning light filtered from a clear sky into the narrow pass-through between two rotting, ramshackle buildings so crusted in the filth of ages that it was impossible to determine what material had been used to construct their walls. Bobby and Frank were standing in knee-deep garbage that had been tossed out of the windows of the two-story structures and left to decompose into a reeking sludge that steamed like a compost pile. Their magical arrival had startled a colony of roaches that scuttled away from them, and caused swarms of fat black flies to leap up from their breakfast. Several sleek rats sat up on their haunches to see what had arrived among them, but they were too bold to be scared off.

The tenements on both sides had some windows completely open to the outside, some covered with what looked like oiled paper, none with glass. Though no people were in sight, from the rooms within the aged walls came voices: laughter here; an angry exchange there; chanting, as of a mantra, softly drifting down from the second floor of the building on the right. It was all in a foreign tongue with which Bobby was not familiar, though he suspected they might be in India, perhaps Bombay or Calcutta.

Because of the ineluctable stench, which by comparison made the stink of a slaughterhouse seem like a new perfume by Calvin Klein, and because of the insistently buzzing flies that exhibited great interest in an open mouth and nostrils, Bobby was unable to get his breath. He choked, put his free hand over his mouth, still could not breathe, and knew he was going to faint facefirst into the vile, steaming muck.

Darkness.

Fireflies.

Velocity.

In a place of stillness and silence, shafts of afternoon sunshine pierced mimosa branches and dappled the ground with golden light. They stood on a red oriental footbridge over a koi pond in a Japanese garden, where sculpted bonsai and other meticulously tended plants were positioned among carefully raked beds of pebbles.

"Oh, yes," Frank said with a mixture of wonder and pleasure and relief. "I lived here, too, for a while."

They were alone in the garden. Bobby realized that Frank always materialized in sheltered places where he was unlikely to be seen in the act, or in circumstances—such as the middle of a cloudburst—that almost ensured even a public place like a beach would be conveniently deserted. Evidently, in addition to the unimaginably demanding task of deconstruction-travel-reconstruction, his mind was also capable of scouting the way ahead and choosing a discreet point of arrival.

Frank said, "I was the longest-residing guest they'd ever had. It's a traditional Japanese inn on the outskirts of Kyoto."

Bobby became aware that they were both totally dry. Their clothes were wrinkled, in need of an ironing, but when Frank had deconstructed them in Hawaii, he had not teleported the molecules of water that had saturated their clothes and hair.

"They were so kind here," Frank said, "respectful of my privacy, yet so attentive and kind." He sounded wistful and terminally weary, as if he would have liked to have stopped his traveling right there, even if stopping meant dying at the hands of his brother.

Bobby was relieved to see that Frank also had not brought with them any of the slime from the narrow alley in Calcutta, or wherever. Their shoes and pants were clean.

Then he noticed something on the toe of his right shoe. He bent forward to look at it.

"I wish we could stay here," Frank said. "Forever."

One of the roaches from that filth-choked alley was now a part of Bobby's footwear. One of the biggest advantages of being self-employed was freedom from neckties and uncomfortable shoes, so he was wearing, as usual, a pair of soft Rockport Supersports, and the roach was not merely stuck on the putty-colored leather but bristling from it and melded *with* it. The roach was not squirming, obviously dead, but it was there, or at least part of it was, some bits of it apparently having been left behind.

"But we've got to keep moving," Frank said, oblivious of the roach. "He's trying to follow us. We have to lose him if—"

Darkness.

Fireflies.

Velocity.

They were on a high place, a rocky trail, with an incredible panorama below them.

"Mount Fuji," Frank said, not as if he had known where they were going but as if pleasantly surprised to be there. "About halfway up."

Bobby was not interested in the exotic view or concerned about the chill in the air. He was entirely preoccupied by the discovery that the roach was no longer a part of the toe of his shoe.

"The Japanese once thought Fuji was sacred. I guess they still do, or some of them do. And you can see why. It's magnificent."

"Frank, what happened to the roach?"

"What roach?"

"There was a roach welded into the leather of this shoe. I saw it back there in the garden. You evidently brought it along from that disgusting alleyway. Where is it now?"

"I don't know."

"Did you just drop its atoms along the way?"

"I don't know."

"Or are its atoms still with me but somewhere else?"

"Bobby, I just don't know."

In Bobby's mind was an image of his own heart, hidden within the dark cavity of his chest, beating with the mystery of all hearts but with a new secret all its own—the bristling legs and shiny carapace of a roach embedded in the muscle tissue that formed the walls of the atrium or a ventricle.

An insect might be *inside* of him, and even if the thing was dead, its presence within was intolerable. An attack of entomophobia hit him with the equivalent force of a hammer blow to the gut, knocking the wind out of him, sending undulate waves of nausea through him. He struggled to breathe, at the same time striving not to vomit on the sacred ground of Mount Fuji.

Darkness.

Fireflies.

Velocity.

They hit more violently this time, as if they had materialized in midair and had fallen a few feet onto the ground. They didn't manage to hold on to each other, and they didn't land on their feet, either. Separated from Frank, Bobby rolled down a gentle incline, over small objects that clattered and clicked under him and poked painfully into his flesh. When he tumbled to a halt, gasping and frightened, he was facedown on gray soil almost as powdery as ashes. Scattered around him, sparkling brightly against that ashen backdrop, were hundreds if not thousands of red diamonds in the rough.

Raising his head, he saw that the diamond miners were there in unnerving numbers: a score of huge insects just like the one they had taken to Dyson Manfred. Caught, as he was, in a whirlpool of panic, Bobby believed that every one of those bugs was fixated on him, all those multifaceted eyes turned toward him, all those tarantula legs churning through the powdery gray soil in his direction.

He felt something crawling on his back, knew what it must be, and rolled over, pinning the thing between him and the ground. He felt it squirming frantically beneath him. Propelled by repulsion, he was suddenly on his feet, without quite remembering how he had gotten up. The bug was still clinging to the back of his shirt; he could feel its weight, its quick-footed advance from the small of his back to his neck. He reached behind, tore it off himself, cried out in disgust as it kicked against his hand, and pitched it as far away as he could.

He heard himself breathing hard and making queer little sounds of fear and desperation. He didn't like what he heard, but he was unable to silence himself.

A foul taste filled his mouth. He figured he had ingested some of the powdery soil. He spat, but his spittle looked clean, and he realized that the air itself was what he tasted. The warm air was thick, not humid exactly but *thick,* like nothing he had experienced before. And in addition to the bitter taste, it had a distinctly different but equally unpleasant smell, like sour milk with a whiff of sulfur.

Turning around, surveying the terrain, he realized that he was standing in a shallow bowl in the land, about four feet deep at its lowest point, and about a hundred feet in diameter. The sloped walls were marked by evenly spaced holes, a double layer of them, and more of the biologically engineered insects were squirming into some of those bores, out of others, no doubt seeking—and returning with—diamonds.

Because it was only four feet deep, he could see above the rim of the bowl. Across the huge, barren, and slightly sloped plain in which this depression was set, he saw what appeared to be scores of similar features, like age-smoothed meteor craters, though they were so evenly spaced that they had to be unnatural. He was in the middle of a giant mining operation.

Kicking at an insect that had crept too close to him, Bobby turned to look at the last quarter of his surroundings. Frank was there, at the far side of the crater, on his hands and knees. Bobby was relieved by the sight of him, but he was definitely not relieved by what he saw in the sky beyond Frank.

The moon was visible in broad daylight, but it was not like the gossamer ghost moon that sometimes could be seen in a clear sky. It was a mottled gray-yellow sphere six times normal size, looming ominously over the land, as if about to collide with the larger world around which it should have been revolving at a respectable distance.

But that was not the worst. A huge and strangely shaped

aircraft hung silently at perhaps an altitude of four or five hundred feet, so alien in every aspect that it brought home to Bobby the understanding that had thus far eluded him. He was not on his own world any longer.

"Julie," he said, because suddenly he realized how terribly far from her he had traveled.

At the far side of the crater, as he was getting to his feet, Frank Pollard vanished.

# 47

AS DAY DIMMED and dark came, Thomas stood at the window or sat in his chair or stretched out on his bed, sometimes reaching toward the Bad Thing to be sure it wasn't coming closer. Bobby was worried when he visited, so Thomas was worried too. A lump of fear kept rising in his throat, but he kept swallowing it because he had to be brave and protect Julie.

He didn't get as close to the Bad Thing as last night. Not close enough to let it grab him with its mind. Not close enough to let it follow him when he quick-like reeled his own mind-string back to The Home. But close. A lot closer than Thomas liked.

Every time he pushed at the Bad Thing to make sure it was still there, up north someplace, where it belonged, he knew the Bad Thing felt him snooping. That spooked Thomas. The Bad Thing knew he was snooping around, but didn't do anything, and sometimes Thomas felt maybe the Bad Thing was waiting like a toad.

Once, in the garden behind The Home, Thomas watched a toad sit real still for a long time, while a bright yellow flutterby, pretty and quick, bounced from leaf to leaf, flower to flower, back and forth, round and round, close to the toad, then not so close, then closer than ever, then way out of reach, then closer again, like it was teasing the toad, but the toad didn't move, not an inch, like maybe it was a fake toad or just a stone that looked like a toad. So the flutterby felt safe, or maybe it just liked the game too much, and it came even closer. *Wham!* The toad's tongue shot out like one of those roll-up tooters they'd let the

dumb people have one New Year's Eve, and it caught the flutterby, and the green toad ate the yellow flutterby, every bit, and
that was the end of the game.

If the Bad Thing was playing a toad, Thomas was going to be
real careful not to be a flutterby.

Then, just when Thomas figured he should start washing himself and changing clothes for supper, just when he was going to
pull back from the Bad Thing, it went somewhere. He felt it go,
bang, there one second and far away the next, slipping past
where he could keep a watch on it, out across the world, going
the same place where the sun was taking the last of the daylight.
He couldn't figure how it could go so fast, unless maybe it was
on a jetplane having good food and a fine whine, smiling at
pretty girls in uniforms who put little pillows behind the Bad
Thing's seat and gave it magazines and smiled back at it so nice
and so much you expected them to kiss it like everybody was
always kissing on daytime TV. Okay, yeah, probably a jetplane.

Thomas tried some more to find the Bad Thing. Then, by the
time day was all gone and night all there, he gave up. He got
off his bed and got ready for supper, hoping maybe the Bad
Thing was gone away and never coming back, hoping Julie was
safe forever now, and hoping there was chocolate cake for dessert.

◆　◆　◆

BOBBY CHARGED across the floor of the diamond-strewn
crater, kicking at the bugs in his way. As he ran he told himself
that his eyes had deceived him and that his mind was playing
nasty tricks, that Frank had not actually teleported out of there
without him. But when he arrived at the spot where Frank had
been, he found only a couple of footprints in the powdery soil.

A shadow fell across him, and he looked up as the alien craft
drifted in blimplike silence over the crater, coming to a full stop
directly above him, still about five hundred feet overhead. It
was nothing like starships in the movies, neither organic looking
nor a flying chandelier. It was lozenge shaped, at least five
hundred feet long, and perhaps two hundred feet in diameter.
Immense. On the ends, sides, and top, it bristled with hundreds
if not thousands of pointed black metal spines, big as church
spires, which made it look a little like a mechanical porcupine

in a permanent defensive posture. The underside, which Bobby could see best of all, was smooth, black, and featureless, lacking not only the massive spines but markings, remote sensors, portholes, airlocks, and all the other apparatus one might expect.

Bobby did not know if the ship's repositioning was coincidental or whether he was under observation. If he was being watched, he didn't want to think about the nature of the creatures that might be peering down at him, and he sure as hell didn't want to consider what their intentions toward him might be. For every movie that featured an adorable alien with the power to turn kids' bicycles into airborne vehicles, there were ten others in which the aliens were ravenous flesh eaters with dispositions so vicious as to make any New York headwaiter think twice about being rude, and Bobby was certain that this was one thing Hollywood had gotten right. It was a hostile universe out there, and dealing with his fellow human beings was scary enough for him; he didn't need to make contact with a whole new race that had devised countless new cruelties of its own.

Besides, his capacity for terror was already filled to the brim, running over; he could contain no more. He was abandoned on a distant world, where the air—he began to suspect—might contain only enough oxygen and other required gases to keep him alive for a short while, insects the size of kittens were crawling all around him, and there was a possibility that a much smaller dead insect was actually fused with the tissue of one of his internal organs, and a psychotic blond giant with superhuman powers and a taste for blood was on his trail—and the odds were billions to one that he would ever see Julie again, or kiss her, or touch her, or see her smile.

A series of tremendous, throbbing vibrations issued from the ship and shook the ground around Bobby. His teeth chattered, and he nearly fell.

He looked for somewhere to hide. There was nothing in the crater to afford concealment, and nowhere to run on the flat plain beyond.

The vibrations stopped.

Even in the deep shadow thrown by the ship, Bobby saw a horde of identical insects begin to scuttle out of the boreholes in the crater walls, one after the other. They had been called forth.

Though no apparent openings appeared in the belly of the ship, a score or more of low-energy lasers—some yellow, some white, some blue, some red—began to play over the floor of the crater. Each beam was the diameter of a silver dollar, and each moved independently of the others. Like spotlights, they repeatedly swept the crater and everything in it, sometimes moving parallel to one another, sometimes crisscrossing one another, in a display that further disoriented Bobby and gave him the feeling that he was caught in the middle of a silent fireworks show.

He remembered what Manfred and Gavenall had told him about the crimson decorations along the rim of the bug's shell, and he saw that the white lasers were focusing only on the insects, busily scanning the markings around each carapace. Their owners were taking roll call. He saw a white beam fidget over the broken corpus of one of the bugs he had kicked, and after a moment a red beam joined it to study the carcass. Then the red beam jumped to Bobby, and a couple of other beams of different hue also found him, as if he was a can of peas being identified and added to someone's grocery bill at a supermarket checkout.

The floor of the crater was teeming with insects now, so many that Bobby could see neither the gray soil nor the litter of excreted diamonds over which they clambered. He told himself that they were not really bugs; they were just biological machines, engineered by the same race that had built the ship hanging over him. But that didn't help much because they still looked more like bugs than like machines. They had been designed to mine diamonds; they were not attracted to him whatsoever; but their disinterest did not make him feel better, because his phobia guaranteed that *he* was interested in *them*. His shadow-chilled skin prickled with gooseflesh. Short-circuiting nerve endings sputtered with false reports of things crawling on him, so he felt as if bugs swarmed over him from head to foot. They were actually creeping over his shoes, but none of them tried to scurry up his legs; he was grateful, because he was sure he would go mad if they began to climb him.

He used his hand as a visor over his eyes, to avoid being dazzled by the lasers that were playing on him. He saw something gleaming in the scanner beams only a few feet away: a curved section of what appeared to be hollow steel tubing. It was sticking out of the powdery soil, partly buried, further concealed by the bugs that scurried and jittered around it. Nevertheless, at first sight Bobby knew what it was, and he was overcome with a horrible sinking feeling. He shuffled forward, trying not to crush any of the insects because, for all he knew, the alien penalty for the additional destruction of property might be instant incineration. When he could reach the glinting curve of metal, he seized it and pulled it loose of the soft earth. It was the missing railing from the hospital bed.

♦ ♦ ♦

"HOW LONG?" Julie demanded.

"Twenty-one minutes," Clint said.

They still stood near the chair where Frank had been sitting and beside which Bobby had been stooping.

Lee Chen had gotten off the sofa, so Jackie Jaxx could lie down. The magician-hypnotist had draped a damp washcloth over his forehead. Every couple of minutes he protested that he could not really make people disappear, though no one had accused him of being responsible for what had happened to Frank and Bobby.

Having retrieved a bottle of Scotch, glasses, and ice from the office wet bar, Lee Chen was pouring six stiff drinks, one for each person in the room, as well as for Frank and Bobby. "If you don't need a drink to steady your nerves now," Lee had said, "you'll need one to celebrate when they come back safe." He had already downed one Scotch himself. The drink he poured now would be his second. This was the first time in his life he had drunk hard liquor—or needed it.

"How long?" Julie demanded.

"Twenty-two minutes," Clint said.

And I'm still sane, she thought wonderingly. Bobby, damn you, come back to me. Don't you leave me alone forever. How am I going to dance alone? How am I going to live alone? How am I going to live?

♦ ♦ ♦

BOBBY DROPPED the bed railing, and the lasers winked off, leaving him in the shadow of the spiny ship, which seemed darker than before the beams appeared. As he looked up to see what would happen next, another light issued from the underside of the craft, too pale to make him squint. This one was precisely the diameter of the crater. In that queer, pearly glow, the insects began to rise off the ground, as if they were weightless. At first only ten or twenty floated upward, but then twenty more and a hundred after that, rising as lazily and effortlessly as so many bits of dandelion fluff, turning slowly, their tarantula legs motionless, the eerie light gone out of their eyes, as if they had been switched off. In a minute or two, the floor of the crater was depopulated of insects, and the horde was being drawn up effortlessly in that sepulchral silence that accompanied all of the craft's maneuvers except for the base vibrations that had called the insect miners from their bores.

Then the silence was broken by a flutelike warble.

"Frank!" Bobby cried in relief, and turned as a gust of vile-smelling wind washed over him.

As the cold, hollow piping echoed across the crater again, there was a subtle change in the hue of the light that issued from the ship above. Now the thousands of red diamonds rose from the ash-gray soil in which they lay and followed the insects upward, gleaming dully here and brightly there, so many of them that it seemed as if Bobby was standing in a rain of blood.

Another whirl of evil-scented wind cast up a cloud of the ashy soil, reducing visibility, and Bobby turned in eager expectation of Frank's arrival. Until he remembered that it might not be Frank but the brother.

The piping came a third time, and the subsequent puff of wind carried the dust away from him, so he saw Frank arrive less than ten feet from him.

"Thank God!"

As Bobby stepped forward, the pearly light underwent a second subtle change. Reaching for Frank's hand, he felt himself become weightless. When he looked down he saw his feet drift off the floor of the crater.

Frank grabbed at his outstretched hand and seized it.

Nothing had ever felt better to Bobby than Frank's firm grip, and for a moment he felt safe. Then he became aware that Frank had risen from the ground too. They were both being drawn upward in the wake of the insects and diamonds, toward the belly of the alien vessel, toward God-only-knew what nightmare inside.

Darkness.

Fireflies.

Velocity.

They were on Punaluu beach again, and the rain was coming down harder than before.

"Where the hell was that last place?" Bobby demanded, still holding fast to his client.

"I don't know," Frank said. "It scares the hell out of me, it's so weird, but sometimes I seem to be . . . drawn there."

He hated Frank for having taken him there; he loved Frank for having returned for him. When he shouted above the rain, neither love nor hate was in his voice, just borderline hysteria: "I thought you could only travel to places you've been?"

"Not necessarily. Anyway, I've been there before."

"But how did you get there the first time, it's another world, it can't have been familiar to you—right, Frank?"

"I don't know. I just don't understand any of it, Bobby."

Though face to face with Frank, Bobby took a while to notice how much the man's appearance had deteriorated since they had teleported from the Dakota & Dakota offices in Newport Beach. Although the storm once more had soaked him to the skin in seconds and left his clothes hanging on him shapelessly, it wasn't just the rain that made him look disheveled, beaten, and sickly. His eyes were more sunken than ever; the whites of them were yellow, as if he had contracted jaundice, and the flesh around them was so darkly bruised that he appeared to have painted a pair of fake shiners on himself with black shoe polish. His skin was paler than pale, a deathly gray, and his lips were bluish, as though his circulatory system was failing. Bobby felt guilty about having shouted at him, so he put his free hand on Frank's shoulder and told him he was sorry, that it was all right, that they were still fighting on the same side of this war, and that everything would turn out just fine—as long as Frank didn't take them back to that crater.

Frank said, "Sometimes it's like I'm almost in touch with . . . with the minds of those people, creatures, whatever they are in that ship." They were leaning on each other now, forehead to forehead, seeking mutual support in their exhaustion. "Maybe I've got another gift I'm not aware of, like for most of my life I wasn't aware of being able to teleport until Candy backed me into a corner and tried to kill me. Maybe I'm mildly telepathic. Maybe the wavelength my telepathy functions on is the major wavelength of that race's brain activity. Maybe I feel them out there, even across billions of light-years of space. Maybe that's why I feel as if I'm being drawn to them, called to them."

Pulling back a few inches from Frank, Bobby looked into his tortured eyes for a long moment. Then he smiled and pinched Frank's cheek, and said, "You devil, you've really done a lot of thinking about this, haven't you, really put the old noodle to work on it, huh?"

Frank smiled.

Bobby laughed.

Then they were both laughing, holding each other up by leaning into each other, the way teepee poles held one another up, and a part of their laugh was healthy, a release of tension, but part of it was that mad laughter that had troubled Bobby earlier. Clinging to his client, he said, "Frank, your life is chaos, you're *living* in chaos, and you can't go on like this. It's going to destroy you."

"I know."

"You've got to find a way to stop it."

"There is no way."

"You've got to try, buddy, you've got to try. Nobody can handle this. I couldn't live like this for one day, and you've done it for seven years!"

"No. It wasn't this bad most of that time. It's just lately, the last few months, it's accelerated."

"A few months," Bobby said wonderingly. "Hell, if we don't give your brother the slip soon and get back to the office and step off this merry-go-ground in the next few minutes, I swear to God I'm going to crack. Frank, I need order, order and stability, familiarity. I need to know that what I do today will determine where I am and who I am and what I have to show for it tomorrow. Nice orderly progression, Frank, cause and effect, logic and reason."

Darkness.

Fireflies.

Velocity.

♦    ♦    ♦

"How long?"

"Twenty-seven . . . almost twenty-eight minutes."

"Where the hell *are* they?"

"Julie," Clint said, "I think you ought to sit down. You're shaking like a leaf, your color's not good."

"I'm all right."

Lee Chen handed her a glass of Scotch. "Have a drink."

"No."

"It might help," Clint said.

She grabbed the glass from Lee, drained it in a couple of long swallows, and shoved it back into his hand.

"I'll get you another," he said.

"Thanks."

From the sofa, Jackie Jaxx said, "Listen, is anyone going to sue me over this?"

Julie no longer sort of liked the hypnotist. She loathed him as much as she had loathed him when they had first met him in Vegas and taken on his case. She wanted to go kick his head in. Though she knew the urge to kick him was irrational, that he really had not been the cause of Bobby's disappearance, she wanted to kick him anyway. That was the impulsive side of her, the quick-to-anger side of which she was not proud. But she couldn't always control it, because it was part of her genetic makeup or, as Bobby suspected, a predilection to violent response that had begun to form in her on the day, in her childhood, when a drug-crazed sociopath had brutally killed her mother. Either way, she knew Bobby was sometimes dismayed by that dark side of her, much as he loved everything else, so she made a bargain with both Bobby and God: *Listen, Bobby, wherever you are—and you listen, too, God—if this just ends well, if I can just have my Bobby back with me, I won't be this way any more, I won't want to kick in Jackie's head any more, or anyone else's head, either, I'll turn over a new leaf, I swear I will, just let Bobby come back to me safe and sound.*

♦ ♦ ♦

THEY WERE on a beach again, but this one had white sand that was slightly phosphorescent in the early darkness. The strand disappeared into a medium-thick fog in both directions. No rain was falling, and the air was not as warm as it had been at Punaluu.

Bobby shivered in the chill, moist air. "Where are we?"

"I'm not sure," Frank said, "but I think we're probably on the

Monterey Peninsula somewhere." A car passed on a highway a hundred yards behind them. "That's probably Seventeen-Mile Drive. You know it? The road from Carmel through Pebble Beach—"

"I know it."

"I love the peninsula, Big Sur to the south," Frank said. "It's another one of the places I was happy . . . for a while."

Their voices were strangely muffled by the mist. Bobby liked the solid ground beneath his feet, and the thought that he was not only on his own planet but in his own country and in his own state; but he would have preferred a place with more concrete details, where fog did not obscure the landscape. The white blindness of fog was another form of chaos, and he had had more than enough disorder to last him for the rest of his life.

Frank said, "Oh, and by the way, back there in Hawaii a minute ago, you were worried about giving Candy the slip, but you don't need to be concerned. We lost him several stops ago in Kyoto, or maybe on the slopes of Mount Fuji."

"For God's sake, if we don't have to worry about leading him back to the office, let's go home."

"Bobby, I don't have—"

"Any control. Yeah, I know, I heard, it's no big secret. But I'll tell you something—you've got control on some level, way down deep in the subconscious, more control than you think you have."

"No. I—"

"Yes. Because you came back to that crater for me," Bobby said. "You told me you hate the place, that it's more frightening than anywhere you've ever been, but you came back and got me. You didn't leave me there with the bed railing."

"Pure chance that I came back."

"I don't think so."

Darkness.

Fireflies.

Velocity.

♦　♦　♦

THEY MADE the soft, pretty *bing-bong* signal come out of the wall, because that was how they told all the people in The Home it was just ten minutes before supper was going to be eaten.

Derek was already out the door by the time Thomas got up from his chair. Derek liked food. Everyone liked food, of course. But Derek liked food enough for three people.

Thomas got to the doorway, and Derek was already down the hall, walking fast in that funny way he did, almost to The Dining Room. Thomas looked back at the window.

Night was at the window.

He didn't like seeing night at the window, which was why he usually kept the drapes closed after the light went out of the world. But after he got himself ready for supper, he had tried to find the Bad Thing out there, and it helped a little to see the night when he was trying to send a mind-string into it.

The Bad Thing was still so far away it couldn't be felt. But he wanted to try once more before going to eat food and Be Sociable. He reached out through the window, up into the big dark, spinning the mind-string toward where the Bad Thing used to be—and it was back. He felt it right away, knew it felt him, too, and he remembered the green toad eating the bouncy yellow flutterby, and he pulled back into his room faster than a toad tongue could snap out and catch him.

He didn't know if he should be happy or scared that it was back. When it was gone away, Thomas was happy, because maybe it was going to be gone away a long time, but he was also a little scared because when it was gone away, he didn't know exactly where it was.

It was back.

He waited in the doorway a while.

Then he went to eat food. There was roast chicken. There was frenched fries. There was carrots and peas. There was coleslaw. There was Homemade bread, and people said there was going to be some chocolate cake and ice cream for dessert, though the people that said it was dumb people, so you couldn't be sure. It all looked good, and it smelled good, and it even tasted good. But Thomas kept thinking about how the flutterby might've tasted to the toad, and he couldn't eat much of anything.

♦  ♦  ♦

BOUNCING like two balls in tandem, they traveled to an empty lot in Las Vegas, where a cool desert wind spun a tumbleweed past them and where Frank said he had once lived in a house that was now demolished; to that cabin at the top of a snowy mountain meadow, where they had first teleported after leaving the office; to the graveyard in Santa Barbara; to the top of an Aztec ziggurat in the lush Mexican jungles, where the humid night air was full of buzzing mosquitoes and the cries of unknown beasts, and where Bobby almost fell down the terraced side of the pyramidal structure before he realized how high they were and how precariously perched; to the offices of Dakota & Dakota—

They were popping around so quickly, remaining in each place such a brief time—in fact, briefer with each stop—that for a moment he stood in a corner of his own office, blinking stupidly, before he realized where he was and what he had to do. He tore his hand away from Frank, and he said, "Stop it now, stop here." But Frank vanished even as Bobby spoke.

Julie was all over him an instant later, hugging him so tightly that she hurt his ribs. He hugged her, too, and kissed her a long time before coming up for air. Her hair smelled clean, and her skin smelled sweeter than he remembered. Her eyes were brighter than memory allowed, and more beautiful.

Though by nature he was not much of a toucher, Clint put a hand on Bobby's shoulder. "God, it's good to see you, good to have you back." There was even a catch in his voice. "Had us worried there for a while."

Lee Chen handed him a glass of Scotch on the rocks. "Don't do that again, okay?"

"Don't plan to," Bobby said.

No longer the smooth and self-assured performer, Jackie Jaxx had had enough for one night. "Listen, Bobby, I'm sure that whatever you have to tell us is fascinating, and you're bound to've come back with a lot of boffo anecdotes, wherever you went, but I for one don't want to hear about it."

"Boffo anecdotes?" Bobby said.

Jackie shook his head. "Don't want to hear 'em. Sorry. It's my fault, not yours. I like show biz 'cause it's a narrow life, you know? A thin little slice of the real world, but exciting 'cause it's all bright colors and loud music. You don't have to *think* in show biz, you can just be. I just want to *be*, you know. Perform, hang out, have fun. I got opinions, sure, colorful and loud opinions about everything, show-biz opinions, but I don't know a damn thing, and I don't *want* to know a damn thing, and I sure as hell don't want to know about what happened here tonight, 'cause it's the kind of thing that turns your world upside down, makes you curious, makes you think, and then pretty soon you're no longer happy with all the things that made you happy before." He raised both hands, as if to forestall argument, and said, "I'm outta here," and a moment later he was.

At first, as he told the others what had happened to him, Bobby walked slowly around the room, marveling at ordinary items, finding wonder in the mundane, relishing the solidity of things. He put his hand on Julie's desk, and it seemed to him that nothing in the world was more wondrous than humble Formica—all those molecules of man-made chemicals lined up in perfect, stable order. The framed prints of Disney characters, the inexpensive furniture, the half-empty bottle of Scotch, the flourishing pothos plant on a stand by the windows—all of those things were suddenly precious to him.

He had been traveling only thirty-nine minutes. He took almost as long to tell them a condensed version. He had popped out of the office at 4:47 and returned at 5:26, but he'd done enough traveling—via teleportation or otherwise—to last the rest of his life.

On the sofa, with Julie and Clint and Lee gathered around, Bobby said, "I want to stay right here in California. I don't need to see Paris. Don't need London. Not any more. I want to stay where I have my favorite chair, sleep every night in a bed that's familiar—"

"Damn right you will," Julie interjected.

"—drive my little yellow Samurai, open a medicine cabinet where the Anacin and toothpaste and mouthwash and styptic pencil and Bactine and Band-Aids are exactly where they ought to be."

By 6:15 Frank had not reappeared. During Bobby's account of his adventures, no one mentioned Frank's second disappearance or wondered aloud when he would return. But all of them kept glancing at the chair from which he had vanished initially and at the corner of the room from which he had dematerialized the second time.

"How long do we wait here for him?" Julie finally asked.

"I don't know," Bobby said. "But I have a feeling . . . a real bad feeling . . . that maybe Frank's not going to regain control of himself this time, that he's just going to keep popping from one place to another, faster and faster, until sooner or later he's unable to put himself back together again."

# 48

WHEN HE CAME straight from Japan into the kitchen of his mother's house, Candy was seething with anger, and when he saw the cats on the table, where he ate his meals, his anger grew into a full-blown rage. Violet was sitting in a chair at the table; her ever-silent sister was in another chair beside her, hanging on her. Cats lay under their chairs and around their feet, and five of the biggest were on the table, eating bits of ham that Violet fed them.

"What're you doing?" he demanded.

Violet did not acknowledge him either with a word or a glance. Her gaze was locked with that of a dark gray mongrel that was sitting as erect as a statue of an Egyptian temple cat, patiently nibbling at a few small bits of meat offered on her pale palm.

"I'm talking to you," he said sharply, but she did not respond.

He was sick of her silences, weary to death of her infinite strangeness. If not for the promise that he had made to his mother, he would have torn Violet open right there and fed on her. Too many years had passed since he had tasted the ambrosia in his sainted mother's veins, and he had often thought that the blood in Violet and Verbina was, in a way, the same blood that had flowed in Roselle. He wondered—and sometimes dreamed—of how his sisters' blood might feel upon the tongue, how it might taste.

Looming over her, staring down as she continued to commune with the gray cat, he said, "This is where I *eat,* damn you!"

Violet still said nothing, and Candy struck her hand, knocking the remaining bits of ham helter-skelter. He swept the plate of ham off the table, as well, and took tremendous satisfaction in the sound of it shattering on the floor.

The five cats on the table were not the least startled by his fury, and the greater number on the floor remained unfazed by the ping and clatter of china fragments.

At last Violet turned her head, tilted it back, and looked up at Candy.

Simultaneously with their mistress, the cats on the table turned their heads to look haughtily at him, too, as if they wished him to understand what a singular honor they were bestowing upon him simply by granting him their attention.

That same attitude was apparent in the disdain in Violet's eyes and in the faint smirk that curled the edges of her ripe mouth. More than once he had found her direct gaze withering, and he had turned away from her, rattled and confused. Certain that he was her superior in every way, he was perplexed by her unfailing ability to defeat him or force him into a hasty retreat with just a look.

But this time would be different. He had never been as furious as he was at that moment, not even seven years ago when he had found his mother's bloody, sundered body and had learned the ax had been wielded by Frank. He was angrier now because that old rage had never subsided; it had fed on itself all these years, and on the humiliation of repeatedly failing to get his hands on Frank when the opportunities to do so arose. Now it was a midnight-black bile that coursed in his veins and bathed the muscles of his heart and nourished the cells of his brain where visions of vengeance were spawned in profusion.

Refusing to be cowed by her stare, he seized her thin arm and jerked her violently to her feet.

Verbina made a soft, woeful sound upon her separation from her sister, as if they were Siamese twins, for God's sake, as if tissue had been torn, bones split.

Shoving his face close to Violet's, he sprayed her with spittle as he spoke: "Our mother had *one* cat, just one, she liked things clean and neat, she wouldn't approve of this mess, this stinking brood of yours."

"Who cares," Violet said in a tone of voice that was at once disinterested and mocking. "She's dead."

Grabbing her by both arms, he lifted her off her feet. The chair behind her fell over as he swung her away from it. He slammed her up against the pantry door so hard that the sound was like an explosion, rattling the loose kitchen windows and some dirty silverware on a nearby counter. He had the satisfaction of seeing her face contort with pain and her eyes roll back in her head as she nearly passed out from the blow. If he had smashed her against the door any harder, her spine might have cracked. He dug his fingers cruelly into the pale flesh of her upper arms, pulled her away from the door, and slammed her into it again, though not as hard as before, just making the point that it *might* have been as hard, that it could be as hard the next time if she displeased him.

Her head had fallen forward, for she was teetering on the edge of consciousness. Effortlessly, he held her against the door, with her feet eight inches off the floor, as if she weighed nothing at all, thereby forcing her to consider his incredible strength. He waited for her to come around.

She was having difficulty getting her breath, and when at last she stopped gasping and raised her head to face him, he expected to see a different Violet. He had never struck her before. A fateful line had been crossed, one over which he never expected to trespass. With his promise to his mother in mind, he had kept his sisters safe from the often dangerous world outside, provided them with food, kept them warm in cold weather and cool in the heat, dry when it rained, but year after year he had performed his brotherly duties with growing frustration, appalled by their increasingly shameless and mysterious behavior. Now he realized that disciplining them was a natural part of protecting them; up in Heaven, his mother had probably despaired of his ever realizing the need for discipline. Thanks to his rage, he had stumbled upon enlightenment. It felt good to hurt Violet a little, just enough to bring her to her senses and to prevent her from spiraling further into the decadence and animal sensuality to which she had surrendered herself. He knew he was right to punish her. He waited eagerly for her to lift her head and face him, for he knew that they had entered a new relationship and that the awareness of these profound changes would be evident in her eyes.

At last, breathing somewhat normally, she raised her head and met Candy's gaze. To his surprise, none of his own enlightenment had been visited upon his sister. Her white-blond hair had fallen across her face, and she stared through it, like a jungle animal peering through its wind-tossed mane. In her icy blue eyes, he perceived something stranger and more primitive than anything he had seen there before. A gleeful wildness. Indefinable hungers. Need. Though she had been hurt when he had thrown her against the pantry door, a smile played on her full lips again. She opened her mouth, and he felt her hot breath against his face as she said, "You're strong. Even the cats like the feel of your strong hands on me . . . and so does Verbina."

He became aware of her long bare legs. The flimsiness of her panties. The way her red T-shirt had pulled up to expose her flat belly. The swell of her full breasts, which seemed even fuller than they were because of the leanness of the rest of her. The sharp outlines of her nipples against the material of the shirt. The smoothness of her skin. Her smell.

Revulsion burst through him like pus from a secret inner abscess, and he let go of her. Turning, he saw that the cats were looking at him. Worse, they were still lying where they had been when he had pulled Violet from her chair, as if they had not been frightened by his outrage even briefly. He knew their equanimity meant that Violet had not been frightened, either, and that her erotic response to his fury—and her mocking smile—was not in the least feigned.

Verbina was slumped in her chair, her head bowed, for she was no more able to look at him directly now than she had ever been. But she was grinning, and her left hand was between her legs, her long fingers tracing lazy circles on the thin material of her panties, under which lay the dark cleft of her sex. He needed no more proof that some of Violet's sick desire had communicated itself to Verbina, and he turned away from her too.

He tried to leave the room quickly, but without looking as if he was fleeing from them.

In his scented bedroom, safely among his mother's belongings, Candy locked the door. He was not sure why he felt safer with the lock engaged, though he was certain it was not because he feared his sisters. There was nothing about them to fear. They were to be pitied.

For a while he sat in Roselle's rocker, remembering the times, as a child, when he'd curled in her lap and contentedly sucked blood from a self-inflicted wound in her thumb or in the meaty part of her palm. Once, but unfortunately only once, she had made a half-inch incision in one of her breasts and held him to her bosom while he drank her blood from the same flesh where other mothers gave, and other children received, the milk of maternity.

He had been five years old that night when, in this very room and in this chair, he tasted the blood of her breast. Frank, seven years old then, had been asleep in the room at the end of the hall, and the twins, who'd only recently reached their first birthday, were asleep in a crib in the room across from their mother's. Being alone with her when all the others slept—oh, how unique and treasured that made him feel, especially since she was sharing with him the rich liquid of her arteries and veins, which she never offered to his siblings; it was a sacred communion, dispensed and received, that remained their secret.

He recalled being in something of a swoon that night, not merely because of the heavy taste of her rich blood and the unbounded love that was represented by the gift of it, but because of the metronomic rocking of the chair and the lulling rhythms of her voice. As he sucked, she smoothed his hair away from his brow and spoke to him of God's intricate plan for the world. She explained, as she had done many times before, that God condoned the use of violence when it was committed in the defense of those who were good and righteous. She told him how God had created men who thrived on blood, so they might be used as the earthly instruments of God's vengeance on behalf of the righteous. Theirs was a righteous family, she said, and God had sent Candy to them to be their protector. None of this was new. But though his mother had spoken of these things many times during their secret communions, Candy never grew tired of hearing them again. Children often relish the retelling of a favorite story. And as with certain particularly magical tales, this story somehow did not become more familiar with retelling but curiously more mysterious and appealing.

That night in his sixth year, however, the story took a new turn. The time had come, his mother said, for him to apply the truly amazing talents he had been given, and embark upon the mission for which God had created him. He had begun to exhibit his phenomenal talents when he was three, the same age at which Frank's far more meager gifts had become evident. His telekinetic abilities—primarily his talent for telekinetic transportation of his own body—particularly enchanted Roselle, and she quickly saw the potential. They would never want for money as long as he could teleport at night into places where cash and valuables were locked away: bank vaults; the jewelry-rich, walk-in safes in Beverly Hills mansions. And if he could materialize within the homes of the Pollard family's enemies, while they slept, vengeance could be taken without fear of discovery or reprisal.

"There's a man named Salfont," his mother cooed to him as he took his nourishment from her wounded breast. "He's a lawyer, one of those jackals who prey on upstanding folks, nothing good about him at all, not that one. He handled my father's estate—that's your dear grandpa, little Candy—probated the will, charged too much, way too much, he was greedy. They're all greedy, those lawyers."

The quiet, gentle tone in which she spoke was at odds with the anger she was expressing, but that contradiction added to the sweet, hypnotic quality of her message.

"I've tried for years to get part of the fee returned to me, like I deserve. I've gone to other lawyers, but they all say his fee was reasonable, they all stick up for each other, they're alike, peas in a pod, rotten little peas in rotten little pods. Took him to court, but judges are nothing except lawyers in black robes, they make me sick, the greedy lot of them. I've worried at this for years, little Candy, can't get it out of my mind. That Donald Salfont, living in his big house in Montecito, overcharging people, overcharging *me,* he ought to have to pay for that. Don't you think so, little Candy? Don't you think he ought to pay?"

He was five years old and not yet big for his age, as he would be from the time he was nine or ten. Even if he could teleport into Salfont's bedroom, the advantage of surprise might not be sufficient to ensure success. If either Salfont or his wife happened to be awake when Candy arrived, or if the first slash of the knife failed to kill the lawyer and brought him awake in a defensive panic, Candy would not be able to overpower him. He wouldn't be in danger of getting caught or harmed, for he could teleport home in a wink; but he would risk being recognized. Police would believe a man like Salfont, even as regarded such a fantastic accusation as murder lodged against a five-year-old boy. They would visit the Pollard place, asking questions, poking around, and God knew what they might find or come to suspect.

"So you can't kill him, though he deserves it," Roselle whispered as she rocked her favorite child. She stared down intently into his eyes as he looked up from her exposed breast. "Instead, what you have to do is take something from him as vengeance for the money he took from me, something precious to him.

There's a new baby in the Salfont house. I read about it in the paper a few months ago, a little girl baby they called Rebekah Elizabeth. What kind of name is that for a girl, I ask you? Sounds high-falutin' to me, the kind of name a fancy lawyer and his wife give a baby 'cause they think them and theirs is better than other people. Elizabeth is a queen's name, you see, and you just look up what Rebekah is in the Bible, see if they don't think way too much of themselves and their little brat. Rebekah . . . she's almost six months now, they've had her long enough to miss her when she's gone, miss her bad. I'll drive you past their house tomorrow, my precious little Candy boy, let you see where it is, and tomorrow night you'll go there and visit the Lord's vengeance on them, my vengeance. They'll say a rat got into the room, or something of the sort, and they'll blame themselves until the day they're dead too."

The throat of Rebekah Salfont had been tender, her blood salty. Candy enjoyed the adventure of it, the thrill of entering the house of strangers without their permission or knowledge. Killing the girl while grownups slept in the adjoining room, unaware, filled him with a sense of power. He was just a boy, yet he slipped past their defenses and struck a blow for his mother, which in a way made him the man of the Pollard house. That heady feeling added an element of glory to the excitement of the kill.

His mother's requests for vengeance were thereafter irresistible.

For the first few years of his mission, infants and very young children were his only prey. Sometimes, in order not to present a pattern to the police, he did not bite them but disposed of them in other ways, and occasionally he took hold of them and teleported out of the house with them, so no body was ever found.

Even so, if Roselle's enemies had all been from in and around Santa Barbara, the pattern could not have been hidden. But often she required vengeance against people in far places, about whom she read in newspapers and magazines.

He remembered, in particular, a family in New York State, who won millions of dollars in the lottery. His mother had felt that their good fortune had been at the expense of the Pollard family, and that they were too greedy to be permitted to live. Candy had been fourteen at the time, and he had not understood his mother's reasoning—but he had not questioned it, either. She was the only source of truth to him, and the thought of disobedience never crossed his mind. He had killed all five members of that family in New York, then burned their house to the ground with their bodies in it.

His mother's thirst for vengeance followed a predictable cycle. Immediately after Candy killed someone for her, she was happy, filled with plans for the future; she would bake special treats for him and sing melodically while she worked in the kitchen, and she would begin a new quilt or an elaborate needlepoint project. But over the next four weeks her happiness would dim like a light bulb on a rheostat, and almost one month to the day after the killing, having lost interest in baking and crafts, she would begin to talk about other people who had wronged her and, by extension, the Pollard family. Within two to four more weeks, she would have settled on a target, and Candy would be dispatched to fulfill his mission. Consequently, he killed on only six or seven occasions each year.

That frequency satisfied Roselle, but the older Candy got, the less it satisfied him. He had not merely acquired a thirst for blood but a craving that occasionally overwhelmed him. The thrill of the hunt also intoxicated him, and he longed for it as an alcoholic longed for the bottle. Not least of all, the mindless hostility of the world toward his blessed mother motivated him to kill more often. Sometimes it seemed that virtually everyone was against her, scheming to harm her physically or to take money that was rightfully hers. She had no dearth of enemies. He remembered days when fear oppressed her; then at her direction all the blinds and drapes were drawn, the doors locked and sometimes even barricaded with chairs and other furniture, against the onslaught of adversaries who never came but who *might* have. On those bad days she became despondent and told him that so many people were out to get her that even he could not protect her forever. When he begged her to turn him loose, she refused and only said, "It's hopeless."

Then, as now, he tried to supplement the approved murders with his forays into the canyons in search of small animals. But those blood feasts, rich as they sometimes were, never quenched his thirst as thoroughly as when the vessel was human.

Saddened by too many memories, Candy rose from the rocking chair and nervously paced the room. The blind was up, and he glanced with increasing interest at the night beyond the window.

After failing to catch Frank and the stranger who had teleported into the backyard with him, after the confrontation with Violet had taken that unexpected turn and left him with undissipated rage, he was smoldering, hot to kill, but in need of a target. With no enemy of the family in sight, he would have to slaughter either innocent people or the small creatures that lived in the canyons. The problem was—he dreaded evoking his sainted mother's disappointment, up there in Heaven, yet he had no appetite for the thin blood of timid beasts.

His frustration and need built by the minute. He knew he was going to do something he would later regret, something that would make Roselle turn her face from him for a time.

Then, just when he felt he might explode, he was saved by the intrusion of a genuine enemy.

A hand touched the back of his head.

He whirled around, feeling the hand withdraw as he turned.

It had been a phantom hand. No one was there.

But he knew it was the same presence that he had sensed in the canyon last night. Someone out there, not of the Pollard family, had psychic ability of his own, and the very fact that Roselle was not his mother made him an enemy to be found and eliminated. The same person had visited Candy several times earlier in the afternoon, reaching out tentatively, probing at him but not making full contact.

Candy returned to the rocking chair. If a real enemy was going to put in an appearance, it would be worth waiting for him.

A few minutes later, he felt the touch again. Light, hesitant, quickly withdrawn.

He smiled. He started rocking. He even hummed softly—one of his mother's favorite songs.

Banking the coals of rage eventually made them burn brighter. By the time the shy visitor grew bolder, the fire would be white hot, and the flames would consume him.

# 49

AT TEN MINUTES to seven, the doorbell rang. Felina Karaghiosis did not hear it, of course. But each room of the house had a small red signal lamp in one corner or another, and she could not miss the flashing light that was activated by the bell.

She went into the foyer and looked through the sidelight next to the front door. When she saw Alice Kasper, a neighbor from three doors down the street, she switched off the dead bolt, removed the security chain from its slot, and let her in.

"Hi, kid. How ya doin'?"

*I like your hair,* Felina signed.

"Do ya really? Just got it cut, and the girl said did I want the same old same old, or did I want to catch up with the times, and I thought what the hell. I'm not too old to be sexy, do ya think?"

Alice was only thirty-three, five years older than Felina. She had exchanged her trademark blond curls for a more modern cut that would require a new source of income just to pay for all the mousse she was going to use, but she looked great.

*Come in. Want a drink?*

"I'd love a drink, kid, and right now I could use six of 'em, but I gotta say no. My in-laws came over, and we're about to either play cards with 'em or shoot 'em—it depends on their attitude."

Of all the people Felina knew in her day-to-day life, Alice was the only one, other than Clint, who understood sign language. Given the fact that most people harbored a prejudice against the deaf, to which they could not admit but on which they acted, Alice was her only girlfriend. But Felina happily would have given up their friendship if Mark Kasper—Alice's son, for whom she had learned sign language—had not been born deaf.

"Why I came over, we got a call from Clint, asking me to tell ya he's not on his way home yet, but he expects to get here maybe by eight. Since when does he work so late?"

*They've got a big case. That always means some overtime.*

"He's going to take ya out to dinner, and says to tell ya it's been an incredible day. I guess that's about the case, huh? Must be fascinating, married to a detective. And he's sweet, too. You're lucky, kid."

*Yes. But so is he.*

Alice laughed. "Right on! And if he comes home this late another night, don't settle for dinner. Make him buy ya diamonds."

Felina thought of the red gem he had brought home yesterday, and she wished she could tell Alice about it. But Dakota & Dakota business, especially concerning an ongoing case in which the client was in jeopardy, was as sacred in their house as the privacies of the marriage bed.

"Saturday, our place, six-thirty? Jack'll cook up a mess of his chile, and we'll play pinochle and eat chile and drink beer and fart till we pass out. Okay?"

*Yes.*

"And tell Clint, it's okay—we won't expect him to talk."

Felina laughed, then signed: *He's getting better.*

"That's 'cause you're civilizing him, kid."

They hugged again, and Alice left.

Felina closed the door, looked at her wristwatch, and saw that it was seven o'clock. She had only an hour to get ready for dinner, and she wanted to look especially good for Clint, not because this was a special occasion, but because she *always* wanted to look good for him. She headed for the bedroom, then realized that only the automatic lock was engaged on the front door. She returned to the foyer, twisted the thumbscrew that slid the dead bolt home, and slipped the security chain in place.

Clint worried about her too much. If he came home and found that she hadn't remembered the dead bolt, he'd age a year in a minute, right before her eyes.

# 50

AFTER BEING off duty all day, Hal Yamataka responded to a call from Clint and came to the offices at 6:35 Tuesday night, to stand a watch in case Frank returned after the rest of them had left. Clint met him in the reception lounge and briefed him there over a cup of coffee. He had to be brought up to date on what had happened during his absence, and after he heard what had gone down, he again wistfully considered a career in gardening.

Nearly everyone in his family either had a gardening business or owned a little nursery, and all of them did well, most of them better than what Hal made working for Dakota & Dakota, some of them a great deal better. His folks, his three brothers, and various well-meaning uncles tried repeatedly to persuade him that he should work for them or come into business with them, but he resisted. It was not that he had anything against running a nursery, selling gardening supplies, landscape planning, tree pruning, or even gardening itself. But in southern California the term "Japanese gardener" was a cliché, not a career, and he couldn't abide the thought of being any kind of stereotype.

He had been a heavy reader of adventure and suspense novels all his life, and he yearned to be a character like one of those he read about, especially a character worthy of being a lead in a John D. MacDonald novel, because John D's lead characters were as rich in insight as they were in courage, every bit as sensitive as they were tough. In his heart Hal knew that his work at Dakota & Dakota was usually as mundane as the daily grind of a gardener, and that the opportunities for heroism in the security industry were far fewer than they appeared to be to outsiders. But selling a bag of mulch or a can of Spectricide or a flat of marigolds, you couldn't kid yourself that you were a romantic figure or had any chance of being one. And, after all, self-image was often the better part of reality.

"If Frank shows up here," Hal said, "what do I do with him?"

"Pack him in a car and take him to Bobby and Julie."

"You mean their house?"

"No. Santa Barbara. They're driving up there tonight, staying at the Red Lion Inn, so tomorrow they can start digging into the Pollard family's background."

Frowning, Hal leaned forward on the reception-lounge sofa. "Thought you said they don't figure ever to see Frank again."

"Bobby says he thinks Frank is coming apart, won't last through this latest series of travels. That's just his feeling."

"So then who's their client?"

"Until he fires them, Frank is."

"Sounds iffy to me. Be straight with me, Clint. What's really got them so committed to this one, especially considering how crazy-dangerous it seems to get, hour by hour?"

"They like Frank. *I* like Frank."

"I said be straight."

Clint sighed. "Damned if I know. Bobby came back here spooked out of his mind. But he won't let go of it. You'd think they'd pull in their horns, at least until Frank shows up again, if he does. This brother of his, this Candy, he sounds like the devil himself, too much for anyone to handle. Bobby and Julie are stubborn sometimes, but they're not stupid, and I'd expect them to let go of this, now that they've seen it's a job big enough for God, not a private detective. But here we are."

♦  ♦  ♦

BOBBY AND JULIE huddled with Lee Chen at the desk, while he shared with them the information he had thus far obtained.

"The money might be stolen, but it's spendable," Lee said. "I can't find those serial numbers on any currency hot sheets—federal, state, or local."

Bobby had already thought of several sources from which Frank might have obtained the six hundred thousand now in the office safe. "Find a business with a high cash flow, where they don't always get to a bank with the receipts at the end of the day, and you've got a potential target. Say it's a supermarket, stays open till midnight, and it's not a good idea for a manager to tote a lot of cash to a bank for automatic deposit, so there's a safe in the market. After the place closes, you teleport inside, if you're Frank, and use whatever other powers you have to open that safe, put the day's receipts in a grocery bag, and vanish. You're not going to find big chunks of cash, a couple hundred thousand at a time, but you hit three or four markets in an hour, and you've got your haul."

Evidently Julie had been pondering the same question, for she said, "Casinos. They all have accounting rooms you can find on the blueprints, the ones the IRS gets into with a little effort. But they've got hidden rooms, too, where the skim goes. Like big walk-in safes. Fort Knox would envy them. You use whatever minor psychic abilities you have to figure the location of one of those hidden rooms, teleport in when it's deserted, and just take what you want."

"Frank lived in Vegas for a while," Bobby said. "Remember, I told you about the vacant lot he took me to, where he'd had a house."

"He wouldn't be limited to Vegas," Julie said. "Reno, Tahoe, Atlantic City, the Caribbean, Macao, France, England, Monte Carlo—anywhere there's big-time gambling."

This talk of easy access to unlimited amounts of cash excited Bobby, though he was not sure why. After all, it was Frank who could teleport, not him, and he was ninety-five-percent sure they were never going to see Frank again.

Spreading a sheaf of printouts across the desktop, Lee Chen said, "The money's the least interesting thing. You remember, you wanted me to find out if the cops are on to Mr. Blue?"

"Candy," Bobby said. "We have a name for him now."

Lee scowled. "I liked Mr. Blue better. It had more style."

Entering the room, Hal Yamataka said, "I don't think I trust the style judgment of a guy who wears red sneakers and socks."

Lee shook his head. "We Chinese spend thousands of years working up an intimidating image for all Asians, so we can keep these hapless Westerners off balance, and you Japanese blow it all by making those Godzilla movies. You can't be inscrutable and make Godzilla movies."

"Yeah? You show me *anybody* who understands a Godzilla movie after the first one."

They made an interesting pair, these two: one slender, modish, with delicate features, an enthusiastic child of the silicon age; the other squat, broad, with a face as blunt as a hammer, a guy who was about as high-tech as a rock.

But to Bobby the most interesting thing was that, until this moment, he had never thought about the fact that a disproportionately large percentage of Dakota & Dakota's small staff was Asian-American. There were two more—Nguyen Tuan Phu and Jamie Quang, both Vietnamese. Four out of eleven people. Though he and Hal once in a while made East-West jokes, Bobby never thought of Lee and Hal and Nguyen and Jamie as composing any subset of employees; they were just themselves, as different from one another as apples are different from pears and oranges and peaches. But Bobby realized that this predilection for Asian-American co-workers revealed something about himself, something more than just an obvious and admirable racial blindness, but he could not figure out what it was.

Hal said, "And *nothing* gets more inscrutable than the whole concept of Mothra. By the way, Bobby, Clint's gone home to Felina. We should all be so lucky."

"Lee was telling us about Mr. Blue," Julie said.

"Candy," Bobby said.

Indicating the data he had extracted from various police records nationwide, Lee said, "Most police agencies began to be computerized and interlinked only about nine years ago—in any sophisticated way, that is. So that's all the further back a lot of electronically accessible files go. But during that time, there have been seventy-eight brutal murders, in nine states, that have enough similarities to raise the possibility of a single perp. Just the possibility, mind you. But FBI got interested enough last year to put a three-man team on it, one in the office and two in the field, to coordinate local and state investigations."

"Three men?" Hal said. "Doesn't sound like high priority."

"The Bureau's always been overextended," Julie said. "And over the last thirty years, since it's been unfashionable for judges to hand out long criminal sentences, the bad guys outnumber them worse than ever. Three men, full time—that's a serious commitment at this stage."

Extracting a printout from the pile on the desk, Lee summarized the essential data on it. "All of the killings have these points in common. First—the victims were all bitten, most on the throat, but virtually no part of the body is sacred to this guy. Second—many of them were beaten, suffered head injuries. But loss of blood, from the bites—usually the jugular vein and carotid artery in the throat—was a substantial contributing factor to the death in virtually every instance, regardless of other injuries."

"On top of everything else, the guy's a vampire?" Hal asked.

Taking the question seriously—as, indeed, they had to consider every possibility in this bizarre case, regardless of how outlandish it seemed—Julie said, "Not a vampire in the supernatural sense. From what we've learned, the Pollard family is for some reason generously gifted. You know that magician on TV, The Amazing Randi, who offers to pay a hundred thousand bucks to anyone who proves they have psychic power? This Pollard clan would bankrupt his ass. But that doesn't mean there's anything supernatural about them. They're not demons, or possessed, or the children of the devil—nothing like that."

"It's just some extra bit of genetic material," Bobby said.

"Exactly. If Candy acts like a vampire, biting people in the throat, that's just a manifestation of psychological illness," Julie said. "It doesn't mean he's one of the living dead."

Bobby vividly remembered the blond giant charging him and Frank on the rainswept black beach at Punaluu. The guy was as formidable as a locomotive. If Bobby had a choice of going up against either Candy Pollard or Dracula, he might choose the undead Count. Nothing as simple as a clove of garlic, a crucifix, or a well-placed wooden stake would effectively deter Frank's brother.

Lee said, "Another similarity. In those instances where victims didn't leave doors or windows unlocked, there was no indication of how the killer gained entrance. And in many instances police found doors dead-bolted from the inside, windows locked from the inside, as if the murderer had gone up the chimney when he was done."

"Seventy-eight," Julie said, and shivered.

Lee dropped the paper onto the desk. "They figure there're more, maybe a lot more, because sometimes this guy has attempted to cover his trail—the bite marks—by further multilating or even burning the bodies. Though the cops weren't fooled in *these* cases, you can figure they were fooled in others. So the count's higher than seventy-eight, and that's just the last nine years."

"Good job, Lee," Julie said, and Bobby seconded that.

"I'm not done yet," Lee said. "I'm going to order in a pizza, do some more digging."

"You've been here more than ten hours today," Bobby said. "That's already above and beyond the call. Got to have downtime, Lee."

"If you believe, as I do, that time is subjective, then you've got an infinite supply. Later, at home, I'll stretch a few hours into a couple of weeks and return tomorrow quite rested."

Hal Yamataka shook his head and sighed. "Hate to admit it, Lee, but you're damned good at this mysterious oriental crap."

Lee smiled enigmatically. "Thank you."

♦   ♦   ♦

AFTER BOBBY and Julie went home to pack an overnight bag for the trip to Santa Barbara, and after Lee returned to the computer room, Hal settled on the sofa in the bosses' office, slipped off his shoes, and put his feet up on the coffee table. He still had the paperback of *The Last One Left,* which he'd read twice before, and which he had started to reread last night in the hospital. If Bobby was right when he said they might never see Frank again, Hal was in for an uneventful evening and would probably get half the book read.

Maybe his happiness at Dakota & Dakota had nothing to do with the prospect of excitement, avoiding a stereotypical job as a gardener, and having the admittedly slim chance to be a hero. Maybe the thing that most affected his career decision was the realization that he simply could not mow a lawn or trim a hedge or plant fifty flats of flowers and read a book at the same time.

♦　♦　♦

DEREK SAT in his chair. Pointed the raygun at the TV and made it be on. He said, "You don't want to watch news?"

"No," Thomas said. He was on his bed, propped up with pillows, looking at the night being dark outside the window.

"Good. Me neither." Derek pushed buttons on the raygun. A new picture came on the screen. "You don't want to watch a game show?"

"No." All Thomas wanted to do was snoop on the Bad Thing.

"Good." Derek pushed buttons, and the invisible rays made the screen show a new picture. "You don't want to watch the Three Stooges pretending to be funny?"

"No."

"What you want to watch?"

"Don't matter. Whatever you want to watch."

"Really?"

"Whatever you want to watch," Thomas repeated.

"Gee, that's nice." He made lots of pictures on the screen until he found a space movie where spacemen in spacesuits were poking around in some spooky place. Derek made a happy sigh and said, "This is good. I like their hats."

"Helmets," Thomas said. "Space helmets."

"I wish I had a hat like that."

When he reached out into the big dark again, Thomas decided not to picture a mind-string unraveling toward the Bad Thing. Instead he pictured a raygun, shooting some invisible rays. Boy, did that work better! *Wham,* he was right there with the Bad Thing in a flash, and he felt it stronger, too, so strong he got scared and clicked off the raygun and got all of himself back into his room with the rest of himself right away.

"They got telephones in their hats," Derek said. "See, they're talking through their hats."

On the TV, the spacemen were in an even spookier place, poking around, which was one of the things spacemen did the most, even though something ugly-nasty was usually in those spooky places just waiting for them. Spacemen never learned.

Thomas looked away from the screen.

At the window.

The dark.

Bobby was scared for Julie. Bobby knew stuff Thomas didn't know. If Bobby was scared for Julie, Thomas had to be brave and do What Was Right.

The raygun idea worked such a lot better it scared him, but he figured it was really good because he could easier snoop on the Bad Thing. He could get to the Bad Thing faster and get away from it faster, too, so he could snoop on it more often and not be scared about it maybe grabbing the mind-string and coming back to The Home with him. Grabbing an invisible raygun ray was harder, even for a thing as fast and smart and mean as the Bad Thing.

So he pictured pushing buttons on a raygun again, and a part of him went through the dark—*wham!*—and to the Bad Thing right away. He felt how mad the Bad Thing was, madder than ever, and thinking lots of thoughts about blood that made Thomas half sick. Thomas wanted to come right back to The Home. The Bad Thing felt him, you could tell. He didn't like the Bad Thing feeling him, knowing he was there with it, but he stayed just a couple clock ticks longer, trying to see any thoughts about Julie in all those thoughts about blood. If the Bad Thing had thoughts about Julie, Thomas would TV a warning right away to Bobby. He was happy he couldn't find Julie in the Bad Thing's mind, and he quick raygunned back to The Home.

"Where you think I could get a hat like that?" Derek asked.

"Helmet."

"Even has a light on it, see?"

Rising up a little from his pillows, Thomas said, "You know what kind of a story this is?"

Derek shook his head. "What kind of story?"

"It's the kind where any second something ugly-nasty jumps up and sucks off a spaceman's face or maybe crawls in his mouth and down his belly and makes a nest in there."

Derek made a disgusted face. "Yuck. I don't like that kind of stories."

"I know," Thomas said. "That's why I warned you."

While Derek made a lot of different pictures come on the screen, one quick after the other, to get far away from the spaceman who was going to get his face sucked off, Thomas tried to think how long he should wait before he snooped on the Bad Thing again. Bobby was real worried, you could tell, even if he tried to hide it, and Bobby was not a Dumb Person, so it was a good idea to check on the Bad Thing pretty regular, in case maybe it all of a sudden thought about Julie and got up and went after her.

"You want to watch this?" Derek asked.

On the screen was a picture of this guy in a hockey mask with a big knife in his hand, going quiet-like across a room where a girl was asleep in a bed.

"Better raygun up another picture," Thomas said.

♦  ♦  ♦

BECAUSE THE rush hour was past, because Julie knew all the best shortcuts, but mainly because she was not in a mood to be cautious or respect the traffic laws, they made great time from the office to their home on the east end of Orange.

On the way Bobby told her about the Calcutta roach that had been part of his shoe when he and Frank had arrived on that red bridge in the garden in Kyoto. "But when we popped to Mount Fuji, my shoe was okay, the roach was gone."

She slowed at an intersection, but she was the only traffic in sight, so she didn't obey the four-way stop. "Why didn't you tell me about this at the office?"

"Wasn't time for every detail."

"What do you think happened to the roach?"

"I don't know. That's what bothers me."

They were on Newport Avenue, just past Crawford Canyon. Sodium-vapor streetlamps cast a queer light on the roadway.

Atop the steep hills to the left, several huge English Tudor and French houses, blazing like giant luxury liners, looked wildly out of place, partly because the insanely high value of such upscale real estate ensured the construction of immense houses out of proportion to the tiny lots they stood on, but partly because Tudor and French architectural styles clashed with the semitropical landscape. It was all part of the California circus, some of which he hated, most of which he loved. Those houses never bothered him before, and given the serious problems he and Julie faced, he couldn't figure why they bothered him now. Maybe he was so jumpy that even these minor disharmonies reminded him of the chaos that had almost engulfed him during his travels with Frank.

He said, "Do you have to drive so fast?"

"Yes," she said curtly. "I want to get home, get packed, get to Santa Barbara, learn what we can about the Pollard family, get finished with this whole damn creepy case."

"If you feel that way, why don't we just drop it here? Frank comes back, we give him his money, his jar of red diamonds, tell him we're sorry, we think he's a prince of a guy, but we're out of it."

"We can't," she said.

He chewed on his lower lip, then said, "I know. But I can't figure why we're compelled to hang in there with this one."

They crested the hill and speeded north, past the entrance to Rocking Horse Ridge. Their own development was only a couple of streets ahead, on the left. As she finally began to brake for the turn, she glanced at him and said, "You really don't know why we can't bug out of it?"

"No. You saying you do?"

"I know."

"Tell me."

"You'll figure it out eventually."

"Don't be mysterious. That's not like you."

She swung the company Toyota into their development, then onto their street. "I tell you what I think, it'll upset you. You'll deny it, we'll argue, and I don't want to argue with you."

"Why will we argue?"

She pulled into their driveway, put the car in park, switched off the lights and engine, and turned to him. Her eyes shone in the dark. "When you understand why we can't let go, you won't like what it says about us, and you'll argue that I'm wrong, that we're just a couple of sweet kids, really. You like to see us as a couple of sweet kids, savvy but basically innocent at the same time, like a young Jimmy Stewart and Donna Reed. I really love you for that, for being such a dreamer about the world and us, and it'll hurt me when you want to argue."

He almost started to argue with her about whether he would argue with her. Then he stared at her for a moment and finally said, "I've had this feeling that I'm not facing up to something, that when this is all over and I realize why I was so determined to see this through to the end, my motivations won't be as noble as I think they are now. It's a weird damn feeling. As if I don't really know myself."

"Maybe we spend all our lives learning to know ourselves. And maybe we never really do—completely."

She kissed him lightly, quickly, and got out of the car.

As he followed her up the sidewalk to the front door, he glanced at the sky. The clarity of the day had been short-lived. A pall of clouds concealed the moon and stars. The sky was very dark, and he was gripped by the curious certainty that a great and terrible weight was falling toward them, black against the black heavens and therefore invisible, but falling fast, faster. . . .

# 51

CANDY KEPT a chokehold on his fury, which strained like an attack dog trying to break its leash.

He rocked and rocked, and gradually the shy visitor grew bolder. Repeatedly he felt the invisible hand on his head. Initially it lay upon him as lightly as an empty silk glove, and it stayed only briefly before flitting away. But as he pretended to be disinterested in both the hand and the person to whom it belonged, the visitor grew more daring, the hand heavier and less nervous.

Though Candy made no effort to probe at the mind of the intruder, for fear of scaring him away, some of the stranger's thoughts came to him nonetheless. He did not think the visitor was aware that images and words from his own mind were slipping into Candy's; they were just leaking out of him as if they were trickles of water seeping from pin-size holes in a rusty bucket.

The name "Julie" came several times. And once an image floated along with the name—an attractive woman with brown hair and dark eyes. Candy wasn't sure if it was the visitor's face or the face of someone the visitor knew—or even if it was the face of anyone who really existed. There were aspects that made it seem unreal: a pale light radiated from it, and the features were so kind and serene that it looked like the holy countenance of a saint in an illustrated Bible.

The word "flutterby" leaked out of the visitor's mind more than once, sometimes with other words, like "remember the flutterby" or "don't be a flutterby." And each time that word flitted through his mind, the visitor quickly withdrew.

But he kept coming back. Because Candy did nothing to make him feel unwelcome.

Candy rocked and rocked. The chair made a soft sound: *creak . . . creak . . . creak . . . creak.*

He waited.

He kept an open mind.

*. . . creak . . . creak . . . creak . . .*

Twice the name "Bobby" seeped from the visitor's mind, and the second time a fuzzy image of a face was linked to it, another very kind face. It was idealized, like Julie's face. Recognition stirred in Candy, but Bobby's visage was not as clear or detailed as Julie's, and Candy did not want to concentrate on it because the visitor might notice his interest and be frightened off.

During his long and patient courtship of the shy intruder, many other words and images came to Candy, but he didn't know what to make of them:

—men in spacesuits—

—"Bad Thing"—

—a guy in a hockey mask—

—"The Home"—

—"Dumb People"—

—a bathrobe, a half-eaten Hershey's bar, and a sudden frantic thought: *Draw Bugs, no good, Draw Bugs, got to Be Neat—*

292

More than ten minutes passed without contact, and Candy started to worry that the intruder had gone away for good. But suddenly he was back. This time the contact was strong, more intimate than ever.

When Candy sensed that the visitor was more confident, he knew the time had come to act. He pictured his mind as a steel trap, the visitor as an inquisitive mouse, and he pictured the trap springing, the bar pinning the visitor to the killplate.

Shocked, the visitor tried to pull away. Candy held him and pushed across the telepathic bridge between them, trying to storm his adversary's mind to find out who he was, where he was, and what he wanted.

Candy had no telepathic power of his own, nothing to equal even the weak telepathic gifts of the intruder; he had never read anyone's mind before, and he did not know how to go about it. As it turned out, he did not need to do anything except open himself and receive what the visitor gave him. Thomas was his name, and he was terrified of Candy, of having Done Something Really Dumb, and of putting Julie in danger; that trinity of terrors shattered his mental defenses and caused him to disgorge a flood of information.

In fact, there was too much information for Candy to make sense of it, a babble of words and images. He tried desperately to sort through it for clues to Thomas's identity and location.

*Dumb People, Cielo Vista, The Home, everybody here has bad eye cues, Care Home, good food, TV, The Best Place For Us, Cielo Vista, the aides are nice, we watch the hummingbirds, the world is bad out there, too bad for us out there, Cielo Vista Care Home. . . .*

With some astonishment, Candy realized that the visitor was someone with a subnormal intellect—he even picked up the term "Down's syndrome"—and he was afraid that he was not going to be able to sort enough meaningful thoughts from the babble to get a fix on Thomas's location. Depending on the size of his IQ, Thomas might not know where Cielo Vista Care Home was, even though he apparently lived there.

Then a series of images spun out of Thomas's mind, a well-linked chain of serial memories that still caused him some emotional pain: the trip to Cielo Vista in a car with Julie and Bobby, on the day they first checked him into the place. This was different from most of Thomas's other thoughts and memories, in that it was richly detailed and so clearly retained that it unreeled like a length of motion-picture film, giving Candy all he needed to know. He saw the highways over which they had driven that day, saw the route markers flashing past the car window, saw every landmark at every turn, all of which Thomas had struggled mightily to memorize because all through the trip he kept thinking, *If I don't like it there, if people are mean there, if it's too scary there, if it's too much being alone there, I got to know how I find the way back to Bobby and Julie anytime I want, remember this, remember all of this, turn there at the 7-11, right there at the 7-11, don't forget that 7-11, and now go past those three palm trees. What if they don't come visit me? No, that's a bad thing to think, they love me, they'll come. But what if they don't? Look there, remember that house, you go past that house, remember that house with the blue roof—*

Candy got it all, as precise a fix as he could have obtained from a geographer who would have spoken precisely in degrees and minutes of longitude and latitude. It was more than he needed to know to make use of his gift. He opened the trap and let Thomas go.

He got up from the rocker.

He pictured Cielo Vista Care Home as it appeared so exquisitely detailed in Thomas's memory.

He pictured Thomas's room on the first floor of the north wing, at the northwest corner.

Darkness, billions of hot sparks spinning in the void, velocity.

♦   ♦   ♦

BECAUSE JULIE was in a let's-move-and-get-it-done mood, they had stopped at the house only fifteen minutes, long enough to throw toiletries and a change of clothes in an overnight bag. At McDonald's, on Chapman Avenue in Orange, she swung by the drive-through window and got dinner to eat on the way: Big Macs, fries, diet colas. Before they reached the Costa Mesa Freeway, while Bobby was still divvying up the extra packets of mustard and opening the containers that held the Big Macs, Julie had clipped the radar detector to the rearview mirror, plugged it in the Toyota's cigarette lighter, and switched it on. Bobby had never before eaten fast food at high speed, but he figured they averaged eighty-five miles an hour north on the Costa Mesa to the Riverside Freeway west to the

Orange Freeway north, and he was still finishing his french fries when they were only a couple of exits away from the Foothill Freeway east of Los Angeles. Though the rush hour was well past and the traffic unusually light, maintaining that pace required a lot of lane changing and nerve.

He said, "We keep this up, I'll never have a chance to die from the cholesterol in this Big Mac."

"Lee says cholesterol doesn't kill us."

"Is that what he says?"

"He says we live forever, and all cholesterol can do is move us out of this life a little sooner. Same thing must be true if I slip up and roll this sucker a few times."

"I don't think that'll happen," he said. "You're the best driver I've ever seen."

"Thank you, Bobby. You're the best passenger."

"The only thing I wonder . . ."

"Yeah?"

"If we don't really die, just move on, and I don't have to worry about anything—why the hell did I bother to get *diet* colas?"

◆ ◆ ◆

THOMAS ROLLED off the bed, onto his feet. "Derek, go, get out, he's coming!"

Derek was watching a horse talking on TV, and he didn't hear Thomas.

The TV was in the room's middle, between the beds, and by the time Thomas got there and grabbed Derek to make him listen, a funny sound was all around them, not funny ha-ha but funny weird, like somebody whistling but not whistling. There was wind, too, a couple of puffs, not warm or cold either, but it made Thomas shiver when it blew on him.

Pulling Derek off his chair, Thomas said, "Bad Thing's coming, you get out, you go, like I said before, *now!*"

Derek just made a dumb face at him, then smiled, like he figured Thomas was pretending to be funny the way the Three Stooges pretended. He'd forgot all about the promise he made Thomas. He'd thought the Bad Thing was going to be poached eggs for breakfast, and when poached eggs never showed up on his plate, he figured he was safe, but now he wasn't safe and didn't know it.

More funny-weird whistling. More wind.

Giving Derek a shove, making him get started for the door, Thomas shouted, "Run!"

The whistling stopped, the wind stopped, and all of a sudden from nowhere the Bad Thing was there. Between them and the open door.

It was a man, like Thomas already knew it was, but it was more than just a man. It was darkness poured in the shape of a man, like a piece of the night itself that came in through the window, and not just because it wore a black T-shirt and black pants but because it was all deep dark inside, you could tell.

Right away Derek was afraid. Nobody needed to tell him this was a Bad Thing, not now when he could see it with his own eyes. But he didn't see it was too late to run, and he went straight at the Bad Thing, like maybe he could push past it, which must have been what he was figuring because even Derek wasn't dumb enough to figure he could knock it down, it was so big.

The Bad Thing grabbed him and lifted him before he had any chance to get around it, lifted him right up off the floor, like he didn't weigh any more than a pillow. Derek screamed, and the Bad Thing slammed him against the wall so hard his scream stopped, and pictures of Derek's mom and dad and brother fell off the wall, not the one where Derek got slammed but another wall all the way around the room from him and over his bed.

The Bad Thing was so fast. That was the worst thing about it, how awful fast it was. It slammed Derek against the wall, Derek's mouth fell open but no more sound came from him, the Bad Thing slammed him again, right away, harder, though the first time was hard enough for anybody, and Derek's eyes went funny. The Bad Thing took him away from the wall and slammed him down on the worktable. The table kind of shivered like it would fall apart, but it didn't. Derek's head was over the table edge, hanging down, so Thomas was looking at his face, upside-down eyes blinking fast, upside-down mouth open real wide but no sound coming out. He looked up from Derek's face, looked right across Derek's body at the Bad Thing, which was looking at him and grinning, like all this was a joke, funny ha-ha, which it wasn't, no way. Then it picked up the scissors on the edge of the worktable, the ones Thomas used to make his picture poems, the ones that almost fell on the floor when it slammed Derek on the table. It made the scissors go into Derek and bring the blood out of him, into poor Derek who wouldn't hurt no one himself, except himself, who wouldn't know *how* to hurt anyone. And the Bad Thing made the scissors go in again and bring more blood out of another place in Derek, and in again, and again. Then blood wasn't coming out of just four places on Derek's chest and belly where the scissors had been made to go in, but out of his mouth and nose too. The Bad Thing lifted Derek off the table, the scissors still sticking out of his front, and threw him like he was just a pillow. No, like he was a garbage bag, threw him the way the Santa Nation Men threw the garbage bags onto their Santa Nation Truck. Derek landed on his bed, on his back on his bed, with the scissors still in him, and didn't move and was gone to the Bad Place, you could tell. And the worst thing was it all happened so fast, faster than Thomas could think what to do to stop it.

Footsteps in the hall, people running.

Thomas yelled for help.

Pete, one of the aides, showed up in the doorway. Pete saw Derek on the bed, scissors in him, blood coming out everywhere, and he got afraid, you could see him get it. He turned to the Bad Thing and said, "Who—"

The Bad Thing grabbed him by the neck, and Pete made a sound like something was stuck in his throat. He put both his hands on the Bad Thing's arm, which seemed bigger than Pete's two arms together, but he couldn't make the Bad Thing let go. The Bad Thing lifted him by his neck, making his chin turn up and his head bend back, and then took hold of him by the belt, too, and pitched him back out the door, into the hall. Pete hit a nurse who came running up just then, and they both went down on the floor out there in the hall, all tangled up, her screaming.

All of this in a few clock ticks. So *fast.*

The Bad Thing made the door shut with a bang, saw you couldn't lock it, then did the funniest thing of all, funny-weird, funny-scary. He held both his hands out at the door, and this blue light came from his hands the way not-blue came from a flashlight. Sparks flew from hinges and around the knob and all around the door edges. Everything metal smoked and turned all soft, like butter when you put it on mashed potatoes. It was a Fire Door. They said you had to keep your door closed if you ever saw fire in the hall, not try to run in the hall, but keep your door closed and stay put. They called it a Fire Door because fire couldn't get through it, they said, and Thomas always wondered why they didn't call it a Fire Can't Get Through It Door, but he never asked. The thing was, a Fire Door was all metal, so it couldn't burn, but now it melted around the edges, and so did the metal frame, they melted together, it didn't look like you could ever get through that door again.

People started pounding on the door from out there in the hall, tried to make it open, couldn't, and shouted for Thomas and Derek. Thomas knew some voices and who they belonged to, and he wanted to yell for them to help quick because he was in trouble, but he couldn't make a sound any better than poor Derek.

The Bad Thing made the blue light stop. Then it turned and looked at Thomas. It smiled at him. It didn't have a nice smile. It said, "Thomas?"

Thomas was surprised he could stand up, he was so scared. He was against the wall by the window, and he thought of maybe making the lock open on the window and push it up and get out, which he knew how to do because of Emergency Drills. But he knew he wasn't fast enough, no way, because the Bad Thing was the fastest he ever saw.

It took a step toward him, and another step. "Are you Thomas?"

For a while he still couldn't find the way to make sounds. He could just move his mouth and sort of pretend to make sounds. Then while he was doing that, he figured maybe if he told a lie and said he wasn't Thomas, the Bad Thing would believe him and just go away. So when all of a sudden he could make sounds, and then words, he said, "No. I . . . no . . . not Thomas. He's gone out in the world now, he's got a big eye cue, he's a high-end moron, so they moved him out in the world."

The Bad Thing laughed. It was a laugh that had no funny in it, the worst Thomas ever heard. The Bad Thing said, "Who the hell are you, Thomas? Where do you come from? How come a dummy like you can do something *I* can't?"

Thomas didn't answer. He didn't know what to say. He wished the people in the hall would stop pounding on the door and find some other way to get in, because pounding wasn't working. Maybe they could call the cops and tell them to bring the Jaws of Life, yeah, the Jaws of Life, like you saw them use on the TV news when a person was in a wrecked car and couldn't get out. They could use the Jaws of Life to pull open the door the way they pulled at smashed-up cars to get people out of them. He hoped the cops wouldn't say, we're sorry but we can only open car doors with the Jaws of Life, we can't open Care Home doors, because then he was finished for sure.

"You going to answer me, Thomas?" the Bad Thing asked.

Derek's TV chair got turned around in the fight, and now it was between Thomas and the Bad Thing. The Bad Thing held one hand out at the chair, just one, and the blue light went *whoosh!* and the chair blew up in splinters, like all the toothpicks in the world. Thomas threw his hands over his face just fast enough so no splinters went in his eyes. Some went in the backs of his hands and even in his cheeks and chin, and he could feel some of them in his shirt, poking his belly, but he didn't feel any hurt because he was so busy feeling scared.

He took his hands from his eyes right away, because he had to see where the Bad Thing was. Where it was was right on top of him, with soft bits of the chair's insides floating in the air in front of its face.

"Thomas?" it said, and it put one of its big hands on the front of Thomas's neck the way it did Pete a while ago.

Thomas heard words coming from himself, and he couldn't believe he was making them, but he was. Then when he heard what he said to the Bad Thing, he couldn't believe he said it, but he did: "You're not Being Sociable."

The Bad Thing grabbed him by the belt and kept hold of him by the neck and lifted him off the floor and pulled him away from the wall, then slammed him into the wall, the same way it did Derek, and, oh, it hurt worse than Thomas ever before hurt in his life.

♦   ♦   ♦

THE INTERIOR garage door had a dead bolt but no security chain. Pocketing his keys, Clint entered the kitchen at ten minutes past eight and saw Felina sitting at the table, reading a magazine while she waited for him.

She looked up and smiled, and his heart thumped faster at the sight of her, just like in every sappy love story ever written. He wondered how this could have happened to him. He had been so self-contained before Felina. He had been proud of the fact that he needed no one for intellectual stimulation or emotional support, and that he was therefore not vulnerable to the pains and disappointments of human relationships. Then he had met her. When he caught his breath, he had been as vulnerable as anyone—and glad of it.

She looked terrific in a simple blue dress with a red belt and matching red shoes. She was so strong yet so gentle, so tough yet so fragile.

He went to her, and for a while they stood by the refrigerator, next to the sink, holding each other and kissing, neither of them speaking in either of the ways they could. Clint thought they would have been happy, just then, even if both of them had been deaf and mute, capable of neither lip reading nor sign language, because at that moment what made them happy was the very fact of being together, which no words could adequately express anyway.

Finally he said, "What a day! Can't wait to tell you all about it. Let me clean up real quick, change clothes. We'll be out of here by eight-thirty, go over to Caprabello's, get a corner booth, some wine, some pasta, some garlic bread—"

*Some heartburn.*

He laughed because it was true. They both loved Caprabello's, but the food was spicy. They always suffered for the indulgence.

He kissed her again, and she sat down with her magazine, and he went through the dining room and down the hall to the bathroom. While he let the water run in the sink to get it hot, he plugged in his electric razor and began to shave, grinning at himself in the mirror because he was such a damned lucky guy.

♦ ♦ ♦

THE BAD THING was right in his face, snarling at him, lots of questions, too many for Thomas to think about and answer even if he was sitting in a chair quiet and happy, instead of lifted off the floor and held against the wall with his whole back hurting so bad he had to cry. He kept saying, "I'm full up, I'm full up." Always when he said that, people stopped asking him things or telling him things, they let him take time to make his head clear. But the Bad Thing was not like other people. It didn't care if his head was clear, it just wanted answers. Who was Thomas? Who was his mother? Who was his father? Where did he come from? Who was Julie? Who was Bobby? Where was Julie? Where was Bobby?

Then the Bad Thing said, "Hell, you're just a dummy. You don't *know* the answers, do you? You're just as stupid as you are stupid-looking."

It pulled Thomas away from the wall, held him off the floor with one hand on his neck, so Thomas couldn't breathe good. It slapped Thomas in the face, hard, and Thomas didn't want to keep crying, but he couldn't stop, he hurt and was scared.

"Why do they let people like you live?" the Bad Thing asked.

It let go of Thomas, and Thomas dropped on the floor. The Bad Thing looked down at him in a mean way that made Thomas angry almost as much as it made him scared. Which was funny-weird, because he almost never was angry. And this was the first time he was ever angry and scared both at the same time. But the Bad Thing was looking at him like he was just a bug or some dirt on the floor that had to be made clean.

"Why don't they kill you people at birth? What're you good for? Why don't they kill you at birth and chop you up and make dog food out of you?"

Thomas had memories of how people, out there in the world, looked at him that way or said mean things, and how Julie always Told Them Off. She said Thomas didn't have to be nice to people like that, said he could tell them they were Being Rude. Now Thomas was angry like he had Every Right To Be, and even if Julie never told him he could be angry about these things, he probably would be angry anyway, because some things you just *knew* were right or wrong.

The Bad Thing kicked him in the leg, and was going to kick him again, you could tell, but a noise was made at the window. Some of the aides were at the window. They broke a little square of glass and reached through, wanting to find the lock.

When the glass made a breaking sound, the Bad Thing turned from Thomas and held its hands up at the window, like it was asking the aides to stop wanting in. But Thomas knew what it was going to do was make the blue light.

Thomas wanted to warn the aides, but he figured nobody would hear him or listen to him until it was too late. So while the Bad Thing's back was turned, he crawled across the floor, away from the Bad Thing, even if crawling hurt, even if he had to go through spots of Derek's blood, all wet, and it made him sick on top of being angry and scared.

Blue light. Very bright.

Something exploded.

He heard glass falling and worse, like maybe not just the whole window blew out on the aides but part of the wall too.

People screamed. Most of the screams cut off quick-like, but one of them went on, it was real bad, like somebody out in the dark past the blown-up window was made to hurt even worse than Thomas.

Thomas didn't look back because he was all the way around the side of Derek's bed now, where he couldn't see the window anyway from where he was on the floor. And, besides, he knew what he wanted now, where he wanted to go, and he had to get there before the Bad Thing got interested in him again.

Quick-like, he crawled to the top end of the bed and looked up and saw Derek's arm hanging over the side, blood running down under his shirtsleeve and across his hand and drip-drip-dripping off his fingers. He didn't want to touch a dead person, not even a dead person he liked. But this was what he had to do, and he was used to having to do all sorts of things he wished he didn't—that was what life was like. So he grabbed the edge of the bed and pulled himself up as fast as he could, trying not to feel the bad hurt in his back and in his kicked leg, because feeling it would make him stiff and slow. Derek was right there, eyes open, mouth open, blood-wet, so sad, so scary, on top of the pictures of his folks that fell off the wall, still dead, off for always and ever to the Bad Place. Thomas grabbed the scissors sticking out of Derek, pulled them loose, telling himself it was okay because Derek couldn't feel anything now, or ever.

"You!" the Bad Thing said.

Thomas turned to see where the Bad Thing was, and where it was was right behind him, all the way around the bed, coming at him. So he shoved the scissors at it, hard as he could, and the Bad Thing's face made a surprised look. The scissors went in the front of the Bad Thing's shoulder. The Bad Thing looked even more surprised. The blood came.

Letting go of the scissors, Thomas said, "For Derek," then said, "for me."

He wasn't sure what would happen, but he figured that making the blood come would hurt the Bad Thing and maybe make it dead, like it made Derek dead. Across the room he saw where the window wasn't any more and where part of the wall wasn't any more, some smoke coming from the broken ends of things. He figured he was going to run over there and go through the hole, even if the night was out there on the other side.

But he never figured on what *did* happen, because the Bad Thing acted like the scissors weren't even in it, like blood wasn't being let loose from it, and it grabbed him and lifted him up again. It slammed him into Derek's dresser, which was a lot more hurt than the wall because the dresser was made with knobs and edges the wall didn't have.

He heard something crack in him, heard something tear. But the funny thing was, he wasn't crying any more and didn't *want* to cry any more, like he'd used up all the tears in himself.

The Bad Thing put its face close to Thomas's face, so their eyes were only a couple inches apart. He didn't like looking in the Bad Thing's eyes. They were scary. They were blue, but it was like they were really dark, like under the blue was a lot of stuff as black as the night out past the gone window.

But the other funny thing was, he wasn't as scared as he was a while ago, like he'd used up all his being scared just like he'd used up his tears. He looked in the Bad Thing's eyes, and he saw all that big dark, bigger than the dark that came over the world each day when the sun went away, and he knew it was wanting to make him dead, *going* to make him dead, and that was okay. He was not so afraid of being made dead as he always thought he would be. It was still a Bad Place, death, and he wished he didn't have to go there, but he had a funny-nice feeling about the Bad Place all of a sudden, a feeling that maybe it wouldn't be so lonely over there as he always figured it was, not even as lonely as it was on this side. He felt maybe someone was over there who loved him, someone who loved him more than even Julie loved him, even more than their dad used to love him, someone who was all bright, no dark at all, so bright you could only look at Him sideways.

The Bad Thing held Thomas against the dresser with one hand, and with its other hand it pulled the scissors out of itself.

Then it put the scissors in Thomas.

This light started to fill up Thomas, this light that loved him, and he knew he was going away. He hoped when he was all gone, Julie would know how brave he was right at the end, how he stopped crying and stopped being scared and fought back. And then all of a sudden he remembered he hadn't TVed a warning to Bobby that the Bad Thing might be coming for them, too, and he started to do that.

—the scissors went in again—

Then he all of a sudden knew something even more important he had to do. He had to let Julie know that the Bad Place was not so bad, after all, there was a light over there that loved you, you could tell. She needed to know about it because deep down she really didn't believe it. She figured it was all dark and lonely the way Thomas once figured it was, so she counted each clock tick and worried about all she had to do before her time ran out, all she had to learn and see and feel and get, all she had to do for Thomas and for Bobby so they'd be okay if Something Happened To Her.

—and the scissors went in again—

And she was happy with Bobby, but she was never going to be *real* happy until she knew she didn't have to be so angry about everything ending in a big dark. She was so nice it was hard to figure she was angry inside, but she was. Thomas only figured it out now, as the light was filling him up, figured out how terrible angry Julie was. She was angry that all the hard work and all the hope and all the dreams and all the trying and doing and loving didn't matter in the end because you were sooner or later made dead forever.

—the scissors—

If she knew about the light, she could stop being angry deep down. So Thomas TVed that, too, along with a warning, and with three last words to her and to Bobby, words of his own, all three things at once, hoping they wouldn't get mixed up:

*The Bad Thing's coming, look out, the Bad Thing, there's a light that loves you, the Bad Thing, I love you too, and there's a light, there's a light, THE BAD THING'S COMING—*

◆　　◆　　◆

AT 8:15 they were on the Foothill Freeway, rocketing toward the junction with the Ventura Freeway, which they would follow across the San Fernando Valley almost to the

ocean before turning north toward Oxnard, Ventura, and eventually Santa Barbara. Julie knew she should slow down, but she
couldn't. Speed relieved her tension a little; if she stayed even
close to the fifty-five-mile-an-hour limit, she was pretty sure that
she would start to scream before they were past Burbank.

A Benny Goodman tape was on the stereo. The exuberant
melodies and syncopated rhythms seemed in time and sympathy with the headlong rush of the car; and if they had been in
a movie, Goodman's sounds would have been perfect background music to the tenebrous panorama of light-speckled
night hills through which they passed from city to city, suburb
to suburb.

She knew why she was so tense. In a way she could never have
anticipated, The Dream was within their grasp—but they could
lose everything as they reached for it. Everything. Hope. Each
other. Their lives.

Sitting in the seat beside her, Bobby trusted her so implicitly
that he could doze at more than eighty miles an hour, even
though he knew that she, too, had slept only three hours last
night. From time to time she glanced at him, just because it felt
good to have him there.

He did not yet understand why they were going north to
check out the Pollard family, stretching their obligation to the
client beyond reason, but his bafflement sprang from the fact
that he was nearly as good a man as he appeared to be. He
sometimes bent the rules and broke the laws on behalf of their
clients, but he was more scrupulous in his personal life than
anyone Julie had ever known. She had been with him once
when a newspaper-vending machine gave him a copy of the
Sunday *Los Angeles Times,* then malfunctioned and returned
three of his four quarters to him, whereupon he had repaid all
three into the coin slot, even though that same machine had
malfunctioned to his disadvantage on other occasions over the
years and was into him for a couple of bucks. "Yeah, well," he'd
said, blushing when she had laughed at his goody-goody deed,
"maybe the machine can be crooked and still live with itself, but
I can't."

Julie could have told him that they were hanging with the
Pollard case because they saw a once-in-a-lifetime shot at really
big bucks, the Main Chance for which every hustler in the world
was looking and which most of them would never find. From

the moment Frank had shown them all that cash in the flight bag and told them about the second cache back at the motel, they were locked in like rats in a maze, drawn forward by the smell of cheese, even though each of them had taken a turn at protesting any interest in the game. When Frank came back to that hospital room from God-knew-where, with another three hundred thousand, neither she nor Bobby even raised the issue of illegality, though it was by that time no longer possible to pretend that Frank was entirely an innocent. By then the smell of cheese was too strong to be resisted at all. They were plunging ahead because they saw the chance to use Frank to cash out of the rat race and buy into The Dream sooner than they had expected. They were willing to use dirty money and questionable means to get to their desired end, more willing than they could admit to each other, though Julie supposed it could be said in their favor that they were not yet so greedy that they could simply steal the money and the diamonds from Frank and abandon him to the mercies of his psychotic brother; or maybe even their sense of duty to their client was a lie now, a virtue they could point to later when they tried to justify, to themselves, their other less-than-noble acts and impulses.

She *could* have told him all that, but she didn't, because she did not want to argue with him. She had to let him figure it out at his own pace, accept it in his own way. If she tried to tell him before he was able to understand it, he'd deny what she said. Even if he admitted to a fraction of the truth, he'd trot out an argument about the rightness of The Dream, the basic morality of it, and use that to justify the means to the end. But she didn't think a noble end could remain purely noble if arrived at by immoral means. And though she could not turn away from this Main Chance, she worried that when they achieved The Dream it would be sullied, not what it might have been.

Yet she drove on. Fast. Because speed relieved some of her fear and tension. It numbed caution too. And without caution she was less likely to retreat from the dangerous confrontation with the Pollard family that seemed inevitable if they were to seize the opportunity to obtain immense and liberating wealth.

They were in a clearing in traffic, with nothing close behind them and trailing the nearest forward car by about a quarter of a mile, when Bobby cried out and sat up in his seat as if warning her of an imminent collision. He jerked forward, pulling the shoulder harness taut, and put his hands on his head, as though stricken by a sudden migraine.

Frightened, she let up on the accelerator, lightly tapped the brake pedal, and said, "Bobby, what is it?"

In a voice coarsened by fear and sharpened by urgency, speaking above the music of Benny Goodman, he said, "Bad Thing, the Bad Thing, look out, there's a light, there's a light that loves you—"

♦   ♦   ♦

CANDY LOOKED down at the bloody body at his feet and knew that he should not have killed Thomas. Instead, he should have taken him away to a private place and tortured the answers out of him even if it took hours for the dummy to remember everything Candy needed to know. It could even have been fun.

But he was in a rage greater than any he had ever known, and he was less in control of himself than at any time in his life since the day he had found his mother's dead body. He wanted vengeance not only for his mother but for himself and for everyone in the world who ever deserved revenge and never got it. God had made him an instrument of revenge, and now Candy longed desperately to fulfill his purpose as he had never fulfilled it before. He yearned not merely to tear open the throat and drink the blood of one sinner, but of a great multitude of sinners. If ever his rage was to be dissipated, he needed not only to drink blood but to become drunk on it, bathe in it, wade through rivers of it, stand on land saturated with it. He wanted his mother to free him from all the rules that had restricted his rage before, wanted God to turn him *loose*.

He heard sirens in the distance, and knew that he must go soon.

Hot pain throbbed in his shoulder, where the scissors had parted muscle and scraped bone, but he would deal with that when he traveled. In reconstituting himself, he could easily remake his flesh whole and healthy.

Stalking through the debris that littered the floor, he looked for something that might give him a clue to the whereabouts of either the Julie or the Bobby of whom Thomas had spoken. They might know who Thomas had been and why he had possessed a gift that not even Candy's blessed mother had been able to impart.

He touched various objects and pieces of furniture, but all he could extract from them were images of Thomas and Derek and some of the aides and nurses who took care of them. Then he saw a scrapbook lying open on the floor, beside the table on which he had butchered Derek. The open pages were full of all kinds of pictures that had been pasted in lines and peculiar patterns. He picked the book up and leafed through it, wondering what it was, and when he tried to see the face of the last person who had handled it, he was rewarded with someone other than a dummy or a nurse.

A hard-looking man. Not as tall as Candy but almost as solid.

The sirens were less than a mile away now, louder by the second.

Candy let his right hand glide over the cover of the scrapbook, seeking . . . seeking . . .

Sometimes he could sense only a little, sometimes a lot. This time he *had* to be successful, or this room was going to be a dead end in his search for the meaning of the dummy's power.

Seeking . . .

He received a name. Clint.

Clint had sat in Derek's chair sometime during the afternoon, paging through this odd collection of pictures.

When he tried to see where Clint had gone, after leaving this room, he saw a Chevy that Clint was driving on the freeway, then a place called Dakota & Dakota. Then the Chevy again, on a freeway at night, and then a small house in a place called Placentia.

The approaching sirens were very close now, probably coming up the driveway into the Cielo Vista parking lot.

Candy threw the book down. He was ready to go.

He had only one more thing to do before he teleported. When he had discovered that Thomas was a dummy, and when he had realized that Cielo Vista was a place full of them, he had been angered and offended by the home's existence.

He held his hands two feet apart, palm facing palm. Sky-blue light glowed between them.

He remembered how neighbors and other people had talked about his sisters—and also about him when, as a boy, he had been kept out of school because of his problems. Violet and Verbina looked and acted mentally deficient, and they probably did not care if people called them retards. Ignorant people labeled him retarded, too, because they thought he was excused from school for being as learning disabled and strange as his sisters. (Only Frank attended classes like a normal child.)

The light began to coalesce into a ball. As more power poured out of his hands and into the ball, it acquired a deeper shade of blue and seemed to take on substance, as if it were a solid object floating in the air.

Candy had been bright, with no learning disabilities at all. His mother taught him to read, write, and do math; so he got angry when he overheard people say he was a deadhead. He had been excused from school for other reasons, of course, mainly because of the sex thing. When he got older and bigger, nobody called him retarded or made jokes about him, at least not within his hearing.

The sapphire-blue sphere looked almost as solid as a genuine sapphire, but as big as a basketball. It was nearly ready.

Having been unjustly tagged with the retarded label, Candy had not grown up with sympathy for the genuinely disabled, but with an intense loathing for them that he hoped would make it clear to even ignorant people that he definitely was not—and never had been—one of *them.* To think such a thing of him—or of his sisters, for that matter—was an insult to his sainted mother, who was incapable of bringing a moron into the world.

He cut off the flow of power and took his hands away from the sphere. For a moment he stared at it, smiling, thinking about what it would do to this offensive place.

Through the missing window and the partially shattered walls, the wail of the sirens became deafening, then suddenly subsided from a high-pitched shriek to a low growl that spiraled toward silence.

"Help's here, Thomas," he said, and laughed.

He put one hand against the sapphire sphere and gave it a shove. It shot across the room as if it were a ballistic missile fired from its silo. It smashed through the wall behind Derek's bed, leaving a ragged hole as big as anything a cannonball could have made, through the wall beyond that, and through every additional wall that stood before it, spewing flames as it went, setting fire to everything along its path.

Candy heard people screaming and a hard explosion, as he did a fadeout on his way to the house in Placentia.

# 52

BOBBY STOOD at the side of the freeway, holding on to the open car door, gasping for breath. He had been sure he was going to throw up, but the urge had passed.

"Are you all right?" Julie asked anxiously.

"I . . . think so."

Traffic shot past. Each vehicle was trailed by a wake of wind and a roar that gave Bobby the peculiar feeling that he and Julie and the Toyota were still moving, doing eighty-five with him holding on to the open door and her with a hand on his shoulder, magically keeping their balance and avoiding roadburn as they dragged their feet along the pavement, with nobody driving.

The dream had seriously unsettled and disoriented him.

"Not a dream, really," he told her. He continued to keep his head down, peering at bits of loose gravel on the paved shoulder of the highway, half expecting a return of the cramping nausea. "Not like the dream I had before, about us and the jukebox and the ocean of acid."

"But about 'the bad thing' again."

"Yeah. You couldn't call it a dream, though, because it was just this . . . this burst of words, inside my head."

"From where?"

"I don't know."

He dared to lift his head, and though a whirl of dizziness swept through him, the nausea did not return.

He said, " 'Bad thing . . . look out . . . there's a light that loves you. . . .' I can't remember it all. It was so strong, so hard, like somebody shouting at me through a bullhorn that was pressed against my ear. Except that's not right, either, because I didn't really hear the words, they were just there, in my head. But they *felt* loud, if that makes any sense. And there weren't images, like in a dream. Instead there were these feelings, as strong as they were confused. Fear and joy, anger and forgiveness . . . and right at the end of it, this strange sense of peace that I . . . can't describe."

A Peterbilt thundered toward them, towing the biggest trailer the law allowed. Sweeping out of the night behind its blazing headlights, it looked like a leviathan swimming up from a deep marine trench, all raw power and cold rage, with a hunger that could never be satisfied. For some reason, as it boomed past them, Bobby thought of the man he had seen on the beach at Punaluu, and he shuddered.

Julie said, "Are you okay?"

"Yeah."

"Are you sure?"

He nodded. "A little dizzy. That's all."

"What now?"

He looked at her. "What else? We go on to Santa Barbara. El Encanto Heights, bring this thing to an end . . . somehow."

♦　♦　♦

CANDY ARRIVED in the archway between a living room and dining room. No one was in either place.

He heard a buzzing sound farther back in the house, and after a moment he identified it as an electric razor. It stopped. Then he heard water running in a sink, and the drone of a bathroom exhaust fan.

He intended to head straight for the hall and the bath, take the man by surprise. But he heard a rustle of paper from the opposite direction.

He crossed the dining room and stepped into the kitchen doorway. It was smaller than the kitchen in his mother's house, but it was as spotlessly clean and orderly as his mother's kitchen had not been since her death.

A woman in a blue dress was sitting at the table, her back to him. She was leaning over a magazine, turning the pages one after the other, as if looking for something of interest to read.

Candy possessed a far greater control of his telekinetic talents than Frank enjoyed, and in particular could teleport more efficiently and swiftly than Frank, creating less air displacement and less noise from molecular resistance. Nevertheless, he was surprised that she had not gotten up to investigate, for the sounds he had made during arrival had been only one small room away from her and, surely, odd enough to prick her curiosity.

She turned a few more pages, then leaned forward to read.

He could not see much of her from behind. Her hair was thick, lustrous, and so black it seemed to have been spun on the same loom as the night. Her shoulders and back were slender. Her legs, which were both to one side of the chair and crossed at the ankles, were shapely. If he had been a man with any interest in sex, he supposed he would have been excited by the curve of her calves.

Wondering what she looked like—and suddenly overwhelmed by a need to know how her blood would taste—he stepped out of the open doorway and took three steps to her. He made no effort to be silent, but she did not look up. The first she became aware of him was when he seized a handful of her hair and dragged her, kicking and flailing, out of her chair.

He turned her around and was instantly excited by her. He was indifferent to her shapely legs, the flare of her hips, the trimness of her waist, the fullness of her breasts. Though beautiful, it was not even her face that electrified him. Something else. A quality in her gray eyes. Call it vitality. She was more alive than most people, vibrant.

She did not scream but let out a low grunt of fear or anger, then struck him furiously with both fists. She pounded his chest, battered his face.

Vitality! Yes, this one was full of life, bursting with life, and her vitality thrilled him far more than any bounty of sexual charms.

He could still hear the distant splash of water, the rattle-hum of the bathroom exhaust fan, and he was confident that he could take her without drawing the attention of the man— as long as he could prevent her from screaming. He struck her on the side of the head with his fist, hammered her before she could scream. She slumped against him, not unconscious but dazed.

Shaking with the anticipation of pleasure, Candy placed her on her back, on the table, with her legs trailing over the edge. He spread her legs and leaned between them, but not to commit rape, nothing as disgusting as that. As he lowered his face toward hers, she first blinked at him in confusion, still rattle-brained from the blows she had taken. Then her eyes began to clear. He saw horrified comprehension return to her, and he went quickly for her throat, bit deep, and found the blood, which was clean and sweet, intoxicating.

She thrashed beneath him.

She was so alive. So wonderfully alive. For a while.

♦    ♦    ♦

WHEN THE deliveryman brought the pizza, Lee Chen took it into Bobby and Julie's office and offered some to Hal.

Putting his book aside but not taking his stockinged feet off the coffee table, Hal said, "You know what that stuff does to your arteries?"

"Why's everyone so concerned about my arteries today?"

"You're such a nice young man. We'd hate to see you dead before you're thirty. Besides, we'd always wonder what clothes you might've worn next, if you'd lived."

"Not anything like what you're wearing, I assure you."

Hal leaned over and looked in the box that Lee held down to him. "Looks pretty good. Rule of thumb—any pizza they'll bring to you, they're selling service instead of good food. But this doesn't look bad at all, you can actually tell where the pizza ends and the cardboard begins."

Lee tore the lid off the box, put it on the coffee table, and put two slices of pizza on that makeshift plate. "There."

"You're not going to give me half?"

"What about the cholesterol?"

"Hell, cholesterol's just a little animal fat, it isn't arsenic."

♦    ♦    ♦

WHEN THE woman's strong heart stopped beating, Candy pulled back from her. Though blood still seeped from her ravaged throat, he did not touch another drop of it. The thought of drinking from a corpse sickened him. He remembered his sisters' cats, eating their own each time one of the pack died, and he grimaced.

Even as he raised his wet lips from her throat, he heard a door open farther back in the house. Footsteps approached.

Candy quickly circled the table, putting it and the dead woman between himself and the doorway to the dining room. From the vision induced by the dummy's scrapbook of pictures, Candy knew that Clint would not be as easy to handle as most people were. He preferred to put a little distance between them, give himself time to size up his opponent rather than take the guy by surprise.

Clint appeared in the doorway. Except for his outfit—gray slacks, navy-blue blazer, maroon V-neck, white shirt—he looked the same as the psychic impression he had left on the book. He had pumped a lot of iron in his time. His hair was thick, black, and combed straight back from his forehead. He had a face like carved granite, and a hard look in his eyes.

Excited by the recent kill, by the taste of blood still in his mouth, Candy watched the man with interest, wondering what would happen next. There were all sorts of ways it could go, and not one of them would be dull.

Clint did not react as Candy expected. He did not show surprise when he saw the woman sprawled dead upon the table; he did not seem horrified, shattered by the loss of her, or outraged. Something major changed in his stony face, though below the surface, like tectonic plates shifting under the mantle of the earth's crust.

Finally he met Candy's gaze, and said, "You."

The note of recognition in that single word was unsettling. For a moment Candy could think of no way this man could know him—then he remembered Thomas.

The possibility that Thomas had told this man—and perhaps others—about Candy was the most frightening turn in Candy's life since his mother's death. His service in God's army of avengers was a deeply private matter, a secret that should not have been spread beyond the Pollard family. His mother had warned him that it was all right to be proud of doing God's work, but that his pride would lead him to a fall if he boasted of his divine favor to others. "Satan," she had told him, "constantly seeks the names of lieutenants in God's army—which is what you are—and when he finds them, he destroys them with worms that eat them alive from within, worms fat as snakes, and he rains fire on them too. If you can't keep the secret, you'll die and go to Hell for your big mouth."

"Candy," Clint said.

The use of his name erased whatever doubt remained that the secret had been passed outside the family and that Candy was in deep trouble, though he had not broken the code of silence himself.

He imagined that even now Satan, in some dark and steaming

place, had tilted his head and said, "Who? Who did you say? What was his name? Candy? Candy who?"

As furious as he was frightened, Candy started around the kitchen table, wondering if Clint had learned about him from Thomas. He was determined to break the man, make him talk before killing him.

In a move as unexpected as his rock-calm acceptance of the woman's murder, Clint reached inside his jacket, withdrew a revolver, and fired two shots.

He might have fired more than two, but those were the only ones Candy heard. The first round hit him in the stomach, the second in the chest, pitching him backward. Fortunately he sustained no damage to head or heart. If his brain tissue had been scrambled, disturbing the mysterious and fragile connection between brain and mind, leaving his mind trapped within his ruined brain before he had a chance to separate the two, he would not have possessed the mental ability to teleport, leaving him vulnerable to a coup de grace. And if his heart had been stopped instantaneously by a well-placed bullet, before he could dematerialize, he would have fallen down dead where he'd stood. Those were the only wounds that might finish him. He was many things, but he was not immortal; so he was grateful to God for letting him get out of that kitchen and back to his mother's house alive.

♦ ♦ ♦

THE VENTURA FREEWAY. Julie drove fast, though not as fast as she had earlier. On the tapedeck: Artie Shaw's "Nightmare."

Bobby brooded, staring through the side window at the nightscape. He could not stop thinking about the blare of words that had seared through him, loud as a bomb blast and bright as a blast-furnace fire. He had come to terms with the dream that had frightened him last week; everyone had bad dreams. Though exceptionally vivid, almost more real than real life, there had been nothing uncanny about it—or so he had convinced himself. But this was different. He could not believe that these urgent, lava-hot words had erupted from his own subconscious. A dream, with complex Freudian messages couched in elaborate scenes and symbols—yes, that was understandable;

after all, the subconscious dealt in euphemisms and metaphors. But this wordburst had been blunt, direct, like a telegraph delivered on a wire plugged directly into his cerebral cortex.

When he wasn't brooding, Bobby was fidgeting. Because of Thomas.

For some reason, the longer he dwelt on the blaze of words, the more Thomas slipped into his thoughts. He could see no connection between the two, so he tried to put Thomas out of mind and concentrate on turning up an explanation for the experience. But Thomas gently, insistently returned, again and again. After a while Bobby got the uneasy feeling there *was* a link between the wordburst and Thomas, though he had no ghost of an idea what it might be.

Worse, as the miles rolled up on the odometer and they reached the western end of the valley, Bobby began to sense that Thomas was in danger. And because of me and Julie, Bobby thought.

Danger from whom, from what?

The biggest danger that Bobby and Julie faced, right now, was Candy Pollard. But even that jeopardy lay in the future, for Candy didn't know about them yet; he was not aware that they were working on Frank's behalf, and he might never become aware of it, depending on how things went in Santa Barbara and El Encanto Heights. Yes, he had seen Bobby on the beach at Punaluu, with Frank, but he had no way of knowing who Bobby was. Ultimately, even if Candy became aware of Dakota & Dakota's association with Frank, there was no way that Thomas could be drawn into the affair; Thomas was another, separate part of their lives. Right?

"Something wrong?" Julie said as she pulled the Toyota one lane to the left, to pass a big rig hauling Coors.

He could see nothing to be gained by telling her that Thomas might be in danger. She would be upset, worried. And for what? He was just letting his vivid imagination run away with him. Thomas was perfectly safe down there in Cielo Vista.

"Bobby, what's wrong?"

"Nothing."

"Why're you fidgeting?"

"Prostate trouble."

♦   ♦   ♦

CHANEL NO. 5, a softly glowing lamp, cozy rose-patterned fabrics and wallpaper . . .

He laughed with relief when he materialized in the bedroom, the bullets left behind in that kitchen in Placentia, over a hundred miles away. His wounds had knit up as if they had never existed. He had lost perhaps an ounce of blood and a few flecks of tissue, because one of the bullets had passed through him and out his back, carrying that material with it before he'd transported himself beyond the revolver's range. Everything else was as it should be, however, and his flesh did not harbor even the memory of pain.

He stood in front of the dresser for half a minute, breathing deeply of the perfume that wafted up from the saturated handkerchief. The scent gave him courage and reminded him of the abiding need to make them pay for his mother's murder, all of them, not just Frank but the whole world, which had conspired against her.

He looked at his face in the mirror. The gray-eyed woman's blood was no longer on his chin and lips; he had left it behind him, as he might leave water behind when teleporting out of a rainstorm. But the taste of it was still in his mouth. And his reflection was without a doubt that of vengeance personified.

Depending on the element of surprise and his ability to target his point of arrival precisely now that he was familiar with the kitchen, he returned to Clint's house. He intended to enter at the dining-room doorway, immediately behind the man, directly opposite the point from which he had dematerialized.

Either the experience of being shot had shaken him more than he realized, or the rage jittering through him had passed the critical point at which it interfered with his concentration. Whatever the reason, he did not arrive where he intended, but by the door to the garage, one-quarter instead of halfway around the room from his last position, to the right of Clint and not near enough to rush him and seize the gun before it could be fired.

Except Clint was not present. And the woman's body had been removed from the table. Only the blood remained as proof that she perished there.

Candy could not have been gone more than a minute—the time he had spent in his mother's room, plus a couple of seconds in transit each way. He expected to return to find Clint bent over the corpse, either grieving or checking desperately for a pulse. But as soon as he realized Candy was gone, the man must have taken the body in his arms and . . . And what? He must have fled the house, of course, hoping against hope that a faint thread of life remained unbroken in the woman, getting her out of the way in case Candy returned.

Cursing softly—then immediately begging his mother's and God's forgiveness for his foul language—Candy tried the door into the garage. It was locked. If he had left by that exit, Clint wouldn't have paused to lock up behind himself.

He hurried out of the kitchen, through the dining room, toward the foyer off the living room, to check out the front lawn and the street. But he heard a noise from deeper in the house, and halted before he reached the front door. He changed direction, cautiously following the hallway back to the bedrooms.

A light was on in one of those rooms. He eased to the door and risked a glance inside.

Clint had just put the woman on the queen-size bed. As Candy watched, the man pulled her skirt down over her knees. He still had the revolver in one hand.

For the second time in less than an hour, Candy heard faraway sirens swelling in the night. The neighbors probably had heard the gunfire and called the police.

Clint saw him in the doorway but did not bring up the gun. He did not say anything, either, and the expression on his stoic face remained unchanged. He seemed like a deaf-mute. The strangeness of the man's demeanor made Candy nervous and uncertain.

He thought there was a pretty good chance that Clint had emptied the gun at him in the kitchen, even though he had teleported out of there with the impact of the second slug. Most likely, he had fired every round reflexively, his trigger finger ruled by rage or fear or whatever he was feeling. He could not have carried the woman into the bedroom and reloaded the gun, too, in the minute or so that Candy had been gone, which meant Candy might be in no danger if he just walked up to the guy and took the weapon away from him.

But he stayed in the doorway. Either of those two shots *could* have been dead-center in his heart. The power within him was great, but he could not exercise it quickly enough to vaporize an oncoming bullet.

Instead of dealing with Candy in any fashion, the man turned away from him, walked around the foot of the bed to the other side, and stretched out beside the woman.

"What the hell?" Candy said aloud.

Clint took hold of her dead hand. His other hand held the .38 revolver. He turned his head on the pillow to look toward her, and his eyes glistened with what might have been unshed tears. He put the muzzle of the gun under his chin, and annihilated himself.

Candy was so stunned that he was unable to move for a moment or think what to do next. He was jolted out of his paralysis by the ululant sirens, and realized that the trail from Thomas to Bobby and Julie, whoever they were, might end here if he did not discover what link the dead man on the bed shared with them. If he ever hoped to learn who Thomas had been, how Clint had known his name, or how many others knew of him, if he wanted to learn how much danger he was in and how he might slide out of it, he couldn't waste this opportunity.

He hurried to the bed, rolled the dead man onto his side, and withdrew the wallet from his pants pocket. He flipped it open and saw the private investigator's license. Opposite it, in another plastic window, was a business card for Dakota & Dakota.

Candy remembered a vague image of the Dakota & Dakota offices, which had come to him in Thomas's room when he had obtained a vision of Clint from the scrapbook. There was an address on the card. And below the name Clint Karaghiosis, in smaller type, were the names Robert and Julia Dakota.

Outside, the sirens had died. Someone was pounding on the front door. Two voices shouted, "Police!"

Candy threw the wallet aside and took the gun out of the dead man's hand. He broke open the cylinder. It was a five-shot weapon, and all of the chambers were filled with expended cartridges. Clint had fired four rounds in the kitchen, but even in his moment of vengeful fury, he had possessed enough control to save the last bullet for himself.

"Just because of a woman?" Candy said uncomprehendingly, as if the dead man might answer him. "Because you couldn't get sex from her any more now? Why does sex matter so much? Couldn't you get sex from another woman? Why was sex with this one so important, you didn't want to live without it?"

They were still pounding on the door. Someone spoke

through a bullhorn, but Candy didn't pay attention to what was being said.

He dropped the gun and wiped his hand on his pants, because he suddenly felt unclean. The dead man had handled the gun, and the dead man seemed to have been obsessed with sex. Without question, the world was a cesspool of lust and debauchery, and Candy was glad that God and his mother had spared him from the sick desires that seemed to infect nearly everyone else.

He left that house of sinners.

# 53

SLUMPED ON the sofa, Hal Yamataka had a slice of pizza in one hand and the MacDonald novel in the other, when he heard the hollow flutelike warble. He dropped both the book and the food, and shot to his feet.

"Frank?"

The half-open door swung slowly inward, not because it was being pushed open by anyone but because a sudden draft, sweeping in from the reception lounge, was strong enough to move it.

"Frank?" Hal repeated.

As he crossed the room, the sound faded and the draft died. But by the time he reached the doorway, the unmelodic notes returned, and a burst of wind ruffled his hair.

To the left stood the receptionist's desk, untended at this hour. Directly opposite the desk was the door to the public corridor that served the other companies on this level, and it was closed. The only other door, at the far end of the rectangular lounge, was also closed; it led to a hallway that was interior to the Dakota & Dakota suite, off which were six other offices—including the computer room where Lee was still at work—and a bathroom. The piping and the wind could not have reached him through those closed doors; therefore, the point of origin was clearly the reception lounge.

Stepping to the center of the room, he looked around expectantly.

The flute sounds and turbulence rose a third time.

Hal said, "Frank," as he became aware, out of the corner of his eye, that a man had arrived near the door to the public hall, to Hal's right and almost behind him.

But when he turned, he saw that it was not Frank. The traveler was a stranger, but Hal knew him at once. Candy. It could be no one else, for this was the man Bobby had described from the beach at Punaluu, and whose description Hal had received from Clint.

Hal was built low and wide, he kept in good shape, and he could remember no instance in his life when he'd been physically intimidated by another man. Candy was eight inches taller than he, but Hal had handled men taller than that. Candy was clearly a mesomorph, one of those guys destined from birth to have a strong-boned body layered with slabs of muscle, even if he exercised lightly or not at all; and he was clearly no stranger to the discipline and painful rituals of barbells, dumbbells, and slantboards. But Hal had a mesomorphic body type, as well, and was as hard as frozen beef. He was not intimidated by Candy's height or muscles. What frightened him was the aura of insanity, rage, and violence the man radiated as powerfully as a week-old corpse would radiate the stink of death.

The instant that Frank's brother hit the room, Hal smelled his mad ferocity as surely as a healthy dog would detect the rabid odor of a sick one, and he acted accordingly. He wasn't wearing shoes, wasn't carrying a gun, and wasn't aware of anything near at hand that might be used as a weapon, so he spun around and ran back toward the bosses' office, where he knew a loaded Browning 9mm semiautomatic pistol was kept in a spring clip on the underside of Julie's desk as insurance against the unexpected. Until now the gun had never been needed.

Hal was not the martial-arts whiz that his formidable appearance and ethnicity led everyone to believe he was, but he did know some Tai Kwan Do. The problem was, only a fool would resort to *any* form of martial arts as a first defense against a charging bull with a bumblebee up its butt.

He made the doorway before Candy grabbed him by his shirt and tried to pull him off his feet. The shirt tore along the seams, leaving the madman with a handful of cloth.

But Hal was wrenched off balance. He stumbled into the office and collided with Julie's big chair, which was still standing in the middle of the room with four other chairs arranged in a semicircle in front of it, as Jackie Jaxx had required for Frank's session of hypnosis. He grabbed at Julie's chair for support. It was on wheels, which rolled grudgingly on the carpet, though well enough to send it skidding treacherously out from under him.

The psycho crashed into him, ramming him against the chair and the chair against the desk. Leaning into Hal, with massive fists that felt like the iron heads of sledgehammers, Candy delivered a flurry of punches to his midsection.

Hal's hands were down, leaving him briefly defenseless, but he clasped them, with his thumbs aligned, and rammed them upward, between Candy's pile-driving arms, catching him in the Adam's apple. The blow was hard enough to make Candy gag on his own cry of pain, and Hal's thumbnails gouged the madman's flesh, skidding all the way up under his chin, tearing the skin as they went.

Choking, unable to draw breath through his bruised and spasming esophagus, Candy staggered backward, both hands to his throat.

Hal pushed away from the chair, against which he had been pinned, but he didn't go after Candy. Even the blow he'd delivered was the equivalent of a tap with a flyswatter to the snout of that bull with the bee up its butt. An overconfident charge would no doubt end in a swift goring. Instead, hurting from the punches to his gut, with the sour taste of pizza sauce in the back of his throat, he hurried around the desk, hot to get his hands on that 9mm Browning.

The desk was large, and the dimensions of the kneehole were correspondingly spacious. He wasn't sure where the pistol was clipped, and he didn't want to bend down to look under because he would have to take his eyes off Candy. He slid his hand from left to right along the underside of the desktop, then reached deeper and slid it back the other way.

Just as he touched the butt of the pistol, he saw Candy thrust out both hands, palms forward, as if the guy knew Hal had found a gun and was saying, *Don't shoot, I surrender, stop.* But as Hal tugged the Browning free of the metal spring clamp, he discovered that Candy didn't have surrender in mind: blue light flashed out of the madman's palms.

The heavy desk abruptly behaved like a wire-rigged, balsa-wood prop in a movie about poltergeists. Even as Hal was raising the gun, the desk slammed into him and carried him backward, into the huge window behind him. The desk was wider than the window, and the ends of it met the wall, which prevented it from sailing straight through the glass.

But Hal was in the center of the window, and the low sill hit him behind the knees, so nothing inhibited his plunge. For an instant the jangling Levolor blinds seemed as if they might restrain him, but that was wishful thinking; he carried them with him, through the glass, and into the night, dropping the Browning without ever having fired it.

He was surprised how long it took to fall six stories, which was not such a terribly great distance, though a deadly one. He had time to marvel at how slowly the lighted office window receded from him, time to think about people he had loved and dreams never fulfilled, time even to notice that the clouds, which had returned at twilight, were shedding light sprinkles of rain. His last thought was about the garden behind his small house in Costa Mesa, where he tended an array of flowers year-round and secretly enjoyed every moment of it: the exquisitely soft texture of a coral-red impatiens petal, and on its edge a single tiny drop of morning dew, glistening—

♦   ♦   ♦

CANDY SHOVED the heavy desk aside and leaned out of the sixth-floor window. A cool updraft rose along the side of the building and buffeted his face.

The shoeless man lay on his back on a broad concrete walk below, illuminated by the amber backsplash of a landscape spotlight. He was surrounded by broken glass, tangled metal blinds, and a swiftly spreading blot of his own blood.

Coughing, still having a little difficulty drawing deep enough breaths, with one hand pressed to the stinging flesh of his battered throat, Candy was upset by the man's death. Actually, not by the fact of it but by the timing of it. First, he'd wanted to interrogate him to learn who Bobby and Julie were, and what association they had with the psychic Thomas.

And when Candy had teleported into the reception lounge, the guy had thought he was Frank; he had spoken Frank's name. The people at Dakota & Dakota were somehow as-

sociated with Frank—knew all about his ability to teleport!—
and therefore would know where to find the mother-murdering
wretch.

Candy supposed the office would hold answers to at least
some of his questions, but he was concerned that police, responding to the dead man's plunge, would necessitate a departure before he turned up all the information he needed. Sirens
were the background music to this night's adventures.

No sirens had arisen yet, however. Maybe he had gotten
lucky; maybe no one had seen the man fall. It was unlikely that
anyone was at work at any of the other companies in the office
building; it was, after all, ten minutes till nine. Perhaps janitors
were polishing floors somewhere, or emptying wastebaskets,
but they might not have heard enough to warrant investigation.

The man had plummeted to his death with surprisingly little
protest. He had not screamed. An instant before impact, the
start of a shout had flown from him, but it had been too short
to attract notice. The explosion of the glass and the tinny clang-
ing of the blinds had been loud enough, but the action had been
over before anyone could have located the source of the sound.

A four-lane street encircled the Fashion Island shopping center and also served the office towers that, like this one, stood on
the outer rim. Apparently, however, no cars had been on it
when the man had fallen.

Now two appeared to the left, one behind the other. Both
passed without slowing. A row of shrubberies, between the sidewalk and the street, prevented motorists from seeing the corpse
where it lay. The office-tower ring of the sprawling complex was
clearly not an area that attracted pedestrians at night, so the
dead man might remain undiscovered until morning.

He looked across the street, at the restaurants and stores that
were on this flank of the mall, five or six hundred yards away.
A few people on foot, shrunken by distance, moved between
the parked cars and the entrances to the businesses. No one
appeared to have seen anything—and in fact it would not have
been that easy to spot a darkly dressed man plunging past a
mostly dark building, aloft and visible for only seconds before
gravity finished him.

Candy cleared his throat, wincing in pain, and spat toward
the dead man below.

He tasted blood. This time it was his own.

Turning away from the window, he surveyed the office, wondering where he would find the answers he sought. If he could locate Bobby and Julie Dakota, they might be able to explain Thomas's telepathy and more important, they might be able to deliver Frank into his hands.

♦　♦　♦

AFTER TWICE responding to an alarm from the radar detector and avoiding two speed traps in the west valley, Julie cranked the Toyota back up to eighty-five, and they dusted L.A. off their heels.

A few raindrops spattered the windshield, but the sprinkles did not last. She switched the wipers off moments after turning them on.

"Santa Barbara in maybe an hour," she said, "as long as a cop with a sense of duty doesn't come along."

The back of her neck ached, and she was deeply weary, but she didn't want to trade places with Bobby; she didn't have the patience to be a passenger tonight. Her eyes were sore but not heavy; she could not possibly have slept. The events of the day had murdered sleep, and alertness was assured by concern about what might lie ahead, not just on the highway before them but in El Encanto Heights.

Ever since he'd been awakened by what he called the "word-burst," Bobby had been moody. She could tell he was worried about something, but he didn't seem to want to talk about it yet.

After a while, in an obvious attempt to take his mind off the wordburst and whatever gloomy ruminations it had inspired, he tried to strike up a conversation about something utterly different. He lowered the volume on the stereo, thereby frustrating the intended effect of Glenn Miller's "American Patrol," and said, "You ever stop to think, four out of our eleven employees are Asian-Americans?"

She didn't glance away from the road. "So?"

"So why is that, do you think?"

"Because we hire only first-rate people, and it so happened that four of the first-rate people who wanted to work for us were Chinese, Japanese, and Vietnamese."

"That's part of it."

"Just part?" she said. "So what's the other part? You think

maybe the wicked Fu Manchu turned a mind-control ray on us from his secret fortress in the Tibetan mountains and *made* us hire 'em?"

"That's part of it too," he said. "But another part of it is—I'm attracted to the Asian personality. Or to what people think of when they think of the Asian personality: intelligence, a high degree of self-discipline, neatness, a strong sense of tradition and order."

"Those are pretty much traits of everyone who works for us, not just Jamie, Nguyen, Hal, and Lee."

"I know. But what makes me so comfortable with Asian-Americans is that I buy into the stereotype of them, I feel everything will go along in an orderly, stable fashion when I'm working with them, and I *need* to buy into the stereotype because . . . well, I'm not the kind of guy I've always thought I was. You ready to hear something shocking?"

"Always," Julie said.

◆　◆　◆

OFTEN, WHEN Lee Chen was laboring in the computer room, he popped a CD in his Sony Discman and listened to music through earphones. He always kept the door closed to avoid distraction, and no doubt some of his fellow employees thought he was somewhat antisocial; however, when he was engaged in the penetration of a complex and well-protected data network, like the array of police systems he was still plundering, he needed to concentrate. Occasionally music distracted him as much as anything, depending on his mood, but most of the time it was conducive to his work. The minimalist New Age piano solos of George Winston were sometimes just the thing, but more often he needed rock-'n'-roll. Tonight it was Huey Lewis and The News: "Hip to Be Square" and "The Power of Love," "The Heart of Rock & Roll" and "You Crack Me Up." Focused intently on the terminal screen (his window on the mesmerizing world of cyberspace), with "Bad Is Bad" pouring into his ears through the headset, he might not have heard a thing if, in the world outside, God had peeled back the sky and announced the imminent destruction of the human race.

◆　◆　◆

A COOL DRAFT circulated through the room from the broken window, but growing frustration generated a compensatory heat in Candy. He moved slowly around the spacious office, handling various objects, touching the furniture, trying to finesse a vision that would reveal the whereabouts of the Dakotas and Frank. Thus far he'd had no luck.

He could have pored through the contents of the desk drawers and filing cabinets, but that would have taken hours, since he didn't know where they might have filed the information he was seeking. He also realized he might not recognize the right stuff when he found it, for it might be in a folder or envelope bearing a case name or code that was meaningless to him. And though his mother had taught him to read and write, and though he had been a voracious reader just like her—until he lost interest in books upon her death—teaching himself many subjects as well as any university could have done, he nevertheless trusted what his special gifts could reveal to him more than anything he might find on paper.

Besides, he had already stepped into the lounge, obtained the Dakotas' home address and phone number, and called to see if they were there. An answering machine had picked up on the third ring, and he had left no message. He didn't just want to know where the Dakotas lived, where they might turn up in time; he needed to know where they were *now*, this minute, because he was in a fever to get at them and wring answers from them.

He picked up a third Scotch-and-soda glass. They were all over the room. The psychic residue on the tumbler gave him an instant, vivid image of a man named Jackie Jaxx, and he pitched it aside in anger. It bounced off the sofa, onto the carpet, without shattering.

This Jaxx person left a colorful and noisy psychic impression everywhere in his wake, the way a dog with poor bladder control would mark each step on his route with a dribble of stinking urine. Candy sensed that Jaxx was currently with a large number of people, at a party in Newport Beach, and he also sensed that trying to find Frank or the Dakotas through Jaxx would be wasted effort. Even so, if Jaxx had been alone now, easily taken, Candy would have gone straight to him and slaughtered him, just because the guy's lingering aura was so brassy and annoying.

Either he had not yet found an object that one of the Dakotas had touched long enough to leave an imprint, or neither of them was the type who left a rich, lingering psychic residue in his wake. For reasons Candy could not fathom, some people were harder to trace than others.

He had always found tracing Frank to be of medium difficulty, but tonight catching that scent was harder than usual. Repeatedly he sensed that Frank had been in the room, but at first he could locate nothing in which the aura of his brother was coagulated.

Next he turned to the four chairs, beginning with the largest. When he skimmed his sensitive fingertips lightly over the upholstery, he quivered with excitement, for he knew at once that Frank had sat there recently. A small tear marred the vinyl on one arm, and when Candy put his thumb upon the rent, particularly vivid visions of Frank assaulted him.

Too many visions. He was rewarded with a whole series of place images, where Frank had traveled after rising from the chair: the High Sierras; the apartment in San Diego in which he had lived briefly four years ago; the rusted front gate of their mother's house on Pacific Hill Road; a graveyard; a book-lined study in which he'd stayed such a short time that Candy could get only the vaguest impression of it; Punaluu Beach, where Candy had nearly caught him. . . . There were so many images, from so many travels, layered one atop another, that he could not clearly see the later stops.

Disgusted, he pushed the chair out of his way and turned to the coffee table, where two more tumblers stood. Both contained melted ice and Scotch. He picked one up and had a vision of Julie Dakota.

♦   ♦   ♦

WHILE JULIE drove toward Santa Barbara as if they were competing in time trials for the Indianapolis 500, Bobby told her the shocking thing: that he was not, at heart, the laid-back guy he appeared to be on the surface; that during his hectic travels with Frank—especially during the moments when he had been reduced to a disembodied mind and a frantic whirl of disconnected atoms—he'd discovered within himself a rich vein of love for stability and order that ran deeper than he could ever have imagined, a motherlode of stick-in-the-mudness; that his delight in swing music arose more from an appreciation for the meticulosity of its structures than from the dizzying musical freedom embodied in jazz; that he was not half the free-spirited man he'd thought he was . . . and far more of a conservative embracer of tradition that he would have hoped.

"In short," he said, "all this time when you thought you were married to an easy-going young-James-Garner type, you've actually been wed to an any-age-Charles-Bronson type."

"I can live with you anyway, Charlie."

"This is serious. Sort of. I've tipped into my late thirties, I'm no child. I should've known this about myself a long time ago."

"You did."

"Huh?"

"You love order, reason, logic—that's why you got into a line of work where you could right wrongs, help the innocent, punish the bad. That's why you share The Dream with me—so we can get our little family in order, step out of the chaos of the world as it is these days and buy into some peace and quiet. That's why you won't let me have the Wurlitzer 950—those bubble tubes and leaping gazelles are just a little too chaotic for you."

He was silent a moment, surprised by her answer.

The lightless vastness of the sea lay to the west.

He said, "Maybe you're right. Maybe I've always known what I am, deep down. But then isn't it unnerving that I've fooled myself with my own act for so long?"

"You haven't. You're easy-going *and* a bit of Charles Bronson, which is a good thing. Otherwise we probably couldn't communicate at all, since I've got more Bronson in me than anyone but Bronson."

"God, that's true!" he said, and they both laughed.

The Toyota's speed had declined to under seventy. She put it up to eighty and said, "Bobby . . . what's really on your mind?"

"Thomas."

She glanced at him. "What about Thomas?"

"Since that wordburst, I can't shake the feeling he's in danger."

"What did that have to do with him?"

"I don't know. But I'd feel better if we could find a phone and put in a call to Cielo Vista. Just to be . . . sure."

She let their speed fall dramatically. Within three miles they exited the freeway and pulled into a service station. There was a full-service lane. While the attendant washed their windows, checked the oil, and filled the tank with premium unleaded, they went inside and used the pay phone.

It was a modern electronic version allowing everything from coin to credit calls, on the wall next to a rack of snack crackers, candy bars, and packages of beer nuts. A condom machine was there, too, right out in the open, thanks to the social chaos wrought by AIDS. Using their AT&T credit card, Bobby called Cielo Vista Care Home in Newport.

It didn't ring or give a busy signal. He heard an odd series of electronic sounds, then a recording informed him that the number he had dialed was temporarily out of service as a result of unspecified line problems. The droning voice suggested that he try later.

He dialed the operator, who tried the same number, with the same results. She said, "I'm sorry, sir. Please call your party later."

"What line problems could they be having?"

"I wouldn't know, sir, but I'm sure service'll be restored soon."

He had tilted the phone away from his ear, so Julie could lean in and hear both sides of the exchange. When he hung up, he looked at her. "Let's go back. I got this hunch Thomas needs us."

"Go back? We're little more than half an hour from Santa Barbara now. Much further to go home."

"He may need us. It's not a strong hunch, I admit, but it's persistent and . . . weird."

"If he needs help urgently," she said, "then we'd never get to him in time, anyway. And if it's not so urgent, it'll be okay if we go on to Santa Barbara, call again from the motel. If he's sick or been hurt or something, the extra driving from here to Santa Barbara and back will only add about an hour."

"Well . . ."

"He's my brother, Bobby. I care about him as much as you do, and I say it'll be all right. I love you, but you've never shown enough talent as a psychic to make me hysterical about this."

He nodded. "You're right. I'm just . . . jumpy. My nerves haven't settled down since all that traveling with Frank."

Back on the highway, a few thin tendrils of fog were creeping in from the sea. Sprinkles of rain fell again, then stopped after less than a minute. The heaviness of the air, and an indefinable but undeniable quality of oppressiveness in the utterly black night sky, portended a major storm.

When they had gone a couple of miles, Bobby said, "I should've called Hal at the office. While he's sitting around there waiting for Frank, he could use some of our contacts with the phone company, the cops, make sure everything's jake at Cielo Vista."

"If the lines are still out when you make the call from the motel," Julie said, "then you can bother Hal about it."

♦   ♦   ♦

FROM THE weak psychic residue on the drinking glass, Candy received an image of Julie Dakota that was recognizably the same face that had seeped from Thomas's mind earlier in the evening—except that it was not as idealized as it had been in Thomas's memory. With his sixth sense he saw that she had gone home from the office, to the address he had obtained earlier from the secretary's Rolodex. She had been there a short time, then had gone somewhere in a car with another person, most likely the man named Bobby. He could see no more, and he wished that the traces she left behind had been as strong as those of Jaxx.

He put down the tumbler and decided to go to her house. Though she and Bobby were not there now, he might be able to find an object that would, like the liquor glass, lead him another step or two along their trail. If he found nothing, he could return here and continue his search, assuming the police had not arrived in response to the discovery of the dead man outside.

♦   ♦   ♦

LEE SWITCHED off the computer, then cut off the CD player too—Huey Lewis and The News were in the middle of "Walking On a Thin Line"—and removed the earphones.

Happy after a long and productive session in the land of silicon and gallium arsenide, he stood, stretched, yawned, and

*331*

checked his watch. A little after nine. He'd been at work for twelve hours.

He should have wanted nothing more than to flop in bed and sleep half a day. But he figured he'd zip back to his condo, which was ten minutes from the office, freshen up, and catch some nightlife. Last week he'd found a new club, Nuclear Grin, where the music was loud and hard-edged, the drinks unwatered, the crowd's politics unconsciously libertarian, and the women hot. He wanted to dance a little, drink a little, and find someone who wanted to screw her brains out.

In this age of new diseases, sex was risky; it sometimes seemed that drinking from the same glass as someone else was suicidal. But after a day in the painstakingly logical microchip universe, you had to get a little wild, take some risks, dance on the edge of chaos, to get some balance in your life.

Then he remembered how Frank and Bobby had vanished in front of his eyes. He wondered if maybe he hadn't already had enough wildness for one day.

He picked up the latest printouts. It was more stuff that he had gleaned from police records, regarding the decidedly weird behavior of Mr. Blue, who would never need to get a little wild for balance, since he was *already* chaos walking around in shoes. Lee opened the door, switched off the lights, went down the hall and through another door into the lounge, intending to leave the printouts on Julie's desk and say goodnight to Hal before splitting.

When he walked into Bobby and Julie's office, it looked like the National Wrestling Federation had sanctioned a match there between tag teams of three-hundred-pound hulks. Furniture was overturned, and Scotch glasses, some of them broken, were scattered over the floor. Julie's desk was aslant and askew: tilting on one shattered leg; the top no longer was properly aligned with the base, as if someone had gone at it with prybars and hammers.

"Hal?"

No answer.

He gingerly pushed open the door to the adjoining bath.

"Hal?"

The bathroom was deserted.

He went to the broken window. A few small shards of glass still clung to the frame. Caught the light. Jagged.

With one hand against the wall, Lee Chen carefully leaned out. He looked down. In a much different tone of voice, he said, "Hal?"

◆　◆　◆

CANDY MATERIALIZED in the foyer of the Dakotas' house, which was dark and silent. He stood quietly for a moment, head cocked, until he was confident that he was alone.

His throat was healed. He was whole again, and excited by the prospects of the night.

He began the search from there, putting his hand on the doorknob in hope of finding some of the residue that, while lacking physical substance, nevertheless provided the nourishment for his visions. He felt nothing, no doubt partly because the Dakotas had touched it only briefly upon entering and departing the house.

Of course, a person could handle a hundred items, leaving psychic images of himself on only one of them, then touch the same hundred an hour later and contaminate every one with his aura. The reason for that was as mysterious, to Candy, as was so many people's interest in sex. He remained as grateful to his mother for this talent as he was for all the others, but tracking his prey with psychometry was not always an easy or infallible process.

The Dakotas' living room and dining room were unfurnished, which gave him little to work with, although for some reason the emptiness made him feel comfortable and at home. That response puzzled him. The rooms in his mother's house were all furnished—as much with mold and fungus and dust these days as with chairs, sofas, tables, and lamps; but he suddenly realized that, like the Dakotas, he lived in such a small percentage of the house that most of its chambers might as well have been bare, carpetless, and sealed off.

The Dakotas' kitchen and family room were furnished and obviously lived in. Though it was unlikely that they had used the family room during their brief stop between the office and wherever they had gone from here, he hoped they might have lingered in the kitchen for a bite of food or a drink. But the handles of the cabinets, microwave, oven, and refrigerator provided him with no images whatsoever.

*333*

On his way to the second floor, Candy climbed the steps slowly, letting his left hand slide searchingly along the oak balustrade. At several points along the way, he was rewarded by psychic images that, while brief and not clear, encouraged him, and led him to believe that he would find what he needed in their bedroom or bath.

# 54

INSTEAD OF immediately dialing 911 to report the murder of Hal Yamataka, Lee ran first to the reception desk and, as he had been trained, removed a small brown notebook from the back of the bottom drawer on the right side. For the benefit of employees, like Lee, who did not often get into the field and seldom interfaced directly with the county's many police agencies but might one day need to deal with them in an emergency, Bobby had composed a list of some of the officers, detectives, and administrators who were most professional, reasonable, and reliable in every major jurisdiction. The brown notebook contained a second list of cops to avoid: those who had an instinctive dislike for anyone in the private investigation and security business; those who were just pains in the ass in general; and those who were always on the lookout for a little green grease to lubricate the wheels of justice. It was a testament to the high quality of the county's law enforcement that the first list was much longer than the second.

According to Bobby and Julie, it was preferable to try to *manage* the introduction of the police into a situation that required them, even going so far as to try to select one of the detectives who would show up at the scene—if it was a scene that needed detectives. Relying on the luck of the draw or a dispatcher's whim was considered unwise.

Lee wondered if he should even call the cops. He had no doubt who had killed Hal. Mr. Blue. Candy. But also he knew that Bobby would not want to reveal more about Frank and the case than was truly necessary; the agency-client privilege was not as legally airtight as that of lawyer-client or doctor-patient, but it was important too. Since Julie and Bobby were on the road and temporarily unreachable, Lee could get no guidance on what and how much to say to the police.

But he couldn't let a dead body lie in front of the building, hoping nobody would notice! Especially not when the victim was a man he had known and liked.

Call the cops, then. But play dumb.

Consulting the notebook, Lee dialed the Newport Beach Police and asked for Detective Harry Ladsbroke, but Ladsbroke was off duty. So was Detective Janet Heisinger. Detective Kyle Ostov was available, however, and when he came on the line he sounded reassuringly big and competent; his voice was a mellow baritone, and he spoke crisply.

Lee identified himself, aware that his own voice was higher than usual, almost squeaky, and that he was speaking too fast. "There's been a . . . well, a murder."

Before Lee could go on, Ostov said, "Jesus, you mean Bobby and Julie know already? I just found out myself. It was pushed on to me to tell them, and I was just sitting here, trying to figure how best to break the news. I had my hand on the phone, going to call them, when you rang through. How're they taking it?"

Confused, Lee said, "I don't think they know. I mean, it must have happened just a few minutes ago."

"A little longer than that," Ostov said.

"When did you guys find out? I just looked, and there weren't any patrol cars, nothing." Finally the shakes hit him. "God, I was talking to him not that long ago, took him some pizza, and now he's splattered all over the concrete six floors down."

Ostov was silent. Then: "What murder you talking about, Lee?"

"Hal Yamataka. There must've been a fight here, and then—" He stopped, blinked, and said, "What murder are *you* talking about?"

"Thomas," Ostov said.

Lee felt sick. He had only met Thomas once, but he knew that Julie and Bobby were devoted to him.

Ostov said, "Thomas *and* his roommate. And maybe more in the fire if they didn't get them all out of the building in time."

The computer that Lee had been born with was not functioning as smoothly as the ones made by IBM in his office, and he needed a moment to grasp the implications of the information that he and Ostov had exchanged. "They've got to be connected, don't they?"

"I'd bet on it. You know of anybody who has a grudge against Julie and Bobby?"

Lee looked around the reception lounge, thought about the other deserted rooms at Dakota & Dakota, the lonely offices on the rest of the sixth floor, and the unpeopled levels below the sixth. He thought of Candy, too, all those people bitten and torn, the giant Bobby had seen on Punaluu Beach, the way the guy could zap himself from place to place. He began to feel very much alone. "Detective Ostov, could you get some people here really fast?"

"I've entered the call on the computer while I've been talking to you," Ostov said. "A couple of units are on the way now."

♦　♦　♦

WITH HIS fingertips, Candy traced lazy circles on the surface of the dresser, then explored the contours of each brass handle on the drawers. He touched the light switch on the wall and the switches on both bedside lamps. He let his hands glide over doorframes on the off-chance that one of his intended prey might have paused and leaned there while in conversation, examined the handles on the mirrored closet doors, and caressed each number and switchpad on the remote-control device for the TV, hoping that they had clicked on the set even during the short time they had been home.

Nothing.

Because he needed to be calm and methodical in his search if he were to succeed, Candy had to repress his rage and frustration. But his anger grew even as he struggled to contain it, and in him the thirst of anger was always a thirst for blood, that wine of vengeance. Only blood would slake his thirst, quench his fury, and allow him an interlude of relative peace.

By the time he moved from the Dakotas' bedroom into the adjoining bath, Candy was possessed of a *need* for blood almost as undeniable and critical as his need for air. Looking at the mirror, he did not see himself for a moment, as if he cast no reflection; he saw only red blood, as if the mirror were a porthole on one of the lower decks of a ship in Hell, on a cruise through a sea of gore. When that illusion faded and he saw his own face, he quickly looked away.

He clenched his jaws, struggled even harder to control himself, and touched the hot-water faucet, searching, seeking. . . .

♦　♦　♦

THE MOTEL ROOM in Santa Barbara was spacious, quiet, clean, and furnished without the jarring clash of colors and patterns that seemed de rigueur in most American motels—but it was not a place in which Julie would have chosen to receive the terrible news that came to her there. The blow seemed greater, the ache in the heart more piercing, for having to be borne in a strange and impersonal place.

She really had thought that Bobby was letting his imagination run away with him again, that Thomas was perfectly fine. Because the phone was on the nightstand, he sat on the edge of the bed to make the call, and Julie watched him and listened from a chair only a few feet away. When he got that recording again, explaining that the Cielo Vista number was temporarily out of service due to line problems, she was vaguely uneasy but still sure that all was well with her brother.

However, when he called the office in Newport to talk with Hal, got Lee Chen instead, and spent the first minute or so listening in shocked silence, responding with a cryptic word or two, she knew this was to be a night that cleaved her life, and that the years to come inevitably would be darker than the years she had lived on the other side of that cleft. As he began to ask questions of Lee, Bobby avoided looking at Julie, which confirmed her intuition and made her heart pound faster. When at last he glanced at her, she had to look away from the sadness in his eyes. His questions to Lee were clipped, and she couldn't ascertain much from them. Maybe she didn't want to.

Finally the call seemed to be drawing to an end. "No, you've done well, Lee. Keep handling it just the way you have been. What? Thank you, Lee. No, we'll be all right. We'll be okay, Lee. One way or another, we'll be okay."

When Bobby hung up, he sat for a moment, staring at his hands, which he clasped between his knees.

Julie did not ask him what had happened, as if what Lee had told him was not yet fact, as if her question was a dark magic and as if the unrevealed tragedy would not become real until she asked about it.

Bobby got off the bed and knelt on the floor in front of her chair. He took both of her hands in his and gently kissed them.

She knew then that the news was as bad as it could get.

Softly he said, "Thomas is dead."

She had steeled herself for that news, but the words cut deep.

"I'm sorry, Julie. God, I'm so sorry. And it doesn't end there." He told her about Hal. "And just a couple minutes before he talked to me, Lee received a call about Clint and Felina. Both dead."

The horror was too much to assimilate. Julie had liked and respected Hal, Clint, and Felina enormously, and her admiration for the deaf woman's courage and self-sufficiency was unbounded. It was unfair that she could not mourn each of them individually; they deserved that much. She also felt that she was somehow betraying them because her sorrow at their deaths was only a pale reflection of the grief she felt at the loss of Thomas, though that was, of course, the only way it could be.

Her breath caught in her throat, and when it flew free, it was not just an exhalation but a sob. That was no good. She could not allow herself to break down. At no point in her life had she needed to be as strong as she needed to be now; the murders committed in Orange County tonight were the first in a domino-fall of death that would take down her and Bobby, too, if misery dulled their edge.

While Bobby continued to kneel before her and reveal more details—Derek was dead, too, and perhaps others at Cielo Vista—she gripped his hands tightly, inexpressibly grateful to have him for an anchor in this turbulence. Her vision was blurry, but she held back the tears with a sheer effort of will—though she dared not make eye contact with Bobby just yet; that would be the end of her self-control.

When he finished, she said, "It was Frank's brother, of course," and was dismayed by the way her voice quavered.

"Almost certainly," Bobby said.

"But how did he find out Frank was our client?"

"I don't know. He saw me on the beach at Punaluu—"

"Yeah, but didn't follow you. He has no way of knowing who you were. And for God's sake, how did he find out about Thomas?"

"There's some crucial bit of information missing, so we can't understand the pattern."

"What's the bastard after?" she said. Now her voice was marked by nearly as much anger as grief, and that was good.

"He's hunting Frank," Bobby said. "For seven years Frank was a loner, and that made him harder to find. Now Frank has friends, and that gives Candy more ways to search for him."

"I as good as killed Thomas when I took the case," she said.

"You didn't want to take it. I had to talk you into it."

"I talked *you* into it, you wanted to back out."

"If there's guilt, we share it, but there isn't any. We took on a new client, that's all, and everything . . . just happened."

Julie nodded and finally met his eyes. Although his voice had remained steady, tears slid down his cheeks. Preoccupied with her own grief, she had forgotten that the friends lost were his as well as hers, and that he had come to love Thomas nearly as much as she did. She had to look away from him again.

"Are you okay?" he asked.

"For now, I have to be. Later, I want to talk about Thomas, how brave he was about being different, how he never complained, how sweet he was. I want to talk about all of it, you and me, and I don't want us to forget. Nobody's ever going to build a monument to Thomas, he wasn't famous, he was just a little guy who never did anything great except be the best person he knew how, and the only monument he's ever going to have is our memories. So we'll keep him alive, won't we?"

"Yes."

"We'll keep him alive . . . until we're gone. But that's for later, when there's time. Now we have to keep ourselves alive, because that son of a bitch will be coming for us, won't he?"

"I think he will," Bobby said.

He rose from his knees and pulled her up from the chair.

He was wearing his dark brown Ultraseude jacket with the shoulder holster under it. She'd taken off her corduroy blazer and her holster; she put both of them on again. The weight of the revolver, against her left side, felt good. She hoped she'd have a chance to use it.

Her vision had cleared; her eyes were dry. She said, "One thing for sure—no more dreams for me. What good is it, having dreams, when they never come true?"

"Sometimes they do."

"No. They never came true for my mom or dad. Never came true for Thomas, did they? Ask Clint and Felina if their dreams came true, see what they say. You ask George Farris's family if they think being slaughtered by a maniac was the fulfillment of their dreams."

"Ask the Phans," Bobby said quietly. "They were boat people on the South China Sea, with hardly any food and less money, and now they own dry-cleaning shops and remodel two-hundred-thousand-dollar houses for resale, and they have those terrific kids."

"Sooner or later, they'll get it in the neck too," she said, unsettled by the bitterness in her voice and the black despair that churned like a whirlpool within her, threatening to swallow her up. But she could not stop the churning. "Ask Park Hampstead, down there in El Toro, whether he and his wife were thrilled when she developed terminal cancer, and ask him how his dream about him and Maralee Roman worked after he finally got over the death of his wife. Nasty bugger named Candy got in the way of that one. Ask all the poor suckers lying in the hospital with cerebral hemorrhages, cancer. Ask those who get Alzheimer's in their fifties, just when their golden years are supposed to start. Ask the little kids in wheelchairs from muscular dystrophy, and ask all the parents of those other kids down there in Cielo Vista how Down's syndrome fits in with *their* dreams. Ask—"

She cut herself off. She was losing control, and she could not afford to do so tonight.

She said, "Come on, let's go."

"Where?"

"First, we find the house where that bitch raised him. Cruise by, get the lay of it. Maybe just seeing it will give us ideas."

"I've seen it."

"I haven't."

"All right." From a nightstand drawer he removed a telephone directory for Santa Barbara, Montecito, Goleta, Hope Ranch, El Encanto Heights, and other surrounding communities. He brought it with him to the door.

She said, "What do you want that for?"

"We'll need it later. I'll explain in the car."

Sprinkles of rain were falling again. The Toyota's engine was still so hot from the drive north that in spite of the cool night air, steam rose from its hood as the beads of rainwater evaporated. Far away a brief, low peal of thunder rolled across the sky. Thomas was dead.

♦　♦　♦

HE RECEIVED images as faint and distorted as reflections on the wind-rippled surface of a pond. They came repeatedly as he touched the faucets, the rim of the sink, the mirror, the medicine cabinet and its contents, the light switch, the controls for the shower. But none of his visions was detailed, and none provided a clue as to where the Dakotas had gone.

Twice he was jolted by vivid images, but they were related to disgusting sexual episodes between the Dakotas. A tube of vaginal lubricant and a box of Kleenex were contaminated with older psychic residue that had inexplicably lingered beyond its time, making him privy to sinful practices that he had no desire to witness. He quickly snatched his hands away from those surfaces and waited for his nausea to pass. He was incensed that the need to track Frank through these decadent people had forced him into a situation where his senses had been so brutally affronted.

Infuriated by his lack of success and by the unclean contact with images of their sin (which he seemed unable to expel from his mind), he decided that he must burn the evil out of this house in the name of God. Burn it out. Incinerate it. So that maybe his mind would be cleansed again as well.

He stepped out of the bathroom, raised his hands, and sent an immensely destructive wave of power across the bedroom. The wooden headboard of the big bed disintegrated, flames leaped from the quilted spread and blankets, the nightstands flew apart, and every drawer in the dresser shot out and dumped its contents on the floor, where they instantly caught fire. The drapes were consumed as if made from magicians' flashpaper, and the two windows in the far wall burst, letting in a draft that fanned the blaze.

Candy often wished the mysterious light that came from him could affect people and animals, rather than just inanimate things, plants, and a few insects. There were times when he would have gone into a city and melted the flesh from the bones of ten thousand sinners in a single night, a hundred thousand. It didn't matter which city, they were all festering sewers of iniquity, populated by depraved masses who worshiped evil and practiced every repulsive degeneracy. He had never seen anyone in any of them, not a single person, who seemed to him to live in God's grace. He would have made them run screaming in terror, would have tracked them down in their secret places, would have splintered their bones with his power, hammered their flesh to pulp, made their heads explode, and torn off the offensive sex things that preoccupied them. If he had been that gifted, he would not have shown them any of the mercy with which their Creator always treated them, so they would have realized, then, how grateful and obedient they should have been to their God, who always so patiently tolerated even their worst transgressions.

Only God and Candy's mother had such unlimited compassion. He did not share it.

The smoke alarm went off in the hall. He walked out there, pointed a finger at it, and blew it to bits.

This part of his gift seemed more powerful tonight than ever. He was a great engine of destruction.

The Lord must be rewarding his purity by increasing his power.

He thanked God that his own saintly mother had never descended into the pits of depravity in which so much of humanity swam. No man had ever touched her *that* way, so her children were born without the stain of original sin. He knew this to be true, for she had told him—and had shown him that it was.

He descended to the first floor and set the living-room carpet on fire with a bolt from his left hand.

Frank and the twins had never appreciated the immaculate aspect of their conceptions, and in fact had thrown away that incomparable state of grace to embrace sin and do the devil's work. Candy would never make that mistake.

Overhead he heard the roar of flames, the crash of a partition. In the morning, when the sun revealed a smoldering pile of blackened rubble, the remains of this nest of corruption would be a testament to the ultimate perdition of all sinners.

Candy felt cleansed. The psychic images of the Dakotas' fevered degeneracy had been expunged from his mind.

He returned to the offices of Dakota & Dakota to continue his search for them.

♦   ♦   ♦

BOBBY DROVE, for he didn't think Julie ought to be behind the wheel any more tonight. She had been awake for more than nineteen hours, not a marathon all-nighter yet, but she was exhausted; and her bottled-up grief over Thomas's death could not help but cloud her judgment and dull her reflexes. At least he had napped a couple of times since Hal's call from the hospital had awakened them last night.

He crossed most of Santa Barbara and entered Goleta before bothering to look for a service station where they could ask for directions to Pacific Hill Road.

At his request, Julie opened the telephone directory on her lap, and with the assistance of a small flashlight taken from the glove compartment, she looked under the Fs for Fogarty. He didn't know the first name, but he was only interested in a male Fogarty who carried the title of doctor.

"He might not live in this area," Bobby said, "but I have a hunch he does."

"Who is he?"

"When Frank and I were traveling, we stopped in this guy's study, twice." He told her about both brief visits.

"How come you didn't mention him before?"

"At the office, when I told you what happened to me, where Frank and I had gone, I had to condense some of it, and this Fogarty seemed comparatively uninteresting, so I left him out. But the longer I've had time to think about it, the more it seems to me that he might be a key player in this. See, Frank popped us out of there so fast because he seemed especially reluctant to endanger Fogarty by leading Candy to him. If Frank's especially concerned about the man, then we ought to have a talk with him."

She hunched over the directory, studying it closely. "Fogarty, James. Fogarty, Jennifer. Fogarty, Kevin. . . ."

"If he's not a medical doctor and doesn't use the title daily, or if 'Doc' is a nickname, we're in trouble. Even if he is a medical doctor, don't bother looking in the Yellow Pages under 'physicians,' because this guy is up in years, got to be retired."

"Here!" she said. "Fogarty, Dr. Lawrence J."

"There's an address?"

"Yes." She tore the page out of the book.

"Great. As soon as you've seen the infamous Pollard place, we'll pay Fogarty a visit."

Though Bobby had visited the house three times, he had traveled there with Frank, and he had not known the precise location of 1458 Pacific Hill Road any more than he had known exactly what flank of Mount Fuji that trail had ascended. They found it easily, however, by following the directions they received from a long-haired guy with a handlebar mustache at a Union 76 station.

Though the houses along Pacific Hill Road enjoyed an El Encanto Heights address, they were actually neither in that suburb nor in Goleta—which separated El Encanto from Santa Barbara—but in a narrow band of county land that lay between the two and that led east into a wilderness preserve of mesquite, chapparal, desert brush, and pockets of California live oaks and other hardy trees.

The Pollard house was near the end of Pacific Hill, on the edge of developed land, with few neighbors. Oriented west-southwest, it overlooked the charmed Pacific-facing communities so beautifully sited on the terraced hills below. At night the view was spectacular—a sea of lights leading to a real sea cloaked in darkness—and no doubt the immediate neighborhood remained rural and free of expensive new houses only because of development restrictions related to the proximity of the preserve.

Bobby recognized the Pollard place at once. The headlights revealed little more than the Eugenia hedge and the rusted iron gate between two tall stone pilasters. He slowed as they went by it. The ground floor was dark. In one upstairs room a light was on; a pale glow leaked around the edges of a drawn blind.

Leaning over to look past Bobby, Julie said, "Can't see much."

"There isn't much to see. It's a crumbling pile."

They drove over a quarter of a mile to the end of the road, turned, and went back. Coming downhill, the house was on Julie's side, and she insisted he slow to a crawl, to allow her more time to study it.

As they eased past the gate, Bobby saw a light on at the back of the house, too, on the first floor. He couldn't actually see a lighted window, just the glow that fell through it and painted a pale, frosty rectangle on the side yard.

"It's all hidden in shadows," Julie said at last, turning to look back at the property as it fell behind them. "But I can see enough to know that it's a bad place."

"Very," Bobby said.

♦   ♦   ♦

VIOLET LAY on her back on the bed in her dark room with her sister, warmed by the cats, which were draped over them and huddled around them. Verbina lay on her right side, cuddled against Violet, one hand on Violet's breasts, her lips against Violet's bare shoulder, her warm breath spilling across Violet's smooth skin.

They were not settling down to sleep. Neither of them cared to sleep at night, for that was the wild time, when a greater number and variety of nature's hunters were on the prowl and life was more exciting.

At that moment they were not merely in each other and in all of the cats that shared the bed with them, but in a hungry owl that soared the night, scanning the earth for mice that weren't wise enough to fear the gloom and remain in burrows. No creature had night vision as sharp as the owl, and its claws and beak were even sharper.

Violet shivered in anticipation of the moment when a mouse or other small creature would be seen below, slipping through tall grass that it believed offered concealment. From past experience she knew the terror and pain of the prey, the savage glee of the hunter, and she yearned now to experience both again, simultaneously.

At her side Verbina murmured dreamily.

Swooping high, gliding, spiraling down, swooping up again, the owl had not yet seen its dinner when the car came up the hill and slowed almost to a stop in front of the Pollard house. It drew Violet's attention, of course, and through her the attention of the owl, but she lost interest when the car speeded up again and drove on. Seconds later, however, her interest was renewed when it returned and coasted almost to a stop, once more, at the front gate.

She directed the owl to circle the vehicle at a height of about sixty feet. Then she sent it out ahead of the car and brought it even lower, to about twenty feet, before guiding it around again to approach the curious motorist head-on.

From an altitude of only twenty feet, the vision of the owl was more than acute enough to see the driver and the passenger in the front seat. There was a woman Violet had never seen before—but the driver was familiar. A moment later she realized that he was the man who had appeared with Frank in the backyard, at twilight that very same day!

Frank had killed their precious Samantha, for which Frank

---

must die, and now here was a man who knew Frank, who might lead them to Frank, and on the bed around Violet, the other cats stirred and made low growling sounds as her passion for vengeance was transmitted to them. A tailless Manx and a black mongrel leaped from the bed, raced through the open bedroom door, down the steps, into the kitchen, out the pet door, around the house, and into the street. The car was moving away, gaining speed, heading downhill, and Violet wanted to pursue it not only by air but on foot, to ensure that she would not lose track of it.

♦ ♦ ♦

CANDY ARRIVED in the reception lounge at Dakota & Dakota. Cool cross-drafts circulated from the broken window in the next room and two open doors in this one, setting up opposing currents. The faint sounds announcing his arrival had evidently been masked by the bursts of static and harsh voices coming from the portable police radios that the cops had clipped to their belts. One policeman stood in the entrance to Julie and Bobby's private office, and the other was at the open door to the sixth-floor corridor. Each of them was talking to someone out of sight, and both had their backs turned to Candy, which Candy knew was a sign that God was still looking out for him.

Though he was angered by this obstacle to his search for the Dakotas, he got out of there at once, materializing in his bedroom, nearly a hundred and fifty miles to the north. He needed time to think if there was some way that he could pick up their trail again, a place where they had been tonight—besides their office and their house—at which he could seek more visions of them.

♦ ♦ ♦

WHEN THEY backtracked to the Union 76 station, the long-haired, mustachioed man who had given them directions to Pacific Hill Road was able to tell them how to find the street on which Fogarty lived. He even knew the man. "Nice old guy. Stops by here for gas now and then."

"Is he a medical doctor?" Bobby asked.

"Used to be. Been retired quite a while."

Shortly after ten o'clock, Bobby parked at the curb in front of Lawrence Fogarty's house. It was a quaint Spanish two-story with the style of French windows that had been featured in the study to which Bobby and Frank had twice traveled, and lights were on throughout the first floor. The glass in the many panes was beveled, at least on the front of the house, and the lamplight inside was warmly refracted by those cut edges. When Bobby and Julie got out of the car, he smelled woodsmoke, and saw a homey white curl rising from a chimney into the still, cool, humid pre-storm air. In the odd and vaguely purple, crepuscular glow of a nearby streetlamp, a few pink flowers were visible on the azaleas, but the bushes were not as laden with early blooms as those farther south in Orange County. An ancient tree with a multiple trunk and enormous branches loomed over more than half the house, so it seemed like a wonderfully cozy and sheltered haven in some Spanish version of a Hobbity fantasy world.

As they followed the front walkway, something dashed between two low Malibu lights, crossed their path, and startled Julie. It stopped on the lawn after passing them, and studied them with radiant green eyes.

"Just a cat," Bobby said.

Usually he liked cats, but when he saw this one, he shivered.

It moved again, vanishing into shadows and shrubs at the side of the house.

What spooked him was not this particular creature, but the memory of the feline horde at the Pollard house, which had raced to attack him and Frank, in eerie silence initially but then with the shrill single-voiced squeal of a banshee regiment, and with a most uncatlike unanimity of purpose. On the prowl alone, swift and curious, this cat was quite ordinary, possessed only of the mystery and haughtiness common to every member of his species.

At the end of the walk, three front steps led up to an archway, through which they entered a small veranda.

Julie rang the bell, which was soft and musical, and when no one answered after half a minute, she rang it again.

As the second set of chimes faded, the stillness was disturbed by the rustle of feathered wings, as some night bird settled onto the veranda roof above them.

When Julie was about to reach for the bell push again, the porch light came on, and Bobby sensed they were being scrutinized through the security lens. After a moment the door opened, and Dr. Fogarty stood before them in an outfall of light from the hall behind him.

He looked the same as Bobby remembered him, and he recognized Bobby as well. "Come in," he said, stepping aside to admit them. "I half expected you. Come in—not that any of you is welcome."

# 55

"IN THE LIBRARY," Fogarty said, leading them back through the hall to a room on the left.

The library, where Frank had taken him during their travels, was the place Bobby had referred to as the study when he had described it to Julie. As the exterior of the house had a Hobbity-fantasy coziness in spite of its Spanish style, so this room seemed exactly the sort of place where one imagined that Tolkien, on many a long Oxford evening, had taken pen to paper to create the adventures of Frodo. That warm and welcoming space was gently illuminated by a brass floorlamp and a stained-glass table lamp that was either a genuine Tiffany or an excellent imitation. Books lined the walls under a deeply coffered ceiling, and a thick Chinese carpet—dark green and beige around the border, mostly pale green in the middle—graced a dark tongue-and-groove oak floor. The water-clear finish on the large mahogany desk had a deep luster; on the green felt blotter, the elements of a gold-plated, bone-handled desk set—including a letter opener, magnifying glass, and scissors—were lined up neatly behind a gold fountain pen in a square marble holder. The Queen Anne sofa was upholstered in a tapestry that perfectly complemented the carpet, and when Bobby turned to look at the wing-backed chair where he'd first seen Fogarty earlier in the day—he twitched with astonishment at the sight of Frank.

"Something's happened to him," Fogarty said, pointing to Frank. He was unaware of Bobby's and Julie's surprise, apparently operating under the assumption that they had come to his house specifically because they had known they would find Frank there.

Frank's physical appearance had deteriorated since Bobby had last seen him at 5:26 that afternoon, in the office in Newport Beach. If his eyes had been sunken then, they were as deep as pits now; the dark rings around them had widened, too, and some of the blackness seemed to have leeched out of those bruises to impart a deathly gray tint to the rest of his face. His previous pallor had looked healthy by comparison.

The worst thing about him, however, was the blank expression with which he regarded them. No recognition lit his eyes; he seemed to be staring through them. His facial muscles were slack. His mouth hung open about an inch, as if he had started to speak a long time ago but had not yet managed to remember the first word of what he had wanted to say. At Cielo Vista Care Home, Bobby had seen only a few patients with faces as empty as this, but they had been among the most severely retarded, several steps down the ladder from Thomas.

"How long has he been here?" Bobby asked, moving toward Frank.

Julie seized his arm and held him back. "Don't!"

"He arrived shortly before seven o'clock," Fogarty said.

So Frank had traveled for nearly another hour and a half after he had returned Bobby to the office.

Fogarty said, "He's been here over three hours, and I don't know what the blazing hell I'm supposed to do with him. Now and then he comes around a little bit, looks at you when you talk to him, even responds more or less to what you say. Then sometimes he's positively garrulous, runs on and on, won't answer your questions but sure wants to talk *at* a person, you couldn't shut him up with a two-by-four. He's told me a lot about you, for instance, more than I care to know." He frowned and shook his head. "You two may be crazy enough to get involved in this nightmare, but I'm not, and I resent being *dragged* into it."

At first glance, the impression that Dr. Lawrence Fogarty made was that of a kindly grandfather who, in his day, had been the type of devoted and selfless physician who became revered by his community, known and beloved by one and all. He was still wearing the slippers, gray slacks, white shirt, and blue cardigan in which Bobby had first seen him earlier, and the image was completed by a pair of half-lens reading glasses, over which he regarded them. With his thick white hair, blue eyes, and gentle rounded features, he would have made a perfect Santa Claus if he had been fifty or sixty pounds heavier.

But on a second and closer look, his blue eyes were steely, not warm. His rounded features were *too* soft, and revealed not gentility so much as lack of character, as though they had been acquired through a lifetime of self-indulgence. His wide mouth would have given kindly old Doc Fogarty a winning smile, but its generous dimension served equally well to lend the look of a predator to the real Doc Fogarty.

"So Frank's told you about us," Bobby said. "But we don't know anything about you, and I think we need to."

Fogarty scowled. "Better that you don't know about me. Better by far for *me*. Just get him out of here, take him away."

"You want us to take Frank off your hands," Julie said coldly, "then you've got to tell us who you are, how you fit into this, what you know about it."

Meeting Julie's gaze, then Bobby's, the old man said, "He's not been here in five years. Today, when he came with you, Dakota, I was shocked, I'd thought I was finished with him forever. And when he came back tonight . . ."

Frank's eyes had not focused, but he had cocked his head to one side. His mouth was still ajar like the door to a room from which the resident had fled in haste.

Regarding Frank sourly, Fogarty said, "I've never seen him like this, either. I wouldn't want him on my hands if he was his old self, let alone when he's half a vegetable. All right, all right, we'll talk. But once we've talked, he's *your* responsibility."

Fogarty went behind the mahogany desk and sat in a chair that was upholstered in the same dark maroon leather as was the wingback in which Frank slumped.

Although their host had not offered them a seat, Bobby went to the sofa. Julie followed and slipped past him at the last moment, sitting on the end of the sofa closest to Frank. She favored Bobby with a look that essentially said, *You're too impulsive, if he groans or sighs or blows a spit bubble, you'll put a hand on him to comfort him, and then you'll be gone in a wink to Hoboken or Hell, so keep your distance.*

Removing his tortoiseshell reading glasses and putting them on the blotter, Fogarty squeezed his eyes shut and pinched the bridge of his nose between thumb and forefinger, as if to banish a headache with an effort of will or collect his thoughts or both. Then he opened his eyes, blinked at them across the desk, and said, "I'm the doctor who delivered Roselle Pollard when she was born forty-six years ago, February of 1946. I'm also the doctor who delivered each of her kids—Frank, the twins, and James . . . or Candy as he now prefers. Over the years I treated Frank for the usual childhood-adolescent illnesses, and I guess that's why he thinks he can come to me now, when he's in trouble. Well, he's wrong. I'm no goddamned TV doctor who wants to be everybody's confidant and Dutch uncle. I treated them, they paid me, and that should be the end of it. Fact is . . . I only ever really treated Frank and his mother, because the girls and James never got sick, unless we're talking mental illness, in which case they were sick at birth and never got well."

Because Frank's head was tilted, a thin, silver stream of drool slipped out of the right corner of his mouth and along his chin.

Julie said, "You evidently know about the powers her children have—"

"I didn't know, really, until seven years ago, the day that Frank killed her. I was retired by then, but he came to me, told me more than I ever wanted to know, dragged me into this nightmare, wanted me to help. How could I help? How can anyone help? It's none of my business anyway."

"But why do they have these powers?" Julie said. "Do you have any clue, any theories?"

Fogarty laughed. It was a hard, sour laugh that would have dispelled any illusions Bobby had about him if those illusions had not already been dispelled two minutes after he'd met the man. "Oh, yes, I have theories, lots of information to support the theories too, some of it stuff you'll wish you never heard. I'm not going to get myself involved in the mess, not me, but I can't help now and then thinking about it. Who could? It's a sick and twisted and *fascinating* mess. My theory is that it starts with Roselle's father. Supposedly her father was some itinerant who knocked up her mother, but I always knew that was a lie. Her father was Yarnell Pollard, her mother's brother. Roselle was a child of rape and incest."

A look of distress must have crossed Bobby's face or Julie's, for Fogarty let out another bark of cold laughter, clearly amused by their sympathetic response.

The old physician said, "Oh, that's nothing. That's the least of it."

♦ ♦ ♦

THE TAILLESS MANX— Zitha by name—took up sentry duty in the concealment of an azalea shrub near the front door.

The old Spanish house had exterior window ledges, and the second cat—as black as midnight, and named Darkle—sprang to another one in search of the room to which the old man had taken the younger man and woman. Darkle put his nose to the glass. A set of interior shutters inhibited snooping, but the wide louvres were only half closed, and Darkle was able to see several cross-sections of the room by raising or lowering his head.

Hearing Frank's name spoken, the cat stiffened, because Violet had stiffened in her bed high on Pacific Hill.

The old man was there, among the books, and the couple as well. When everyone sat down, Darkle had to lower his head to peer between another pair of tilted louvres. Then he saw that Frank was not only one of the subjects of their conversation but actually present in a high-backed chair that stood at just enough of an angle to the window to reveal part of his face, and one hand lying limply on the wide, maroon-leather arm.

♦ ♦ ♦

LEANING OVER his desk and smiling humorlessly as he talked, Doc Fogarty resembled a troll that had crawled out from its lair beneath a bridge, not content to wait for unsuspecting children to pass by, prepared to forage for his grisly dinner.

Bobby reminded himself not to let his imagination run away with him. He needed to keep an unbiased perspective on Fogarty, in order to determine the truthfulness and value of what the old man had to tell them. Their lives might depend on it.

"The house was built in the thirties by Deeter and Elizabeth Pollard. He'd made some money in Hollywood, producing a bunch of cheap Westerns, other junk. Not a fortune, but enough that he was fairly sure he could give up films and Los Angeles, which he hated, move up here, get into some small businesses, and do all right for the rest of his life. They had two children. Yarnell was fifteen when they came here in 1938, and Cynthia was only six years old. In forty-five, when Deeter and Elizabeth were killed in a car crash—hit head-on by a drunk driving a truck full of cabbages down from the Santa Ynez valley, if you can believe it—Yarnell became the man of the house at the age of twenty-two, and the legal guardian of his thirteen-year-old sister."

Julie said, "And . . . forced himself on her, you said?"

Fogarty nodded. "I'm sure of it. Because over the next year, Cynthia became withdrawn, weepy. People attributed it to the death of her folks, but it was Yarnell using her, I think. Not just because he wanted the sex—though she was a pretty little thing, and you could hardly fault his taste—but because being man of the house appealed to him, he liked authority. And he was the type who wasn't happy until his authority was absolute, his dominance complete."

Bobby was horrified by the words "you could hardly fault his taste" and what they implied about the depth of the moral abyss in which Fogarty lived.

Oblivious of the disgust with which his visitors were regarding him, Fogarty continued: "Yarnell was strong-willed, reckless, caused his folks a lot of heartache before they died, all kinds of heartache but mostly related to drugs. He was an acidhead before they had a name for it, before they even had LSD. Peyote, mescaline . . . all of the natural hallucinogens you can distill from certain cactuses, mushrooms and other fungi. Wasn't the drug culture back then that we have now, but crap was around. He got into hallucinogens through a relationship he had with a character actor who appeared in a lot of his father's movies, got started when he was fifteen, and I tell you all this because my theory is it's the key to everything you want to know."

"The fact that Yarnell was an acidhead," Julie said. "That's the key?"

"That and the fact he impregnated his own sister. The chemicals probably did genetic damage, and a lot of it, by the time he was twenty-two. They usually do. In his case some very *strange* genetic damage. Then, when you add in the fact that the gene pool was very limited, being as Cynthia was his sister, you might expect there's a high chance the offspring will be a freak of some kind."

Frank made a low sound, then sighed.

They all looked at him, but he was still detached. Though his eyes blinked rapidly for a moment, they did not come back into focus. Saliva still drooled from the right corner of his mouth; a string of it hung from his chin.

Though Bobby felt that he should get some Kleenex and blot Frank's face, he restrained himself, largely because he was afraid of Julie's reaction.

"So about a year after their parents died, Yarnell and Cynthia came to me, and she was pregnant," Fogarty said. "They had this story about some itinerant farmworker raping her, but it didn't ring true, and I pretty much figured out the real story just watching how they were with each other. She'd tried to conceal the pregnancy by wearing loose clothes and by staying in the house entirely during her last few months, and I never could understand that behavior; it was as if they thought the problem would just go away one day. By the time they came to me, abortion was out of the question. Hell, she was in the early stages of labor."

The longer he listened to Fogarty, the more it seemed to Bobby that the air in the library was foul and growing fouler, thick with a humidity as sour as sweat.

"Claiming that he wanted to protect Cynthia as much as possible from public scorn, Yarnell offered me a pretty fat fee if I'd keep her out of the hospital and deliver the baby right in my office, which was a little risky, in case there were complications. But I needed the money, and if anything went really wrong, there were ways to cover it. I had this nurse at the time who could assist me—Norma, she was pretty flexible about things."

Just great, Bobby thought. The sociopathic physician had found himself a sociopathic nurse, a couple who would be right in the social swim of things among the medical staff at Dachau or Auschwitz.

Julie put a hand on Bobby's knee and squeezed, as if the contact reassured her that she was not listening to a mad doctor in a dream.

"You should have seen what came out of that girl's oven," Fogarty said. "A freak it was, just as you'd expect."

"Wait a minute," Julie said. "I thought you said the baby was Roselle. Frank's mother."

"It was," Fogarty said. "And she was such a spectacular little freak that she'd have been worth a fortune to any carnival sideshow willing to risk the anger of the law to exhibit her." He paused, enjoying their anticipation. "She was an hermaphro-dite."

For a moment the word meant nothing to Bobby, and then he said, "You don't mean—she had both sexes, male and fe-male?"

"Oh, but that's exactly what I mean." Fogarty bounced up from his chair and began to pace, suddenly energized by the conversation. "Hermaphroditism is an extremely rare birth de-fect in humans, it's an amazing thing to have the opportunity to deliver one. You have *traverse* hermaphroditism, where you have the external organs of one sex and the internal of the other, lateral hermaphroditism . . . several other types. But the thing is . . . Roselle was the rarest of all, she possessed the complete internal and external organs of both sexes." He plucked a thick medical reference book from one of the shelves and handed it to Julie. "Check page one forty-six for photos of the kind of thing I'm talking about."

Julie handed the volume to Bobby so fast it seemed as if she thought it was a snake.

Bobby, in turn, put it beside himself on the sofa, unopened. The last thing he needed, with his imagination, was the assis-tance of clinical photographs.

His hands and feet had gone cold, as though the blood had rushed from his extremities to his head, to nourish his brain, which was spinning furiously. He wished that he could *stop* thinking about what Fogarty was telling them. It was gross. But the worst thing about it was, judging by the physician's strange smile, Bobby sensed that what they had heard thus far was all just the bread on this horror sandwich; the meat was yet to come.

Pacing again, Fogarty said, "Her vagina was about where you'd expect, the male equipment somewhat displaced. Urina-tion was through the male part, but the female appeared repro-ductively complete."

"I think we get the picture," Julie said. "We don't need all the technical details."

Fogarty came to them, stood looking down at them, and his eyes were as bright and lively as if he were recounting a charm-ing medical anecdote that had bewitched legions of delighted companions at dinner parties over the years. "No, no, you must understand what she was, if you're going to understand all that happened next."

◆  ◆  ◆

THOUGH HER OWN mind was split into many parts—
sharing the bodies of Verbina, all the cats, and the owl on Fogarty's porch roof—Violet was most acutely aware of what she
was receiving through the senses of Darkle, as he perched upon
the windowsill outside the study. With the cat's sharp hearing,
Violet missed not a word of the conversation, in spite of the
intervening pane of glass. She was enthralled.

She seldom paused to think about her mother, although Roselle was still in this old house in so many ways. She seldom
thought about *any* human being, for that matter, except herself
and her twin sister—less often Candy and Frank—because she
had so little in common with other people. Her life was with the
wild things. In them emotions were so much more primitive
and intense, pleasure so much more easily found and enjoyed
without guilt. She hadn't really known her mother or been close
to her; and Violet would not have been close, even if her mother
had been willing to share affection with anyone but Candy.

But now Violet was riveted by what Fogarty was telling them,
not because it was news to her (which it was), but because
anything that had affected Roselle's life this completely also had
profound effects on Violet's life. And of the countless attitudes
and perceptions that Violet had absorbed from the myriad wild
creatures whose minds and bodies she shared, a fascination with
self was perhaps paramount. She had an animal's narcissistic
preoccupation with grooming, with her own wants and needs.
From her point of view, nothing in the world was of interest
unless it served her, satisfied her, or affected the possibility of
her future happiness.

Dimly she realized that she should find her brother and tell
him that Frank was less than two miles away from them. Not
long ago she had heard the wind-music of Candy's return.

◆  ◆  ◆

FOGARTY TURNED away from Bobby and Julie and circled behind his desk again, where he walked along the bookshelves, snapping his finger against the spines of the volumes to
punctuate his story.

As the physician spoke of this family that had seemingly

*sought* genetic catastrophe, Julie could not help but think of how Thomas's affliction had been visited upon him even though his parents had lived healthy and normal lives. Fate played as cruelly with the innocent as with the guilty.

"When he saw the baby's abnormality, I think Yarnell would have killed it and thrown it out with the garbage—or at least put it in the hands of an institution. But Cynthia wouldn't part with it, she said it was her child, deformed or not, and she named it Roselle, after her dead grandmother. I suspect she wanted to keep it largely because she saw how it repulsed him, and she wanted to have Roselle around as a permanent reminder to him of the consequences of what he had forced her to do."

"Couldn't surgery have been used to make her one sex or another?" Bobby asked.

"Easier today. Iffier then."

Fogarty had stopped at the desk, where he had removed a bottle of Wild Turkey and a glass from one of the side drawers. He poured a few ounces of bourbon for himself and recapped the bottle without offering them a drink. That was fine with Julie. Though Fogarty's house was spotless, she wouldn't have felt clean after drinking or eating anything in it.

After taking a swallow of the warm bourbon, neat, Fogarty said, "Besides, wouldn't want to remove one set of organs only to discover that, as the child grew older, it proved to look and act more like the sex you denied it than like the one it was permitted. Secondary sex characteristics are visible in infants, of course, but not as easily read—certainly not in 1946. Anyway, Cynthia wouldn't have authorized surgery. Remember what I said—she probably welcomed the child's deformity as a weapon against her brother."

"You could have stepped between them and the baby," Bobby said. "You could've brought the child's plight to the attention of public health authorities."

"Why on earth would I want to do that? For the psychological well-being of the child, you mean? Don't be naive." He drank some more bourbon. "I was paid well to make the delivery and keep my mouth shut about it, and that was fine by me. They took her home, stuck to their story about the itinerant rapist."

Julie said, "The baby . . . Roselle . . . she had no serious medical problems?"

"None," Fogarty said. "Other than this abnormality, she was

as healthy as a horse. Her mental skills and her body developed right on schedule, like any child, and before long it became obvious that, to all outward appearances, she was going to look like a woman. As she grew even older, you could see she'd never be an attractive filly, mind you, more on the sturdy side than a fashion model, thick legs and all that, but quite feminine enough."

Frank remained vacant-eyed and detached, but a muscle in his left cheek twitched twice.

The bourbon apparently relaxed the physician, for he sat behind his desk again, leaned forward, and clasped his hands around the glass. "In 1959, when Roselle was thirteen, Cynthia died. Killed herself, actually. Blew her brains out. The following year, about seven months after his sister's suicide, Yarnell came to the office with his daughter—that is, with Roselle. He never called her his daughter, maintaining the fiction that she was only his bastard niece. Anyway, Roselle was pregnant at fourteen, same age at which Cynthia had given birth to her."

"Good God!" Bobby said.

The shocks kept piling one atop another with such speed that Julie was almost ready to grab the whiskey bottle off the desk, drink straight from it, and never mind that it was Fogarty's booze.

Enjoying their reactions, Fogarty sipped the bourbon and gave them time to absorb the shock.

Julie said, "Yarnell raped the daughter he had fathered by his own sister?"

Fogarty waited a little longer, savoring the moment. Then: "No, no. He found the girl repellent, and I'm confident he wouldn't have touched her. I'm sure what Roselle told me was the truth." He sipped more bourbon. "Cynthia had developed quite a religious streak between the time she gave birth to Roselle and the day she killed herself, and she had passed on that passion for God to Roselle. The girl knew the Bible backward and forward. So Roselle came in here, pregnant. Said she'd decided she should have a child. Said God had made her special—that's what she called hermaphroditism, *special!*—because she was to be a pure vessel by which blessed children could be brought into the world. Therefore she had collected the semen from her male half and mechanically inserted it into her female half."

Bobby shot up from the sofa as if one of its springs had broken under him, and he grabbed the bottle of Wild Turkey from the desk. "You have another glass?"

Fogarty pointed to a bar cabinet in the corner, which Julie had not noticed before. Bobby opened the double doors, revealing not only more glasses but additional fifths of Wild Turkey. Evidently the physician kept a bottle in his desk drawer only so he would not have to walk across the room for it. Bobby poured two glasses full, with no ice, and brought one back to Julie.

To Fogarty, she said, "Of course, I never thought Roselle was barren. She did bear children, we know that. But I assumed you meant the male part of her was sterile."

"Fertile as a male *and* as a female. She couldn't actually join herself to herself, so to speak. So she resorted to artificial insemination, as I said."

Late that afternoon, in the office in Newport, when Bobby had tried to explain how traveling with Frank was like a bobsled ride off the edge of the world, Julie had not really understood why he was so unnerved by the experience. Now she thought she had an inkling of what he had meant, for the chaos of the Pollard family's relationships and sexual identities made her skin crawl and filled her with a dark suspicion that nature was even stranger and more hospitable to anarchy than she had feared.

"Yarnell wanted me to abort the fetus, and abortion was a fairly lucrative sideline in those days, though illegal and hush-hush. But the girl had hidden her pregnancy from him for seven months, as he and Cynthia had tried to hide a pregnancy fourteen years earlier. It was much too late for an abortion then. The girl would've died, hemorrhaging. Besides, I would no more have aborted that fetus than I'd have shot myself in the foot. Imagine the degree of inbreeding involved here: the hermaphroditic child of brother-sister incest impregnates herself! Her child's mother is also its father. Its grandmother is also its great-aunt, and its grandfather is its great-uncle! One tight genetic line—and genes damaged by Yarnell's use of hallucinogenics, remember. Virtually a guarantee of a freak of one kind or another, and I wouldn't have missed it for the world."

Julie took a long swallow of the bourbon. It tasted sour and stung her throat. She didn't care. She needed it.

"I'd become a doctor because the pay was good," Fogarty

said. "Later, when I gravitated toward illegal abortions, the pay was better, and it became my main business. Not much danger, either, because I knew what I was doing, and I could buy off an authority now and then if I had to. When you're getting those fat fees, you don't have to schedule many office visits, you can have a lot of free time, money and leisure, the best of both worlds. But having settled for a career like that, what I *never* figured was that I'd encounter anything as medically interesting, as fascinating, as *entertaining* as this Pollard mess."

The only consideration that caused Julie to refrain from going across the room and kicking the crap out of the old man was not his age but the fact that he would leave the story unfinished and some vital piece of information unrevealed.

"But the birth of Roselle's first child wasn't the event I'd thought it would be," Fogarty said. "In spite of the odds, the baby she produced was healthy and, from all indications, perfectly normal. That was 1960, and the baby was Frank."

In the wingback chair, Frank whimpered softly but remained in his semicomatose condition.

◆　◆　◆

STILL LISTENING to Doc Fogarty through Darkle, Violet sat up and swung her bare legs over the edge of the bed, dispossessing some of the cats from their resting places, and eliciting a murmur of protest from Verbina, who was seldom content to share just a mental link with her sister and needed the reassurance of physical contact. With cats swarming at her feet, seeing through their eyes as well as her own and therefore not blinded by the darkness, Violet started toward the open door to the lightless upstairs hall.

Then she remembered that she was nude, and she turned back for panties and T-shirt.

She wasn't afraid of Candy's disapproval—or of Candy himself. In fact, she would welcome his violent attentions, for that would be the ultimate game of hunter and prey, hawk and mouse, brother and sister. Candy was the only wild creature into whose mind she couldn't intrude; though wild, he was also human and beyond the reach of her powers. If he tore out her throat, however, then her blood would get into him, and she would become a part of him in the only manner she ever could.

Likewise, that was the only way he could get into her: by biting his way in, by chewing into her, the only way.

On any other night, she would have called to him and let him see her nude, with the hope that her shamelessness would at last provoke him to violence. But she could not pursue her fondest desire right now, not when Frank was nearby and still unpunished for what he had done to their poor puss, Samantha.

When she had dressed, she returned to the hall, moved along it in the gloom—still in complete touch with Darkle and Zitha and the wild world—and stopped before the door to their mother's room, into which Candy had moved upon her death. A thin line of light showed along the sill.

"Candy," she said. "Candy, are you there?"

♦   ♦   ♦

LIKE A MEMORY from wars past or a presentiment of an ultimate war to come, a searing flash of lightning and a sky-shattering crash of thunder shook the night. The windows of the study vibrated. It was the first thunder Bobby had heard since the faint and distant peal when they had come out of the motel, nearly an hour and a half ago. In spite of the fireworks in the sky, rain was not yet falling. But though the tempest was slow-moving, it was almost upon them. The pyrotechnics of a storm was an ideal backdrop to Fogarty's tale.

"I was disappointed in Frank," Fogarty said, taking a second bottle of bourbon from his capacious desk drawer and refilling his glass. "No fun at all. So normal. But two years later, she was pregnant again! This time the delivery was every bit as entertaining as I'd expected Frank's to be. A baby boy again, and she called him James. Her second virgin birth, she said, and she didn't mind at all that he was as much of a mess as she was. She said that was just proof that he, too, was favored by God and brought into the world without a need to wallow in the depravity of sex. I knew then that she was as mad as a hatter."

Bobby knew he had to remain sober, and he was aware of the danger of too much bourbon after a night of too little sleep. But he had a hunch that he was burning it off as fast as he drank it, at least for now. He took another sip before he said, "You're not telling us that beefy hulk is hermaphroditic too?"

"Oh, no," Fogarty said. "Worse than that."

♦  ♦  ♦

CANDY OPENED the door. "What do you want?"
"He's here, in town, right now," she said.
His eyes widened. "You mean Frank?"
"Yes."

♦  ♦  ♦

"WORSE," Bobby said numbly.

He got up from the sofa long enough to put his glass on the desk. It was still three-quarters full, but he suddenly decided that even bourbon would not be an effective tranquilizer in this case.

Julie seemed to reach the same conclusion, and put her glass aside too.

"James—or Candy, if you wish—was born with four testes instead of two, but with no male organ. Now, at birth, male infants all carry their testes safely in their abdominal cavity, and the testes descend later, during infant maturation. But Candy's never descended and never could, because there was no scrotum for them to descend into. And for another thing, there's a strange excrescence of bone that would prevent their descent. So they've remained within his abdominal cavity. But I would guess they've functioned well, busily producing quite large amounts of testosterone, which is related to development of musculature and partly explains his formidable size."

"So he's incapable of having sex," Bobby said.

"With his testicles undescended and no organ for copulation, I'd say he's got a shot at being the most chaste man who ever lived."

Bobby had come to loathe the old man's laugh. "But with four gonads, he's producing a flood of testosterone, and that does more than help build muscles—doesn't it?"

Fogarty nodded. "To put it in the language of a medical journal: excess testosterone, over an extended period of time, alters normal brain function, sometimes radically, and is a causative factor of socially unacceptable levels of aggression. To put it in layman's language: this guy is seriously stoked with sexual tension he can't possibly release, he's rechanneled that energy into other outlets, mainly acts of incredible violence, and he's

362

as dangerous as any monster any moviemaker ever dreamed up."

♦  ♦  ♦

ALTHOUGH SHE HAD released the owl as the storm drew near, Violet still inhabited Darkle and Zitha, taking their fear away from them when the lightning flared and the thunder boomed. Even as she stood before Candy, at the door to his room, she was listening to Fogarty tell the Dakotas about her brother's deformity. She knew about it already, of course, for within the family their mother had referred to it as God's sign that Candy was the most special of all of them. Likewise, and in some way Violet had been aware that this deformity was related to the great wildness in Candy, the thing that made him so powerfully attractive.

Now she stood before him, wanting to touch his huge arms, feel the sculpted muscles, but she restrained herself. "He's at Fogarty's house."

That surprised him. "Mother said Fogarty was an instrument of God. He brought us into the world, four virgin births. Why would he harbor Frank? Frank's on the dark side now."

"That's where he is," Violet said. "And a couple. His name's Bobby. Hers is Julie."

"Dakota," he whispered.

"At Fogarty's. Make him pay for Samantha, Candy. Bring him back here after you've killed him, and let us feed him to the cats. He hated the cats, and he'll hate being part of them forever."

♦  ♦  ♦

JULIE'S TEMPER, not always easily controlled, was dangerously near the flashpoint. As lightning shocked the night outside and thunder again protested, she counseled herself about the necessity for diplomacy.

Nevertheless, she said, "You've known all these years that Candy is a vicious killer, and you've done nothing to alert anyone to the danger?"

"Why should I?" Fogarty asked.

"Haven't you ever heard of social responsibility?"

"It's a nice phrase, but meaningless."

"People have been brutally murdered because you let that man—"

"People will always and forever be brutally murdered. History is full of brutal murder. Hitler murdered millions. Stalin, many millions more. Mao Tse-tung, more millions than anyone. They're all considered monsters now, but they had their admirers in their time, didn't they? And there're people even now who'll tell you Hitler and Stalin only did what they had to do, that Mao was just keeping the public order, disposing of ruffians. So many people *admire* those murderers who are bold about it and who cloak their bloodlust in noble causes like brotherhood and political reform and justice—and social responsibility. We're all meat, just meat, and in our hearts we know it, so we secretly applaud the men bold enough to treat us as what we are. Meat."

By now she knew that he was a sociopath, with no conscience, no capacity for love, and no ability to empathize with other people. Not all of them were street hoodlums—or even high-class, high-tech thieves like Tom Rasmussen, who had tried to kill Bobby last week. Some got to be doctors—or lawyers, TV ministers, politicians. None of them could be reasoned with, for they had no normal human feelings.

He said, "Why should I tell anyone about Candy Pollard? I'm safe from him because his mother always called me God's instrument, told her wretched spawn I was to be respected. It's none of my business. He's covered his mother's murder to avoid having the police tramping through the house, told people she moved to a nice oceanside condo near San Diego. I don't think anybody believes that crazy bitch would suddenly lighten up and become a beach bunny, but nobody questions it because nobody wants to get involved. Everybody feels it's *none of their business.* Same with me. Whatever outrages Candy adds to the world's pain are negligible. At least, given his peculiar psychology and physiology, his outrages will be more imaginative than most.

"Besides, when Candy was about eight, Roselle came to thank me for bringing her four into the world, and for keeping my own counsel, so that Satan was unaware of their blessed presence on earth. That's exactly how she put it! And as a token of her appreciation, she gave me a suitcase full of money, enough to make early retirement possible. I couldn't figure where she'd gotten it. The money that Deeter and Elizabeth piled up in the thirties had long ago dwindled away. So she told me a little bit about Candy's ability, not much, but enough to explain that she'd never want for cash. That was the first time I realized there was a genetic boon tied to the genetic disaster."

Fogarty raised his glass of bourbon in a toast that they did not return. "To God's mysterious ways."

◆  ◆  ◆

LIKE THE ARCHANGEL come to declare the end of the world in the Book of the Apocalypse, Candy arrived just as the heavens sundered and the rain began to fall in earnest, although this was not black rain as would be the deluge of Armageddon, nor was it a storm of fire. Not yet. Not yet.

He materialized in the darkness between two widely spaced streetlamps, almost a block from the doctor's house, to be sure that the soft trumpets that unfailingly announced his arrival would not be audible to anyone in Fogarty's library. As he walked toward the house through the hammering rain, he believed that his power, provided by God, had now grown so enormous that nothing could prevent him from taking or achieving anything he desired.

◆  ◆  ◆

"IN SIXTY-SIX, the twins were born, and physically they were as normal as Frank," Fogarty said as rain suddenly splattered noisily against the window. "No fun in that. I couldn't believe it, really. Three out of four of the kids, perfectly healthy. I'd been expecting all sorts of cute twists—harelips at the very least, misshapen skulls, cleft faces, withered limbs, or extra heads!"

Bobby took Julie's hand. He needed the contact.

He wanted to get out of there. He felt burnt out. Hadn't they heard enough?

But that was the problem: he didn't know what was left to hear, or how much of it might be crucial to finding a way of dealing with the Pollards.

"Of course, when Roselle brought me that suitcase full of money, I began to learn that the children *were* all freaks, men-

365

tally if not physically. And seven years ago, when Frank killed her, he came to me, as if I owed him something—understanding, shelter. He told me more about them than I wanted to know, too much. For the next two years, he'd periodically return here, just appear like a ghost that wanted to haunt *me* instead of a place. But he finally understood there was nothing for him here, and for five years he stayed out of my life. Until today, tonight."

In his wingback chair, Frank moved. He shifted his body and tipped his head from the right to the left. Otherwise, he was no more alert than he had been since they had entered the room. The old man had said that Frank had come around a few times and had been talkative, but it couldn't be proved by his behavior during the past hour or so.

Julie, who was the closest to Frank, frowned and leaned toward him, peering at the right side of his head.

"Oh, my God."

She spoke those three words in a bleak tone of voice that was as effective a refrigerant as anything used in an air conditioner.

With a chill skittering up his spine, Bobby slid along the sofa, crowding her against the other end, and looked past her at the side of Frank's head. Wished he had not. Tried to look away. Couldn't.

When Frank's head had been tilted to his right, almost lying against his shoulder, they had not been able to see that temple. After leaving Bobby at the office, still out of control, traveling against his will, Frank evidently had returned to one of those craters where the engineered insects shat out their diamonds. His flesh was lumpy all the way along his temple to his jaw, and in some places the rough gemstones that were the cause of the lumpiness poked through, gleaming, intimately melded with his tissue. For whatever reason, he had scooped up a handful to bring with him, but when reconstituting himself he had made a mistake.

Bobby wondered what treasures might be buried in the soft gray matter within Frank's skull.

"I saw that too," Fogarty said. "And look at the palm of his right hand."

Although Julie protested, Bobby pinched the sleeve of Frank's jacket and pulled until he twisted the man's arm off the chair and revealed his palm. He had found the partial roach that had once been welded into his own shoe. At least it appeared to be the same one. It was sprouting from the meaty part of Frank's hand, carapace gleaming, dead eyes staring up toward Frank's index finger.

♦  ♦  ♦

CANDY CIRCLED the house in the rain, passing a black cat on a windowsill. It turned its head to glance at him, then put its face to the windowpane again.

At the rear of the house, he stepped quietly onto the porch and tried the back door. It was locked.

Vague blue light pulsed from his hand as he gripped the knob. The lock slipped, the door opened, and he stepped inside.

♦  ♦  ♦

JULIE HAD heard and seen enough, too much.

Eager to get away from Frank, she rose from the sofa and walked to the desk, where she considered her unfinished bourbon. But that was no answer. She was dreadfully tired, struggling to repress her grief for Thomas, striving even harder to make some sense out of the grotesque family history that Fogarty had revealed to them. She did not need the complication of any more bourbon, appealing as it might look there in the glass.

She said to the old man, "So what hope do we have of dealing with Candy?"

"None."

"There must be a way."

"No."

"There must be."

"Why?"

"Because he can't be allowed to win."

Fogarty smiled. "Why not?"

"Because he's the bad guy, dammit! And we're the good guys. Not perfect, maybe, not without flaws, but we're the good guys, all right. And that's why we have to win, because if we don't, then the whole game is meaningless."

Fogarty leaned back in his chair. "My point exactly. It *is* all meaningless. We're not good, and we're not bad, we're just meat. We don't have souls, there's no hope of transcendence for a slab of meat, you wouldn't expect a hamburger to go to Heaven after someone ate it."

She had never hated anyone as much as she hated Fogarty at that moment, partly because he was so smug and hateful, but partly because she recognized, in his arguments, something perilously close to the things she had said to Bobby in the motel, after she had learned about Thomas's death. She had said there was no point in having dreams, that they never came true, that death was always there watching even if you *were* lucky enough to grasp your personal brass ring. And loathing life, just because it led sooner or later to death . . . well, that was the same as saying people were nothing but meat.

"We have just pleasure and pain," the old physician said, "so it doesn't matter who's right or who's wrong, who wins or loses."

"What's his weakness?" she demanded angrily.

"None I can see." Fogarty seemed pleased by the hopelessness of their position. If he had been practicing medicine in the early 1940s, he had to be nearing eighty, though he looked younger. He was acutely aware of how little time remained to him, and was no doubt resentful of anyone younger; and given his cold perspective on life, their deaths at Candy Pollard's hands would entertain him. "No weaknesses at all."

Bobby disagreed, or tried to. "Some might say that his weakness is his mind, his screwed-up psychology."

Fogarty shook his head. "And I'd argue that he's made a strength of his screwed-up psychology. He's used this business about being the instrument of God's vengeance to armor himself very effectively from depression and self-doubt and anything else that might trip him up."

In the wingback chair, Frank abruptly sat up straighter, shook himself as if to cast off his mental confusion the way a dog might shake water from its sodden coat after coming in from the rain. He said, "Where . . . Why do I . . . Is it . . . is it . . . is it . . . ?"

"Is it what, Frank?" Bobby asked.

"Is it happening?" Frank said. His eyes seemed slowly to be clearing. "Is it finally happening?"

"Is what finally happening, Frank?"

His voice was hoarse. "Death. Is it finally happening? Is it?"

♦ ♦ ♦

CANDY HAD crept quietly through the house, into the hallway that led to the library. As he moved toward the open door on the left, he heard voices. When he recognized one of them as Frank's, he could barely contain himself.

According to Violet, Frank was crippled. His control of his telekinetic talent had always been erratic, which is why Candy had enjoyed some hope of one day catching him and finishing him before he could travel to a place of safety. Perhaps the moment of triumph had arrived.

When he reached the door, he found himself looking at the woman's back. He could not see her face, but he was sure that it would be the same one that had been suffused in a beatific glow in Thomas's mind.

Beyond her he glimpsed Frank, and saw Frank's eyes widen at the sight of him. If the mother-killer had been too mentally confused to teleport out of Candy's reach, as Violet had claimed, he was now casting off that confusion. He looked as if he might pop out of there long before Candy could lay a hand on him.

Candy had intended to throw the library into a turmoil by sending a wave of energy through the doorway ahead of him, setting the books on fire and shattering the lamps, with the purpose of panicking and distracting the Dakotas and Doc Fogarty, giving him a chance to go straight for Frank. But now he was forced to change his plans by the sight of his brother trembling on the edge of dematerialization.

He entered the room in a rush and seized the woman from behind, curling his right arm around her neck and jerking her head back, so she—and the two men—would understand at once that he could snap her neck in an instant, whenever he chose. Even so, she slashed backward with one foot, scraping the heel of her shoe down his shin, stomping on his foot, all of which hurt like hell; it was some martial-art move, and he could tell by the way she tried to counterbalance his grip and stance that she had a lot of training in such things. So he jerked her head back again, even harder, and flexed his biceps, which pinched her windpipe, hurting her enough to make her realize that resistance was suicidal.

Fogarty watched from his chair, alarmed but not sufficiently to rise to his feet, and the husband came off the sofa with a gun in his hand, Mr. Quick-Draw Artist, but Candy was not concerned about either of them. His attention was on Frank, who had risen from his chair and appeared about to blink out of there, off to Punaluu and Kyoto and a score of other places.

"Don't do it, Frank!" he said sharply. "Don't run away. It's time we settled, time you paid for what you did to our mother. You come to the house, accept God's punishment, and end it now, tonight. I'm going there with this bitch. She tried to help you, I guess, so maybe you won't want to see her suffer."

The husband was going to do something crazy; seeing Julie in Candy's grip had clearly unhinged him. He was searching for a shot, a way to get Candy without getting her, and he might even risk firing at Candy's head, though Candy was half crouching behind the woman. Time to get out of there.

"Come to the house," he told Frank. "You come into the kitchen, let me end it for you, and I'll let her go. I swear on our mother's name, I'll let her go. But if you don't come in fifteen minutes, I'll put this bitch on the table, and I'll have my dinner, Frank. You want me to feed on her after she tried to help you, Frank?"

Candy thought he heard a gunshot just as he got out of there. In any event, it had been too late. He rematerialized in the kitchen of the house on Pacific Hill Road, with Julie Dakota still locked in the crook of his arm.

# 56

No LONGER CONCERNED about the danger of touching Frank, Bobby grabbed handsful of his jacket and shoved him backward against the wide-louvred shutters on the library window. "You heard him, Frank. Don't run. Don't run this time, or I'll hang on to you and never let go, no matter where you take me, I swear to God, you'll wish you'd put your neck on Candy's platter instead of mine." He slammed Frank against the shutters to make his point, and behind him he heard Lawrence Fogarty's soft, knowing laughter.

Registering the terror and confusion in his client's eyes, Bobby realized that his threats would not achieve the effect he desired. In fact, threats would almost certainly frighten Frank into flight, even if he wanted to help Julie. Worse, by stooping to violence as a first resort, he was treating Frank not as a person but as meat, confirming the depraved code by which the corrupt old physician had led his entire life, and that was almost as intolerable as losing Julie.

He let go of Frank.

"I'm sorry. Listen, I'm sorry, I just got a little crazy."

He studied the man's eyes, searching for some indication that sufficient intelligence remained in the damaged brain for the two of them to reach an understanding. He saw fear, stark and terrible, and he saw a loneliness that made him want to cry. He saw a lost look, too, not unlike what he had sometimes seen in Thomas's eyes when they had taken him on an excursion from Cielo Vista, "out in the world," as he had said.

Aware that perhaps two minutes of Candy's fifteen-minute deadline had passed, trying to remain calm nonetheless, Bobby took Frank's right hand, turned it palm up, and forced himself to touch the dead roach that was now integrated with the man's soft white flesh. The insect felt crisp and bristly against his fingers, but he did not permit his disgust to show.

"Does this hurt, Frank? This bug mixed up with your own cells here, does it hurt you?"

Frank stared at him, finally shook his head. No.

Heartened by the establishment of even this much dialogue, Bobby gently put his fingertips to Frank's right temple, feeling the lumps of precious gems like unburst boils or cancerous tumors.

"Do you hurt here, Frank? Are you in pain?"

"No," Frank said, and Bobby's heart pounded with excitement at the escalation to a spoken response.

From a pocket of his jeans, Bobby removed a folded Kleenex and gently blotted away the spittle that still glistened on Frank's chin.

The man blinked, and his eyes seemed to focus better.

From behind Bobby, still in the leather chair at the desk, perhaps with a glass of bourbon in his hand, almost certainly with that infuriatingly smug smile plastered on his face, Fogarty said, "Twelve minutes left."

Bobby ignored the physician. Maintaining eye contact with his client, his fingertips still on Frank's temple, he said quietly, "It's been a hard life for you, hasn't it? You were the normal one,

371

the most normal one, and when you were a kid you always wanted to fit in at school, didn't you, the way your sisters and brother never could. And it took you a long time to realize your dream wasn't going to happen, you weren't going to fit in, because no matter how normal you were compared to the rest of your family, you'd still come from that goddamned house, out of that *cesspool,* which made you forever an outsider to other people. They might not see the stain on your heart, might not know the dark memories in you, but *you* saw, and *you* remembered, and you felt yourself unworthy because of the horror that was your family. Yet you were also an outsider at home, much too sane to fit in there, too sensitive to the nightmare of it. So all your life, you've been alone."

"All my life," Frank said. "And always will be."

He wasn't going to travel now. Bobby would have bet on it.

"Frank, I can't help you. No one can. That's a hard truth, but I won't lie to you. I'm not going to con you or threaten you."

Frank said nothing, but maintained eye contact.

"Ten minutes," Fogarty said.

"The only thing I can do for you, Frank, is show you a way to give your life meaning at last, a way to end it with purpose and dignity, and maybe find peace in death. I have an idea, a way that you might be able to kill Candy and save Julie, and if you can do that, you'll have gone out a hero. Will you come with me, Frank, listen to me, and not let Julie die?"

Frank didn't say yes, but he didn't say no, either. Bobby decided to take heart from the lack of a negative response.

"We've got to get moving, Frank. But don't try teleporting to the house, because then you'll just lose control again, pop off to hell and back a hundred times. We'll go in my car. We can be there in five minutes."

Bobby took his client's hand. He made a point of taking the one with the roach embedded in it, hoping Frank would remember that he had a fear of bugs and perceive that his willingness to overrule the phobia was a testament to his sincerity.

They crossed the room to the door.

Rising from his chair, Fogarty said, "You're going to your death, you know."

Without glancing back at the physician, Bobby said, "Well, seems to me, you went to yours decades ago."

He and Frank walked out into the rain and were drenched by the time they got into the car.

Behind the wheel, Bobby glanced at his watch. Less than eight minutes to go.

He wondered why he accepted Candy's word that the fifteen-minute deadline would be observed, why he was so sure that the madman had not already torn out her throat. Then he remembered something she had said to him once: *Sweetcakes, as long as you're breathing, Tinkerbell will live.*

Gutters overflowed, and a sudden wind wound skeins of rain, like silver yarn, through his headlights.

As he drove the storm-swept streets and turned east on Pacific Hill Road, he explained how Frank, through his sacrifice of himself, could rid the world of Candy and undo his mother's evil the way he had wanted to undo it—but had failed—when he had taken the ax to her. It was a simple concept. He was able to go over it several times even in the few minutes they had before pulling to a stop at the rusted iron gate.

Frank did not respond to anything that Bobby said. There was no way to be sure he understood what he must do—or if he had even heard a word of it. He stared straight ahead, his mouth open an inch or so, and sometimes his head ticked back and forth, back and forth, in time with the windshield wipers, as if he were watching Jackie Jaxx's crystal pendant swinging on its gold chain.

By the time they got out of the car, went through the gate, and approached the decrepit house, with less than two minutes of the deadline left, Bobby was reduced to proceeding entirely on faith.

◆   ◆   ◆

WHEN CANDY brought her into the filthy kitchen, pushed her into one of the chairs at the table, and let go of her, Julie reached at once for the revolver in the shoulder holster under her corduroy jacket. He was too fast for her, however, and tore it from her hand, breaking two of her fingers in the process.

The pain was excruciating, and that was on top of the soreness in her neck and throat from the ruthless treatment he had dealt out at Fogarty's, but she refused to cry or complain. Instead, when he turned away from her to toss the gun into a drawer beyond her reach, she leapt up from the chair and sprinted for the door.

He caught her, lifted her off her feet, swung her around, and body-slammed her onto the kitchen table so hard she nearly passed out. He brought his face close to hers and said, "You're going to taste good, like Clint's woman, all that vitality in your veins, all that energy, I want to feel you spurting in my mouth."

Her attempts at resistance and escape had not arisen from courage as much as from terror, some of which sprang from the experience of deconstruction and reconstitution, which she hoped never to have to endure again. Now her fear doubled as his lips lowered to within an inch of hers and as his charnel-house breath washed over her face. Unable to look away from his blue eyes, she thought these were what Satan's eyes would be like, not dark as sin, not red as the fires of Hell, not crawling with maggots, but gloriously and beautifully blue—and utterly devoid of all mercy and compassion.

If all the worst of human savagery from time immemorial could be condensed into one individual, if all of the species' hunger for blood and violence and raw power could be embodied in one monstrous figure, it would have looked like Candy Pollard at that moment. When he finally pulled back from her, like a coiled serpent grudgingly reconsidering its decision to strike, and when he dragged her off the table and shoved her back into the chair, she was cowed, perhaps for the first time in her life. She knew that if she exhibited any further resistance, he would kill her on the spot and feed on her.

Then he said an astonishing thing: "Later, when I'm done with Frank, you'll tell me where Thomas got his power."

She was so intimidated by him that she had difficulty finding her voice. "Power? What do you mean?"

"He's the only one I've ever encountered, outside our family. The Bad Thing, he called me. And he kept trying to keep tabs on me telepathically because he knew sooner or later you and I would cross paths. How can he have had any gifts when he wasn't born of my virgin mother? Later, you'll explain that to me."

As she sat, actually too terrified either to cry or shake, in a storm's-eye calm, cradling her injured hand in the other, she had to find room in her for a sense of wonder too. Thomas? Psychically gifted? Could it be true that all the time she worried about taking care of him, he was to some extent taking care of her?

374

She heard a strange sound approaching from the front of the house. A moment later, at least twenty cats poured into the kitchen through the hall doorway, tails sweeping over one another.

Among the pack came the Pollard twins, long-legged and barefoot, one in panties and a red T-shirt, the other in panties and a white T-shirt, as sinuous as their cats. They were as pale as spirits, but there was nothing soft or ineffectual about them. They were lean and vital, filled with that tightly coiled energy that you always knew was in a cat even when it appeared to be lazing in the sun. They were ethereal in some ways, yet at the same time earthy and strong, powerfully sensual. Their presence in the house must have cranked up the unnatural tensions in their brother, who was doubly male in the matter of testes but lacking the crucial valve that would have allowed release.

They approached the table. One of them stared down at Julie, while the other hung on her sister and averted her eyes. The bold one said, "Are you Candy's girlfriend?" There was unmistakable mockery of her brother in the question.

"You shut up," Candy said.

"If you're not his girlfriend," the bold one said, in a voice as soft as rustling silk, "you could come upstairs with us, we have a bed, the cats wouldn't mind, and I think I'd like you."

"Don't you talk like that in your mother's house," Candy said fiercely.

His anger was real, but Julie could see that he was also more than a little unnerved by his sister.

Both women, even the shy one, virtually radiated wildness, as if they might do anything that occurred to them, regardless of how outrageous, without compunctions or inhibitions.

Julie was nearly as scared of them as she was of Candy.

From the front of the moldering house, echoing above the roar of the rain on the roof, came a knocking.

As one, the cats dashed from the kitchen, down the hall to the front door, and less than a minute later they returned as escort to Bobby and Frank.

♦   ♦   ♦

ENTERING THE KITCHEN, Bobby was overcome with gratitude—to God, even to Candy—at the sight of Julie alive.

375

She was haggard, gaunt with fear and pain, but she had never looked more beautiful to him.

She had never been so subdued, either, or so unsure of herself, and in spite of the banshee chorus of emotions that roared and shrieked in him, he found capacity to contain a separate sadness and anger about that.

Though he was still hoping that Frank would come through for him, Bobby had been prepared to use his revolver if worse came to worst or if an unexpected advantage presented itself. But as soon as he walked in the room, the madman said, "Remove your gun from your holster and empty the cartridges out of it."

As Bobby had entered, Candy had moved behind the chair in which Julie sat, and had put one hand on her throat, his fingers hooked like talons. Inhumanly strong as he was, he could no doubt tear her throat out in a second or two, even though he lacked real talons.

Bobby withdrew the Smith & Wesson from his shoulder holster, handling it in such a way as to demonstrate that he had no intention of using it. He broke out the cylinder, shook the five cartridges onto the floor, and put the revolver down on a nearby counter.

Candy Pollard's excitement grew visibly second by second, from the moment Bobby and Frank appeared. Now he removed his hand from Julie's throat, stepped away from her, and glared triumphantly at Frank.

As far as Bobby could tell, it was a wasted glare. Frank was there in the kitchen with them—but not there. If he was aware of everything that was happening and understood the meaning of it, he was doing a good job of pretending otherwise.

Pointing to the floor at his feet, Candy said, "Come here and kneel, you mother-killer."

The cats fled from the section of the cracked linoleum which the madman had indicated.

The twins stood hipshot but alert. Bobby had seen cats feign indifference in the same way but reveal their actual involvement by the prick of their ears. With Violet and Verbina, their true interest was betrayed by the throbbing of their pulses in their temples and, almost obscenely, by the erection of their nipples against the fabric of their T-shirts.

"I said come here and kneel," Candy repeated. "Or will you

really betray the only people who ever lifted a hand to help you in these last seven years? Kneel, or I'll kill the Dakotas, both of them, I'll kill them *now.*"

Candy projected the awesome presence not of a psychotic but of a genuinely supernatural being, as if his name were Legion and forces beyond human ken worked through him.

Frank moved forward one step, away from Bobby's side.

Another step.

Then he stopped and looked around at the cats, as if something about them puzzled him.

Bobby could never know if Frank had intended to evoke the bloody consequences that ensued from his next act, whether his words were calculated, or whether he was speaking out of befuddlement and was as surprised as anyone by the turmoil that followed. Whatever the case, he frowned at the cats, looked up at the bolder of the twins, and said, "Ah, is Mother still here, then? Is she still here in the house with us?"

The shy twin stiffened, but the bold one actually appeared to relax, as if Frank's question had spared her the trouble of deciding on the right time and place to make the revelation herself. She turned to Candy and favored him with the most subtly textured smile Bobby had ever seen: it was mocking, but it was a would-be lover's invitation, as well; it was tentative with fear, but simultaneously challenging; hot with lust, cool with dread; and above all, it was wild, as uncivilized and ferocious as any expression on the face of any creature that roamed any field or forest in the world.

Her smile was met by Candy with an expression of stark horror and disbelief that made him appear, briefly and for the first time, almost human. "You didn't," he said.

The bold twin's smile broadened. "After you buried her, we dug her up. She's part of us now, and always will be, part of us, part of the pack."

The cats swished their tails and stared at Candy.

The cry that erupted from him was less than human, and the speed with which he reached the bold twin was uncanny. He drove her against the refrigerator with his body, crushed her against it, grabbed her by the face with his right hand and slammed her head against the yellowed enamel surface, then again. Lifting her bodily, his hands around her narrow waist, he tried to throw her as a furious child might cast away a doll, but cat-quick she wrapped her limber legs around his waist and locked her ankles behind him, so she was riding him with her breasts before his face. He pounded at her with his fists, but she would not let go. She held on until the blows stopped raining on her, then loosened her lock on him so she slid down far enough to bring her pale throat near his mouth. He seized the opportunity that she thrust upon him and tore the life out of her with his teeth.

The cats squealed hideously, though not as one creature this time, and fled the kitchen by several routes.

To the sound of his anguished screams and her eerily erotic cries, Candy extinguished his sister's life in less than a minute. Neither Bobby nor Julie attempted to intervene, for it was clear that to do so would be like stepping into the funnel of a tornado, ensuring their death but leaving the storm undiminished. Frank only stood in that curious detachment that was now his only attitude.

Candy turned immediately to the shy twin and destroyed her even more quickly, as she offered no resistance.

As the psychotic giant dropped the brutalized corpse, Frank at last obeyed the order he had been given, closed the distance between them, and surprised his brother by taking his hand. Then, as Bobby had hoped, Frank traveled and Candy went with him, not under his own power but as a sidecar rider, the way Bobby had gone.

After the tumult, the silence was shocking.

Sweating, clearly ill from what she had witnessed, Julie pushed back her chair. The wooden legs stuttered on the lino-leum.

"No," Bobby said, and quickly came to her, stooped beside her, encouraging her to sit down. He took her uninjured hand. "Wait, not yet, stay out of the way. . . ."

The hollow piping.

A blustery whirl of wind.

"Bobby," she said, panicking, "they're coming back, let's go, let's get out of here while we have the chance."

He held her in the chair. "Don't look. I have to look, be sure, make certain Frank understood, but you don't need to see."

The atonal music trilled again, and the wind stirred up the scent of the dead women's blood.

"What are you talking about?" she demanded.

"Close your eyes."

She did not close her eyes, of course, because she had never been one to look away or run away from anything.

The Pollards reappeared, back from the brief visit they had made in tandem to someplace as far away as Mount Fuji or as close as Doc Fogarty's house, more likely to several places. Recklessly rapid and repeated travel was key to the success of the trick, just as Bobby had outlined it to Frank in the car. The brothers were no longer two distinct human beings, for Frank's had been the guiding consciousness on their journeys, and his ability to shepherd them through error-free reconstitution was declining rapidly, worse with each jaunt. They were fused, more biologically tangled than any Siamese twins. Frank's left arm disappeared into Candy's right side, as if he had reached in there to fish among his brother's internal organs. Candy's right leg melted into Frank's left, giving them only three to stand on.

There were more strangenesses, but that was all Bobby could comprehend before they vanished again. Frank needed to keep moving, stay in control, give Candy no chance to exert his own power, until the scramble was so complete that proper reconstitution of either of them would be impossible.

Realizing what was happening, Julie sat perfectly still, her broken hand curled in her lap, holding fast to Bobby with her good hand. He knew she understood, without being told, that Frank was sacrificing himself for them, and that the least they could do for him was bear witness to his courage, just as they would keep Thomas and Hal and Clint and Felina alive in memory.

That was one of the most fundamental and sacred duties good friends and family performed for one another: they tended the flame of memory, so no one's death meant an immediate vanishment from the world; in some sense the deceased would live on after their passing, at least as long as those who loved them lived. Such memories were an essential weapon against the chaos of life and death, a way to ensure some continuity from generation to generation, an endorsement of order and of meaning.

Piping, wind: the brothers returned from another series of rapid deconstructions and reconstitutions, and now they were essentially one creature of cataclysmic biology. The body was large, well over seven feet tall, broad and hulking, for it incorporated the mass of both of them. The single head had a nightmare face: Frank's brown eyes were badly misaligned; a slanted mouth gaped between them where a nose should have been; and a second mouth pocked the left cheek. Two tortured, screaming voices filled the kitchen. Another face was set in the chest, mouthless but with two eye sockets, in one of which lay an unblinking eye as blue as Candy's; the other socket was filled with bristling teeth.

The slouching beast vanished, then returned once more, after less than a minute. This time it was an undifferentiated mass of tissue, dark in some places and hideously pink in others, prickled with bone fragments, tufted with sparse clumps of hair, marbled with veins that pulsed to different beats. Along the way, Frank had no doubt visited that alleyway in Calcutta or someplace like it, for he had conveyed with him dozens of roaches, not just one, and rats as well; they were incorporated into the tissue everywhere that Bobby looked, further ensuring that Candy's flesh was too diffused and polluted ever to be properly reconstituted. The monstrous and obviously dysfunctional assemblage fell to the floor, flopped and shuddered, and finally lay still. Some of the rodents and insects continued to quiver and writhe, trying to get free; inextricably bonded to the dead mass, they also would soon perish.

# 57

THE HOUSE WAS SIMPLE, on a section of the coast that was not yet fashionable. The back porch faced the sea, and wooden steps led down to a scrubby yard that ended at the beach. There were twelve palm trees.

The living room was furnished with a couple of chairs, a love seat, a coffee table, and a Wurlitzer 950 stocked with records from the big-band era. The floor was bleached oak, tightly made, and sometimes they pushed the furniture to the walls, rolled up the area rug, punched up some numbers on the juke, and danced together, just the two of them.

That was mostly in the evenings.

In the mornings, if they didn't make love, they pored through recipe books in the kitchen and whipped up baked goods together, or just sat with coffee by the window, watched the sea, and talked.

They had books, two decks of cards, an interest in the birds and animals that lived along the shore, memories both good and bad, and each other. Always, each other.

Sometimes they talked about Thomas and wondered at the gift he'd possessed and had kept secret all his life. She said it made you humble to think of it, made you realize everyone and everything was more complex and mysterious than you could know.

To get the police off their backs, they had admitted working on a case for one Frank Pollard from El Encanto Heights, who believed his brother James was trying to kill him over a misunderstanding. They said they felt James may have been a complete psychotic who had killed their employees and Thomas, merely because they had dared to try to settle the matter between the brothers. Subsequently, when the Pollard house up north was found torched with gasoline, with a confusing array of skeletal remains in the aftermath, police pressure was slowly lifted from Dakota & Dakota. It was believed that Mr. James Pollard had killed his twin sisters and his brother, as well, and was currently on the run, armed and dangerous.

The agency had been sold. They didn't miss it. She no longer felt she could save the world, and he no longer needed to help her save herself.

Money, a few more red diamonds, and negotiation had convinced Dyson Manfred and Roger Gavenall to invent another source for the biologically engineered bug when, eventually, they published their work on it. Without the cooperation of Dakota & Dakota, they would never know the actual source, anyway.

In the finished attic of the beach house, they kept the boxes and bags of cash they had brought back from Pacific Hill Road. Candy and his mother had tried to compensate for the chaos of their lives by storing up millions in a second-floor bedroom, just as Bobby and Julie had suspected before they had ever gotten to El Encanto Heights. Only a small portion of the Pollards' treasure was now in the beach-house attic, but it was more than two people could spend; the rest had been burned, along with everything else, when they'd torched the house on Pacific Hill Road.

In time he came to accept the fact that he could be a good man and still sometimes have dark thoughts or selfish motives. She said this was maturity, and that it wasn't such a bad thing to live outside of Disneyland by the time you reached middle age.

She said she'd like a dog.

He said fine, if they could agree on a breed.

She said you clean up its poop.

He said you clean up its poop, I'll take care of the petting and Frisbee throwing.

She said she had been wrong that night in Santa Barbara when, in her despair, she had claimed no dreams ever came true. They came true all the time. The problem was, you sometimes had your sights set on a particular dream and missed all the others that turned out your way: like finding him, she said, and being loved.

One day she told him she was going to have a baby. He held her close for a long time before he could find the words to express his happiness. They dressed to go out for champagne and dinner at the Ritz, then decided they would rather celebrate at home, on the porch, overlooking the sea, listening to old Tommy Dorsey recordings.

They built sandcastles. Huge ones. They sat on the back porch and watched the incoming tide wreck their constructions.

Sometimes they talked about the wordburst he had received in the car on the freeway, from Thomas at the moment of his death. They wondered about the words "there is a light that loves you," and dared to consider dreaming the biggest dream of all—that people never really die.

They got a black Labrador.

They named him Sookie, just because it sounded silly.

Some nights she was afraid. Occasionally, so was he.

They had each other. And time.